Praise for
CHER AMI AND MAJOR WHITTLESEY

"If you haven't yet discovered the offbeat genius of Kathleen Rooney, start here with a novel both heartbreaking and sharply funny. It justifies its own premise on the first page, and quickly surpasses that premise. *Cher Ami and Major Whittlesey* is brilliant and surprising at every turn."
—Rebecca Makkai, Pulitzer Prize finalist for *The Great Believers*

"Imaginative and audacious . . . Rooney uses Cher Ami's bird's-eye view and curious afterlife to exhilarating, comic, and terrifying effect, while Whit's tragic fate is exquisitely rendered. . . . Unforgettable . . . A celebration of animal intelligence, and tribute to altruism and courage."
—*Booklist* (starred review)

"Hands down, one of the best books of the year. *Cher Ami and Major Whittlesey* is a magnificent achievement and everything I want from a novel. I *loved* it."
—J. Ryan Stradal, bestselling author of
The Lager Queen of Minnesota

"You'll be amazed at the depths of character Rooney plumbs from a literal bird's-eye-view, and by how she entwines the voices of a messenger pigeon and a witty, disconsolate veteran to craft a story based on true events."
—*Chicago Magazine*

"A properly mysterious, warmly convincing work of bright imagination. A pigeon and a haunted man returned generously, gently, to the story of the world."
—Sebastian Barry, Booker Prize–shortlisted
author of *Days Without End*

"*Cher Ami and Major Whittlesey* is a splendid novel; so smart, so beautifully written—a heroic tale of the cross-species relationship between pigeon and man during the Great War. Affecting and imaginative, this story vibrated deep in my heart because it all felt so very true."
—Annie Hartnett, author of *Rabbit Cake*

"Her well-researched novel touches on the folly of war (particularly *this* war), the sentience of animals, and—especially—survivor guilt and imposter syndrome. Rooney's writing has a delicate lyricism. . . . She injects humor and whimsy into an otherwise solemn story. A curiosity but richly imagined and genuinely affecting."
—*Kirkus Reviews*

PENGUIN BOOKS

CHER AMI AND MAJOR WHITTLESEY

© Beth Rooney

Kathleen Rooney is a founding editor of Rose Metal Press and a founding member of Poems While You Wait. She is the author, most recently, of the novel *Lillian Boxfish Takes a Walk* (St. Martin's Press, 2017) and the co-editor of *René Magritte: Selected Writings* (University of Minnesota Press, 2016). Her previous work includes poetry, fiction, and nonfiction and has appeared in *The New York Times Magazine*, *Allure*, *Salon*, *Chicago Tribune*, *The Nation*, and elsewhere. She teaches English and creative writing at DePaul University and lives in Chicago with her spouse, the writer Martin Seay.

Look for the reading group discussion guide in the back of this book. To access Penguin Readers Guides online, visit penguinrandomhouse.com.

ALSO BY KATHLEEN ROONEY

FICTION

Lillian Boxfish Takes a Walk
The Listening Room: A Novel of Georgette and Loulou Magritte
O, Democracy!

NONFICTION

René Magritte: Selected Writings
For You, For You I am Trilling These Songs: Essays
Live Nude Girl: My Life as an Object
Reading with Oprah: The Book Club That Changed America

POETRY

Robinson Alone
That Tiny Insane Voluptuousness (with Elisa Gabbert)
Oneiromance (an epithalamion)

CHER AMI
and
MAJOR
WHITTLESEY

KATHLEEN ROONEY

PENGUIN BOOKS

PENGUIN BOOKS

An imprint of Penguin Random House LLC
penguinrandomhouse.com

LIBRARY OF CONGRESS CATALOGING-IN-PUBLICATION DATA
Names: Rooney, Kathleen, 1980– author.
Title: Cher Ami and Major Whittlesey / Kathleen Rooney.
Description: [New York] : Penguin Books, [2020]
Identifiers: LCCN 2019051665 (print) | LCCN 2019051664 (ebook) |
ISBN 9780143135425 (paperback) | ISBN 9780525507093 (ebook)
Subjects: LCSH: World War, 1914–1918—Campaigns—Meuse River Valley—
Fiction. | Cher Ami (Pigeon)—Fiction. | GSAFD: Historical fiction.
Classification: LCC PS3618.O676 C47 2020 (ebook) | LCC PS3618.O676 (print) |
DDC 813/.6—dc23
LC record available at https://lccn.loc.gov/2019051665

Printed in the United States of America
1 3 5 7 9 10 8 6 4 2

Set in LinoLetter Std
Designed by Sabrina Bowers

This is a work of fiction based on actual events.

IN TOKEN

OF MY ADMIRATION FOR HIS GENIUS,

THIS BOOK IS INSCRIBED

TO

MARTIN SEAY.

In the great majority of animals there are traces of physical qualities and attitudes, which qualities are more markedly differentiated in the case of human beings. For just as we pointed out resemblances in the physical organs, so in a number of animals we observe gentleness and fierceness, mildness or cross temper, courage or timidity, fear or confidence, high spirits or low cunning, and, with regard to intelligence, something akin to sagacity.

—Aristotle, *History of Animals*

We want men, men, men.
—General Joseph Joffre to President Woodrow Wilson, April 1917

CHER AMI
and
MAJOR
WHITTLESEY

CHAPTER 1

CHER AMI

Monuments matter most to pigeons and soldiers.

I myself have become a monument, a feathered statue inside a glass case.

In life I was both a pigeon and a soldier. In death I am a piece of mediocre taxidermy, collecting dust in the Smithsonian Institution's National Museum of American History.

The museum has closed, and everyone has gone home. The last guests took their leave at five thirty, as they do every weekday, and even the janitorial staffers have finished their tasks: miles of floors polished and pine-scented, acres of displays gleaming and silent. A few hours remain before midnight. This is the eve of the one-hundred-year anniversary of what, according to the United States Army, was the most important day of my avian life: October 4, 1918.

I'm not sure I agree. That day was an important one, certainly, but days don't carry the same meaning for pigeons as they do for humans, and my life comprised other days, days that might be equally worth note, if not to the army then at least to me and to those I loved.

Pigeons can love.

Pigeons cannot fight. Yet I was once as well known to schoolchildren and grown-up citizens alike as any human hero of what was then called the Great War.

Hence the stuffing of my mangled body. Hence my enshrinement here, in the grandmother's attic of the entire country.

I hear the tale of my heroism—the simple version—over and over. I used to hear it daily from patriotic patrons who knew it by rote. Time having passed, other wars having superseded my own, nowadays I hear it every week or so from history-buff parents—usually French or British but sometimes American—as they lead their kids from case to case. Or I hear it from precocious children themselves, animal lovers fascinated by what I did. In their reedy voices, birdlike in their own right, they tell the tale as follows: *During that big war in France, some American soldiers got trapped in enemy territory. They were called the Lost Battalion because they got surrounded by the Germans. They released homing pigeon after homing pigeon with messages for help. They watched and watched as the little birds fell, shot down by enemy fire. But the last pigeon, Cher Ami right here, wasn't going to let that stop him. Even though he got shot through the chest and the leg, the brave bird struggled on, carrying his note for forty kilometers—* American kids say *twenty-five miles—until, close to death, he arrived at his loft at the American base. Thanks to Cher Ami, all the soldiers were saved.*

Their parents will smile and say, *Very good.*

Occasionally a child who doesn't know the story of the Lost Battalion will glance my way as she goes by. Catching sight of my single orange leg, she will ask, *Why? Why does the pigeon only have one foot?*

Balanced there on my polished oak base, I will want to explain. Naturally, I can't.

The little girl and her parents will see that I am displayed near a Yeoman (F) uniform and a field telephone. They'll read the plaque beneath the black-and-white photograph of an infantryman's back as he trails a spool of wire through the woods, toward the front: TELEPHONES WERE ONE OF SEVERAL NEW TECHNOLOGIES DEPLOYED IN THE SERVICE OF WAGING WAR, it states. TROOPS STRUNG MILES OF TELEPHONE WIRE IN THE FIELD, ALLOWING INSTANT COMMUNICATION. BUT THE LINES PROVED VULNERABLE, AND THE ARMY OFTEN RELIED ON TRADITIONAL MEANS TO RELAY MESSAGES—HUMAN RUNNERS AND CARRIER PIGEONS.

The little girl and her parents will look at the engraved silver band around my remaining leg, identifying me as National Union of Racing Pigeons Number 615. I've never thought of myself that way, only as Cher Ami, my given name: French, meaning "Dear Friend," though I was a British bird.

The family will read my placard, quite brief, which states:

CHER AMI, ONE OF THE 600 CARRIER PIGEONS
DEPLOYED BY THE U.S. ARMY SIGNAL CORPS,
WAS AWARDED THE FRENCH CROIX DE GUERRE
WITH PALM FOR HIS HEROIC SERVICE.

Huh, they'll say, and wander off, satisfied. And I, too, will feel satisfied, partly, at the knowledge they've gained.

The placard gets my name at least, if not my gender. Even now, more than a century after I was first misidentified, that error still grates. Though originally registered as a Black Check cock, I'm really a Blue Check, and when I was being taxidermied, they discovered that I was—that I am—a hen. The man doing the job informed them as much, but since they'd already had the placard made and budgets were tight, they didn't pay to change it. *Good enough for government work,* they said, and laughed. I've been wrongly called a cock bird ever since, in history books and military records.

I never behaved like a typical hen, it's true. But I am a female, and female war heroes are rarely given their due.

This erasure annoys me.

I do appreciate that placard for its refusal to overemphasize me: one of six hundred. There were so many of us, and so many of us could be called heroic. My fellow pigeon President Wilson, for instance, my fond companion during the war who joined me for a time in this display case, this eternal institutional afterlife. They shipped him over to the Pentagon in 2008, I think. I miss him.

Though he's not the bird I miss the most.

Pigeons have an almost bottomless capacity for longing.

I've still got Sergeant Stubby in here with me, sleeping now. He and I talk and talk and talk when we're both awake.

He was the mascot of the 102nd Infantry, 26th Division, accompanying his unit in the hellish French trenches, awarded a gold medal by General John J. Pershing. A consummate joiner, as are most dogs, he was made a lifetime member of the Red Cross, the Young Men's Christian Association, and the American Legion. He stands over there by the canteen, the bread tin, the wire cutters, the first-aid kit, the mess kit, and the trench periscope, looking as pert and ferocious as he did in life, or so he assures me.

His paws, quick and light, look ready to leap from his mahogany block mount, and even in repose his underslung jaw seems ready to bite the enemy or eat a treat. His ears appear as though they could still rotate to hear an incoming shell, and his studded leather collar gives his stalwart adorability the slight sharpness that befits an army pup. I never call him Stubby; I call him Sarge, because my doing so pleases him. He's a dog of uncertain breed but seems mostly Boston terrier in appearance and temperament. He's also the only dog— as he'll tell you, repeatedly—to have been nominated for rank and promoted to sergeant through combat.

I don't much care about rank. Most of us pigeons are less fixated on titles and decorations than on missions completed. In this respect we resemble the flying aces—or so I gather; we had no contact with them during the war and certainly never sought to emulate them. Something about performing one's duties alone, aloft above the carnage, may engender this attitude.

Dogs, on the other hand, are infantry through and through, not to mention rule-bound and craving of human regard. Sarge deserves the regard that he received. He served eighteen months on the front, in seventeen battles. He gave comfort to the wounded, saved his regiment from a mustard-gas attack, and stopped a German soldier by clasping the seat of his pants in his terrier jaws until human reinforcements arrived to complete the capture.

He, unlike me, is excited about my centenary. But as I said, dogs are like that. I am to wake him at midnight so he and I can celebrate. Knowing Sarge, this will mean that we will reminisce and sing "Auld Lang Syne." Dogs love singing. And I love Sergeant Stubby. His uncomplicated good cheer and patience remain constant even in death, and I can see why the men of the Yankee Division adored him. His owner had his pelt mounted on a plaster cast after he died in his sleep in 1926, and Sarge passed into the heterogeneous holdings of the Smithsonian in 1956, where he still greets each day as though this placement were the best and most unexpected surprise.

Sarge is, however, not immune to indignation and is given to wondering aloud why the army hasn't seen fit to present either of us—or, for that matter, the many other creatures who served alongside us, birds and horses and mules and dogs—with the Distinguished Service Cross. The DSC was not, I remind him, an honor customarily presented to animals, at least not while any of us were alive. *Well, a posthumous award is still an award,* he always replies, snuffling.

General Pershing did give me a small silver medal, but it was just a made-up thing. Though aren't all honors, really? Either we believe that they matter or we don't.

Still, I like having my Croix de Guerre here next to me. *Next to,* not *on,* as it's too large and heavy for a pigeon to wear, and I haven't a uniform on which to pin it. The French have long been more willing to perceive valor in sapient creatures of species other than human. Their citation notes that I—NURP Number 615, Cher Ami, *un pigeon voyageur*—was responsible for the safe delivery of twelve battlefield messages in France. Here in the States, I'm remembered only for that final voyage, but I flew many missions before being invalided out trying to save my Lost Battalion.

That was just my tiny corner of the war. Even from my

bird's-eye perspective, the magnitude of our forces' involve-
ment was hard to take in. Within little more than a year of its
late entry into the long conflict, the United States military
raised, trained, and transported an army of two million men
to France. Despite the brevity of our participation, 53,402
American soldiers lost their lives in combat; 204,002 were
wounded. Over a million Americans—more soldiers than had
served in the entire Confederate army—fought in the forty-
seven days of the Meuse-Argonne Offensive, advancing thirty-
four miles against enemy lines, ending the stalemate.

I think of these numbers all the time. I have so much time
to think and think.

I think of the eight million horses who died in the Great
War, roughly the same number killed as all the soldiers of all
the human armies.

I think of how humans used over a hundred thousand of
us pigeons on the battlefield, and with a 98 percent success
rate. Of how twenty thousand of us lost our lives in combat.

Can humans ever atone for dragooning beasts into their
own conflicts on such a colossal scale? What form could such
atonement take?

A few of them try. They ascribe to us their own fraught-
ness and foibles. And with animals' honors, the light of our
heroism shines on the personnel who worked with us as well.

I like to believe that here in the Smithsonian I stand as a
steadfast sentinel, reminding those whose eyes fall upon me
of untold immensities of mute sacrifice. But perhaps I am just
a tatty mass of feathers and a couple of glass eyes in this
small display case for an enormous war.

I like to think that I betoken memory. But then I think of
the scant relics of my cherished commander, Charles Whittlesey: Galloping Charlie, our captain-then-major, known as
Whit to my beloved Bill Cavanaugh, and therefore to me.
Whit's helmet and other articles reside in the library of his
alma mater, Williams College, where nobody ever goes to see
them, not really. People at least accidentally see me on their

way to more popular exhibits: Julia Child's kitchen or all of World War II.

World War II, which happened even though the horrors of the Great War were said to have obviated all future war.

When he is awake, Sergeant Stubby and I debate over that. He thinks we should forgive the humans and that they meant well. I am not so sure.

These days the children passing by are not impressed with us, so accustomed have they become to zoos and aquariums, where they stare and stare at living animals, active and un-stuffed in their cages, their tanks, their habitats. But even here, as in those places, we animals stare back. Humans make their mighty interventions in our lives—hunting, tam-ing, training, breeding, eating; warping our bodies and in-stincts away from nature, toward their own ends—and they imagine that their great power puts them beyond our regard, beyond our judgment. But we observe, even as we are ob-served. Most humans forget that.

My beloved Bill Cavanaugh, the 308th Infantry Regiment's greatest pigeon man, understood this and always looked me in the eye with a feeling of reciprocity. Whit did, too. What-ever Bill wanted him to do, he did.

In life my eyes were golden. Most of us have eyes that range from red—*ruby*, if you use the fancy lexicon of the pi-geon fancier—through orange to yellow.

The taxidermist who prepared me used standard orange-and-black, two dull disks popped into my empty sockets. I was already missing one eye, shot out on that final flight by the same bullet that carried away my right leg. An injury every bit as horrifying as I hope it sounds.

Pigeons can feel pain.

I wanted to protest, to say to the taxidermist, *Pardon me, but if I am to be preserved because of my sacrifice in the war, does it make any sense to erase the signs of that sacrifice? I want to have only one false eye, because people should see what the war did to me. And I want that eye to be golden!*

But even had I been alive, the man, as a man, would not have been capable of understanding my language—would not have even perceived it *as* language. It doesn't matter, I guess. I can still see through this flat glass. In my state of being now, I can see most everything.

Men shot the eyes out of their fellow men, too. I first saw such an injury through the wicker basket weave of my coop, bouncing upon Bill Cavanaugh's back. The man in question was walking toward us as we were supposed to be advancing. One of the officers yelled at him that he was going the wrong way. "Stragglers are to be shot," the officer said.

The man, sweaty and shaking, stopped there in the dark woods and laughed like a maniac.

"You think that order is funny, Private?" the officer said, releasing the strap on his sidearm holster.

"Shot?" the man said. "I already have been. I've lost a lamp."

He tilted up his helmet-shaded face and pointed to his socket with his left hand, opening his right to show the orb in bloody proof. Grinning.

He kept grinning, and the officer nodded, approving the man's return to the first-aid stations in the rear.

Their exchange was quick, and I looked away, shuddering. Afterward I had to ask my basketmate Buck Shot if it had really happened. It had, he said.

We kept on our way, quieter then. I huddled against Buck Shot's dingy white feathers, saddened and repulsed by what I'd seen, but not quite imagining that such a wicked injury could—would—happen to me.

When it did, it wasn't what killed me. I lived on with my wounds—bodily and otherwise—until June 13, 1919. The taxidermist did his work, and I ended up here not long after.

Like my fellow hero Major Whittlesey, I had expected the Great War to be a temporary interruption. I'd settle back into my original orbit once the guns fell silent. Instead, within eight strange and painful months of my famous flight, I was dead. Three years after he and his mutilated band of survivors were freed from the Pocket, Whit was, too. Well prior to our respective deaths, he and I both realized—and suffered considerably from the realization—that after a war there can be no getting back to the original plan.

In the Great War's immediate aftermath, many seemed to think that honor and glory ought to be more than adequate compensation for our inability to recuperate our lives to a state of normalcy. When he was still in here with me, my pigeon buddy President Wilson would rag me, joking but jealous, about all the ink committed to Whit and me in newsprint, magazines, the pages of books.

But so much of it was wrong, and so much of it was terrible. The worst was a phenomenally popular poem, titled "Cher Ami," by Harry Webb Farrington. I can still hear President Wilson reciting it in a mocking voice:

> The finest fun that came to me
> Was when I went with Whittlesey;
> We marched so fast, so far ahead!
> "We all are lost," the keeper said . . .

Dreadful, for so many reasons.

But heartbreaking, too, as a reminder of an era when a man like Farrington—a Methodist revivalist, a university graduate, the athletic director for the French troops during the war—might be moved to grind out such a commemorative poem, indeed a whole book of them, with the certainty that he was creating an enduring memorial to noble events. Many men who served in the war displayed this sort of rough-and-ready, well-rounded masculinity, as sensitive to the value of abstractions like Art and Poetry as they were to Honor and Glory. Few who saw combat managed to retain this attitude, at least without a great deal of effort.

And this is as it should be. The worst thing about Farrington's poem is that it presents the vast obscenity that was the Great War as a jolly adventure—but in fact any war story, no matter how unsparing or how true, warns against war only if its audience wants to be warned.

Even my story. Over the years the crowds that pass by my case have taught me that.

Paraphernalia of violence surrounds me here and seems to thrill at least as many as it appalls: an entrenching shovel, a .30-caliber machine gun, an artillery shell for a French howitzer.

I, too, have become paraphernalia of violence.

A German hand grenade, nicknamed "turtle" by Allied forces, interests me particularly, as does everything that humans make and then give an animal's name. What purpose do these nicknames serve? Do they make the lethal apparatus seem more natural and therefore inevitable? Therefore no one's fault?

Sergeant Stubby considers this interest morbid. I tell him it's simply a matter of taste—a human concept I picked up but still don't completely understand. Is it tasteful to have stuffed us and put us in the Smithsonian?

Even now, on this side of it, death perplexes me. Unlike human beings, birds tell no stories about what follows death; I expected the void. Now I'm here, free from all bodily needs, watching and remembering. I'm not sure how long I'll continue like this. I don't know whether my and Sergeant Stubby's wakeful states are the result of taxidermy or—somehow—of the adulation we earned during our brief lives. Maybe death is like this for every animal. The ancient Greeks associated message-bearing pigeons with oracles; from where I perch, it would seem that there's something to that belief.

A common rhetorical situation following the Great War involved the dead speaking. "We are the Dead," for instance, begins a line from John McCrae's well-known poem "In Flanders Fields." And we are, I am, dead and speaking, speaking in a way that would be called "from beyond the grave" if I'd been given a grave instead of this bright glass case.

Even in the throes of the archivist mania that I esteem

among the staff here, no curator would ever taxidermy a human soldier. But even if the Smithsonian was so disposed to flout taboo, it couldn't have the man it wanted the most: it couldn't do Charles Whittlesey.

Whit, it seems, wanted the opposite of what I got. His family put up a marker in the cemetery in Pittsfield once it was clear that he was gone for good. But it's an IMO: In Memory Only.

The name of the exhibit that my body is in, here with good ol' Sergeant Stubby, is *The Price of Freedom*. When they point from the other side of the glass, *Freedom isn't free*, I hear the patriots say. *Blah, blah, blah.* They're right, but not for the reasons they think they are.

The Great War cost me a lot, and although it's not a competition, on this, the eve of my centenary, I can honestly conclude that it cost Whit more.

CHAPTER 2

CHARLES WHITTLESEY

~~~~~~~~~

Monuments matter most to pigeons and soldiers.

Some matter more than others. None matter more to me than the Soldiers' and Sailors' Monument on Riverside Drive on the Upper West Side.

It's not a monument for my war, the Great War, the war that has caused me to be known these past three years as "Go to Hell" Whittlesey, heroic commander of the Lost Battalion. Instead its white marble gleams for the Union army, which won the Civil War almost sixty years ago.

The Soldiers' and Sailors' Monument has a personal significance for me, one that has nothing to do with war. It's where I—fresh from Harvard Law School, naïve and lonesome—met the man who would be my entrée into the double life I led until I chose to let the war interrupt it.

My thoughts keep returning to it tonight, though Marguerite and I are currently a couple of miles away, walking from the Rivoli movie palace on Broadway toward her midtown apartment. The November breeze blows chill and damp. I'm wearing my best fall jacket, which feels a bit ostentatious—it's already discomfiting that the Rivoli's ushers invariably make a show of recognizing me—but Marguerite likes the pomp of seeing a film there, the spectacle of the other moviegoers who pack the Greek Revival building being as interesting to her as anything on the screen. She works in advertising, and even on her weekends she harbors a professional interest in human behavior. Knowing better than to apply her gimlet amateur psychologist's eye to me, she has to exert her analytic capacity on strangers.

I enjoy the program of musicians—soloists, organ, and orchestra—who accompany the movies there. Enjoy turning invisible for a while in the darkness, no one asking for stories of the front in France.

As we arrive at the door of her kitchenette apartment building at Fifth Avenue and Fifty-fourth Street, Marguerite drops my arm. I have told her that I'm going away for the weekend, which is true. I've also let her think that it's to check on my parents in Pittsfield, which is not.

"Thank you, Charlie," she says, reaching into her reticule to find her key. "As always, it's been a lovely evening. Maybe when you get back, you can see somebody about that cough."

"I might," I say, though I won't. I've already been to the specialist that Bayard—her brother-in-law, my best friend and former law partner—recommended; the man told me that he was sorry but that not much can be done for gas-related TB. Not even for a *war hero*.

"Well, I hope you do," she says, her eyes meeting mine from behind her glasses—a couple of gangly four-eyes, that's Marguerite and me. "I need to keep you around for a while. My Friday nights would feel aimless without you."

I make myself smile. Even at thirty-five—a certified Old Maid, as she puts it cheerily—she looks young and bright. When I no longer monopolize her free time, she might get into greater social circulation. She deserves more vivacious companions than solitary, wheezing me, looking every day of my thirty-seven years and then some.

My little sister, Annie, might've grown up to look like Marguerite, I think for the millionth time. And been every lick as smart, probably. Ever since I met her, Marguerite has been like a sister to me.

She squeezes my hand, and I kiss her on the cheek, which smells faintly of geraniums. "Don't get too close!" she says, kissing mine back. "I'm a regular bed of garlic."

We went to Barbetta for dinner, Marguerite's choice. She had insisted, as she often did, on theming our evening: we were seeing a Valentino picture, she reasoned, and Valentino hails from Italy. The meal was delicious. Rather than a red-sauce-ladling joint with checked tablecloths, Barbetta was a Piedmontese place, upscale and a bit eccentric. I paid, of course, not minding the price. Though she doesn't know it yet, this evening will be Marguerite's parting memory of me, and I want it to be perfect.

The movie was ridiculous, as we knew it would be, having seen Valentino earlier that spring in *The Four Horsemen of the Apocalypse* on another of our Friday outings. We snickered in the upper balcony, far back above the crowd. His dandyish poses! The purple prose of the title cards! His randy leers revealing the whites all the way around his smoldering eyes! But we had to admit that the Latin Lover did possess a titillating magnetism, as the papers all said.

Marguerite's face—thin, full-cheeked, pale under her dark hair—glows in the streetlamps. I am struck by a pang of sorrow and fear at the small precious goodness that the world contains and that I will shortly abandon, but I believe I succeed in keeping it from my expression, which in any case the lamps have cast in darkness.

"Adieu and good night, Marguerite," I say. "Dream, if you can, of Valentino."

"Same to you." She affects a swooning, moony gaze like that of Agnes Ayres in *The Sheik* and steps inside, laughing that laugh of hers, a sound like a china plate breaking. She might have waved, but I'd already turned away.

At a safe remove from her windows, I stop to light a cigarette. Even with my cough, I smoke so much these days that I could use a Pershing boot as an ashtray. At this point I've no good reason to stop.

From here I'll head back to Broadway, then north to Eighty-ninth, to the monument on the banks of the Hudson. It will take me a while to get there, even at my pace: Galloping Charlie, tall as a weed and always marching double time. My ship doesn't hoist anchor until eleven tomorrow morning,

and the radium hour hand of my army-approved wristlet—
my trench watch—glows at ten forty-five. I should make it to
the monument by eleven thirty, and I won't take long bidding
my farewell. Tonight I'm interested only in the place itself,
not the men who haunt it, as I might have been in the past.

I've always enjoyed strolling the streets, whether with the
intent to remain solitary or to meet someone. Lately my walks
have been almost exclusively nocturnal: in the dark no one
recognizes me, and this anonymity reminds me of my former
freedom.

But walking at night also makes it more likely that I'll lose
my bearings, which is something I no longer enjoy. Before
the war few pastimes afforded me greater pleasure than
wandering through the city, ending up somewhere strange.
But now, having been twice officially lost—lost as in waylaid,
misplaced, unreachable, doomed, lost as in the Lost Battalion—
I find the appeal is itself somewhat lost to me. I need to know
where I am. I want a magnet in my beak, like Bill Cavanaugh
said pigeons have, always able to seek and find home. *Cher
Ami, my savior, I grieve you*, I think absurdly, eyes to the sky.
All the pigeons are roosting, of course. The sky stares back,
empty.

A slight, dapper man at the corner adjusts his hat atop his
perfectly slicked hair: a type that's come to be known as the
Vaselino. I smile as I pass, picturing him wearing a kaffiyeh
and perched atop a steed, but I take care not to meet his gaze.

I suppose I shouldn't mock Valentino; he may be a ham,
but he's a better actor than I.

The Lost Battalion: that's the straightforwardly named picture they convinced me to appear in, rushed through pro-
duction in 1919. I agreed to play myself. Myself! I didn't feel
as though I could tell them no, not in light of the case made
by Major General Alexander—who also played himself, with
greater enthusiasm—that this movie would be good for the
reputation of the troops who served, and for the army as a
whole, and also good for the memory of the dead, the dead for

whom (I felt, although Alexander did not say) I must claim responsibility. My trusty second-in-command, George McMurtry, played himself, too, as did Cullen and McKeogh, Jordan and Hershkowitz, Cepaglia and Bergasse, Munson—poor Munson—and Krotoshinsky.

The producer didn't ask much of me: put on fatigues and a trench helmet, pose with my former subordinates, pretend to consult a map. Since my scenes were shot in a Westchester County meadow, not in the Charlevaux Ravine, I didn't even have to spend a night away from home. They assured me that my performance, such as it was, would be blended so seamlessly with actual battle footage from the Argonne Forest that the audience would be convinced I was there.

I *was* there, of course. The experience seems far stranger in retrospect than it did at the time: a day spent playacting the most horrible events of my life in order to help someone produce a largely false depiction of it that will almost certainly supplant the real thing in popular consciousness. Marguerite couldn't believe that I would consider it, tried to reassure me that I was within my rights to refuse. *Why on earth would you want to relive that?* she asked. I replied with a muddled paraphrase of Alexander's appeal to my sense of duty.

The truth was that I was reliving it every day anyway.

I, unlike Valentino, am by no means handsome enough to spark collective sexual fantasies among the moviegoing public. When I saw myself in *The Lost Battalion* at its New York premiere, I squirmed in my seat at how awkward my performance seemed: stiffer than the manufactured sets wherein actors playing brave enlistees bade farewell to actors playing proud parents. I realize now that my and my fellow veterans' filmed behavior *was* quite natural, or nearly so, given the odd circumstances. It was the context—cast onto the silver screen—that made us appear cringing and gauche, out of place, simply because we weren't rolling our eyes and thrashing about like Valentino and Ayres. I and my men were in the film to grant it authenticity, yet somehow we were the least convincing thing in it. The whole experience was a pungent reminder—a reminder I didn't need—that in a contest against passion, truth always makes a poor showing.

In any event the reviewers thought my stoic taciturnity apt. *"American deadpan,"* said one of the notices. *"A man of infinite class and a true gentleman,"* said another.

I wished they would all shut up.

The film flopped in New York City, but they still trot it out as a reliable fund-raiser at American Legion halls all over the country. All right with me—the wounded and their families need the money—so long as I never have to see it again. I fled celebrity after *The Lost Battalion*'s retreat from theaters, but celebrity follows. Even here on Broadway, I look over my shoulder, half expecting to find it behind me.

In another sense—a sense that Valentino might or might not understand—I am quite the performer. Canyons of incomprehension yawn between me and most other human beings, and I keep acting as if it's possible for me to reach across and join them on their side, to span the gap between who they believe me to be and who I really am. Theater of war, theater of life. I'll always have to be an actor if I stay.

Rounding Columbus Circle, I look up at the statue of the man who discovered America, this America that bore me toward enlistment aboard ideals that still bind me: Honor and Duty. Not merely words to be carved in the marble of tombstones. Like the angel holding the globe on the statue's pedestal, we infantry tried to hand the world back to itself intact, though we who fought have been blown apart. Whether the world will hold together remains to be seen.

On the October day when we reached and were trapped in the Pocket, we learned that for an infantryman a successful attack can be worse than a defeat. I will dream forever of men with blown-off legs attempting to run. Of skin shreds and scraps of American uniforms. Of the whistle of a shell and the pulverized chunk of flesh that's left of the man who'd just been next to you. Corpses annihilated, no hope of a marked grave. War as magician. War as vanishing act.

Immediately after we were rescued, ordinary activities, like brushing my teeth—mechanical before—felt stunningly enjoyable. Now almost nothing does. To go from living like a soldier, thinking only from minute to minute, to having once again to think far into the fields of the future is more than many minds can muster.

My hand shakes as I light another cigarette, but I smile anyway, because happiness has crept back to me now that it's almost time to execute my escape. A woman on the corner startles at my face, illuminated by my match, grinning like a jack-o'-lantern. I want to reassure her—*Believe me, lady, you have nothing to fear from me*—but she hurries to the next block.

Passing Seventy-ninth Street, I recall my brother Melzar's wedding a little over a year ago—September 27, 1920—at All Souls Unitarian Church on the Upper East Side, straight across Central Park from where I'm walking now. Though the ceremony was tiny, I had Marguerite there with me, just as we'd stood up together in her sister's wedding. Melzar and his bride, Addie, live today not three blocks from the church, and Melzar, a pillar of respectability, works for the Phelps Dodge Corporation. His life runs in a comfortable furrow from their home to his offices on John Street, and I am glad that there's no chance of bumping into him here.

Though I've been walking for almost an hour, I don't feel tired as I reach Riverside. Amid the misty rain and the fog of the Hudson, the Soldiers' and Sailors' Monument rises before me like a decrepit ghost.

A compact approximation of a Corinthian temple, the design was called "The Temple of Fame." From the looks of it, the columns and eagles began to decay instantly upon its dedication in 1902, which certainly reflects my experience of fame. But the marble blocks, dissolving and sugary, don't depress me as they might have in the years between the standoff in the Pocket and my new resolve. I laugh out loud at my own bathos, which likely makes me look crazy, but that's all right; I don't want to be approached.

The usual wooden benches line the chalky promenade, just as they did when I first came to the city with little experience but great desire. Banking and contractual law filled my days, and I soon sought ways to fill my nights.

I was expected to have a strong handshake and broad shoulders, to be a man's man as well as a woman's man and a Christian, and not to be weak-kneed, thin-skinned, effeminate, sissified. I kept my hair up, as Felix would later teach me to say.

At Williams, and then at Harvard, all the surfaces had had a haughty, hygienic varnish, and I'd affected just such a varnish myself. In truth I preferred the smut and dirt of the city. The oily filth of the leather straps on the subway. The hints on the street of things done in darkness, away from the lamps and their nimbuses of gnats. Yet this dirtiness held a kind of purity, a virgin allure.

When I came back after the war, I could no longer access this.

At Williams I'd gained the reputation of someone who worked too hard to spare time for the ladies. At Harvard the same. In the city, too, I maintained a decorous fiction about who I was and for whom I spared time. When renting my lodgings, I asked my landlady if I could have women in my rooms. "Why, certainly," she replied. "This is your home." I have always appreciated the polite ways by which New Yorkers in close quarters remain aloof, granting one another privacy. But I never hosted even one woman in my rooms.

I discovered quickly that for someone with my proclivities, one of the most private places is actually the street. The term I now know to use is "cruising": I went cruising. One of the many bits of slang that Felix—whom I first met right here, at the monument—taught me. I wore out my shoes that first summer, drifting after dinner and before bed. What led me to the Soldiers' and Sailors' Monument, which Felix told me was a well-established pickup spot, I'll never know. Some kind of instinct, I suppose.

That August night in 1908, strolling in the cool breeze off the Hudson, I simply felt an impulse to look up. Felix sat on a bench at the base of the one-hundred-foot-tall cylindrical rotunda, a structure whose phallic suggestiveness was not lost on me.

I sit now where he and I first sat, and I light another cigarette. He was smoking then, too. Calmly intelligent and dressed with a trim elegance, he looked nothing like the swishes and obvious types—which is not to say I resented them, as some men did. They didn't bother me then and don't bother me now; I've just never been interested. I like masculine men. Felix was masculine, middle-aged but unlined, and youthful, his skin tallowy somehow, his jaw strong, his hair blond.

"Need a light?" he asked. Exciting me, for I knew that that was not all he was offering.

I sat beside him, apprehensive yet finding something safe about him, too, discreet and distant, like a mathematical theorem.

We went to bed together only once, that night, at his place, the Dakota, quite nearby, very big, very private. And it was fine: less sweaty and furtive, more practiced and unhurried than any of my student tumbles. Yet not something to repeat—not because I felt guilty but because we simply enjoyed each other more as friends. Professorial in manner, Felix took an interest in mentoring me. He taught me where else I might go in the city to find what I sought—what restaurants and bars I could try if I tired of the streets.

Soon enough I had my round of places to meet men—men like me: respectable and professional and bourgeois in their normal lives. Men bound by an unspoken code to never betray our shared secret. But I still visited the monument on occasion for nostalgia's sake.

Now that I, too, am a war veteran like those it commemorates, the monument is doubly significant to me. Perhaps triply: just like the structure, I am falling apart. Fame has all but foreclosed my previous life. I am so much more identifiable now, potentially subject to blackmail. I have permitted myself only a couple of assignations since my return.

If I sit here too long tonight, someone will read me as seeking a tryst. I don't want to speak to anyone, so I stand and walk past the monument toward the Hudson.

A seagull sits on a post near the shoreline, huddled up but not asleep, its beady eye shining in the light reflected off the water. I wish I had some bread to feed it. The river stinks, but I've smelled worse.

"You can never know," I tell the seagull. "And I can never show you."

The bird's neck telescopes slightly upward; its sharp teardrop head ticks toward me.

Because there's some purchase to be gained through acting a little cracked, I continue. "The war. The trenches and the funkholes, all festering cesspools breathing forth the toxic reek of guts and shit. American. German. French. Horse. Atrocious, barbarous—it stank. Words falter. Fetid and stygian, a river in Hades. I missed flush toilets. Those long days in the Pocket, I had many wishes, but selfishly, among them—among those blood-filled holes and dying men—frankly one was to no longer have to touch and dwell in my own excrement. Like animals do. But not wild animals, or mostly wild ones like you. Like animals in confinement. Forced to find a home in horror. Forced by men like me."

The seagull makes that cruel face that all seagulls make and turns away. I do the same. Wishing again that pigeons were here at night—much kinder birds—but such is not their way. They are all home, as I should be.

Rain falls as I walk back south. I should return by the path I came, take the most direct route to where I live. Bachelors' quarters, as they say.

Instead I turn on Amsterdam. Straight through Hell's Kitchen, where Bill Cavanaugh used to live. I do not know his old address, though I could probably find it through the army. His mother's still there, with his little sister, Annie. He described the place when we were in France. I've never visited.

Geographically speaking, Hell's Kitchen is not far from my place in Midtown. In every other sense, it's a world away. A block into the neighborhood, the atmosphere changes, I hear voices dropping and feel eyes tracking me, and the full dimensions of the foolhardiness of my detour begin to become clear. These streets are more orderly now than when Bill was growing up here, but that order, I recall, is imposed by gangs, not by the police department, which evidently will patrol it only in sizable packs. Thanks to Prohibition, the commercial prospects of the old tanners' warehouses along the river have been reinvigorated by rumrunners; the previously senseless violence of the local hooligans has found fresh purpose.

A slender, tidy fellow in spectacles and a dinner jacket must make for quite a sight among the tenements. While most of the inhabitants no doubt bear me no ill will, one or two are enough to make trouble, and it's not hard to imagine some toughs accosting me out of simple curiosity, much as John James Audubon might have hastened to shoot an unfamiliar bird. My pulse quickens, as does my step, and I laugh at myself. What, at this point, have I to fear?

As luck would have it—both the gangsters' luck and mine, for I can hardly imagine what disastrous effect the casual murder of a national hero might have on their criminal enterprise—I arrive unmolested at Tenth and Fiftieth, the heart of Hell's Kitchen. I allow myself a moment's pause, imagining I'll find some sign that will show me where Bill hailed from, but there's nothing, or almost nothing. The streets smell wet, and gently of horses, and I can see the outlines of pigeon coops atop some of the roofs. Bill always smelled like tobacco and hay.

At the doorway of the building on the corner, some resident has planted a statue of St. Francis of Assisi. The Cavanaughs can't possibly live there—what odds would those be?—but Bill was our regiment's best pigeon handler, and that's how I picture him: St. Francis standing with an armful of birds.

Saints fast and give their worldly possessions away until there's nothing left to give. I have done something similar, though I am no saint.

Sentimental narratives are ever popular, but especially in times of decline. I cut left on Fiftieth and strive to be unsentimental—about Bill or about his treasured Cher Ami, whose very name bespeaks sentimentality: *Dear Friend*. Oh, dear.

For years I've felt like a rotten egg trying to hide beneath a fresh white shell.

The Neo-Gothic spires of St. Patrick's Cathedral tower in the night. Even to an unbeliever, the church's beauty refuses to be denied. Bill was Irish Catholic, and faithful. The taste of him, I imagine, like sweet and healthy candy. How I wish I could have loved him without fear. His charisma without guile. World without end, Amen. The church's roseate stained-glass window regards me like a judgmental eye.

Forgive me, I think as I skirt Grand Central, where Marguerite thinks I'll go tomorrow to take the train to Pittsfield. I put my younger brother Elisha on that train last week. He'd been living by me—his own room in the same spartan building—but I sent him home to be with our parents. He was an ambulance driver in France before I went over, he got gassed as well, and his resulting TB was a horror, truly. The whole quarters could hear him coughing through the walls at night, louder than me. Now that I am leaving, I don't want him to be here on his own.

And here indeed I am again: 136 East Forty-fourth, my home for one more night. I let myself in and head to my room.

For years, whenever I've come home, I've felt like a suitcase dumped out at a hotel: secret disarray behind a closed door. But this past week I have packed myself tightly, everything in its right place, and I am happy to be taking myself away. The doctor to whom Bayard sent me gave me some pills to help my cough and to help me sleep. "We can mask the symptoms at least," he said. For weeks I took them, not with water but with whiskey. His pharmacist dispensed it to me, as so many pharmacists have been doing lately, in keeping with the requirements of Prohibition.

The bottle helps me endure what I can't when sober. It doesn't make me forget. Nothing makes me forget. It merely lets me be in proximity to the memories without being sliced by them. My memories of the Argonne do not merely get on my nerves; they scrape across my mind like a cheese grater. But not tonight. I take no whiskey, no pills, having thrown them all away, not wanting anyone to find them.

And for once I feel as though I don't need them. The clothes I'll wear tomorrow are already laid out on the chair, my army-issue pistol in the pocket of my coat, loaded, even though I don't plan to need it. On my trip I'll take no baggage aside from one change of clothes, and my dress uniform, and the eight letters I've typed up this past week, stacked neatly beneath the lamp on my desk, addressed to the people I am most sorry to be leaving. Mother and Father and Marguerite, Melzar and Elisha, Bayard and McMurtry, et cetera, et cetera. My ticket for the *Toloa* is on top of the heap. I undress. Touch the ticket once before I flip out the light.

I fall asleep in peace for the first time in years, the city noise soothing me, the sounds of tires outside hissing over dim, wet streets.

———————

I wake to a gray morning and the clinks downstairs of Mrs. Sullivan cooking breakfast. I requested that she have mine at eight. When she knocks to bring the tray, I am dressed and ready.

"You're looking cheery today, Mr. Whittlesey," she says as she brings the meal in, enlivening the small space with the roasted scent of coffee.

"Am I?" I smile, smelling the food: heat and grease. A man hit by a shell disintegrates into bits, like an overcrisped slice of bacon when bitten.

"I hope you have a fine time with the family," she says, black skirts rustling, her widow's weeds. "Please tell Elisha that I've been praying for his recovery."

"I will," I say, though I won't, and anyway no amount of praying will heal his lungs. "Mrs. Sullivan, here's my check for next month's rent. If you could do me the courtesy, would you cash it right away?"

"Of course, Mr. Whittlesey, of course," she says, her eyes puzzled beneath her steel-gray eyebrows.

But I know that she'll do it, as she's a woman of her word. Given the unorthodox nature of my plans, I want to spare her any financial inconvenience.

"Thank you for breakfast," I say as she makes for the door. "Thank you for everything."

The coffee and eggs go down delectably, and I look around my furnished room, humble in the pearly light.

Almost none of what remains in the space is mine, and none of it would I desire to own, save perhaps the dresser: bird's-eye maple and nicer than any other item Mrs. Sullivan had scrounged up. Its drawers held the belongings of unknown lodgers preceding me and will hold those of my successors with the same impartiality. Atop the tiny swirls disrupting the smooth lines of the grain rests the last memento that I've allowed myself to keep, the only one that I'm taking with me: Marguerite's calling card.

She gave it to me the day we met, almost a decade ago, in that halcyon time before the war when people still used them. "Marguerite Babcock" in elegant script on card stock the pale beige of a Communion wafer.

Early summer up the Hudson Valley. A garden party at

Bayard's parents' mansion in Kinderhook, in honor of his engagement to Marguerite's sister, Elsie. The flora and fauna were doing their best Garden of Eden impression: butterflies in the lilacs and stone fruits forming on the trees. Family and friends in weekend frocks and togs, looking as hand-tinted as a picture postcard. Yet in these outlandishly serene surroundings, I recognized in Marguerite the same watchful distance that I'd cultivated myself—a kind of superimposition, as if she were in the scene but not of it.

When Elsie and Bayard introduced us and I took her extended hand in mine, I thought of my Williams College physical-science class: atoms bonding to form a molecule.

"Would you care to go for a stroll around the grounds?" I asked, unafraid that Bayard or any of the other attendees would fear impropriety, as we'd remain in view of the group no matter how far we walked. Not to mention that, honestly, both he and Elsie would have been happy if Marguerite and I had turned out to be a love match. Both had worried in my presence about how unusual and solitary Marguerite was for a woman, how inexplicably devoted to her career.

She was not a beauty, Bayard had warned me, like Elsie, a veritable Gibson Girl, with hourglass figure and corona of hair. As if I cared. No, he cautioned, Marguerite had a soft chin, weak eyes, thin arms, a flat figure.

But there, in the supersaturated green of the garden, Marguerite looked lovely: kindred, sympathetic to the likes of me.

"Somehow I don't think you're one of those mashers who'll paw my knee on a bench as soon as we're around the bend," she said, a smile not quite visible at the corners of her thin lips.

Disarmed by her forthrightness, I could only laugh and confirm reports of my confirmed bachelorhood.

And I felt, as we walked, unaccountably that I could tell her anything, a sensation that I hadn't had since Annie died. Because of that first day with Marguerite, I will forever associate the scent of dogwood blossoms with pungent candor.

We paused at a gazebo to gaze back at the party. Men and women in pairs, celebrating the practice of pairing. "Do you ever wish that you could be like everyone else?" I asked, pulling a white flower from a branch. "That it could be easier?"

"No," she said, taking the flower and tucking it into the band of her hat. With the incisiveness that I would soon learn made her such a good advertising woman and would make her such a good friend, she added, "I like being the way I am. Don't you?"

No one before had ever asked me directly. I had never, in such terms, posed the question to myself.

"I do," I said, and realized I meant it.

"There are plenty of people who do things the normal way," she said, nodding at the patio of guests. "What's the harm in not? Besides, motherhood seems like less than a bargain for the ladies."

As if to illustrate her point, one of the children on the patio dropped a chocolate ice cream down the front of her dress. Her mother rushed over to scold and comfort.

"I look forward to being the outré aunt to Elsie and Bayard's children," she said. "And I know they plan to make you a godfather. We'll likely be seeing more of each other."

"I'd like that very much," I said. "In fact, I'd prefer to see you again before they have time to reproduce themselves."

"That can be arranged," she said, smiling without reservation and handing me her card. "Find me when we're back in the city."

"I promise," I said.

I stack the dishes on the tray, and put the letters in my suitcase, and figure that I might as well be on my way.

I place my key on the bedspread and leave the door unlocked. I imagine Mrs. Sullivan keeps a spare key, but I've never asked, and I can't now, and I don't want to oblige her to break it down or pay for a locksmith. Grateful not to run into any of my fellow lodgers on the stairs, I depart without saying anything further to anybody.

Rain taps the awnings and slicks the pavement, but I'm going to walk. Heading to lower Manhattan, I imagine it will be almost as though I'm going to work, though it's a Saturday.

The *Toloa* departs for Cuba from Pier 16, where all the United Fruit steamships dock. I've walked by countless times on breaks from my law office, admiring the blinding sun on the spotless hulls and its reflections on the tan faces of the sailors. United Fruit paints all its reefers pure white—to ward off the banana-spoiling solar heat—and each ship looms from its berth like a New England church, promising cool relief, conveyance to the next world.

The letter I've written to Bayard feels heaviest in my suitcase: *"Just a note to say good-bye. I'm a misfit by nature and by training, and there's an end of it."*

My one-way ticket sits in my breast pocket, a lucky charm.

CHAPTER 3

CHER AMI

———— ❧ ————

The desire to be something other than what one is is a cruel affliction, and I am finally cured.

I no longer wish that I could be a human. But when I was young, growing up in the Cotswolds, humans seemed to me the most admirable creatures.

This was because the first human I knew was John. He was an exceptional man of the kind whom I had the good fortune to meet several times over the course of my relatively short life. By that I mean: this fellow was mad for pigeons.

Here in the Smithsonian, I've gathered that our reputation as a species is not as sterling as it used to be. I overhear snide comments about "rats with wings." Although I'm no fan of rats—no one who served in the trenches is—I hesitate to take offense at ignorant remarks like these. Rats, too, have stronger character and more admirable habits than humans tend to credit.

In life I preened. I kept clean. We pigeons carry disease no more readily than any other being. When I hear patrons outside my glass case say hateful things, I wish I could remind them of our intertwined history.

"It's in their Bible," I've said to Sergeant Stubby—often enough that he's probably weary of hearing it, although being a dog he's too kind to say as much. "Noah sent a raven to find dry land, but the raven failed him and didn't return. Then he sent a dove, who did come back after finding only water. When Noah sent the dove out again, she found dry earth, and instead of staying put she returned to the Ark with an olive branch. As dogs are loyal, pigeons are trustworthy."

John understood that about us, and more. He got as much from caring for us as we got from his care. With us in the dovecote off the barn, he felt safe in a feather-lined pocket of time. He loved all the earthbound animals on Wright Farm, too, the ducks and the sheep and the horses and especially the dogs. But though he fed them tidbits and taught them to shake with their paws, he preferred the rugged claws and craggy feet of us pigeons, the rootlike way we tendriled our toes around his finger perch.

I was born into a family of achievers. Monogamous like all pigeons and quick to breed, my parents had been together for four years by the time I arrived in 1916 and had raised many babies, always two at once, as was the clockwork case with my twin sister and me.

Our father, Big Tom, kept our two eggs warm for eighteen days, never missing a turn. Our mother, Lady Jane, did the same for eighteen nights. Dad was handsome, a red cock with copper feathers, famous throughout our county for his record race times. Mum was a silvery hen with black-and-white checkered wings, elegant and regal as her name suggested, known for her ability to traverse prodigious distances without getting tired.

Farmer and Mrs. Wright granted John full authority over bestowing our names. He wasn't what you'd call an educated man, but as an autodidact who read in the evenings when his chores were complete, he took the responsibility seriously. Sometimes he aspired to timeless simplicity, hence my older siblings Twilight and Dawn. Others he went literary, hence my brother Thomas Hardy, or theatrical, hence my sister Sarah Bernhardt. He christened us, too, according to personality traits, hence our friend Sweet Sam, or in line with some aspiration he had for us: racing homers all. John was avid in competition, and therefore a bird born a few weeks before my sister and me he called Fast Time.

John's only son was fighting in the Great War when my sister and I hatched, and so he named me Cher Ami, thinking of his boy in France—and thinking me, mistakenly, a boy; else I'd be Chère Amie. Unsure how to feel about this error, I was annoyed at being misperceived, but mostly I was reminded that sex is a much bigger to-do for humans than it is for us pigeons. Unlike a lot of birds, whose males and females look like different species—peek at a peacock next to a peahen—it's not something we pigeons tend to fret about until humans insist.

My sister received the appellation Miss America to express his wish, shared by many of his countrymen, that that nation across the pond would join in the bloodshed and end the attrition.

During those first few days in the snug, soft loft, John saw to it that Big Tom and Lady Jane had every comfort they required to raise Miss America and me. The two of them kept the two of us warm with their bodies' downy expanses and took turns feeding us pigeon milk: our mother by night and our father by day.

The fact that birds can produce milk surprises most humans and their mammalian cousins, who assume themselves to hold a monopoly on lactation. I should clarify that pigeon milk, rather more solid than liquid, is secreted by our crops, the elastic pouches below our throats where we store our meals. By contrast to the glands that give mammals their name—and that serve as a sign of sexual difference from which, I gather, many complications follow—the crops of both mother and father pigeon produce milk, and both parents equally share the task of feeding.

I should note, too, that most birds do not produce crop milk. Doing so is one of the defining characteristics of pigeons and doves—one of several, I have often thought, that place us in a peculiar middle ground between the avian kingdom and that of our furry, suckling friends.

Six days after my sister and I broke through the shells of our eggs, pure white and not much bigger than those of a robin, we opened our eyes to see our parents and our flock of dovecote-mates. These were not the plump, strutting park pigeons who coo through public squares and splash in fountains; no, John bred his racing homers to be slender and wiry, alert and faster than some of the express trains we'd see speeding through the countryside during our practice flights.

With his leathery hands and raspy voice, John devoted himself to the notion that the mental attitude of us, his birds, was the key that would unlock our promise in both racing and showing. He handled each of us each day and spoke to us constantly, his theory being that a creature will have no fear of accustomed things.

"In the showroom," he said, paraphrasing a book he'd been reading, "the pigeon meets coops handling, the judge's stick, and crowds for the first time. A frightened bird loses poise and type and does not show well."

He spoke of the showroom most in relation to my sister. Miss America was red, with wings in a lacy, cream-colored stencil, and she possessed the dainty mien of a ballerina. "I am a very original type," she told me, echoing John's refrain and tilting her head to show her profile like a queen on a coin.

I, on the other hand, was the spitting image of my mother, Lady Jane, said John, though she was silvery and I was blue. "Don't feel jealous of your sister, Cher Ami." I hadn't been, but I appreciated his concern for my state of mind. "Blue's the most common color of domestic pigeons, because blue is the color of your wild ancestor, *Columba livia*, the rock dove."

I bobbed my head in assent, and he laughed and stroked my slate-blue back.

"I been told that that Latin translates loosely as 'a leaden-colored bird that bobs its head,'" he said, "and you are shaping up to be a textbook picture of racing perfection."

He went about putting out our oats and hemp, our dried peas and lentils, keeping up his running conversation. John fed us twice a day, not throwing the food in, as he did for the chickens, but sitting in our pen and allowing us to peck from his hand, then filling the pans and cups as well, rarely scattering the grains on the floor, being a tidy man. He changed our water for drinking and bathing, then swept the floors and checked our nests. He liked to experiment with nesting materials, and while we usually had hay, he'd leave us long-leaf pine needles, oat straw and wheat straw, alfalfa and twigs, and even excelsior, sawdust, and burlap bags.

"You and Miss America are squabs no longer," he said, making sure our feed troughs were clean. "You're a couple of squeakers, going on youngsters. Soon it'll be time to start our training."

The day I first flew home was the day I knew the meaning of true purpose.

John carried us to a spot he'd chosen about a mile from our dovecote, nestled in the rolling green hills outside Chipping Norton. A "liberation point," he called it, using the parlance of pigeon racers: a term that refers to our liberation from the basket in which he'd transported us.

My own feelings about the term—and liberty in general—are complicated.

On the one hand, the feeling of emerging from enclosure, of launching away from the inert ground, of negotiating with the air's invisible thickness to resist and exploit the tug of gravity, amounts to an ecstatic release that I pity terrestrial beings for never knowing. Humans, fond of lists and categories, regard themselves as possessing five senses; pigeons have at least seven, some of which language does not name. Those that we share with you—sight, smell, touch—are so refined in us as to be barely analogous to yours. But the senses of pigeons are truly awakened only when we are in flight: from a thousand feet up, our side-set eyes take in the full vastness of the landscape along with its finest detail, our nostrils sort and source a panoply of odors, our feathers parse intricate patterns of breeze and gust, and still other perceptions map our position precisely above the turning earth. I do not remember my sightless escape from my egg-shell; therefore I think of that first flight home—bursting skyward into an overwhelming wealth of sensation—as my true birth.

But I do not think of it as a point of liberation. Because while it was the moment when I first became aware of my extraordinary capabilities for navigation and travel, my awakening was accompanied not by an impulse to wander and explore but by an intense and all-consuming drive to return to the Wright Farm dovecote by the best possible route. Do not think that this homeward drive of ours is fearful, lit by a desire to retreat to the safety of confinement. Rather, we seize upon these pathways with the same ruthless zeal shown by lions as they pounce upon gazelles. Our need to fly home pushes through all other concerns—including self-preservation, thus our usefulness on the battlefield. It's braided into the fibers of our muscles and the barbules of our feathers. It gives us our purpose, and therefore our power.

It does not, however, make us free.

Although John released Miss America and me simultaneously on that first flight, I outpaced my sister—rocketing high, noting my position relative to sun and hills, decoding from the chaos of wind the familiar smells of the Wrights' sheep and our own excrement-bedecked dovecote—and I beat her back to the loft, where I bragged to my parents with no small amount of conceit.

"I don't even know where Miss America is!" I said, flapping with excess energy, more exalted than tired. "I left her so far behind."

"You're a speedy one, as your father and I suspected you'd be, Cher Ami," said Mum, giving me a kiss on the top of my head. "Now, drink some water—not too much—and wait for your sister. The time has come for us to tell you something."

When Miss America returned, happy and panting, Dad and Mum took us out to the flypen, beneath the blue sky and the shining sun. John, who liked to smoke his pipe strolling home over the meadows, would take a while to make it back and confirm our arrival.

"Now, listen, you two," our mother began. "It's time you understood something about birds and humans. We pigeons of John's are fortunate. We are his companions, and he has for us grand plans. But born on any other farm, you could just as easily have ended up meat."

Miss America and I cocked our heads, less horrified than perplexed.

"Nowadays it's mostly chickens, and sometimes ducks and geese," our father said, "but humans once ate all sorts of birds. Did you see the waterfowl in the pond as you were flying?"

Miss America and I nodded. Our parents must have delivered a version of this speech to our siblings, too, careful and rehearsed.

"Those were their food once," he said. "Swan and stork, crane and heron, peacock and bustard. But pigeons, particularly squab"—and here he gestured at the Wrights' milk cow, velvety and limpid, munching grass in her pasture—"were thought to be the most delicious. Veal from the clouds."

Next to me Miss America quivered. Humans ate lots of other animals, too, I knew, but it didn't seem real to me, the idea of being harmed by a human. It wouldn't until I got to the war.

"Happily," said our mum, taking up the thread, "some birds they came to see more as cohorts than as livestock."

At this, Miss America brightened. "We became pets!" she said.

"Not pets," Mum said, her tone gentle but firm. "Pets are animals that depend on humans. We are animals that humans depend on."

"Like hunting dogs," Dad said. "Or mules. Or, even better, like Thoroughbreds."

"We're the racehorses of the skies!" I said, recollecting the wind as it lofted my feathers.

"Now, dear," our mother said, "there's no need to borrow

dignity from other creatures. Besides, a racehorse can run at thirty-five miles per hour for a single mile, which I suppose is impressive for a big, flightless animal with a man on its back. But I, a homing pigeon—one pound of feathers and flesh—can fly five hundred miles in a day at over sixty miles per hour. I can do it without stopping to eat or drink. And I can find my way home from places I've never seen. Alone, by my wits, without anyone tugging my reins."

Our parents' speech was meant to foster pride in our capabilities, and indeed it did, particularly since I was still luxuriating in the thrill of that first flight over the hills.

But my newfound confidence also inclined me toward contrariness. "You do this because John wants you to, no?" I said. My parents were impressive, but John was intriguing.

Our father—always one for pigeon pride, which he had in abundance, one could even say in excess—puffed out his breast at this question. "John provides an occasion for our feats," he said. "But we perform them out of our inherent fiber. And while it's true that over thousands of years our human keepers have helped us become the extraordinary creatures that we are, so, too, have we shaped their history. Our line is descended from the pigeons who constituted the private post of the Rothschilds in London. Our forebears delivered them news of Napoleon's defeat at Waterloo a full day before the rest of the city heard it!"

This meant nothing to Miss America and me. "Darling, you digress," our mother said, rubbing her iridescent head against his shoulder. "What you must always remember, children, is that in the air no creature is our equal. Our wings, as the two of you found today, are shaped ideally for ease in lengthy flight. Our necks are muscular and flexible, allowing us vision in all directions. Our heads are large because our brains are large. Our vital parts are well protected against attacks."

"Rather more so than those of the mammals, including John and his ilk," our father said, an aside directed more toward me than Miss America. I wouldn't understand what he meant until the trenches of France.

"Most astonishing of all," my mother said, "is the quality after which these humans have named us: our ability to home."

"This is our home," said Miss America, craning her exquisite neck at the wire screen above us, which let in fresh breezes and the smell of clover. "Provided by the Wrights and maintained by John."

"We live in a home," said our mum. "That's correct. But for us home is a verb, too—a thing to do as well as a place to be."

"It would do many humans well to think in those terms," my father said. "The world would be a better place. Not so many people marching in conquest. Or stepping out for cigarettes, never to be seen by their families again."

"Even we pigeons don't know what enables us to do this," our mother continued, accustomed to his puzzling interruptions. "To return, if necessary, from a point we've never been, a thousand miles away. To humans it's evidently rather unusual and mysterious, a riddle that remains unsolved." She laughed, a bit ruefully. "What fun it would be to explain it to them! But we can't, of course. It comes so naturally to us, as you've just seen, and fundamental things are always the hardest to explain. Imagine describing the color red to one of the farm dogs! It simply can't be done."

"Practice is important," our father said. "As John continues your training, you'll encounter interference, danger, disorientation, and you'll learn to overcome it all. But experience isn't enough. You'll also develop strength of wing and steadiness of mind, keenness of eye and a sharp sense of direction, but these, too, are incidental to your innate and irreducible ability to home, to whatever site you regard as your home, from any location."

Pigeons have no belief in God nor any need for such belief, but like most creatures we have our rituals. That day our parents taught us about *the voice*—a voice that speaks from both within and outside each of us, that urges us homeward and reassures us that we'll get there. Every pigeon knows this voice. I still hear it in the Smithsonian every morning, though it's been a hundred years since I last took flight.

Our mother ended their talk to us with a truth that still astonishes me. "Now, Miss America and Cher Ami, the two of you must always listen to that voice, the voice humans intuit but cannot experience. Heed it at the start of every journey and you'll never be unable to home to your home."

"I'll want to home because home is where *you* are!" said Miss America, always sweeter than I.

"Me, too," I said, though truthfully I was more eager for the crossing of strange distances than for the many happy returns.

"You're good birds," our father said, and took us inside to show us how best to eat to restore our energy postflight.

My wait to practice listening for the voice was not a long one. John came the next day—and the next, and the next, always at the same time—carrying us off in a basket and liberating us from various points a mile from Wright Farm. Then he began strapping our basket onto a bicycle to take us farther—five miles, he said. Then he borrowed the Wrights' motorcar, and we flew for ten.

With each toss from John's hand, I could hear a voice behind my beak resonate with increasing clarity: *Cher Ami!* it said—it knew my name!—*Home to Wright Farm!* And home I went.

The day that John first liberated us at twenty miles, he came in early, the morning sun shining through the door of the dovecote, illuminating the feathers and dust motes, making the air sparkle.

"Cher Ami and Miss America," he said, crooked teeth smiling beneath his bushy mustache, "I've brought you some jewelry."

He scooped me up and set me in his lap, then put a narrow band on my left leg above my pink claw.

"Aluminum," he said as I balanced on my right foot atop his corduroy-clad thigh, his thick fingers delicate as they fastened the anklet. "Your first race is coming up, and we've got to have you registered. 'National Union Racing Pigeon, Number 615,' it says. But don't worry—you'll always be Cher Ami to me."

I flapped uneasily when he released me, testing the new weight on my leg. The band felt strange and cumbersome at first, but then soon like nothing at all, like a part of me, which it might as well have been. Although I didn't yet fully understand what it meant, I knew that I had crossed another threshold, had become more completely myself.

John did the same for Miss America, who held her foot out and admired the accessory before John popped us into our wicker basket and put us in the motorcar, on the seat, while he cranked the engine and drove us out.

Tossed, I spiraled, the band encircling my left ankle a badge rather than a burden, an indication of the seriousness of my purpose. I caught the breeze and made it back to our roost at a mile a minute, faster than John could have traveled in the car.

Miss America struggled, showing up late, taking three times as long. "The bracelet puts too much pressure on," she said, cleaning herself in the bathing water.

It wasn't long before John gave up on racing her and committed her to being a show bird, which suited her fine; she won many prizes. If my parents were disappointed, they didn't say so, but I could feel the pleasure that they took in my speed.

Early the next spring—the start of my second year, 1917—John sent me along with nine other birds, including Fast Time, to what would be my first race: five hundred miles, with a five-hundred-pound prize. John put almost every penny he won back into us, his hobby. I wanted to win for him, for the loft, and for myself.

We all fit into a single large shipping basket—a bit crowded, but John gave us ample food and water and drove us to the rail station at Chipping Norton. When John bade us farewell with final encouraging words and left us in the care of a porter, I flapped in alarm, but Fast Time calmed me with faint exasperation. "Easy, Cher Ami," she said. "We'll see John again soon enough, won't we?"

"But who'll toss us from the basket?" I asked.

"What a silly question," she said. "Does it matter? Out is out."

As we sat on the platform waiting to be loaded onto the train, we took note of garish images lining the walls. They were propaganda posters, many depicting the Germans as savage beasts: raping and pillaging, shelling and killing. DE-STROY THIS MAD BRUTE, one read across its top, and below that a German soldier in the form of a gorilla clutching Europe— personified as a lady, limp and partially clothed—in his hairy left arm, civilization in ruins on the horizon behind him.

Pigeons are capable of neither hatred nor patriotism. But there on the platform I began to see that humans had difficulty understanding the war without animal metaphors. "The fighting is raging like a tiger," someone on the platform said.

None seemed to understand that the war had come from them.

Another poster showed a picture of a pup in a Red Cross uniform beneath the headline EVEN A DOG ENLISTS, and across the bottom, WHY NOT YOU? It was meant to recruit men, but I thought about the question for hours and hours on the swaying train, dark in a freight car, silent and stoic. Half a dozen pigs squeaked and complained in the same car, but not we pigeons.

We arrived in Inverness the following morning, and after a confusion of strange hands and all-but-unintelligible voices and a bumpy ride into the countryside, when the men in charge of the race set us free, I thrilled to the familiar happiness of being high up and homing. The voice said, as it did every time, *Cher Ami! Home to your loft by the airway! Home to Wright Farm!* For a moment I was flummoxed by the alien topography of the Scottish Highlands, utterly different from the gentle hills of Chipping Norton. And then I knew where I was.

I flew as low as I could, for it was windy, and left the rest behind. The air was choked with grit blown up from the ground below, and my nictitating membranes skimmed my eyes constantly to keep them clear and bright. Like other birds, pigeons have a transparent third eyelid, a thin, glassy film that sweeps the eyeball like a windscreen wiper, rewetting it and swabbing away dust without interrupting our vision. It's always struck me as remarkable that humans must go blind for an instant each time they blink, but then again humans aren't routinely obliged to hurl their hollow-boned bodies between tree limbs at breakneck speed.

I needed sharp eyes for my journey. In the late afternoon, I was chased for two miles by a bird of prey, a falcon, broad-winged eater of ducks and chickens and pigeons. But not racing pigeons, at least not this one; I got away.

Then I ran into a thick pewter fog, as dangerous to homing as was any predator. I had to wait on the roof of a house for an hour, drinking from the wet shingles and thinking of how I longed to be home with John and corn, John and peas. When the fog lifted at dusk, I flew on at almost a hundred miles per hour to make up time, but soon night fell, and pigeons can't fly at night, or rather can't home. The world pours clues at us, as it always does, but when the sun's gone, they stop adding up.

I found shelter in a barn among fowl, a turkey and some hens, none too friendly, jealous maybe of my relative freedom. I stayed in the hayloft, pecked at stray seeds, and resolved to be off again at dawn.

I awoke to the prismatic blue eyes of a Siamese cat eyeing me hungrily and made my escape through a hole in the roof, probably cut for some other homer.

By the time I rang the bell later that morning on the landing board of my own loft, I'd lost a full three ounces of my total sixteen. I was welcomed home by Big Tom and Lady Jane, Miss America and my fellow birds. I was the first of the ten from Wright Farm to return, faster even than Fast Time, but I hadn't won the race, John told me gently. A hen from another loft had completed all five hundred miles the day before. But he said to never mind that, that one day I'd make a name for myself.

He was right. In every race after that, I finished in the top three. All through 1917 I raked in prize money with my clawed feet.

Only two apprehensions, gray nimbuses, floated low and indistinct on our otherwise sunny horizon.

The first was the war. Sometimes on the darkest nights, we could hear a German bomber fly over the countryside in search of targets. The warplanes sought ports and factories, not modest farms, but their navigation was bad and their aim was worse. The sound of their engines frightened John and the other farmworkers and therefore frightened us, too. John spoke to us often about his soldier son and also told us that pigeons—Belgian, Italian, French, and English birds on one side, German birds on the other—had been dying alongside men in the war. They flew like I flew, not for prize money but as messengers. I thought of them often.

The second apprehension was breeding. Most pigeons mature sexually at around seven months of age, and given my gifts as a homer, John had high hopes for my progeny. Miss America, always indifferent to racing but delighted at the prospect of becoming a mum, was already raising her first pair of squabs, and John didn't understand why I hadn't taken to producing babies with any of the lady birds in the cote. Despite his considerable expertise in avian physiology, he had mistaken me for male, and I could sense his quiet dismay as he confronted the growing likelihood that my talents were doomed to die with me.

In John's defense the sex of pigeons is not an entirely straightforward subject. Our external anatomy provides few hints in this department, so it's mostly behavior that signals our gender, and I certainly *acted* like the males did, particularly in the affection I showed toward other females.

"Breeding pigeons is an art, they say," John told me somewhat apologetically as he put me in a private cage with Fast Time. "A careful balancing of beauty and form. You're my two finest homers, and I can only imagine what your broods might do. Pigeon hearts have their own reasons, I'm sure, but I do hope you'll give this arrangement some consideration."

While I don't wish to be prurient, at this point a few words on the subject of pigeon coitus may be in order. To be blunt, we, like most birds, have no genitals but only a cloacal opening from which we dispense excrement and through which male pigeons secrete—and female birds admit—sperm. Copulation, though pleasurable, is fleeting and consists only of light cloaca-to-cloaca contact. No penetration.

Because he had observed my sexual interactions with other female pigeons and had no fertilized eggs to show for it, John believed that I had failed in my efforts to impregnate, and he trimmed the feathers around my cloaca prior to arranging my dalliance with Fast Time, thinking it would improve my chances of making an effective deposit. But though she and I enjoyed our liaison, with respect to breeding it was to no avail.

I once overheard a discussion between John and another experienced pigeon man from a neighboring farm on the phenomenon of "henny cocks" and "cocky hens"—birds whose characteristics and mannerisms don't align neatly with their supposed sex—but John never recognized me as one of the latter. The men speculated that these "unnatural" conditions might be caused by abnormalities of our invisible interior gonads or of the hormones they secrete. In my case this was probably correct; unlike Miss America, exactly my age and an excellent layer, I never produced an egg.

Their conversation bothered me for some time. Partly this was because I wanted to inform John, who in most ways was so sensitive and perceptive, of his mistake. Partly, too, it was because I never *felt* unnatural. I never had any idea of what it might *mean* to feel unnatural.

Now, drained of my innards, wood-stuffed and wire-skeletoned, perched one-legged on my base for eternity, I have a much clearer sense of what this means.

By the spring of 1918, John had largely given up on breeding me, his mind busy with other concerns. One early morning he entered the dovecote with Farmer and Mrs. Wright. The farmer had a newspaper under his arm, and I could make out a headline announcing the long-awaited arrival in Liverpool of American troops, the first wave to pass through the UK on their way to France.

"We have almost fifty," the farmer said, surveying us in our nesting boxes. "I should think we could spare a dozen for the Allied cause."

John nodded, grim-faced. Mrs. Wright said she was sorry but encouraged him to think of how the birds might help his son in some way. "This war has upended the normal duties of men and women," she said. Short and round and ruby-cheeked, in her orange apron she had the look of a chrysanthemum. "It's no wonder, is it, that it's finally come to upend the birds, too?"

"I'll pick out a dozen tonight and have 'em ready to go by noon," John said, tipping his tweed flat cap.

He waited until the farmer and his wife had gone back to the big house, then took up speaking to us as he always did. "Those Yanks coming to help are going to need things," he said. "Their General Pershing asked for two thousand homers, to be used as messengers in the army. England has offered to send five hundred directly. And not just five hundred but the five hundred best. Many of you are among the best, true and tested. So there's no way around it. You're off to help our boys."

The dovecote bubbled in a cooing cacophony. John came to me straightaway, as I knew he would. Sad, I could tell, to give me up. But I wasn't a breeder, I had already won the best purses in Britain, and my talents called out for a fresh challenge. I had no future on the farm.

Everyone feels old when they're sad, even children. Even pigeons. During my stay in the dovecote, I'd felt young and happy much of the time, but I never felt that I belonged there, and I'd always felt the pull of an unidentified desire just beyond my reach. I came closest to catching whatever it was when I was in the sky. Looking down at the towns and the land, I had a yearning to be a part of something larger and the sense that I could be. But back at the farm, that feeling of oldness would creep in again, and I couldn't say why. Maybe in France that would change.

Miss America whispered, "I'm glad it's not me." Lady Jane told her to hush.

Big Tom reminded me always to listen to the voice. "Don't take any risks over there," he said. "Do your best, do your duty, and we'll see you when it's over."

I kissed them all, a quick beak-to-cheek, and John reached in, speaking low as ever. "You're a fine, odd creature, Cher Ami," he said. "That's why I've always loved you."

He brought me close to his mouth, and his soft, soothing voice dropped to a whisper, as if to confide something he didn't want even the other birds to hear. "Save my son," he said.

My heart beat hard against his clasping hand. I'd be a liar if I said that I wasn't excited. I wanted to fly with the best homers in Britain. I wanted to save John's son, and others. I felt sure that I was approaching the brink of my destiny.

I wasn't mistaken.

How was I to know that I'd never see John—or Big Tom, or Lady Jane, or Miss America, or any of the rest—ever again?

CHAPTER 4

CHARLES WHITTLESEY

~~~~~~

The desire to be something other than what one is is a cruel affliction, and I am finally cured.

The *Toloa* sailed without fanfare this morning, without anyone knowing that Charles "Go to Hell" Whittlesey is among her passengers. Last week I bought my ticket under the name C. W. Whittlesey—no first name, no "Lieutenant Colonel."

I've stowed myself in a cabin on the starboard side, one I chose from the chart at the American Express office based on its proximity to the upper promenade deck. To get there I need only pass through two doors and ascend two sets of stairs—or "ladders," as sailors are wont to call them—and I'm confident that the engines' drone will cover any openings and closings and footfalls I generate in my egress.

Here on the open sea, my plan finally under way, the finely wrought nerves I've fought to keep in control feel so at ease that I don't blanch when the bellhop recognizes me. I let him alert his commander that he has a celebrity aboard, and I accept an invitation to dine at the captain's table this evening. Why not? Soon I'll be free of all obligations; one more won't hurt.

I was the last man on earth whom one would expect to become a war hero. Soon I won't have to live up to anyone's expectations.

I set about unpacking. I've already arranged for the disposition of most of my significant possessions, which would be of no use to me where I'm going, and the stack of letters I've brought will take care of the rest. The one addressed to George McMurtry—my second-in-command in the Pocket—

encloses the original copy of the German surrender request, the one to which I am alleged, falsely, to have replied, "Go to hell." My Congressional Medal of Honor I've left to my mother, along with all my other property. That assemblage of ribbon and bronze-coated copper rests in a safe-deposit box with my will at the Mercantile Trust Company back in Manhattan. I never wanted it. All it did was remind me of those doomed men, steadfast in their refusal to complain or give in.

But it will be a comfort to Mother. She'll put it over the mantel in the drawing room, where its star and eagle will be on display but out of the sun so the blue ribbon won't fade. I'm sad I'll never go back to visit anymore but glad I won't have to see it—showy, embarrassing.

Gallantry, the quality ascribed to me in the newspaper stories about my citation, is in fact not in my nature. My nature is to feel, still, every bit of the horror that we encountered in the Pocket. I can't blame Mother, though, for wanting to be proud. Her life has not been easy, and she has always thought me her oddest child.

"You stand out because of your suppressed nervous temperament," my mother told me one day when I came home complaining about school. The teacher always called on me because I always knew the answers, and I didn't want the other pupils to despise me as a know-it-all. I understood even then that when my parents described me to their friends as "sensitive" and "bookish," those were not meant strictly as compliments.

I was born January 20, 1884, and raised for my first ten years in Wisconsin, the second-oldest of six boys. I had a brother Frank, named after my father, who died at his first birthday, so I was for all intents the eldest. I loved my brothers, but Annie Elizabeth, my only sister, was my dearest friend. Two years younger than I, she was sweet and kind and equipped with a poetic sense of humor. Nobody got her jokes the way I did.

"What do you call a sheep with no legs?" she asked one

afternoon as we walked home from the one-room school-house beneath a cotton-balled blue sky.

There was no way to predict her punch lines that refused to behave like punch lines.

"A cloud!" she said. As cryptic as it was, we fell to the ground laughing and had to pick leaves from each other's hair when we stood up again.

My family moved back east the year of Annie's death. Just shy of her eighth birthday, she was cut down by the black diphtheria epidemic then scything the North Woods. We moved not to get away from bad memories, though that was a benefit, but because my father had taken a job as a General Electric purchasing agent. From Connecticut, he missed New England.

Ours was a well-heeled family, and we fit comfortably into the western Massachusetts ethos, with its belief in hard work, and duty, and hell and damnation for those who sinned—though this last was mildly expressed in our Unitarian household.

My father is silver-haired now but still straight of spine. My mother's eyes are blue as steel. Growing up, I never asked them for permission to shoot birds, as all my brothers did. "Remember, son, that this is not a toy," my father would say each time he held out the muzzle-up family rifle to their eager hands.

I have learned few enduring truths in my too-short, too-long life, and here is one: if something must be stated repeatedly, ritualistically, then it is almost certainly not true. The gun *is* a toy, as much for grown men as for foolish boys.

My father goaded me over my disinterest, not quite calling me a coward yet wondering, "What are you afraid of, son?" He didn't expect me to be a hunter but wanted me to hold a weapon in my hands without flinching.

Silent of mouth, I would reply in my mind, *This device is made to kill at worst, to maim at best.* But I made myself say, "Nothing, Father. I'm not afraid."

So I learned to shoot.

Quieter after Annie's death than before, I inclined toward literature and poetry. I felt more at ease with girls than I did with boys, the latter discomfiting me with their crudeness and violence. For a while this preference was indulged by my parents and teachers, first with knowing sighs as natural melancholy at the loss of Annie and then laughed off. I must be, they joked, a pint-size Romeo pining for my crushes. But when at last I imagined myself as a Romeo, it was Mercutios, not Juliets, for whom I was yearning.

More than anything I was alone. I took long solitary walks through the Berkshires, examining plants and watching birds. Among many other things, my time in the Argonne Forest spoiled woods for me.

Everyone feels old when they're sad, even children. Roaming the hills of western Massachusetts, I felt old much of the time. Aware in a vague way of my fundamental difference from other boys, I thought a lot about how, if not to be more like them, then to be the sort of person whom they'd like. When I matriculated at Pittsfield High, I deliberately set out to become more popular, with a grim understanding that this would amount to concealing, not expressing, my inner life. I succeeded, at first through sheer effort and then with increasing ease as I came to enjoy my new niche as a storyteller with a sense of humor more accessible, I suppose, than Annie's had been. "Laconic" and "sarcastic," as the men in my regiment would later invariably describe me. Classic New England.

At Williams College—twenty miles from Pittsfield, a different academic world but an overlapping social scene—I grew to my full height of six feet two inches, towering over my classmates. But my eyesight was poor: I wore spectacles then as I do to this day, and I was never seen with a ball in my hands. I compensated for my athletic deficiency with an upright bearing and an impeccable style of dress that earned me the nickname "the Count"—one bestowed with affection, as I was good-humored about my own foibles. In spite of my determination to be a gentleman, I allowed myself to become known as a "regular guy," then the highest compliment that a man could give another man. "Chick," they said—another of my innumerable nicknames—"is always up for a beer and a late-night bull session."

This was all true. But even as I maintained my respectable standing within the comfortable cloche of Williams, I'd begun to take an interest in the vaunted postcollegiate world that we were about to enter, to be reflective and serious about how I'd contribute. To say that I was an idealist in my youth understates the case. I flirted with socialism. I composed verse as a member of St. Anthony Hall. I wrote in my yearbook that the purpose of a college education is "learning to judge correctly, to think clearly, to see and to know the truth, and to attain the faculty of pure delight in the beautiful." All achievements that proved conspicuously useless a few years later when I was watching my men get shot and gassed and blown to pieces.

After I took my law degree from Harvard, my parents hoped I'd remain in Cambridge—to be closer to them and to marry some fine Boston girl named after a virtue: Faith or Patience—but I moved to Manhattan. I said it was to embark on a Wall Street career, and that wasn't a lie, as I soon found a position at Murray, Prentice & Howland, which is in fact on Wall Street. But so, too, was my move prompted by the liberty that the city would afford me to live as I chose.

Those years between the Panic of 1907 and the establishment of the Federal Reserve were, believe it or not, a fascinating time to practice law. The intricacies of contracts and the evolving stringency of the rules governing banks absorbed and grounded me, even as my entanglements with men—queer men, as Felix taught me to say—gave my body and heart the occasional flight. No one suspected, with the possible exception of Bayard—J. Bayard Pruyn, that is, my Williams classmate and closest male friend, through whom

I'd soon meet Marguerite—and Bayard would never mention it, or even let on that he knew. Intensely loyal, cheerfully tolerant to an almost irritating degree, Bayard could forgive or brush off any lapse by his confederates, always secure in his conviction that they were pure at heart. If they reneged on deals, or seduced typists, or had trysts in public parks with other men . . . well, it was all more or less the same to Bayard: disappointing, but even the best of us makes mistakes, so what's to be gained by shaming anyone?

After three years with our respective firms, Bayard and I had learned enough and built professional reputations strong enough to go into business for ourselves. We formed a partnership and founded a firm of our own. It was a struggle at first to make a go of it, but our list of clients grew, and we settled into a comfortable routine. Even my discreet meetings with men, once a source of such anxiety, had come to seem manageable, unremarkable, just another part of my life in the city.

Then, in May of 1915, the Germans sank the *Lusitania*, killing twelve hundred passengers and crew, including 128 Americans.

I'd been following the war since it began in August, but my residual socialism had left me with deep—and, as it turns out, valid—concerns about exactly which citizens of the belligerent nations would shoulder the burden of combat and therefore inclined me to be a pacifist. Not so my brother Elisha. He had moved to the city, too, and was living at the same boardinghouse as I. Always a patriot, an adventurer, and frankly a hothead, he took the U-boat's act of aggression as his cue to join the fight. America hadn't entered the war yet, but by that fall he'd figured out how to become an ambulance driver in France.

———————

We sent each other letters. With every missive he invoked the glory he felt in emulating our ancestors who fought in both the Revolutionary and Civil wars. "Our nation is shame-fully unprepared," he wrote. "Our men must be made ready."

I was not ready, and it had never occurred to me that there was anything I ought to feel ready for. The only drafting in my world was that of drafting a contract and handing it off to a typist. Since we were boys, I had kept a careful distance from Elisha's masculine world because I looked down on it as cheap bravado. But Elisha's service showed me that there could be nobility in such brotherhood. I confess that I ceased to find the prospect of becoming a manful-man repugnant. When manifested in football and fraternity pranks, this roughhousing seemed stupid and shallow, but now that it was for ideals that I could admire, I saw the appeal. I felt challenged by Elisha's example and, embarrassingly, by the fact that our parents were far prouder of him as a son than they'd ever been of me.

Plenty of powerful Americans agreed with Elisha, including Lindley Garrison, the secretary of war. Garrison overran President Wilson in his support for the Preparedness Movement, which organized volunteer camps that provided professional men the chance to play citizen-soldier, attaching them to regular army units for a month or so in the summer with no requirement to enlist. In the papers I read over the breakfasts Mrs. Sullivan prepared, I often saw the one in upstate Plattsburgh referred to as "Business Men's Camp": the hundreds of men there were mostly older, in their thirties and forties. Educated. A lot of attorneys. Even Quentin Roosevelt, Theodore's youngest son, attended. He'd later die in the war at the age of twenty.

And so in the summer of 1916, convinced that Europe would bleed itself white if we didn't eventually put an end to it, I went, too, up to Plattsburgh. Bayard was surprised, as I was hardly the soldier type, but said he could keep up the practice in my absence, no trouble. Summer was generally an idle time, made even more so by many of our peers' sudden interest in putting aside their briefs and covenants to try marching in formation.

Marguerite, predictably, was both amused and horrified. I told her that I was doing it for Elisha, that I was doing it for democracy. These were both true. But if I am honest, so, too, did I do it out of romantic yearning for a purely masculine environment, a desire to unite with other men in common purpose. At Williams and Harvard, I had felt inklings of what such an environment might be like, but there our ostensible seriousness was constantly being adulterated by social obligations, fatuous demands that we demonstrate our good breeding. At camp, I imagined, we'd have no time for such frivolity; the business of living moment to moment would eclipse any jockeying for status or making of future plans.

By "romantic," I should clarify, I do not mean "erotic." While I had no doubt that I'd encounter other queer men in the camp—with greater frequency, maybe, than I did in the city—we'd be there to serve our country, not to pursue our own liaisons.

Training at Plattsburgh did not disappoint. Far upstate on Lake Champlain, two dozen miles from the Canadian border, the camp did have the atmosphere of the old college spirit. By day we went on drills and hikes and sat in classes on history and tactics. Evenings we gathered around actual campfires to roast Frankfurter sausages—or "hot dogs," in keeping with prevailing sentiments toward the Germans—and to hear various eminent speakers, such as Elihu Root and Major General Leonard Wood.

Although that first summer I was technically a private—Company L, Seventh Training Regiment—I and my fellow volunteers weren't treated as such: the assumption was that if we formally enlisted, we'd serve as commissioned officers. We learned about "kitchen police" detail—i.e., KP, i.e., Cinderella Duty—a task that we'd be able to assign as punishment to men who might one day be under our command and require discipline by way of coal-shoveling, potato-peeling, dish-washing, ashcan-cleaning, and floor- and bench- and table-scrubbing, all tasks regarded as particularly loathsome and humiliating, since they were the work of women. But though we learned the language and structure of the army's hierarchy, only the top of the pyramid was present: we had no one to command.

Though many a fellow went off to Plattsburgh equipped with a firm undergraduate grasp of the classics and imagining himself as an epic hero in the offing, the poetic genre best matched to that July was the pastoral idyll. We walked out each morning into the muzzy yellow light filtered by the clouds over the lake and did our drills amid the torpid bobbing of dragonflies. Days off, we walked the woods and swam the cold waters, and I liked how I looked when I removed my clothes to do so: my former paleness tanned lightly by the sun, my thinness less spindle, more sinew.

As predicted, I met the occasional man like me, queer but manly, and when I returned to the city that August, a couple of them did look me up at my invitation. Usually we dined at the Williams Club, which I had helped to found. The building, donated by the wife of a famous graduate, was conveniently close to the Midtown neighborhoods where I and many other young men, single and working in offices, resided. We'd eat and retire to my fellow Plattsburgher's place, always the perfect picture of discretion.

I was at the Williams Club, in fact, on April 2, 1917, when I read President Wilson's declaration of war. I'd intended to order dinner and read the later editions, as I did most evenings, but the announcement left me agitated, without appetite. *It is a fearful thing,* the president said, *to lead this great peaceful people into war.* But we would fight, he pledged, *for a universal dominion of right by such a concert of free people as shall bring peace and safety to all nations and make the world itself at last free.*

I put down the paper and told the waiter that I had changed my mind: no dinner this evening, no thank you, good night. I went out into the streets, not the only one with that idea. Bands played—mostly airs from the Civil War, the last major conflict in which we'd involved ourselves—and men and women and children waved flags.

I had trained. I could fight. But should I?

What finally tore it for me in the days that followed were the placards going up left and right. I had never imagined myself to be susceptible to the crude inducements of a recruitment poster, yet the one I saw that balmy April evening that asked ON WHICH SIDE OF THE WINDOW ARE YOU? demanded an answer.

You could see at a glance—as I did, staring at a post-office wall—that the sides in question were clearly defined. In the foreground a dapper, effeminate man stood hiding behind the curtain of his darkened home, while outside, a group of robust lads in uniform marched proudly in the sunlight beneath a billowing American flag. Put one of them behind the wheel of an ambulance and you had Elisha. Put some glasses on the young fop and he could've been me. I flushed tomato red on the sidewalk.

The image deftly played on fears that middle- and upper-class males had become too soft at the cost of their manhood. Later I'd meet—briefly, before they were killed—many men who'd agreed with this sentiment, who had believed, before they saw the shit- and bloodstained reality, that war brought the prospect of adventure and heroism. A way to shunt, like a train, from a familiar track. Their one great chance for excitement and risk.

The next morning I signed up to go back to Plattsburgh, not as a curious private but as an officer in training. Bayard, that prince of a man, held my position at our firm from May through August, but when I finished at Plattsburgh, obtained my commission as captain, and received orders to report to Camp Upton, I tendered my resignation.

_____

Magic tricks that are easy to learn are not worth learning. At Camp Upton the magic trick by which we transformed the men into soldiers who could reasonably call themselves part of an army was difficult indeed.

Sixty miles from New York City, Camp Upton had gone up in haste over the remains of an old oak forest, with some stumps still in need of removal when we arrived: "forest dentistry," they called it, and wasted no time in assigning it to the new recruits. The ten-thousand-acre tract lacked the bucolic atmosphere of Plattsburgh, consisting of sand and scrub, stunted oaks and windblown pines, desolate and isolated save for Yaphank, a nondescript village on the route of the Long Island Rail Road, unremarkable save for its ugly name.

A few gaunt pinewood barracks straggled up from the mud toward an indifferent sky, and the white tents resembled half-inflated balloons. Heaps of lumber and swearing workmen with their teams and wagons and motor trucks suggested the place might never be finished. We were shown around to the bathhouses—which contained no baths, just cold-water showers—and given instructions on how to form messes. Suddenly gentlemen who had previously hosted formal dinner parties—or who, like me, had relied on their landladies—found ourselves dining in rustic surroundings.

We officers were informed that two thousand drafted men were scheduled to arrive on September 10. George McMurtry—fellow captain, fellow Harvard grad, and fellow Wall Street attorney, my first and best friend at Upton and throughout the war—declared himself to be "as excited as a young girl preparing for her debut"—a sincere sentiment but hilarious coming from him. A hulking Scotch-Irishman who'd delayed the pursuit of his juris doctor to serve with the Rough Riders in the Spanish-American War, he was one of the few among us who'd actually been in combat, having seen action in the battles of Las Guasimas and San Juan Hill.

I did not consider myself a snob—though the conscripts regarded every officer to be one by default, and they had their reasons—but I was astonished by the gulf between the concept and the reality of the drafted men pouring into Camp Upton. In training we'd learned that the army was deeply committed to the popular understanding of Americans as durable individualists, hardy descendants of pioneers. Their eagle eyes would make them sturdy riflemen! Their ruggedness would show those womanly Europeans wasting in their trenches a thing or two about initiative!

But as my fellow war hero Sergeant Alvin York would later quip, for every turkey-shooting frontiersman who reported for duty, there were hundreds of city boys who'd never held a gun in their lives and who when called upon to fire one "missed everything but the sky." And that, I should add, was when they could get rifles at all: the army, chronically undersupplied, often had our men drilling with broomsticks.

Some of the recruits alighted in the Yaphank station bearing tennis rackets, bathing suits, and bathrobes, as if they expected to be guests at an elegant resort. Others might as well have been refugees: short, gaunt, hollow of eye and cheek. Plenty were illiterate. Upon their arrival at camp, many received adequate dental and medical care for the first time in their lives. Ditto nutrition. They feasted on cantaloupe, fried liver, cornflakes, creamed cauliflower, chili, pudding, stewed peaches, and iced tea. Animals fattening for the slaughter.

Many were animalistic in other ways. Even had he not later given me countless reasons to remember him, I would never have forgotten the figure that Philip Cepaglia cut on arrival, stumbling off the train in a red silk shirt and a pink bow tie: a sweaty valentine still drunk from an all-night wedding reception in Little Italy. The other Bronx men in the battalion called him Zip, so that's how we all came to know him; it was, I later learned, a derogatory term, one that Neapolitans who'd been in the States for decades applied to newer immigrants from Sicily, supposedly because their Italian was too fast to understand.

When I first tried to address him, I discovered that Cepaglia could speak only three words of English, two of which were "Merry Christmas" and the third of which was "fuck."

These were the men who would make up the 77th Infantry Division of the United States Army. They came from a total of forty-three countries, which earned us our nickname, the Metropolitan.

"Well, Captain," McMurtry said as we stared into that melting pot, "we've got to get them from 'Alla right, boss' to 'Very good, sir,' and we've got to do it double time."

"At roll call tomorrow," I said, "I'll explain that in the trenches the order to duck will be given in English, and if they don't understand it, their heads may be blown off."

Attendance at English classes among my men was high, but I'm sorry to say that many of their heads were blown off anyway.

In the barracks that first night, the new privates swore like virtuosos and urinated out the windows. After lights-out they parted the dark with belches and barking, yelled conversations, real and mock farts. McMurtry, whom I studied closely in my search for a leadership style, did not resort to the screamed vulgarity favored by many of the sergeants, engaging the men instead with a perpetual finesse, one that allowed him to mix and joke with them but still assert his superiority and bend them to his will.

"All right, all right!" he called into the din. "You're a rowdy crowd, not prone to doze. Come morning we'll start your training, and I'll bet dollars to doughnuts you'll sleep soundly tomorrow night."

We officers couldn't be everywhere all the time, so in order to discourage certain recurring behaviors we put up certain signs, of which I took a hand in the composition. Given how I'd been living in Manhattan, I hardly considered myself a prude, but I must admit to being ill at ease with my regiment's coarse talk and lewd humor, their contempt for authority, and their streetwise cockiness. I did not want to be perceived as a martinet or a cold CO, so my signs addressed them in language they could understand. PLEASE DO NOT SHIT IN FENCE CORNERS, read one I that recall with particular satisfaction. They proved effective.

So, too, did I find myself ordering men who were accustomed to changing their clothes seasonally to wash themselves every morning, change uniforms often, and take pride in a neat appearance. This wasn't easy, as the supply sergeants handed out coats and breeches ill-fitting and mismatched. Men with thirty-two-inch chests found themselves given thirty-sixes and told to be grateful to have anything to wear at all. They looked like badly pulled taffy, and on more than one occasion I had to order them to swap.

Given my own double life, I didn't feign hypocritical disapproval of what my men did on their days off or leave time, provided their activities didn't leave them sick, dead, or in jail. I left moralizing concerns to the representatives of the Young Men's Christian Association, who strove like choirboys to keep the troops from harlots and strong drink. Like all the men, I was grateful for the forums that the YMCA established throughout Upton—eight huts and a three-thousand-seat auditorium—upon the stages of which we could watch boxing matches, motion pictures, and theatrical productions as well as religious programs on Sundays. The YMCA was proud to inform us officers of the significant demand for Bibles from the men in camp; I didn't have the heart to tell them that the Good Book wasn't always being put to its intended use. The onionskin pages evidently made perfect rolling papers; one Sunday a private told me that he'd "smoked through the New Testament as far as Second Corinthians."

This was a test: he'd disclosed a small, arguable transgression to see how I'd react, the better to gauge the breadth of my tolerance. That he'd hazard this experiment at all was proof of how far the battalion had come in terms of cohesion—but it

represented a risk for me, too. If my response were dispro-
portionate, they'd make me out to be a prig, or so insecure in
my authority as to feel the need to pounce on the mildest
lapse. If I laughed along with him and his fellows, I'd put
myself on their level, smudging a line of command that on the
battlefield would need to be straighter and brighter than a
searchlight's beam.

So at first I said nothing, only met his gaze with an even
smile. Then, when his courage seemed to flicker, "That's resourceful," I said. "Along those same lines, Private, if you're
feeling peckish, you might check the chaplains' schedules
and take Communion as a second breakfast."

As jokes go, it was unlikely to make the pages of the *Lam-
poon*, but it seemed to do the trick, returning the soldier's
serve, not surrendering the point. A couple of onlookers suppressed nervous laughter, and I walked away.

But I honestly wasn't sure quite how the exchange had
come off until weeks later, at the Harvard Club in Manhattan, where I and some of the other officers had gone on leave
for dinner and a drink. "I heard a story about you, Whit," Mc-
Murtry said, and proceeded to recount my exchange with the
private, fairly accurately in substance if not in my exact
phrasing. Wary, I allowed that it was true.

Marshall Peabody—a brash and friendly banker from a
family of bankers, now a second lieutenant in the 306th Machine Gun Battalion—cackled heartily at this, as he did at
most things. "You keep it pretty well hidden," he said, "but
you've got a wit as keen as a safety blade."

I appreciated that, but I was most concerned about Mc-
Murtry's judgment. He knew it and with a hint of mischief let
me suffer in suspense. "Many who served in the 1st Volunteer Cavalry," he said at last, "cannot finish a conversation
without mentioning that fact. I try to be more sparing, but in
this case I hope you'll indulge me. One of the many lessons I
learned from watching Colonel Roosevelt during our scrapes

in Cuba is that a well-timed jest can spur the troops better
than the finest bugler. If you've got your wit, then you've got
your *wits*, and men know they can follow you without fear.
That's something the army doesn't teach its officers, but you
seem to have puzzled it out on your own."

"We'll see how my sense of humor holds up under fire," I
said, an honest bit of modesty to mask my pride and my
relief.

My sense of humor held up well enough for the rest of that
evening, at any rate. With the help of the Harvard Club's good
scotch whiskey—still flowing freely in those happy days before
the Volstead Act—McMurtry's endorsement put me enough at
ease that I relaxed my customary reserve and ventured a few
mordant observations about the goings-on at camp, thoughts I
had previously relegated to my letters to Marguerite and otherwise kept to myself. These, as it happened, were so well received as to leave my companions teary-eyed with laughter,
alternately roaring and gasping for breath, and the commotion
earned me an even larger audience as civilian men from
nearby tables joined our group. In short order I stowed my profound uncertainty as an untested officer and entered territory
familiar from my student days: the domain of the raconteur.
This odd paradox—i.e., sometimes the best place to hide oneself is center stage—was one I took so thoroughly to heart in
my youth that I almost forgot I'd learned it, but it came back to
me then with invigorating force.

Throughout the war I looked back on that evening at the
Harvard Club with great fondness, recalling it as the moment
when I found my footing among the officers and struck up
some of my truest friendships. But then the Pocket tainted
my nostalgia, as it tainted everything else. Now what I remember most acutely about that night are the uncharitable
gibes I made at the expense of my conscripted men, their
styles of dress and habits of hygiene, their malapropisms and
infelicitous grammar. Men who, though pressed into service

against their wills, would come to display poise and courage
to equal Hector's. Men whom I would lead to their deaths.

As I bade my tipsy companions good night under a clear
sky of autumn stars, I felt a sense of complete well-being.
Though my place was a straight six blocks east, past Grand
Central Station, I walked south with McMurtry to give myself a chance to thank him for his encouraging words.

He waved my gratitude away like a cloud of gnats. "Balder-
dash," he said. "Just stating plain facts." He stopped, gave me
a kindly, appraising glance, and shook my hand. "You know,
Whit, when I met you, I took you for a reticent, professorial
sort. And that's fine. The army can use such fellows. But now
I see you're a regular guy. Which, to be frank, I prefer."

He set out for home. Not quite ready to do so myself, I stood
and contemplated the columns and lions of the public library,
that cool and orderly warehouse of wisdom. Other men may
thrill to the sight of Old Glory rippling in the breeze, but for
me the library was a better symbol of what I had taken up
arms to defend.

I walked around its pale expanse and turned the corner
into Bryant Park, where I met a young plasterer—drunken
and sullen, curly hair still powdered like a periwig with the
gypsum of his trade—and brought him almost wordlessly
home, taking care not to disturb Mrs. Sullivan.

———————

Like the whole of the 77th Infantry, we men of the 308th
Regiment all hailed from the five boroughs of New York City.
In terms of our attitudes and experiences, however, we officers held less in common with the enlisted men than we
might have with bankers and barristers from Bolivia, or Fiji,
or the Planet Mars. My youthful excursions into socialism
had fostered sympathy for the workers of the world but had
given precious little guidance when it came to encountering
them in person. I thought constantly about esprit de corps—
words whose French origin, I knew, would be a cause for

mockery or irritation among the privates if I spoke them aloud.

"The trouble with this outfit," one often heard it said at Camp Upton, in both the polished tones of majors and the rumpled burrs of privates, "is that all the officers come from below Fulton Street and all the men from above it." Concord on the topic of discord, as it were. The enlisted men and draftees were immigrants, Bowery boys, Lower East Side roustabouts, educated on the streets. They pegged us "the Fighting Eggheads" and wondered how such men, many of whom had never so much as sustained or inflicted a bloody nose in a humdrum bout of Saturday-night fisticuffs, could expect to command them to kill. Many of us wondered the same.

The great amplifier of trouble at Camp Upton was boredom. We officers had the wherewithal to return to the city on leave, but many of the enlisted men did not and so remained in camp, at loose ends. When idle and alone, one might be moved to compose lyrical ballads; when idle in the company of other idlers, one's thoughts inevitably turn toward petty intrigues and grievances. Days spent preparing to face a deadly enemy whom one never actually meets are long and fraught days indeed.

We officers tried to provide relief when we could, but in that tense atmosphere any generous act might also be taken as an affront to dignity. Dignity, I was often reminded, is something that most men prize above their very lives. My men were prepared to risk the latter for me, and in return they expected me to honor—and defend—the former.

With winter closing in, every barracks wanted a phonograph, and those of the 308th were no exception. One of the lieutenants brought me Corporal Walter Baldwin to ask my permission on the company's behalf. I liked Baldwin: quiet, judicious, even-tempered, a soldier the others listened to. He was training to become the battalion's message clerk. Later he'd be among the few men who'd walk out of the Pocket alive.

"We're going to do it the usual way, sir," he said. "Taking up a collection. Only if it's all right with you."

"What do you expect to ask from each man, Corporal?"

"A dollar per man," he said, looking at his shoes. Weighing whether to ask if I'd like to contribute.

I handed him five, which he tried to reject, but I insisted. He blushed, almost with a wince, and seemed eager to take his leave, already worrying about how he'd recount this conversation to his bunkmates, anticipating their contempt at my high-handedness, dreading the prospect of defending me. I had put him in a fix.

"One thing I suggest," I said. "Ask a dollar per man, just as you're planning. But remember that some of these fellows are already sending every spare cent home to wives and children. Trust that they'll earn their music in other ways. Take up the collection, but don't tell anyone what anyone else has paid. That includes me."

His knotted face loosened, and I knew I'd thrown him the life buoy he needed. I dismissed him before he could muster another round of thanks.

That became my preferred practice: helping to ease the troops' burdens when I could while avoiding public gestures that made me stand out as different, privileged, more refined. But when faced with another monetary collection going on at the same time, I could not maintain my silence.

Orders had come down: officers were to sign up every man in camp—from the highest-paid to the poorest conscript—for the Liberty Loan Drive. Congress had authorized the issuance of nearly six billion dollars in bonds to fund what was sure to be a military mobilization of unprecedented scale, but the bonds weren't selling well, trading much below par, something that the Treasury and their allies in the banks attributed nebulously to German sabotage or investors' lack of patriotism, rather than to their own misunderstanding of the bond market. With the shortfall beginning to take on the dimensions of a scandal, they indulged in the time-honored tradition of curing economics with politics and called upon the military to squeeze dollars from their soldiers.

Major General Franklin Bell—then in charge of the 77th Division, an accomplished soldier who'd been army chief of staff under Roosevelt and Taft and who maintained facility in the political realm—did not hesitate to implement this directive, asserting that the success of our mission depended no less on raising funds than on wielding arms and informing his colonels that the men were to be told forthwith to allot a portion of their salaries toward Liberty Bonds.

When our commander, Colonel Nathan K. Averill, asked whether the 308th had made these allotments, I indicated that it had not and would do no such thing.

Colonel Averill reacted as if he simply hadn't understood what I'd said. My fellow officers in Headquarters Company—among whom I was renowned for fretting over regulations and checking every detail—also reacted with ill-concealed shock. I was the last man they had expected to question an order.

But while I might have been as green as a spring meadow on many aspects of battlefield command, as a Wall Street attorney I understood the Liberty Bond push as well as anyone at Camp Upton. Per my entirely deserved reputation as a stickler, I also knew the army's rules, which in their tedious elegance bound us officers no less than the enlisted men.

"The War Risk Insurance Act, as amended," I explained to the colonel—and shortly thereafter, per the colonel's request, to the major general himself—"draws a clear distinction between compulsory and voluntary allotments. It also sets a limit on what portion of a soldier's pay can be allotted without his consent. When you add up the current allotments for family and insurance, most of our men are at that cap now, or near to it. So while we can, and no doubt should, make our men aware of an investment opportunity that helps to fund our operations, we also have to tell them it's strictly voluntary. Furthermore, we have to mean it."

General Bell was not pleased, but to his credit he immediately understood my concern and cut off the discussion by saying he'd ask the JAG Corps for an opinion. I had the unquantifiable sense that Bell found the order distasteful himself, though he was too much the professional soldier to let that show. I never had a chance to speak with him about it privately; not long after, he left Camp Upton for France to observe the front, then failed a physical exam on his return and was removed from command of the 77th. Like many at Camp Upton, he'd be dead within a year, though his last breath would be snuffed not by gas or shell burst but pneumonia, in an infirmary on Governors Island.

If the legal officer ever wrote an opinion on the subject, I never saw it—but neither were the officers of the 308th asked about the progress of bond allotments again. Later that winter, when Averill was reviewing the troops, a sergeant asked him, "Sir, about the loan drive. Some of the men have been wondering. We know the army wants us to sign up, and a lot of us have. But there's a bit of confusion, sir. Is it an order? Or is it our choice?"

Colonel Averill looked at me, more amused than annoyed. "Captain Whittlesey," he said, "will you answer the question on the regiment's behalf?"

"It's a voluntary allotment, Sergeant," I said. "The men can make up their own minds." And a cheer went up in the barracks, musky and close with the smell of male bodies.

As for the phonograph, it was cheery to have music. To hear reveille followed cheekily by "It's Nice to Get Up in the Morning (But It's Nicer to Lie in Bed)" or after retreat at sunset to hear taps echoed by "Give Me the Moonlight, Give Me the Girl."

One evening in December, when the music was playing and it had begun to snow, I was walking alone toward my own quarters and happened upon Corporal Baldwin, probably returning from a YMCA hut. I returned his salute, complimented his successful stewardship of the phonograph plan, and inquired generally about the sentiments of the men. Baldwin had an innate genius for communication: a sense of what it would best serve me to know and the grace to tell me without betraying confidences.

"Spirits are high, Captain," he said. "We feel like an army now. We're eager to get over there. Nervous, naturally. We try to keep up with the war as best we can, newspapers being hard to come by. Some of the men can't read too well, as you know, sir. So when we do have one, a fellow reads it aloud, for the benefit of all."

"Can't listen to the phonograph all the time, I suppose," I said.

"I wonder, sir," he said, looking toward the lights of the barracks, avoiding my eyes. "Some of the men want to know, and I want to tell them right. If it's okay to ask, were you in a war before, sir?"

"It's okay to ask, Corporal. Had I been conscripted in as a private, I'm sure I'd want to put the same question to my commanders. No, I've never been to war. I'm a lawyer. I trained at Plattsburgh, and now I'm here."

Baldwin seemed satisfied and nodded. "Some of the things we learned about. Verdun. The Somme." His mispronunciations were those of someone self-taught by reading, not through chatter at the club. "I guess no one's ever been in a war like this one."

Laughter cut through the night air: a group of soldiers debating the correct lyrics to "It's Been a Long, Long Time Since I've Been Home."

"Captain," Baldwin said, "I wanted to tell you that the men think—well, sir, we think you're okay. We know if you're bossing the job, then it's going to be done right."

I was glad of the darkness, which hid my discomfort at

receiving praise. I wanted to respond to Baldwin with the same generosity, the same reassurance that all would be well, but I could not. And there was rank to consider; there was command.

"You should get back to the phonograph, Baldwin. It sounds as though you're needed. At the rate they're going, those men will never puzzle through that last verse before lights-out."

And Baldwin laughed, departing with a crisp salute.

At Christmastime—fine rain, melting icicles—I further improved my standing with both the officers and the enlisted men, although my motives for doing so weren't entirely noble. Half the division got a forty-eight-hour pass at Christmas, and the other half would get the same on either side of New Year's Eve. From brigadier generals to buck privates, most wanted Christmas and planned to spend it with their families in the city.

But my family would be gathering in Pittsfield, and the trip there and back wouldn't be feasible in two days' time. Thus, if I took the Christmas pass, I'd probably return to Manhattan, too—and were I back in Manhattan with no family to visit, I would probably go cruising. Sordid sadness being the saddest sadness, the prospect seemed too depressing to abide.

But I could make the most of a New Year's Eve in New York City. So I volunteered to spend Christmas in camp, causing everyone to think me quite the altruist.

That night had the pall of a glum soiree, poor weather and an anxious mood prevailing. To conjure some cheer, we got approval to decorate a thirty-foot pine tree that grew near headquarters and that had somehow escaped the forest dentistry of the Quartermaster Corps. We also helped the Red Cross distribute packages of food and cigarettes, as well as wholesome cards—each from a girl, unknown and therefore lovely—offering glad tidings.

After the New Year, we felt our call to ship out drawing nearer. The army wanted us to be seen before we departed, so the city could marvel at the magic we'd wrought.

On February 4, 1918, Colonel Averill led the 308th Infantry in parade up Eighth Avenue and down Fifth. A West Point instructor well liked by the soldiers, he was determined to reassure the Manhattanites gathered on the sidewalks that the hordes plucked from their midst by the draft had been ennobled. The men seemed determined to prove it, too.

The crowd was huge and ready to be dazzled, despite a driving snowstorm and a bitter wind. Face upon cheering face appraised us as we filed by, snowflakes on our olive drab, slush under our boots. Marguerite and Bayard watched us pass, as did men from the Williams and Harvard clubs, and men whom I had met on the street and taken home and then never met again. On the march, though, I had no impression of individual identities, either among the spectators or in our uniformed column. We seemed to become two huge organisms, one watched and the other watching, creatures at once new to the world and utterly ancient, enacting a ritual older than history itself.

Dazzle we did, and with such effectiveness that enlistments soared throughout the city during the next week, and the army issued orders for infantry units all over the country to do the same in their cities.

I should have been proud. Instead all I felt was ineffable sadness, which—I did not understand at the time but realize now, aboard the *Toloa*—was due to the fact that we were about to take these men whom we had improved so much physically and mentally to Europe and erase all traces not just of that improvement but of their entire existence.

Here at sea I put on my dress uniform and hang my regular clothes in the tiny wardrobe. I might as well look the part of war hero tonight at the captain's table, as it will be expected of me. The very last expectation that I'll be required to meet.

CHAPTER 5

CHER AMI

~~~~~~~

Hannibal took elephants across the snow-covered Alps, the better to bring his war to the Roman Republic. We pigeons took trains across the green Cotswold Hills, south to the Channel port of Dover, the better to carry our message-bearing prowess to France.

In the motorcar on the way to the station at Chipping Norton, John recited "Channel Firing" in honor of the poet's namesake, my brother Thomas Hardy, the only one of my siblings also chosen for my batch: the Wright Farm Dozen, soon to be scattered across the Argonne Forest. Narrated by bodies in their coffins, it tells of how the stupidity of war disrupts divine order enough to wake the dead. Dead now and conscious forever, I remember his choice as not merely apt but also prophetic.

> "I wonder,
> Will the world ever saner be,"
> Said one, "than when He sent us under
> In our indifferent century!"

As directed by a soldier, John loaded our wicker basket onto a military train. It was a dulcet day in early May. Even the snorts of the engines and the stink of the coal smoke couldn't disguise the luxuriant smells of damp and dirt and unfurling plants. By way of farewell, John checked the food and water in our basket and patted its top shut with his great paw of a hand—that hand which had a hand in raising us all.

"Well, my birds," he said, his voice bearing an unaccustomed rasp, "I wish you bon voyage and good luck. When the Hun marched off to the front in August of '14, the kaiser told 'em, 'You will be home before the leaves have fallen.' Now, if it ain't the spring of 1918. I hope you lot can help the Yanks put the stop to it."

He waved and turned, and the soldier slid the door to the boxcar shut. The circumstances of our transportation seemed so normal that I had to remind myself, as my eyes adjusted to the half-light, that this was no typical Saturday trip; John wasn't shipping us off to a race.

Aboard the boxcar with us and adding to the odor— comforting, mind you, to us country pigeons—were half a dozen horses and a pair of mules. Wood chips and dust, leather and molasses, sweat and manure. Most pigeons are fond of horses. Once we put aside the obvious difference in size that inclines us to think of them in almost geographical terms, we find them quite easy to understand and sympathize with.

The train pulled out, heading south and west toward the junction at Kingham, and we animals settled in place, braced against the boxcar's rocking. "Are you messenger pigeons?" one of the mares asked.

(The reader may be forgiven for wondering how animals of different species—indeed of different genera, families, or- ders, and classes—are able to communicate, whereas hu- mans' speech is often entirely unintelligible to others of their kind who reside only a sea's or a mountain range's breadth away. The answer is that I don't know. I might also respect- fully add that we animals find it very odd that humans have such trouble understanding one another, and add further that we suspect this might be due to their rather impover- ished notions of what qualifies as language.

But here, too, I question myself, because in fact the ani- mals to whom I have felt the closest kinship have always been those whose lives are most closely bound up with humans—dogs, horses—as well as the human animals them- selves.)

"We are indeed messenger pigeons," said Thomas Hardy, his voice raised above the train whistle's shriek. "Are you warhorses?"

"So they've told us," the mare replied. "Though we'd rather not be."

"Why not?" I asked. "I thought horses love war."

The mare snorted, as did her five compatriots. "Men love war," she said. "Kings love it, and so do their poets. 'Theirs not to make reply, / Theirs not to reason why, / Theirs but to do and die. / Into the valley of death rode the six hundred!' Twelve hundred if you count the horses. Most of those men survived the Charge of the Light Brigade. Most of those horses didn't. The poets don't rhyme about that, do they?"

That struck me as cynical but not false.

The horse kept her head low, shifting her hooves to the train's chuff as it picked up speed. "Our groom told us that horses can't even charge in this war," she said. "The battle-field's all pits and barbed wire. We'll just haul supplies to the front lines."

"What's wrong with hauling supplies?" said one of the mules in her heavy canvas halter.

"Nothing at all, Edna dear," said the horse, clearly accustomed to placating her comrade. "I'm just explaining to these birds how far removed our war will be from the gallant cavalry exploits of old."

"Just because you dray horses can trace a sliver more of your heritage back to Alexander's stallion Bucephalus, that doesn't make you authorities on combat," said Edna. "Many animals of many sorts will help our humans win their war. After all, who's to say what they need from us, exactly? I've heard a story about sailors on the HMS *Glasgow* who keep a pig as a mascot. They took him from a German cruiser they sank and kept him for a lucky charm instead of eating him."

"An exception that proves the rule," said the horse. "The sailors know they're no different from the pig. They spared it just as they'd want to be spared and because sparing it made them feel powerful, although they're not. If they thought any of us were ever coming back, then the British government wouldn't have to force the farmers to donate us. You're not here on your own accord, are you, birdies?"

"Of course we're not," I answered, the fresh straw in the basket fragrant beneath my claws. "But we're honored to be going. We're ready to put our skills to use for something besides winning prize money."

The horse hoisted her head to peer at me with her beetle-black eye. "I suppose if I were flying over the trenches instead of toiling in the muck, then I might think the same. None of us has a choice, so it really doesn't matter. As for me, I'll do my job, but I'll do it with my eyes wide open, not fogged with slogans of shared sacrifice. Our injured stableman told me a tale about the children of Lord Kitchener and a letter they wrote him. 'Please spare our pony Betty. It would break our hearts to let her go.'"

"And was Betty spared?" asked Edna the mule.

"You bet your tail she was," said the mare with a toss of her mane.

We sank into a momentary silence. From inside our basket, between the planks of the boxcar, we could see the countryside clipping along. Land that only a few weeks ago had been brown and drab beneath us on our practice flights now flashed by in verdant grass and blinking bloom—apple, cherry, and pear trees filling the air with blossoms.

"I still say they'd be lost without us," Thomas Hardy piped up, cheerful as was his welcome way, a way I never shared but miss. "The humans, I mean. They wouldn't know what to make of themselves. I've heard that they call Georges Clemenceau 'the Tiger' to make him sound brave."

Edna brayed. "I've heard that they call Lloyd George 'the Goat,'" she said, "because he's as randy as a billy when it comes to the ladies."

"They also say," said another of the horses, "that he's hung like one of us, as the phrase goes."

And so the ride went on, from Kingham through Oxford toward London along the Thames, stopping now and then for water or coal or to be shunted onto a longer train. And our conversation, too, went on in this crasser vein, which I would learn is typical among man and beast alike in times of war: talk of death giving way to talk of sex.

As we rolled on, I also thought about what Thomas Hardy had said—the idea that humans need animals to understand themselves. Later, on the battlefield, I would come to see soldiers befriend the field mice and wrens who ventured into the trenches seeking morsels of food. Even the smallest creature—a spider on her web—could give a man the mercy of taking his mind off the violence raging at all hours, reminding him that the earth still retained some forms of order even within the catastrophe.

Attunement with another creature feels magical, a brief stay against dread. It's true for humans, and it's true for us pigeons.

Our longest stop was at Victoria Station in London, a city whose immensity I could sense from the track. Our supply train's arrival—according to the American Expeditionary Forces, we qualified as supplies—coincided with that of a train full of troops, Americans like those we were going to aid.

Their accents were strange. They complained as they stretched their legs on the platform and received cups of English war coffee, evidently weak and terrible-tasting to their tongues. "Coffee in name only," said one of them, spitting onto the rails.

Bored of the beverage, the soldier dug into the pocket of his uniform and threw a penny toward a group of soot-cheeked young boys near a newsstand, thereby inciting a frantic scramble that reminded me, surprisingly, of us—the way we pigeons would dart and squeeze and shove to get our share of the fresh feed that John supplied. One of the boys flung himself to the ground, scooping up the paltry treasure in his grimy fist. The others followed its arc to the American soldiers, many of whom began to pull pennies from their own pockets and toss them into the mob. Little boys of all sizes piled up, swearing and squeaking when punched or stepped on, elbowing one another, hats flying off, coat sleeves yanked, until a sergeant ordered his men to knock it off and get back on the train. The boys scattered like raindrops shaken from a wing, jumping in every direction to get out of the way.

I thought for the rest of the journey how very like hungry birds those little boys had been, or how like them we were. On the farm we'd never seen children idle like that—idle and desperate—and I realized that most were probably war orphans, their fathers killed in France.

When the train arrived in Dover, an American soldier slid open the boxcar door. Before we could say good-bye to the horses, adieu to the mules, he took Thomas Hardy and me and our ten Wright Farm dovecote-mates out to the docks, briny with salt spray, crowded with hundreds of baskets identical to ours. Stevedores lashed our carriers to the hurricane deck of a channel steamer and covered us with a tarp.

The water was choppy and fogged, and the whole way across, the men talked about the weather. In the Great War, everyone adored the meteorologist. Artillery officers relied on reports about air and moisture, temperature and wind; they needed to know if shells could be fired. And everyone needed to know if roads would be passable. The preoccupation was familiar to me, since I thought about weather all the time when I was homing.

"I wish we could fly over," I said. "This boat ride is rough on the stomach."

"Come on, Cher Ami," said Thomas Hardy, nuzzling against me, hale and encouraging. "We can't have you being seasick in the basket. You'll make everyone else ill."

The tarp blew off into the bitter blue water, and cold mist swept over us, punctuated with occasional freezing splashes.

"Well, here's a silver lining," Thomas Hardy said. "Now you can keep your nausea at bay by looking at the horizon."

John had done his best at selecting names for us, but his aim was often off: flubbing my sex, for instance, and christening Thomas Hardy after an English writer whom I gather is among the most relentlessly pessimistic of his era. While my brother's cheerfulness could be overbearing at times, I was glad of it during that crossing.

And I miss it badly now. When I was recovering from the injuries that I suffered in the Pocket, I met another wounded bird who'd been Thomas Hardy's basketmate on the battlefield and who'd seen him die. He'd been pulverized in midair, his fluids spurting everywhere, a few white feathers floating down—*like someone shot open a child's snow globe*, the pigeon said. At the time I didn't understand the reference; it's one of the many things I've learned during my long decades in the museum. It still strikes me as a strange metaphor for a pigeon to use, but then again we have a very limited apprehension of violence, much as humans have a rudimentary understanding of flight.

I didn't watch the horizon during that crossing to France. Instead I watched the Royal Navy blimp overhead, on alert for the approach of U-boats. I envied it, because it was airborne and I was trapped, but it also seemed grotesque. A bloated parody, swollen like a tick.

Airplanes have always seemed more honorable to me: pathetic in their way, but expressive of an honest desire for the mitigated plunge, the intense negotiation with unseen forces that is proper flight. My landlords at the Smithsonian Institution have an entire building devoted to human achievements in this area. I've never seen it. I remain in my glass case, earthbound, a monument instead to loss.

CHAPTER 6

CHARLES WHITTLESEY

―――――――――――― ᎱᎱᎱᎱ ――――――――――――

Hannibal took elephants across the snow-covered Alps, the better to bring his war to the Roman Republic. We men of the 77th Division took steamships across the gray Atlantic—fifteen hundred men in each, like skyscrapers laid on their sides—the better to fight the war to end all wars.

Here on the promenade deck of the *Toloa*—in international waters now, en route to Cuba—I try to concentrate on my impending escape, but as always the present streams by me, trailing hooks to drag me back toward the past. With each wave split by the white ship's prow, recollections of my first Atlantic voyage beat against my brain.

A man traveling alone has the luxury of being meticulous to a much greater degree than do those moving en masse. After interminable anticipation, the order for the 77th to ship out came with little warning and much alacrity, haste making the waste that one might expect.

We, the 308th Infantry Regiment, left Camp Upton for France in the second convoy, which embarked on April 6, 1918, one year to the day after America's declaration of war. Hurry and discomfort characterized our leaving. Squads were detailed to destroy everything left in the white pine buildings that was not the property of the United States government. Pictures were ruthlessly torn from the walls. The treasured phonograph was lugged away, to cheer us no more. Books both trashy and high-minded, civilian clothes both shabby and modish, boxes and packages both worthless and valuable were all seized and burned, though many a hard word was spoken by the men. The stuff was cherished but inessential to the fight; thus it perished.

The night before had blown in chilly, but we officers had had to order our soldiers to turn in their bedding and sleep on the bare spring mattresses or the naked floors. I could have exerted the privilege of rank and kept mine, but I surrendered it in solidarity. Before dawn I dug my hip bones out of the hard wood to the sound of reveille, then went to the mess hall with everyone else for a quick cold breakfast and further instructions.

"The sun never rose more beautiful, did she?" said George McMurtry, passing my table in a flurry of olive drab and hail-fellow-well-met.

By 5:00 A.M. we'd fallen in facing east, where the sun had begun to lace the clouds. We received our orders and snapped into action, stepping out for the trains to Long Island City and the waiting ferries, which took us and our gear to the North River Piers. Each of our three battalions was assigned to a huffing transport ship, its sides pimpled with rivets. Swarms of sailors swung derrick nets, hoisting blue denim barracks bags and hauling them away.

My 1st Battalion and Headquarters Unit boarded a Red Star Liner by the name of *Lapland*, with the 2nd and 3rd on the *Cretic* and the *Justicia*. We filed up the gangplanks and checked in with an officer, shouting over the din, then received our deck and mess and bunk assignments as well as our cork life belts, which we were ordered to put—and keep—on.

Our departure was meant to be secret, and therefore we received no grand send-off dockside, which didn't bother me. I was still rattled by the spectacle of our parade through the city—the sense of a species shaking off its humanity in answer to some darker impulse. The eerie tension between near chaos and stealth befitted my ambivalence. When it seemed as though the deck railings might give way from the pressure of bodies craning for a last look homeward, we officers ushered most of the men to the bowels of the ship, where they clustered around the cloudy portholes.

Just as Manhattan was knocking off work for the day, the steam whistle shrilled a single, splendid note. The civilians heading home knew who we were and where we were headed, and as we turned down the Hudson and made for the sea, they spotted our trio and cheered us. Ferries blew their horns, and the residents of the buildings along the water waved white towels and handkerchiefs.

I had a spot on one of the open lower decks, jammed with men, but my height granted me a view of the Statue of Liberty receding in the golden light, a sentimental sight that nevertheless provoked my sentiments. How many crimes, I wonder now—how many blunders worse than crimes—get committed in her name?

As the stars came out, we were ordered below. The captain of the *Lapland* passed around the promise of a reward: one hundred pounds to any man who spotted a sub. Thinking of the torpedoes that sank the *Lusitania* and of the Germans' proclamation of unrestricted submarine warfare, we eyed the waves as if we were gulls hunting prey, motivated less by the contest than by the reminder of peril. I heard many a man remark that an Atlantic crossing that might have been a pleasure in peacetime was anything but in a time of war.

For the second night in a row, I had difficulty sleeping, it being vexing to expect one's ship to be fired upon at any hour. But despite many false alarms of sub sightings from the overexcited men, we never saw one.

To call the shipboard food terrible was to overpraise it. Our meals were prepared by English cooks, evidently committed to safeguarding their reputation for awfulness. Boiled potatoes, rice, tapioca, and marmalade—no salt, no sugar, no seasoning of any kind. For lunch that day, we'd had rabbit stew, which tasted as if the cooks had left the fur on. Coffee was served from garbage cans. Seasick men puked thickly over the sides: "feeding the fishes," they called it.

By April 8 we'd reached Nova Scotia, where we stopped to load the scuppers with coal and to take on more supplies. Supplies, supplies, always more supplies! I didn't yet fully appreciate the degree to which wars are fought and won by quartermasters or the quantity of killing that was accomplished through lack. France would teach me that lesson, with the Pocket as my final examination.

We spent an afternoon conducting lifeboat drills in the Halifax Harbor. Dropping the boats and rowing around the icy chop of the bay provided a welcome break from the crowded ship, which I had come to imagine as a floating tenement—or as how I imagined a tenement would be, since unlike the majority of the enlisted men, I had never set foot in one. With the regiment in action, it was easier to picture the *Lapland* as a beehive—honeycombed with bulkheads and decks and infinite compartments—and the men as a purposeful swarm.

We departed from Halifax the following evening to a much livelier send-off than we'd been granted in New York. Women and kids waved; bands played "There'll Be a Hot Time in the Old Town Tonight" and "La Marseillaise" and "The Girl I Left Behind Me." The men seemed especially moved by this last one; many had sweethearts, or even fiancées. I sympathized, feeling a tinge of yearning myself—not for anyone in particular but rather for my habits in the city, where I had freedom, and privacy, and Marguerite as a trusted friend. Melancholy and relief in equal measure rushed at me through the salty air; I was sailing farther and farther from my double life.

That night, like every night, provided a beautiful sunset, a golden yellow disk sinking into the water like a coin into a slot.

That night, like every night, strict light discipline limited our activities. We'd given up our matches upon boarding the ship; absolutely no smoking was permitted outside at night, as the glow of a cigarette could be seen at sea from half a mile. Portholes were kept closed, and the only illumination came from tiny blue bulbs.

Once the bands were out of earshot, most of the men drifted belowdecks. Though it had begun to mist, I stayed above in the briny sea air to watch the sun's last traces vanish, in no hurry to return to the fetid stench among the bunks below. From the rear deck, all I could see was deep blue water in every direction. The only sounds were the engine's thump, like a giant heart, and the faint applause of waves against the hull. I liked the nights best, with blackest darkness all around. Sharing solitude with these fifteen hundred men made the isolation that I had always felt seem external as well, a quality of the night itself: a pathetic fallacy that made me feel less alone.

The morning after our departure from Nova Scotia, I rose early to catch the sunrise—no less spectacular—and to beat my fellow soldiers to the decks, where we'd all go to smoke in the open air.

That morning, April 10, was the first time I set eyes on Bill Cavanaugh.

I didn't notice him at first, a slim figure leaning aslant the opposite railing, utterly motionless, his back turned to the horizon's glow. His elbows were braced so he could hold something close to his face at an odd angle: a book. He was reading. He and I had both been craving first light, but he was using the dawn to inhale knowledge, while I'd just been impatient to safely strike an army match. I was amused, and impressed, and a little ashamed.

I didn't want to disturb him—or, honestly, to speak to anyone at that hour—and had decided to pursue my original aim of sunrise-watching by drifting farther along the starboard side when he looked up and saw me.

"Good morning, Captain Whittlesey," he said, coming to attention and saluting. It was the most perfect salute I had ever seen—perfect, I realized later, because its perfection was achieved for its own sake, not to impress me. As he turned, the copper light from the east caught him, shrinking the pupils of his sapphire eyes. I detected no nervousness in his expression, and its absence reminded me of its ubiquity in the other enlisted men who chanced upon me. His face showed only guarded readiness and a trace of good humor, like that of a skilled tennis player awaiting a serve. He carried his book smartly at his waist, saving his place with the tip of a little finger.

"At ease, Private," I said. "What brings you out so early? Most men don't want to prolong these dull days by waking up any sooner than reveille requires."

He lowered his hand, nodded toward the open sea. "I've never been on a boat before, sir," he said. "Not even the Weehawken Ferry. It's a thrill for me. I figure from here on I'll be seeing and doing a lot of things for the first time, not all of them this pleasant. So why not make time for the sunrise?"

"And for study?"

He brought up the book, held it in both hands. *"The Homing Pigeon,"* he said, "by Edgar Chamberlain. I'm a pigeon man, sir—I mean, I'll be handling pigeons for the regiment— but I keep birds at home as well. I want to learn everything I can about them."

"I'm impressed you managed to get that book out of Upton."

"It took some convincing, sir," he said. "The roundup of personal effects was pretty thorough. But I told them that it's related to my army work, and they understood."

This was a good answer—explaining the situation without suggesting that anyone hadn't done his job—and he didn't seem to offer it with care, only honesty. His face was stunningly symmetrical, perfectly proportioned, like that of an antique statue, and I understood at once how convincing he could be.

"What's your name, Private?"

"It's Cavanaugh, sir. Bill Cavanaugh."

"Lucky for the regiment to have an experienced pigeon man in its ranks. And lucky for you, too, I suppose, that the army has put you to work doing something you enjoy."

"It is, sir," Cavanaugh said. "It really is. To hold a pigeon and to feel it enjoy being held . . . well, sir, it's a pleasure un-matched by any other."

Though I took it at first for a trick of the morning light, a closer look confirmed that he was blushing. This soldier who'd converse with a captain or a king as easily as with a fellow private would, I'd come to learn, turn boiled-lobster red whenever he spoke of something he loved. And he loved many things, though none, I think, more than pigeons.

"Being in the loft with my homers," he went on, "quiets all the troubles of life. It's like growing roses, I imagine. Pursu-ing beauty, cultivating it, but never reaching it completely. Not that my family ever had space for a garden."

It felt rare, almost unsafe, to hear a grown man speak so openly of his passions. My mind alit at once on my own com-parable pursuits, in much the same way that one's hand might reach automatically for one's wallet while navigating a crowded street. To be clear, I'm referring not to my dalliances with men—an appetite is not a passion—but rather to my dal-liances with poetry, which I had written seriously since I was a boy and for which I had earned modest acclaim at Williams. Even at work in Manhattan, I would still sometimes hit upon a promising string of iambs and cancel engagements in order to spend the weekend coaxing them into a sonnet or a vil-lanelle. But no one in the army or back at my law office knew that I did this, and I had never for a moment considered tell-ing them, or sharing my verses with anyone but Marguerite. It had never occurred to me that I might do so.

I tried to steer Cavanaugh back toward practicalities. "So you breed and race them?"

"Yes, sir. They really are a lot like roses. Flying flowers! All different colors, different degrees of hardiness. To appreci-ate them you can't just go by how they look but also what they can do in the air. Their power and their smarts."

"How did you come by this hobby? Has your family always raised pigeons?"

"Oh, no, sir, not at all. Though Ma likes that I keep the birds.

They're a better thing to spend money on than drink, which is where my father's wages go, I'm afraid. There was an old guy in our building who kept them for years and who taught me about them. He told me once that they gave him an intelligent and profitable pastime. 'They keep the harp of life in tune,' he said."

This conversation was by a wide margin the longest I had ever had with an enlisted man and certainly among the strangest, given its topic and the many bald-faced disclosures it had included. Cavanaugh's candor was almost insubordinate; it certainly seemed heedless of the hierarchies that defined every aspect of our lives and our mission. Without question I should have brought our exchange to a swift end, perhaps with a reprimand.

But there on the deck with him—we two quite alone, our first morning on the open sea, the horizon visible in every direction, a clouded and violent future ahead—I could not. I reassured myself that this was a special case, that as a pigeon man Cavanaugh would likely be attached to the regiment's command staff, that he wasn't simply another interchangeable private whom I might have to tactically sacrifice, and that therefore this intimate dialogue was appropriate and constructive.

This was all hogwash. I was captivated.

"So, do you," I asked, feeling all the authority that I had carefully constructed over the past months crumble like a gingerbread castle being demolished by a pig, "have a favorite pigeon you've left behind?" Never before had I possessed an ounce of care for pigeons.

"I surely do. Her name is Annie."

"That was my little sister's name," I said, before I could stop myself.

"My little sister's Annie, too! She was jealous of the birds for all the time I spent with them, so I told her I'd name one in her honor, my sweetest and fastest. I have a photograph. May I show you?"

Without waiting for my reply, he pulled a flat brass object from his breast pocket, looked at it, and blushed anew. "I'm a waiter at Rector's," he said, "and one of my regulars is a photographer. He told me—"

"Rector's? On Broadway?" I knew it well, Marguerite and I dined there often, and I wondered how I had never seen him there—or whether I *had* seen him and had paid him no mind, which hardly seemed possible given how stricken I'd been by our encounter that morning. His employment at a see-and-be-seen restaurant in the Theater District helped explain not only his creamy indoor complexion but also how such a working-class fellow as himself might possess such ease when among the high and mighty.

"Yes, sir, that's the place. This photographer wanted to do my portrait, and he said that in return he'd give me some pictures." Cavanaugh paused to laugh and shrug, showing neither discomfort nor any conspiratorial acknowledgment that what he was describing was almost certainly—must have been—a queer advance. "But I don't need any pictures of myself. So he offered to let me choose my subject. And here we are."

He held out the object for my examination: a locket containing a sepia portrait of a flaxen-haired girl who looked like him—heart-shaped face, freckles across the bridge of her nose, smart smiling eyes—standing next to her pigeon namesake, perched blurrily atop a globe.

"*The Feathered World*," I said, reading aloud the legend printed across the bottom.

"Yes, sir," said Bill. "The photographer said I could give it a title if I wanted, and that's what I came up with: *The Feathered World*. Those two Annies are the queens of my heart."

The artistic poses of girl and bird, the caption, the earnestness of it all—it was almost too much to bear. I was scattered, divided against myself. I felt some interior policeman cautioning me to suppress my laughter, but I also recognized that the impulse welling within me was not laughter at all but something more like terror, or rapture. I had never before felt this way toward any living being. Why had I come up here this morning and happened upon Bill Cavanaugh? Why couldn't I have ended our conversation sooner, turned and walked the other way?

Cavanaugh and I both realized that I'd been staring flummoxed at the photograph for quite some time. He returned it to his pocket without a hint of awkwardness. "What about you, Captain Whittlesey?" he asked. "What brings you out so early this morning?"

Robbed of the capacity to make even the most innocuous statement about myself, I stared sternly out to sea. "'Eternal vigilance is the price of safety,'" I said, quoting the pamphlet we'd each been handed as we stepped aboard, orienting us to nautical life and telling us to consider ourselves self-appointed lookouts.

"'It takes a force of only nine pounds to explode a modern mine,'" he replied, laughing.

"You must really be devoted to reading if you've committed that to memory," I said. "Where are you from?"

"Hell's Kitchen," he said, and finally for an instant he looked self-conscious, both proud and embarrassed. "Most of the boys in my barracks are not what you'd call literary-minded."

"Oh, I don't know about that," I said. "I remember when your group arrived in Upton, you brought a banner. It was quite poetic."

Cavanaugh grinned. "'We're from Hell's Kitchen! We'll keep the kaiser itchin'!' I thought it was pretty funny. But I'm not so eager to kill as those fellows. I'm glad to be a pigeon man."

The words were out of my mouth before I could properly shape them. "You'll be expected to fight, too," I said. It felt to me like a lament, but it sounded like an admonition.

For an instant a crease appeared in Cavanaugh's otherwise placid forehead. "Oh, I know, sir," he said. "No need to worry about me. I'm no shirker." His smile returned, a bit stiffer. "Well, I'd best be going in now, sir."

Watching the rhythm of his receding back, I wanted, insanely, to touch him, to prove such a handsome and thoughtful man real. But that would have been madness—I was his commanding officer, and there was no evidence to suggest that he would have welcomed, even covertly, the impassioned advances of my silliest fantasies. Instead I clenched my fists in silence. But even as I tried to resist, I could feel: he had let the bird of my heart come out of its cage.

The crossing lasted ten more days, and there was little to do, so I took my entertainment where I could find it. Some of us officers got French lessons; a few played bridge, while the privates played poker. Chores like abandon-ship drills and cleaning our quarters became almost pleasurable relief from boredom. We chatted, we watched the other ships in the convoy, we counted down the hours until the next bad meal.

Apart from occasional concerts by the regiment's musicians, the primary group diversions were religious ceremonies. Though I wasn't sure I believed in God then, and I certainly don't now, I took to attending the daily Mass held by Father Halligan, one of the Catholic chaplains, a practice that my Unitarian family would have thought very strange. I had been told, quite correctly, that Halligan was an excellent speaker and a charismatic man, which partly accounted for my interest. I also guessed that men hailing from Hell's Kitchen would likely be among the flock.

It was a theatrical scene: the padre there on the lower aft deck, sunlight on his vestment and wind in his candle flames, counseling his listeners to trust in God and each other and the justness of our cause. The men sang hymns, led by a badly mutilated piano that they'd hauled up from the hold: a relic of the *Lapland*'s previous service as a luxury liner. Halligan drew a crowd, and I couldn't find Bill Cavanaugh's face amid the other faces.

Afterward I saw James Larney, our signalman, exchanging

greetings with the other congregants. Older than most of the men and always with a just-scrubbed air, Private Larney worked as a civil engineer in civilian life. He was alert and adept at complex tasks, which led to his assignment as signal-man; on the battlefield he'd have to carry and use communication apparatus ranging from flags to lamps to mirrors, and he'd have to keep track of a constantly shifting system of codes. He had excelled during training, and I hoped his performance would carry over to combat. I imagine he hoped the same about me.

"Captain Whittlesey," he said, surprised to see me. "I didn't think you were in the fold."

"I'm not. But I've been told that Father Halligan is worth hearing regardless. Say, Larney," I added, feeling impatient and adventuresome, "do you happen to know a private called Bill Cavanaugh?"

"The pigeon man?" said Larney. "Yes, sir, I do. Now, there's a soldier who's suited to his job, Captain. He lives and breathes pigeons. He knows a lot about the wireless radio aboard the ship, too. Interesting guy, very curious about communications. That's him there, in fact."

As the crowd broke up into pockets, I saw Cavanaugh seated at Halligan's battered piano—it was customary, I later learned, for it to be put to secular use after Mass concluded—and as I watched, he began to play with fluid, unassuming confidence.

"He says he learned to play in Hell's Kitchen saloons," said Larney. "Can't read music, not a note, but if he hears a tune once, he can play it back exactly."

"Billy!" somebody shouted from somewhere. "Strike it up, why don't you, and play 'Over There'!"

Cavanaugh obliged. It had become customary to sing "Over There" in grim, humorous paraphrase—substituting "when" for "till"—to mock or accept the prospect of death. That's how the men sang it that morning to Cavanaugh's accompaniment, which made up in verve what it lacked in refinement: "And we won't come back when it's over over there!"

I liked watching him in the center of the circle, happy and necessary, but when the twist to the lyrics arrived, my breath caught, though I'd heard it sung that way dozens of times before.

The notion that Cavanaugh might not return made me realize that at that moment my strongest desire was to see him in Manhattan, going about his everyday life in a nation at peace. Then a second realization struck, like the cross that follows a jab: I, to a great extent, was responsible for whether he and every other man singing on the aft deck came home alive. I knew this, of course; I had thought of it constantly since receiving my commission. But the responsibility felt different, weightier, when I considered the specificity of what might be lost.

I felt desperate that my Manhattan should have Bill Cavanaugh in it. He did not seem queer. Nor did he seem like trade, as Felix would have put it: a working-class man who would provide sexual favors to other men but who expected eventually to marry and have a family. In his blue-eyed, impenitent enthusiasm, Cavanaugh seemed almost to stand outside sex, with all its complications and distractions.

Still, I thought I could go see him at Rector's at least. I could take Marguerite there, and Bill Cavanaugh would be our waiter. I could tell him that I was interested in taking up pigeon racing, maybe, and ask him to teach me how to do it.

It seems stupid now, looking back.

The days slipped by, and we strained our eyes as we smoked on the decks, until one morning we spotted a low dark streak, dismissed at first as a cloud on the horizon. Then the cry went up—*Land! Land!*—as if we were explorers of old, conquistadors in reverse.

And land it was: Ireland. The soldiers of Irish extraction—Bill Cavanaugh included—saluted the motherland as we passed through the Irish Sea.

On the evening of April 19, our convoy dropped its anchors in the river Mersey, within sight of Liverpool. We stayed on the ship that night as there was nowhere better to put us, though we were mad to get out, a tin of stinking sardines come back to life.

The next morning the *Lapland* berthed at last, and the men whooped and hollered down the gangways toward terra firma. "Nice to have something before our eyes besides wave after wave," said McMurtry as we watched the men hand over stacks of Soldiers' Mail postcards to a Military Postal Express Service crew. I imagined Cavanaugh's sister, Annie, getting one from him, rushing to show to their mother, maybe going all the way to the roof to read it aloud to her pigeon namesake.

Dockside, a group of elderly women greeted us. We were hungry for anything that hadn't been cooked on the ship, and they were selling ginger buns and hot coffee. We still had only American money, but we settled on a nickel as the equivalent of the price of the breakfast, which they quoted as tuppence, ha'penny.

The story soon went around of an old Scouser woman, widow's black shawl wrapped about her stocky frame, who held out a steaming cup to one of our men and asked him, "Did ye come over to die?"

The man, nonplussed, nearly dropped his mug. "Not if I can help it, lady," he said.

The woman's eyes went wide, abashed. "No, no!" she said. "What I mean is, did ye just arrive?"

The accents took some getting used to, but we didn't have much time to adjust. Before we'd stopped feeling the phantom roll of waves beneath our feet, we'd been loaded onto railcars and sent south through the English countryside to Dover, where we'd make the Channel crossing to Calais.

Our steamship went under the escort of the Dover Patrol, as well as a Royal Navy blimp, placid and watchful above scudding gray clouds. I kept my eyes on it, transfixed, wondering what it might be like to fight the war in the air.

From the deck of the *Toloa*, I can't say for sure how far we are from land, only that land is completely out of view. Yet here swoop the seagulls, even this far out. How do they do it?

During burials at sea, the officiant says, "We therefore commit his body to the deep." What about a burial in air, when one dies in the sky and falls, the lifeless impact like a second death? Plenty of men died in midair during the Great War, and plenty of birds did, too, Bill Cavanaugh's included.

CHAPTER 7

CHER AMI

※※※

We heard that the Germans had a proverb: "He liveth best who is always ready to die." We soon learned that their army fought that way.

The practicality, hard-heartedness, and hint of perversion mixed in that maxim seemed to strike our men as stereotypically German, which is probably why we heard them quote it so often. I never met a German bird who could confirm or deny it.

We Allied pigeons did, however, receive frequent briefings from our keepers about our German counterparts, inevitably shaded with envy and concern. The enemy's pigeons were better prepared, Germany being one of the first nations to establish military lofts in Danzig, Stettin, Tönning, and Wilhelmshaven, places whose names we knew by rumor and reputation. Metz and Cologne, too, each said to hold over four hundred trained pigeons at any given moment, all ready to carry messages from cog to cog in the giant Teutonic machine of war.

After we landed in Calais, we began to hear stories that even a century later leave me heartbroken and horrified. Whenever they occupied Belgian or French territory, the Germans would order all pigeons in the region destroyed. Anyone found owning or selling birds, combatant or noncombatant, would be punished for possessing contraband. One million pigeons were confiscated and killed in Belgium alone.

Unlike some species—crows, cowbirds, cuckoos—pigeons are not vengeful. But some part of me was eager to take to the air on behalf of these slaughtered birds, if not to avenge their deaths then to fly for the side that hadn't committed such an atrocity.

When the basket containing me and Thomas Hardy and the rest of the Wright Farm Dozen finally reached France alongside innumerable other conscripted pigeons, the landscape that met us was bleak and sunless, nothing like the green Cotswold Hills. The soldiers unloading us wondered aloud whether the previous three and a half years of steady gunfire and explosions along the Western Front had seeded the clouds, making the weather wetter.

"Oh, look," said Thomas Hardy, his usual good cheer finally veering toward sarcasm. "We get to ride another train."

Mucking through the final miles by truck, we arrived at the American pigeon lofts in Langres, an old French city, walled and fortified since the days of the Romans, its towers peering from a limestone promontory, the red-roofed houses coiling up and around the hill like beads on a string.

Langres was far from the front and hadn't undergone the destruction we'd see in other towns, but it was cold and somber all the same. The men plucked us from the trucks and put us in whatever lofts had space. I flew slowly to a perch— more of a hop, really, its being so crowded—and looked out at the complex: hundreds upon hundreds of us, rippling like water, all shades and colors, all army birds.

"This isn't any better than the basket," I said to Thomas Hardy, longing to stretch my wings and soar. "Being cooped up in here makes me feel more like livestock than a racing homer. Are they fattening us for slaughter?"

"They'll send you to the front soon enough," said a voice from the perch beside us. "Then you'll see what slaughter means."

It was a baleful-looking black cock with frizzled feathers and horny feet. He spoke with his eyes barely open, without turning toward us, as if conserving his energy. "When I first came to the war," he said, "I met a bird who'd been attached to a French battalion during the Nivelle Offensive. When the mutiny started, the soldiers being marched to the line began bleating."

"Lambs led to the slaughter?" I said.

"Their officers could do nothing to stop it," he said. "Unseemly, perhaps. But the poilus have my sympathy."

His orange eye opened and stared straight into mine. His small pupil was ringed with yellow, reminiscent of a bull's-eye, though I'd soon learn that he was gifted at evading shrapnel and bullets: an almost—almost—unhittable target.

"Who are you?" said Thomas Hardy, in a friendlier tone than I'd have managed.

"President Wilson's the name," he said, puffing his oil-black breast like a head of state.

"You're American?" I asked. I had never met an American—man or bird—and was intrigued to meet a representative of what was to be our side.

"No, French," he said. "It's just a patriotic moniker. And you?"

"Cher Ami," I said. "And this is my brother, Thomas Hardy. We're English."

"An English bird with a French name here to fly for the Americans," said President Wilson. "And your name is masculine, but you're a hen, unless I miss my guess. *Mon Dieu*, life in wartime!"

"It's complicated," I said.

Amid the cacophony of the thronged loft, from somewhere on the dropping-dappled straw floor, a soft sound caught my ear: a rattling cough.

Below me hunkered a silvery hen, not doing well but trying to hide it. Private and stoic, she was, even in her obvious illness, the most beautiful bird I had ever seen. The ends of her feathers were tinted faintly pink, like low clouds at sunrise or the smoldering ruins of an ancient city. But it was her smell that nearly knocked me from my perch: the hint of white roses at the edge of happiness.

Without speaking another word to President Wilson, I flew

down next to her and asked, "Who are you?" I knew that she might make me sick, too, but I didn't care.

"USA 15431," she said, her voice like cinders.

"No, your real name. Where did you come from? What's wrong?"

"Baby Mine," she said. "I came all the way from the States in a dark crate. Storms. Five thousand miles. Sick and sad. It's pneumonia, I think."

Had John come along to care for his Wright Farm birds, as I believe he wanted to, he'd have helped Baby Mine. Anything that ailed a pigeon was curable in his hands. Would these American pigeoneers bustling in their khaki take notice?

If you want to tell whether a human is the type who truly loves animals, the eyes are a giveaway. When Corporal George Gault opened the loft door to cast us our feed, I saw care in his eyes. His accent and the tone of his voice were nothing like John's, but he had the same patient manner and a similar mustache, though his was pure chestnut with no strands of gray.

When the seed hit the troughs—vaster than those at Wright Farm, for we were such a huge flock—the other birds flapped over to eat, wings clapping as though in an ovation to the corporal. I remained in the straw next to Baby Mine, looking up and cooing.

"What have we got here?" the corporal said, gently pushing me aside to lift Baby Mine in a spruce, agile hand. "Come on, sweet Baby Mine, we'll get you fixed in no time. And, Cher Ami, if you aren't the best-named pigeon this fella's ever met! Don't worry about your new friend."

Carrying her with the same reverence and professionalism that a museum curator might show toward a precious antiquity, he shut the loft door behind them, leaving a faint waft of chocolate in his wake: he always kept it in his pocket, and among us sharp-sniffing pigeons it became a cherished herald of his approach.

But I took little notice of it at the time, or for that matter of the meal the corporal had provided and after which my new loftmates were flapping and jostling. My mind was fixed on Baby Mine—her voice, her smell—trying to braid every strand of her into my memory, as I might work to memorize landmarks and traces that would lead me home.

When Corporal Gault returned to refresh our water the following morning, he did not bring Baby Mine back, and I stood at the rim of the bathing pan, bereft.

"Stiff upper lip," said President Wilson, alighting beside me. "Isn't that what the men say in your country? Baby Mine is in good hands. Gault is a gem among pigeoneers. He'll nurse her back to health, if anyone can."

This was typical of President Wilson—he'd offer a few authoritative words of reassurance, then follow them with a shrug of doubt meant to protect him from ever being wrong—but I was too morose to challenge him.

Our training regimen left me little time to pine, though. To an accomplished racer, the exercises seemed remedial: allowing ourselves to be held without protest, accepting bulky message canisters on our legs, and taking stock of the sights and sounds and smells of Langres from the roof of the loft while confined to our baskets.

I felt frustrated at our slow progress, irritated by our close quarters, and constantly aware that once released I could simply fly home to Wright Farm. The sluggish, meandering journey to France by truck and train and ship notwithstanding, I knew that Chipping Norton was about four hundred miles from Langres, manageable for any pigeon willing to brave the poor visibility and unpredictable winds over the Channel. In fact, I had a clear idea of the route I'd take, the speed and altitude I'd maintain, the sights by which I'd navigate—which, I suddenly realized, is exactly why the corporal had kept us in our baskets. We had a job to do in France; we knew it, and we *wanted* to do it. But when at last we were airborne from Gault's hands, would *the voice* understand our purpose here? Or would it simply send us hurtling back to our birthplace, as it had always done?

Gault's gentle attention and a steady supply of tasty tic beans and maple peas did their work. When the corporal finally transported us to a spot south of the city walls and tossed me skyward, the voice spoke clearly: *Cher Ami! Home to your loft by the airway! Home to Langres!*

Relieved, I flew back to the loft, reveling in the long-withheld rush through open air. Only later that night, as I perched sleeplessly, did a note of disquiet find me. Something that I had taken as fixed had shifted, had *been* shifted. I felt the world grow larger, myself grow smaller in it, and Wright Farm and my family grow farther away.

Once Corporal Gault finally granted us liberty, I began to enjoy my training, just as I had when John had trained us back in England. The French landscape sprawled below in a pleasing pattern, villages and countryside ceilinged by glorious sky of crisp and solitudinous blue, only a permeable layer of other birds seeming to abide between earth and heaven.

"This really is a beautiful place," Thomas Hardy remarked upon his return from a long flight. He spoke between pecks at grains of rice and cinquintina maize, his reward from Gault for a route well flown.

"You should go ahead and enjoy it," President Wilson advised, forever behaving like everyone's dad, "because it is teaching you absolutely nothing about the battlefields we'll soon be sent to."

He said this offhandedly, while grooming his velvety black breast. I cocked my head at him and stamped a foot—by then I had outflown every pigeon in the loft, and I was in no mood to be deferential—but he took no apparent notice. The other birds, however, were watching my reaction closely, alert for a shift in the balance of power.

I chose to stand down. Jealous though he might have been of my skill in the air, President Wilson was a veteran of many missions, and he'd earned his authority on the topic he'd raised. Like the other birds, I wanted to know what he knew of war. The human notion of fighting in an organized, mechanized way—with the principal aim of claiming and holding areas of ground while killing as many other humans as possible—remained incomprehensible. We had no real understanding of what a battlefield was, much less of what flying over one might be like. Since our arrival President Wilson had spoken only cryptically of his experiences under fire; now, perhaps, his wounded pride presented an opportunity to draw him out.

"All right," I said. "Do tell."

And tell he did, that evening and for many evenings thereafter. He spoke in the same indifferent, matter-of-fact tone that he used for all his stories, but what he described was so preposterously awful as to resemble folktales invented to terrify gullible squabs. He told us about German snipers who could launch metal projectiles across hundreds of yards to kill men and pigeons alike. He told us about poison gases that the Germans used against our soldiers, gases that would kill us even faster thanks to our active metabolism. He told us about exploding shells that would fall among our troops and cast jagged shrapnel everywhere. He told us about soldiers—our own soldiers!—who fell backward and crushed the baskets of pigeons they carried, or who panicked and left their baskets behind, or who, starving after weeks without supplies, wrung the necks of their birds in order to roast and eat them.

When he heard this story, Thomas Hardy burst into deranged laughter. "What's so funny?" the rest of us demanded, and then we were laughing, too.

"You might expect," President Wilson told us one night after a long flight back to the loft, breaking a weary silence that had settled among us, "that one advantage to homing from a battlefield is that the violence of war will have banished and replaced all the usual dangers we face on our journeys. This is wrong."

Silhouetted against the twilight, he spoke with his eyes closed, as if imparting this warning were a final task keeping him from sleep. "The Argonne Forest is still full of buzzards and sparrow hawks. The war has driven the mice from the fields into the woods, and so the raptors are healthy and plentiful. Also, the Germans have trained falcons for the specific purpose of taking *pigeons voyageurs*. Even the most dead-eyed rifleman has trouble shooting a bird on the wing—and unlike the Americans, the Germans don't use shotguns—so to supplement their bullets they conscript the fastest birds of prey to capture and kill us. This is always the way with humans, you see. Pigeons home; it is our nature. And falcons hunt pigeons; this is natural, too. But the humans pervert our respective natures toward their own ends. And by doing this perhaps they express their own nature. Who can say?"

This didn't seem right. The care and training that we got from John on Wright Farm, that we were getting from Corporal Gault at Langres, didn't feel like a perversion of anything to me. It felt like collaboration, maybe even like love. I didn't feel as though I'd been warped in their custody but instead as though I'd become more completely myself.

I wasn't sure how to argue this, so I kept silent, pretending to be asleep until, without intending to, I slept.

For the next few weeks, cars and motorcycles came and went, gradually taking all my Wright Farm loftmates away, including Thomas Hardy. I wanted to go, too—but I was also afraid I'd go before Baby Mine returned or before I learned what had become of her.

Our lofts provided a good vantage from which to observe the American troops whom we'd be supporting, and much of what we saw did not put us at ease. Even though these soldiers understood themselves to be saving the French, they could act like invaders themselves. Medical officers tried to establish sanitation and in the process denigrated the villagers' habits. When the doughboys got paid, they spent their salaries haphazardly, insensate to the greed they exercised and the jealousy they inspired. And if I sometimes grew frustrated at being unable to make myself understood in human language, it was nothing compared to the frustration that emerged between doughboy and villager, both so reliant on speech and yet mutually unintelligible. The failure of words to function as accustomed caused many a minor disagreement to become major.

The local French children helped bridge this divide. They ran free as roosters all over the streets, and I credit them with teaching the doughboys the little smattering of French they were able to acquire.

Knowledge flowed in the other direction, too. Day in, day out, the cheeky *enfants* loitering near the doughboy quarters learned the men's drills quite well. Their little leader, a tow-headed and toughly cherubic boy, gave the commands in fine English, not omitting the profane. "Parade rest, you flea-bit fuckers!" he'd shout, augmenting his piping voice with a sergeant's growl.

Late one afternoon I watched this same urchin, snaggly teeth giving him the air of a field mouse, run up to a soldier and ask for a cigarette, *s'il vous plaît.*

"Mais tu es bien trop petit!" the man said with a laugh, stating the obvious: the boy was too little.

"C'est pour mon père!" said the boy, though there were no *pères* in that village, nor *pères* anywhere, all of them having been sent to the front.

The soldier didn't have enough French to continue the debate, and sadness stole over him, as if he were thinking of the boy's father's fate, or of his own. He relented, and the boy hopped off with his treasure like a sparrow to his nest.

I remembered myself as a fledgling in the Wright Farm loft, after I left the nest but before I mastered flight, under normal circumstances the most perilous time of any bird's life. Although my parents and John looked after me well, I was always in danger from hawks and cats and foxes. I was a fledgling for only a few terrifying weeks; human children pass entire years before they're able to fend for themselves. For the thousandth time, I wondered how such a delicate species—slow runners, poor kickers, ineffective biters thanks to the peculiar placement of their all-but-useless noses—came to dominate the earth.

The group of children, having witnessed their leader's success, now clustered around the same soldier, their filthy hands outstretched. "How do they learn to forage like this?" I wondered aloud. "No one is training them."

"Hunger is a good teacher for any animal, I suppose," said a voice from behind me, a voice like cinders.

It was Baby Mine. I was staggered by how much more beautiful she was in health. Some of her feathers were the color of violets.

Without quite deciding to, I flew to her, cooing low and pecking lightly at her ravishing neck. She welcomed my attention, pecking in return. "I didn't know if you'd ever come back!" I said.

"I have," she said. "And it's all thanks to you, for getting me the care I needed."

"Oh, Gault is a quality pigeon man," I demurred. "He'd have noticed you without my help. He'd never let a perfect bird like you die."

"Well, you helped him find me faster, and I'm not sure how much longer I could have lasted. So thank you. Gault says it will be a while before I'm ready to train near the front, but I'm well enough now to be back in the flock."

Another bird intruded alongside us with a series of ungraceful flaps—a bird with feathers so purely and brilliantly white that his every arrival was like a signal flare or a loud noise. "You're doubly lucky, then," he said. "Not sick but not going into battle either."

This was Buck Shot, a recent arrival from near Chicago. Striking though he was in appearance, he was a tactless bumbler, lacking the humor to see the grim comedy in our circumstances, much less in his ironic name. Among birds and men alike, a sense of humor was a critical asset in war, far more important than skill or courage.

Buck Shot had a standard litany of complaints through which he constantly cycled, and in Baby Mine he saw a fresh audience. "Do I look like a bird who belongs on a battlefield? Look at me! Pure white! I'm practically a fancy pigeon. I have no business flying around with messages on my legs. I'm an emblem of peace, and they're sending me to a bloodbath. Not to mention how easy I'll be to spot in flight!"

"Buck Shot!" President Wilson called sternly from the floor of the loft. "As you may be aware, there are certain counter-measures that pale birds like yourself can employ to decrease visibility in the air. Why don't you leave those two alone, fly down here, and let me tell you about them?"

I was grateful for his intervention, but it turned out to be unnecessary. The door to the loft swung open, and Corporal Gault walked in. His eyes easily located Buck Shot and Baby Mine, then pivoted to plain me perched beside them. "Your dear friend is back, Cher Ami!" he said. "I'm glad you got to see her now, as I'm afraid you'll soon be separated again."

For a moment I was concerned that Baby Mine might still be ill, but then I saw the way Gault looked at Buck Shot and me, and I knew: our time had come. The two things I'd been waiting for were happening at once, and one was taking me away from the other.

Baby Mine and I exchanged pained looks, our warm necks lightly entwined, both flummoxed as to what to say.

"Well," said President Wilson, staring philosophically through the loft's open door, "there's nothing to be gained from mooning about. This is what war is: Saying good-bye. Just saying good-bye, friends. Might as well get used to it."

He was, as usual, half right. If war was saying good-bye, it was equally finding oneself at a loss about what to do with sudden hellos, unexpected connections made as the world fell to pieces.

Baby Mine gave me a peck on the beak just as the corporal

scooped up Buck Shot and expertly lifted me in his other hand. I tried not to look back, tried to accept that I'd never see her again, that to hope otherwise was childish, that our separation was for the best. While our fellow pigeons did not regard bonds between hens as unnatural, the humans who kept us certainly seemed to—and in any case such a pairing could serve no human purpose, as it would yield no champion racers, no progeny at all. While I preferred to think of us as the humans' partners and collaborators—and we were; I wasn't wrong—we were also their property and their tools. What did I expect?

Gault placed us in our wicker basket along with a few other birds whom I didn't know, then carried us outside, where a tall, narrow, four-wheeled cart awaited our arrival.

"It looks like a covered wagon," said Buck Shot.

I didn't know what a covered wagon was. Mobile Loft Number 11, my third home, had large barred windows to admit breezes, and its front end was crowned with a caged-in alighting board, beyond which we could hear the commotion of many other pigeons. Gault gently placed us on the board, and we advanced through swinging wires to join eighty other homers from all over the Langres complex, fluttering amid brightly colored nests.

Gault closed the cage, lowered thick blinds over the windows, hitched the loft to a truck, and off we went. The ride was terrible, jouncing us around, all the more nauseating since we couldn't see. It grew as dark outside as in—we were traveling with lights off through the inky night, since we didn't want airplanes to see us—and at one point we were nearly upended when the truck towing us became stuck in a shell hole.

We went through Neufchâteau and Bar-le-Duc to the thunderous accompaniment of guns and shells. Buck Shot trembled, and I didn't blame him. Others beat their wings. All I could manage was to hold very still. During my short life, I had been well cared for, had encountered very little danger.

I thought of the falcon that chased me on my first race from Scotland back to Wright Farm. I was young then, and it had seemed like no more than a game, not something that could have meant the end of me. I had stayed so far ahead that I'd barely glimpsed the killer bird. But for many nights after I returned to the loft, the image of the falcon came back to me, jolting me from sleep aflutter. I began to imagine the curved speck of the falcon as a hole punched in the world, one through which I might slip to my doom. Ever since I'd heard President Wilson describe the birds of prey that stalked the front, I had begun to picture the war as a swirling mass of these holes, vast as the horizon and all but impossible to escape.

As dawn was breaking, we finally pulled up to Rampont, barely a wide spot on the dirt road bordering the forty-mile length of the Argonne Forest. Another mobile loft, Number 9, was there, too, settled in under the care of more American pigeoneers.

The forest birds were in the midst of unfamiliar morning songs, and for a moment I thought I heard an English lark among them—but it was Corporal Gault, whistling "It's a Long Way to Tipperary" as he opened the cages to let in the light and feed us. There was a bathing pan sunk into the floor, and he uncovered that, too. Being passed among freight handlers during my travels to races had shown me that men can be careless, or indifferent, or simply ignorant of pigeons' needs, and it was a comfort to see Gault's dependable face, particularly as distant explosions shook the earth and air.

I made my way to the edge of the loft to see the lay of the land: what trees were nearby, and what roads. I took in as much information as I could about the loft itself, particularly its smells—the wood and paint and iron and rubber, the nests and feed and down and droppings—knowing I'd have time to learn it by sight soon enough, to plot the best approaches to its landing board. Mobile Loft Number 9 was next to us in parallel, and it looked just like Mobile Loft Number11. *Not my loft!* I told myself. I must not confuse them.

"At any hour you might be needed," said Corporal Gault each time he took us out to train, carrying our baskets in the sidecar of a motorcycle, releasing us to head back. He threw me into the air every day, sometimes alone and sometimes with others, first near and then farther and farther, until I could find my way quickly and unfailingly to Mobile Loft Number 11. *Mine, mine, mine,* I thought.

Home, Cher Ami! said the voice, softly at first, then more steadily. *Home to your loft by the airway! Home to Rampont!*

Beside the alighting board hung a small silver bell. Corporal Gault and the other pigeon men paid close attention to that bell and would reward any bird who rang it upon returning from a long flight with praise and a few delicious bits of corn. Not so different than returning from a race.

Mobile Loft Number 11, we learned, was where we'd be delivering messages from the battlefield. Soldiers waiting for the sound of the bell would take them from our legs, transcribe them, and then relay them by telegraph or by telephone in code to commanding officers headquartered far from the front. Almost everything about human communication made little sense to us, but we intuited the preciousness of the rolls of paper.

During my training flights at Langres, everything below had appeared calm and orderly, nature in perfect balance with human cultivation. Above Rampont the earth looked like a dumping ground for ashcans. What not long ago had been primeval forests and pastel meadows had been displaced by German narrow-gauge railroads and trenches that gaped like fatal wounds. I could see bicyclists distributing chocolate and tobacco and mail, pedaling along as if on a pleasure ride in the country, except the country was a hellscape.

At Langres, flying far behind the lines, I would often smell the perfumes of what the soldiers called—among other things—women of ill repute: musk and gardenia, storax and jasmine. These odors were not to be found near the Argonne Forest. Instead I flew through wafts of darker scents, nature accommodating itself to a land of death: mushrooms in the woods, reeking like glue or creosote, particularly a toxic lollipop called the destroying angel. I'd soon learn that these bad smells were nothing compared to those of actual battlefields.

Then one day on the way back to Rampont, I smelled white roses at the edge of happiness. Baby Mine had arrived. I spotted her in the air by her flower-petal feathers; she was coming home from a training flight, headed for Mobile Loft Number 9. For the first time in my life, I was able to quiet the voice for a moment, to deviate from my route enough to meet her in the air.

We flew together, her movements fluid and linear like the steady unspooling of time itself.

"I don't know if it's being thrown in with each other in the war like this," she said, "or if I'm crackers, or what. But back at Langres, after you left, I couldn't stop thinking of you. And it isn't just because you saved my life when I was sick. I was afraid that I'd lost the chance to tell you, but now that I haven't, I want you to hear it: I love you. And if I die, I loved you."

"I love you, too," I said, hardly able to believe my ears. We pigeons are forthright in our declarations of love, but to receive one from her was more than I had dared to dream. "And we're not going to die. We'll make it through."

"I don't know if we will," she said. "I sometimes wonder what our lives would be like if we were free to choose our own destinations. If we didn't have to follow the voice."

This was a radical notion, one I had never heard spoken before, one I had never even quite managed to think. "I'm not sure what we'd be if we didn't."

"We wouldn't be tools of war," she said. "We know that at least."

"That's true," I said, unable to dispute her sense of impending peril. "If you *could* choose where to fly, where would you go?"

"That's just the thing," she said. "It's impossible to imagine. But if I could, I'd want to fly there with you."

And with that, Mobile Lofts Number 9 and 11 came into view, and we went our separate ways to ring our separate bells. I wished that I could gather her to me at the end of the day, as dusk gathers itself to itself. All that night my heart beat harder, knowing how close she was.

I was further along than she in my training and was therefore always released farther from Rampont, so I would keep my eyes and nose alert for her on each flight back, usually to no avail. But sometimes I found her, and we'd fly together, speaking desperately of our youths in England and America, of adventures we'd had on races, of the small things that gave us pleasure in the world.

These rendezvous began to add minutes to my return times, which did not go unnoticed. The pigeoneers began to fear that my homing skill—and therefore my usefulness—was on the wane.

"War waits for neither man nor pigeon," Corporal Gault told me one morning, with what seemed like sincere regret. And I knew then—or I strongly felt—that I was about to be parted from Baby Mine for the last time.

The hour had come to go into combat.

Gault plopped me into a two-bird shipping basket, a large silver cock on the other side. No point in making introductions. Gault covered us up with heavy meshed wire, put a loose canvas bag with a drawstring over that, then piled us into a motorcycle's sidecar and hopped in with us. A private whom I'd never seen drove us twenty kilometers to the edge of the woods. We came to a narrow path where two other pigeoneers in a second motorcycle waited to take us another twenty kilometers farther on.

"Adieu for now, Cher Ami," said Gault, and I breathed deeply so as not to forget his scents of chocolate bars and shaving cream. "When all else fails, and it often does, we'll rely on you to carry the news. I hope to see you back at Rampont, and soon."

They dropped us in Grandpré, ravaged and dour, where we were immediately carried down into a deep, dark hole, larger and darker than any I'd ever seen or been in. Though we are aerial animals, pigeons have no aversion to the earth—our wild ancestors often nested in shallow cliffside caves, and back on Wright Farm some of us liked to wallow in the deep pits that Bobs, John's big black hound, compulsively dug, the dust bath fabulous between our feathers—but this was not like that. This was a trench, twisting for miles under fields, miles under woods, wide enough for hundreds of soldiers to lurk in and sleep in and fire guns from.

I waited in my basket, dark and cold and wet. A pigeoneer was supposed to feed me corn and peas and water every day, and mostly that happened, but sometimes it didn't. I was prepared to risk my life by outflying falcons and bullets, but I hadn't been prepared to become an unloved piece of furniture. I was thankful for the wire that covered my cage, for a gruesome gray rat with a cruel face stared at me each night, night after night.

The wire also kept out fragments of shells that exploded nearby, and the canvas kept us safe from gas attacks. Whenever a gas shell burst, the pigeoneer—nondescript, no aficionado like John or Corporal Gault, just a man doing his job—pulled the drawstring and kept us covered until the all-clear.

One leaden morning, after days of waiting, the pigeoneer lifted me. He took the commander's message on a small piece of thin paper and slipped it into the canister. Then, around my right leg, he affixed the tube with two narrow copper wires. The message was written in code; if I got killed, the Germans wouldn't be able to read it.

The pigeoneer—who never spoke a word to me during all my time there—threw me at the patch of dingy sky above the trench. Circling to gain altitude, I pushed the thought of my death aside. Fiery-edged clouds contrasted and harmonized with rifle fire: silvery muzzle flashes, silvery bullets. I thought of turkeys and geese and other table birds as I felt myself basted in a hot shower of metal.

But so, too, did I feel the slap of cold air on my beak and the joy of being loosed, and I heard the voice: *Cher Ami! Home to your loft by the airway! Home to Rampont!*

In twenty-five minutes, I flew thirty kilometers, back to the landing board of Mobile Loft Number 11. Corporal Gault rushed to me at the sound of the bell and phoned my first message to headquarters, far from the loft and the front. Baby Mine was long gone by then, in some other basket in some other trench, but for the rest of the day I got to coo with my friends and eat and bathe and sit on the roof in the sun. Home. That night Gault patiently explained the significance of the message I had delivered, and although I understood little of it, I'd be lying if I said I didn't take pride in my accomplishment.

Of course I had to go back: on the motorcycle, in the basket, in the air, all summer long. Sometimes the wind came in gales and the rain fell in torrents, but I flew the thirty kilometers in under a half hour every time, over and over.

CHAPTER 8

CHARLES WHITTLESEY

―――――――⟫⟫⟫⟪⟪⟪――――――――

We heard that the Germans had a proverb: "He liveth best who is always ready to die." I never asked any of our prisoners to confirm or deny this, but we would soon find out they fought that way.

The British soldiers with whom we were attached for training outside Calais warned us that the devils in field gray had emplaced across the Meuse-Argonne—which we planned to overtake—four *Stellungen*, or belts of fortification. As in some blood sport dreamed up by demons, we Allied troops would have to pass through parallel rows of pillboxes and bunkers that on maps looked like the spiked collars of malevolent dogs. In a Teutonic touch both silly and terrifying, the belts were all named after characters from the *Nibelungenlied*, an epic poem I knew mostly via Wagner works that Marguerite and I had been bludgeoned by at the Met; the third and worst *Stellung*, for instance, was called Kriemhilde, after the vengeful bride of the hero Siegfried.

When our assault on those fortifications came later that fall, it would be less *grand opéra* than Grand Guignol: prolonged, yes, and massive in scale, but possessing neither art nor glamour.

Any man among us who expected cries of *"Vive les Américains!"* when we landed in Calais was due for disappointment. Nobody cheered; they'd seen it before. The port city's buildings, bombed so often by German airplanes, stood windowless beside the water like blinded faces, mute and empty. Aside from German prisoners working the docks alongside

Chinese laborers, and soldiers from every Allied nation, Calais was a ghost town.

It was the first place we'd been that felt like it was at war, and for most of us our arrival was sobering. Not for all of us, however.

"Hail, hail, the gang's all here!" sang Lieutenant Maurice Revnes as he led his men through the streets. Revnes was a showboat, an actor in civilian life who'd produced a few one-act plays in New York before volunteering for the Plattsburgh camps. He'd been the theatrical director at Upton, and he'd resume that role on this side of the ocean, gathering musicians, singers, and vaudevillians to form the Argonne Players. Talented but mean was how I'd pegged him, and seeing him make his entrance in Calais did nothing to change my opinion: a toothy smile and scornful eyes, bluff and swaggering, his performance a poor fit for a city marred by tragedy. I exchanged glances with McMurtry, a little down the column, and he shook his head in disgust.

If Revnes noticed, he paid it no mind. *"Hail, hail, the gang's all here!"* he sang again, louder, his gaudy tenor echoing off the chalky walls.

"We're going to get the kaiser, going to get the kaiser!" sang some of the men in reply as we awaited the order to march to our quarters.

Nearby a French captain with his right arm in a sling leaned against the base of an old stone watchtower, smoking with his good hand. He called to Revnes, "You remind me of me in 1914."

"Merci, mon ami," Revnes replied, doffing his cap to reveal the handsome sheen of his close-cropped blue-black hair.

"I saw this all the time at the front," the soldier continued in English, accented but clear. "You want to attack. You are ready. But when the moment comes, perhaps you change your mind. Often when one has never done something, it seems quite easy to do."

At our camp outside town, we began to hear similar sentiments from the British soldiers—the Tommies—who took charge of our education in throwing grenades and firing machine guns. Fights broke out occasionally, and then regularly, between our sergeants and those of the British army; our boys were deaf to the gradations of class that defined the Tommies' service, while also being unaccustomed to the tartness of the admonishments they received in training, and I spent an alarming amount of my time smoothing over conflicts and supervising reluctant handshakes. But somewhat to my chagrin, I discovered that I had a better rapport with the British officers than with many of my fellow Americans.

"At first it was exciting," admitted the captain whom I was shadowing, as we watched the men learn the thrusts of a bayonet drill. I'd often heard tell of the famous English reserve and encountered it often in Calais, but this officer was refreshingly open, even urgent, in his disclosures, and he had the kindly if unsettling mien of a haunted soothsayer.

"The training was dull, of course, as was all the waiting," he said. "But I was slow to appreciate the extent to which our expectations had been shaped by the way we all spoke. Elevated by an almost feudal language. A friend was a 'comrade,' a friendship a 'fellowship.' Horses were 'steeds' and actions 'deeds,' and the enemy was 'a foe,' and danger was 'peril.' The dead on the field would be 'the fallen.' We would not be fast, we would be 'swift.' We would not sleep, we would 'slumber,' and we'd gaze not into the sky but into 'the heavens.' In the end that shaped us more than the training did."

"This is scholarship of a different sort than I know from Williams or Harvard," I said as my men drove and lunged.

"But the Oxford view I'd had of war could not long stand," he said. "Those were not our 'limbs' strewn over the fields but our arms and legs. None of us who've survived this long can ever hear the word 'machine' without his poor brain following it with 'gun.' It's really done us." He smiled: sorrowful, not cruel.

The war drew closer. Its approach was less like the coming of a storm, more the onset of a sickness. We could feel it changing us.

Periodically we'd march the men eight kilometers to the nearest train depot to pick up supplies. The army was loath to admit how unprepared it was in regard to combat gear; much of the equipment we were issued was French and British, particularly the weapons. The light machine gun was a French model called the Chauchat; the men nicknamed it the "Sho-Sho" and within a few weeks began calling it the "Shit-Shit," based on its habit of jamming after firing only a few rounds. The best means of clearing a jam in the Chauchat, per an oft-repeated quip, was to throw it away.

We were somewhat better provisioned with defensive gear. The train delivered an adequate supply of steel helmets, which replaced our wool caps; the mass of us donning them around the depot was like a sudden bloom of hard gray flowers.

"One of the most versatile pieces of equipment imaginable," said McMurtry as we stood near the boxcars. "It sheds water like a roof, serves as a chair in the mud. It can be instantly turned into a candlestick in the dark. I'll take it over a rifle any day."

"If it can dissuade the occasional piece of shrapnel, then I'm sold," I said, rapping its edge and making it ding.

The army also provided maps of the countryside for use on practice marches. I studied mine alongside Omer Richards, one of our battalion's pigeon men, so he'd understand where his birds might need to go. Lanky and pale-cheeked, with a sweaty face and peculiar topaz eyes, his most notable feature was that he wasn't Bill Cavanaugh. But I was charmed by the French-Canadian private's delight at noticing a hamlet on the map north of us called Saint-Omer, his namesake.

To and from the depot we marched, through town after beautiful town brought to ruin: unchanged and of little significance for hundreds of years, then reduced to rubble by explosive shells and incendiary bombs. Houses disemboweled, guts pouring forth into sunless streets. Skeletons of churches, their entrances blocked by fallen chimes. Sometimes we'd pass a single shop left intact amid a row of destruction, a mannequin in its window raising a hand like Christ in blessing over a wrecked civilization.

Whenever we passed a tavern, Revnes would complain that the beer in France tasted more like rain, watery despite the exorbitant prices French farmers demanded. The men around him always laughed and agreed. Revnes, I'd begun to notice, had the ham actor's habit of speaking to his platoon while really addressing other audiences: men in other units, or the French townsfolk, or, most often, me and the other commanding officers. The trick allowed him to skirt insubordination while maintaining the escape route of having been misunderstood. I began to mentally review punishments I might impose without recourse to a court-martial, just to be prepared.

It was hard to keep track of thousands of men, but I did my best to know at least something about each of those with whom I was in regular contact. A few were troublemakers like Revnes, but many more were guys so wholesome that one could imagine them drinking nothing harder than root beer and eating nothing more exotic than white bread slathered with butter. I did my best to be worthy of leading them.

One afternoon, in the last emaciated husk of a village we passed on our way back to camp, an old woman in a peasant scarf with a face as dry and lined as a walnut emerged from a shop that I'd taken as abandoned. *"Cartes postales?"* she called out—postcards—desperate to sell them. The men had been performing well and were due for a break, so we halted the column and let the company fall out.

The soldiers passed through the small shop a few at a time, and the woman fanned her cards out on a battered counter. Some showed sylvan scenes, others bucolic landscapes of what this place must have looked like before the war. Others slipped casually between the respectable ones bore pictures of nude women, or of men and women locked in carnal embraces. The woman asked the men if these cards were *bon*, and many replied *oui*. Some bought them and tucked them into their pockets with varying degrees of embarrassment.

I made a point of letting these transactions proceed, literally looking the other way. The men, I imagine, took my averted eyes as indicative of my self-imposed restraint and steady moral code. In fact I simply wasn't tempted, or especially interested: the cards weren't at all artful, and their prurient appeal was lost on me.

Instead I watched Bill Cavanaugh. He didn't buy any cards either—politely refusing the old woman's inducements, slipping her some coins anyway—and this pleased me. For a moment, when he noticed me noticing his gesture, I met his gaze, blue as the cornflowers that lined the ditches. But he immediately looked down and away.

"All right, Sergeant," said McMurtry, "let's line 'em up."

"One more kilometer, boys!" shouted an overeager corporal as the men filed out, only to have some wiseacre answer, "Kill-o-meter? More like kill-yourself."

That day's supply run hadn't delivered the bedding the army had promised, so back at camp the men dozed off under used blankets, crusted with blood and reeking of delousing solution.

Early June it was time. We had orders to occupy the Baccarat defensive sector, east of Nancy in Lorraine, at the western foot of the Vosges Mountains. I had enjoyed the British sector and often found myself fondly recalling the Tommies' attitudes and expressions, particularly the infrequently bestowed compliment "Good show!" I resolved to do my best to put on such a show every day I was in command.

One summery morning, warm and gilded, we marched back to the Calais station to ship south in boxcars labeled HOMMES 40, CHEVAUX 8. We filled them with *hommes*, there being a shortage of horses given how many had been killed in the almost four years of fighting.

The upstate men felt awkward crammed and standing in the cars, but those from the boroughs felt right at home. "A fella feels just like he's riding the subway," called Bill Cavanaugh from a corner. The air vibrated with excitement, the men exhilarated to be going somewhere again, finally. I felt less electric and more liquid, lonely and anxious, still suspecting my own fraudulence and wishing, always, for more time.

We stayed overnight near the station in Nancy, then continued the trek on *camions*, French motortrucks. The trucks had no shock absorbers, so the journey felt like being sloshed for hours in a cocktail shaker. As we drew close to the trenches, we got out and walked: fifty minutes of marching to ten minutes of rest, as usual.

"No-man's-land" had a specific meaning in the war: the fatal flyway for bullets that separated opposing trenches. But the term seemed applicable to the villages we passed, too: no men of military age remained in any of them.

True to form, Revnes led the regiment in a vulgar marching song:

> Lulu took the farmer's horse and team
> To drive to the country store,
> But she eloped with the old studhorse
> And won't come back no more!
> Bang, bang Lulu!
> Bang her good and strong!
> What'll we do for banging
> When Lulu's dead and gone?

I longed to be the sort of carefree person who'd join the ribald chorus, but also congratulated myself on not being such a person.

The song passed the time, and it would have been pointless for me to look askance. But when some of the men began pilfering grapes from vineyards along the roadway, I couldn't stay silent, sympathetic though I might have been to their hunger for the tough-skinned fruit, the largest quantity of fresh produce we'd seen in months. "Remind your platoons," I said to the assembled lieutenants, "that we are here to rescue this country, not to sack it. We help these people; we do not threaten their livelihoods by stealing from them. Any soldier who forgets that shall be assigned extra duty for not less than thirty days. I trust that I have made myself clear."

Baccarat was a "quiet" sector—given our near-total lack of combat experience, from officers down to privates, the Allied strategists had wisely opted not to plunge us into the thick of battle—but it still wasn't safe to march too close to the front in daylight, so we bivouacked until nightfall and continued in the direction of the billets we'd been promised.

June 21 was a Friday night, the bright moon like a pearl. We, the Metropolitan Division, were many of us thinking of what we'd be doing in the city were we still at home. Midway through the woods, we passed the Fighting 69th, part of the Rainbow Division that we were relieving. Amid the splintered trees, with moonlight burnishing their faces, the city men sang "Sidewalks of New York" together and called out streets and home addresses. I held back—this was a working-class salute—but I wished I could share their panache and neighborhood pride. What would I call out? Midtown, by Grand Central? Or, worse yet, Wall Street? Not likely. When I heard Cavanaugh call out "Hell's Kitchen!" I turned to catch his silvery face, as fine in profile as Mercury's on a dime.

After the woods our good cheer was quelled by the faint first whiff of a real battlefield, a gagging combination of shit and gunpowder, gas and blood, decaying flesh and muddy rot. Though still distant, it was almost unbelievably awful, sending a spark of panic up my spine. I glanced down the column at McMurtry for reassurance, as I often did, only to see him as pale and stone-faced as I was. I immediately understood that all our training—the rehearsal of thoughts and actions, the merging of individual identities into a coordinated and interdependent force—was done in anticipation of this very moment, to stanch the fundamental impulse to flee from such terror. We smelled that death—perhaps the death of civilization—and we kept moving toward it, thereby becoming something more and less than human. Much of what happened to us later, I now believe, simply followed from that moment.

At last we arrived at our billets, old barns with dirt floors and starlight streaming through the roofs and walls, holes for windows, chickens everywhere, rats eating from manure piles shat by years-dead cattle. Late as it was, depressing as the accommodations seemed, some of the men still had energy for jokes, most of which took on a cruel and antic cast all too well suited to our circumstances. One private showed such a fear of rats that he was certain to become a figure of fun; every time he fell asleep, one of his buddies would run a bayonet up the seam of his pant leg, and he'd bolt awake and scream loud enough to wake men in adjacent barns. Laughter and merriment. Annoying, yes, but who was I to ruin their fun?

For the 77th was to be the first American division to enter the line.

For three weeks we had French mentors, and they told us stories. Proud and dignified, they were also respectful, and down-to-earth, and grateful for the relief. "It's the least we can do, after that hand you lent us back in 1778," McMurtry said.

It was interesting, and sobering, to see the change that came over McMurtry during our discussions with the French. He was still as buoyant and steady as ever, but his relaxed mien was gone, replaced by minute attention to our counterparts' every word. We were now, I realized, approaching conditions of which my battle-hardened friend was as ignorant as were the rest of us.

Not every combat veteran among our commanders, of which

there were several, seemed to share his concern, and the French intuited this. "Please understand," a patch-eyed colonel told us, "that the devastation you will witness along the front has no military precedent. Even in the fall of Carthage, the Romans had at their disposal no poison worse than salt."

I wanted to see no-man's-land, to be prepared, so I signed up one night for a Cook's tour of sorts, along with a handful of other officers. We crept through the trenches in small groups to reduce the likelihood of the division's commanders all being wiped out by a single burst of shrapnel, then took turns peering over the edge toward German territory. The occasional star shell illuminated the barbed wire and the churned earth, the heaps of rags and meat that had once been human beings. That alien landscape, devoid of comforting common objects to put the vista into scale, did not seem real and taught me nothing. It settled into my bones like the chill that heralds a fever.

When we got behind the line again, the French colonel bade us adieu with one final tale. "There is no purpose in terrifying you further," he said, wearily sipping his coffee, "but I have heard rumors of a battalion-size group of ghoulish deserters from both sides, British and Australian and French and German, who hide in abandoned trenches and come out only at night, looting supplies from the corpses. They have secret lairs everywhere, and long beards, and they wear rags and uniforms covered in patches. Barely human, more like carrion dogs. The generals don't know what to do. They'll need to be eradicated, but it will have to wait until after the war. Perhaps we will gas them. *Naturellement*," he concluded with a hint of mischief, "the most superstitious among the troops speculate that these men cannot be killed, because they are already dead yet do not know it. But this is beyond the scope of our concerns."

"Surely this war is horrible enough," I said, smiling, "without enlisting the supernatural."

The colonel shrugged, then spit contemplatively. "I hadn't yet told that story to anyone from your army," he said. "It is difficult to know how properly to report such a thing. But I think of it often, and I had to get it out. A good-bye present for you, my friends, along with the sector, which we leave to you tomorrow. *Merci* and *bonsoir*."

For the next three weeks, Baccarat was ours alone: the first time an American division had held a section of the Western Front independently. The time passed without notable incident, apart from the sensation of that which had been abstract becoming real, then routine. The unseasonably wet weather we'd seen since our arrival continued, the raindrops like the ticking of a billion tiny clocks: mud, potatoes, mud, black coffee, and mud. Continually cold, continually wet, we feared influenza as much as we did the enemy. Every type of supply was short, and many of the men took to using coffee for shaving, given that it was hot and more plentiful than water. A popular pastime—particularly in Lieutenant Revnes's platoon—became damning the generals for living in relative luxury far behind the lines.

One muggy night a few of us officers went on liberty to the nearest town, which like all towns close to the front had a bustling trade in goods and activities favored by soldiers, given that military paychecks were the only source of revenue. McMurtry was keen to enjoy a mediocre beer, as were most of the other officers.

My biggest delight was being back in civilization, walking amid the storefronts, however pitiful, and seeing the people and the signs. On a chipping plaster wall on the way to the tavern, I saw a poster that the Signal Corps had put up, clearly for the benefit of our own men:

BROKEN LINK IN VITAL COMMUNICATIONS:

DON'T SHOOT!

THE CARRIER PIGEON!

The letters were emblazoned above a cartoon image of a dead bird, X's over its little eyes.

"Now, who would do a damn fool thing like that?" I asked Lieutenant Peabody. His boots and mine were marching in step across the cobblestones, not out of intention but habit.

"Some bored man itching to shoot his rifle, I guess. Not one of my machine-gunners, that's for certain. Wouldn't be any fun." He laughed, then shrugged. "Or someone very hungry."

The importance of battlefield communications, and therefore of pigeons, had been so thoroughly drilled into us during our training as officers that I tended to forget that the enlisted men might not have an equal understanding of the topic. The Signal Corps did its best to run telephone wires to frontline units, but the infantry usually outpaced them—and if the wires weren't secured along their full lengths, the enemy could listen in. A soldier sent to deliver a written message could be killed or captured. Radios were mostly useless in the field, fragile and unwieldy, and even when they worked, their transmissions could be picked up from the air.

But pigeons remained as fast and as reliable as they'd been since the time of Alexander the Great. I thought of Bill Cavanaugh and how it would grieve him to see one of our birds killed, much less eaten by his fellow soldiers.

The tavern was hazed with tobacco smoke and dotted with oak tables, each topped with bottles and ringed by other American soldiers. A pregnant French girl—her baby's father probably gone with the French force we'd relieved—took our order, *deux bières* for Peabody and McMurtry and *vin blanc* for me.

"Lieutenant Revnes is also on liberty tonight, isn't he?" I said. "I don't see him here."

"We can rule out the other taverns," Peabody said, "because there aren't any."

"He's probably cooped up memorizing a monologue by Shakespeare, or Shaw, or Ibsen, or whomever," said McMurtry. "There's no reason to worry about him."

"I can think of any number of reasons to worry about him," I said.

"Well, he's on liberty, Whit," McMurtry said. "We can't very well expect our men to defend freedom if they're not allowed to enjoy it now and again. Sure, he's probably up to no good. But if he's not hurting anyone and he's still able to discharge his duties when he returns, then let's leave him be."

I could see several holes in that argument, but I chose not to attack them and smiled instead. "McMurtry, you're an example to all of us," I said. "You always see the best in everything, be it person or incident."

"Oh, like hell," he said, concealing his embarrassment with a sip of his beer. "Charging me with Pollyannaism will be a tough case to prove."

"Now, hear me out, fellows. I'm being uncharacteristically sincere. Were McMurtry to be told, hypothetically, that one of our men had stolen a thousand francs, he would most likely say, 'Oh, I don't believe that! He's quite incapable of such a thing.' If proof of the man's guilt were provided . . . well, then he'd say, 'If you're sure, then he probably did. But there must have been some reason for it that we don't know anything about. You notice that he didn't steal two thousand, which he might easily have done.' Am I mistaken, gentlemen?"

The other officers laughed. "Let's have a toast to McMurtry," Peabody said. "If the czar and the kaiser shared his generosity of spirit, we might be raising our glasses at Broadway and Thirty-ninth Street tonight."

We drank another round, then settled up with the girl. The bell in the church spire chimed ten o'clock as the tavern door swung shut behind us, closing the songs and cigar smoke and lamplight off from the sleepy street.

It did not remain sleepy, alas. *"Good night, ladies!"* came a lubricious tenor voice from the terrace of the battered house next door. *"Good night, ladies! Good night, ladies! We're going to leave you now!"*

Revnes staggered down its steps and into our path, a bottle

of cognac dangling from his right hand, a woman barely wearing a slip enfolded in his left. In the silence following his command performance, the splashing of the fountain in the square sounded like mocking laughter. Haughty as an insolent housecat, he all but ignored our presence on the otherwise empty street.

"Lieutenant," I said, barely above a whisper, hating the impression of Americans he was giving the town's beleaguered residents. "Collect yourself."

I snatched the cognac from his wilted grasp and handed it to the whore. *"Merci, Capitaine,"* she said, clutching the bottle and drawing herself up into a posture of elegance despite her smeared lipstick. "Perhaps you and your friends would like to come in?"

"Non, merci," I said, shifting Revnes's weight to my own shoulder and leading him from the doorway. "Lieutenant, your liberty has come to an end, I'm afraid."

"But O Captain, my Captain!" Revnes declaimed into my ear at unnecessary volume. "I have only been on liberty from the Army of Mars. I am on the march in the Army of Venus!" He sank into me, boneless as a scarecrow.

"You're only in one army, Revnes. And it demands better of you, even on liberty. Do you really expect your platoon to show discipline if this is the example you set?"

"But a soldier must be a *complete man.* Don't you agree, Captain? Not an automaton. I have been exercising my virility to better serve our nation! My every undertaking proves my loyalty."

"Your conduct is unbecoming of an officer, Revnes, and I'll take action to that effect if you don't come back quietly. We can dock your pay and confine you to quarters. Do you understand?"

"Oh, you're a smart one, Captain, just like they all say," drawled Revnes, yawning a stagy and feline yawn, revealing the carmine interior of his mouth. "A real clever kid. But what this army needs are idiots! Idiots like me. Tell me,

Captain, is there any law in the United States that says you can't be an idiot?"

"We're not in the States," McMurtry cut in. "As perhaps you've noticed. And being an idiot here has consequences— for you, which we don't care a damn about, but more to the point for your men."

McMurtry had hesitated to intervene, but I appreciated the help. Revnes respected McMurtry more than he did me, and after that we got him back with little fuss.

I reported the incident, and Revnes received a formal reprimand, but the experience galled. I had the unshakable suspicion that among the many thousands of New York men who constituted the 77th Infantry Division there must be at least one or two with firsthand knowledge of what the army would broadly term my "sexual depravity," and although my personal conduct since arriving in France had been unimpeachable, disciplining the sexual misadventures of others felt like hypocrisy, even if it wasn't. Revnes was right: I *had* been a clever kid, at least so far, and I intended to continue.

In Calais we found that the French took a permissive attitude toward sexual matters; their local officials refused to cooperate with efforts to suppress prostitution near our bases. Meanwhile the army had launched shock-tactics campaigns to curb venereal disease—mostly to protect our health and combat-readiness but also from a touching if presumptuous concern with preserving the sexual morality of young men from rural homes. (City boys were assumed to be a lost cause.) We were all regularly instructed to shun contact with prostitutes and other loose women.

The campaigns—promulgated with the assistance of the YMCA—were so histrionic in their portrayal of females as sources of infection that many soldiers came to regard them as much more dangerous than sodomites and other such "degenerates" criminalized under the Articles of War. I had to laugh inwardly at this rhetorical emphasis, for the YMCA facilities in New York and elsewhere had a well-established reputation as pickup hubs for queer men.

Though I never engaged in degenerate behavior in France, I knew from the men's talk that there were "cocksuckers" around, both in our ranks and in the towns. So there would have been opportunities. But I could see the danger that men like Revnes posed to the division—due not to their erotic pre-dilections but to their lack of restraint—and to earn the au-thority to safeguard order, I held myself to a higher standard of duty than I held those under me. I didn't relish enforcing puritanical dictates, but Revnes had left me with little choice.

Between this unsavory business and the interminable rain, a sourness settled over me and persisted for weeks. In a pattern that would recur often, that bad thing was eventually scattered by something worse—in this case the news that we'd be moving to an active sector.

The sounds of war are complex as any orchestra; one could make a study of their subtleties. Shrapnel or high explosives scream and then explode with a roar. Gas shells warble, then bang, cracking open to exhale sickness and death.

I learned this on the banks of the Vesle River—by Ameri-can standards more of a sluggish stream, not thirty feet wide and maybe six to eight feet deep.

On August 12 we were sent to relieve the 4th or "Ivy Divi-sion" and occupy the Vesle sector, which was anything but quiet. The river snaked through a broad marshland, brush and barbed wire snarling its banks. Above it rose bare chalk ridges, six hundred feet high and riddled with caves. The Germans had dug in on the northern heights.

Each day we lost men to artillery fire, some of whom we never found enough of to identify. Most of the officers slept in dugouts, but I remained aboveground like the enlisted men, figuring myself not indispensable and wanting to prove something to my troops, and myself.

Vesle was even more rugged and filthy than Baccarat had been, and baths became distant memories, almost embarrassing, like fairy castles and treasure chests we read about as children.

But we had some mild nights, some misty stars. And though I wasn't a glory hunter, I found to my surprise that I was, for lack of a better way of putting it, good at war.

Leading my men against the Germans, I displayed "tactical finesse and taciturn courage," as Colonel Averill said when they bumped me up from HQ captain to regimental operations officer, responsible for conceiving and implementing battle plans. Though Averill and I had had a tense exchange over war-bond allotments back at Upton, like most of the men I admired the old cavalry officer, and his admiration meant much in return.

Beyond commendation and advancement, there was a rigid passion, a stiff exhilaration, to be had from achieving success under such straitened circumstances. And I'd be lying if I said that this fulfillment—egotistical at its core—didn't lead, on occasion, to error.

Phosgene and mustard were the two types of gas we were trained to beware of. Phosgene was an urticant, raising hives on the skin and overstimulating the lungs until a man drowned from the inside; it smelled of new-mown hay, or rotting bananas. Mustard gas, the Germans' favorite, was a vesicant with the strong smell of mustard seed; it killed by blistering and burning. Inhaled or swallowed, it seared everything on the way down. If one so much as brushed against trees or dirt that mustard gas had settled on, the residue clung. At Vesle I saw a private—John J. Munson, one of my battalion's bravest men—take off his service coat after a gas attack only to have a layer of skin come off with it.

Among the most insidious qualities of mustard gas was the fact that the onset of its effects was slow, sometimes taking a full day to manifest. But the tiniest breath of it could cause diarrhea, potentially fatal when water was scarce. Wisps in the air or on the ground dried out one's fingertips until they split and bled. Enough in the eyes could cause permanent blindness. Most relevant to my own mistake, inhaled gas also caused a heavy, dry, chest-deep cough that might never subside. This had happened to my younger brother, Elisha, during his service as an ambulance driver. But when one has excelled in war, one tends to convince oneself that one is invincible, and I refused to consider that it could happen to me.

Naturally it did. On August 21 a hail of shells made Swiss cheese of the roof of the farmhouse that was the 308th Regimental HQ. Most of the men inside were struck by shrapnel, or gassed, or both. A signal officer, Lieutenant Meredith Wood, rescued several men, dragging them from the splintered timber and crumbled plaster. Gassed in the process, he was in the hospital until mid-October.

I got gassed, too, and as severely. Wood, helping me out of the building, insisted that I report it. I never did. They would have taken me off the line, like they did him. My sense of duty could not accept it.

Had I sought treatment in that instant for the poison in my lungs, so much might have turned out otherwise. If I, like Wood, had convalesced until mid-October, neither the Small Pocket nor the Pocket might have occurred. Bill Cavanaugh and hundreds of other men might not have died, at least not under my command.

And I might not be in the boat—literally—that I find myself in now.

At the time I felt proud for sticking it out.

I stand wheezing at the rail of the *Toloa*, my nose running incessantly and my lungs feeling like fire. Hateful as it is, the cough is hardly the worst thing that haunts me.

CHAPTER 9

CHER AMI

~~~~~~

After our inculcation into the army tradition of hurry-up-and-wait, the rapidity of the orders and the intensity of the bloodshed in late September and early October were bewildering.

So many of my bird comrades had been killed by then that I'd come to think of the war as a pigeon shoot: thousands of feathers sashaying down from the clouds. Back at Wright Farm, in an unusually macabre mood, John had told us once about this so-called sport, practiced by so-called sportsmen: pigeons released from beneath worn-out bowler hats by the tug of a string, then shotgunned from the air. Participants also shot blackbirds, sparrows, purple martins, and bats. When a man has a gun, evidently, anything can be a target.

Many birds were not killed outright in these shoots but only maimed, left on the ground as the firing went on. Twitching in pain, they lay, I imagined, like the soldiers whose comrades couldn't make their way across no-man's-land to rescue them.

If I could write my own wall text here in the Smithsonian—or, better yet, if I could speak as humans do and record my testimony as an audio guide—then I would try to warn of these things.

Spending most of a century in a museum has taught me much about humans and flight: how they envy and desire it. Since 1884, when the French invented the dirigible, and since 1903, when the Americans invented the airplane, the sky had changed. All the old myths—the dreams of Daedalus, the hubris of Icarus—had been achieved, then surpassed.

Aerial combat seduced the public. Both sides in the Great War displayed captured aircraft as trophies and morale boosters—much as President Wilson and I have been displayed, though we pigeons are seen as sweet, not scary, never a source of awe, never striking fear into anyone's heart. Fine by me. You can't mount a gun on a pigeon.

Each of my flights provided an all-encompassing view that humans could never have, not even generals. All summer long I watched the sweeping away of life's illusions. The charnel trenches. One man hanging his canteen off a dead man's foot. Muddy holes, constant floods of mud, mud up to the knees, mud in the bunks, in the food, entire subterranean cities of mud.

Then the summer got hot, and I felt parched after I flew. As the weeks went on, the land grew more sullen. Water carts bogged down in the brushwood. Duckboard tracks spanned the landscape. The earth drank in blood as if thirsty for it.

Each time I returned to Rampont with a message, the villagers seemed more accepting of the heretofore outlandish idea of infinite war, no longer sure that the Americans could end this.

On the battlefield every regiment hummed with the same banal dread. Before each advance—what the commanders called it when they drove the infantry over the tops of the trenches into maws of the machine guns—there'd be a final inspection. The men would put their affairs in order: who would get their pistols, their money belts and any contents, their watches, their compasses, their water, and their scraps of food.

Events that should have been singular and era-defining became commonplace, like an ancient stone bridge blown up, or a church collapsed by the tremor of the guns, or a cedar tree that had stood for four centuries splintered to kindling by a shell. Men's bodies sustained the same damage, but this ceased to be worthy of remark.

But if I were to narrate all this to the Smithsonian's visitors,

I fear it would fail in its intended effect. I'd be making war sound interesting—or, even worse, sublime. Humans can read glory into the most abhorrent circumstances. They believe that stories help them understand, but in fact they often merely help them pay attention. The idea that the war can be known by way of a few representative accounts of heroism and misery is a falsehood.

Perhaps it's simpler to give the numbers. Sixty-five million men were mobilized worldwide. Thirteen percent of them died. Thirty-three percent were wounded to the point of disfigurement and/or disability. Twelve percent were taken prisoner or declared missing. The overall casualty rate was 58 percent.

At what point must we consider whether the human species was trying to destroy itself? Or at least—and this is more in keeping with the evidence—to reduce its male population?

"I was prepared to die," I once heard a private named John J. Munson say, "but not to die in stages." First you're a living man, he said, then a writhing animal, wounded and gasping. And then you're a thing: dead.

I took no offense at his pejorative use of "animal"; he was an ordinary person trying to make sense of something too wide for his mind, or anyone's.

Munson was a member of the unit to which Corporal Gault assigned me after I flew my tenth mission back home to Rampont, a unit that would soon be known throughout the world as part of the Lost Battalion. That summer it was still simply the 1st Battalion of the 308th Regiment of the United States Army's 77th Infantry Division, under the command of newly minted Major Charles White Whittlesey.

Before I encountered Whit, or any of the other men whose names would be bound up with mine in the annals of history, my heart leapt into my beak at the sight of Buck Shot, in the same wicker carrier that Gault had popped me into. Though he'd been a bit of a nuisance at Langres, the sight of familiar eyes was a joy, lending a momentary sense of order.

But Buck Shot did not look happy to see me; he did not look happy about anything anymore. His prized white feathers had taken on the dingy hue of city snow, and his eyes were rheumy.

"Buck Shot!" I said, brushing past six other pigeons to join him. In war, I'd found, one had to behave as if one had privacy, though one was never alone, except in the air.

He shrank from my affectionate peck. "What's wrong, my friend?" I asked. For an instant I took his watering eyes for tears of sorrow—I had certainly seen plenty of those from the men.

"Gas," he said. "Mustard. The pigeoneer didn't get the canvas over us in time. The other birds died. The pigeoneer was killed by flamethrowers. Smelled like roast meat."

"Oh, Buck Shot," I said, carefully preening his wings, wanting to restore him to his pristine dove-self. "You're lucky to be alive!"

"You think so?" He didn't reciprocate my preening but didn't pull away either. "I've been with the 308th before. They have one decent pigeon man. I hope we end up with him."

"I hope so, too," I said, "but we'll pull through regardless. I'm just happy that Gault has thrown us together again." My confidence was overstated for Buck Shot's benefit; he needed reassurance. Some pigeons, like some men, are able to meet the demands of war while others crumble. There's no way to predict what you can stand until you stand it.

"All summer," said Buck Shot, not meeting my eyes, "flying all those missions, when I'd look down, what I saw reminded me of the Chicago Stockyards. Soldiers waiting in the trenches while other soldiers went over the top, like they were livestock waiting for other animals to be hung and skinned and gutted."

"I've never seen a stockyard," I said. "But I've heard some of the men make the same comparison."

"No matter how high I fly," said Buck Shot, "I can't stop smelling it. The rotting flesh in these fields makes the slaugh-

terhouses seem like rose gardens. Slaughterhouses are organized, after all. They get cleaned. They don't waste. When I
first saw one, I couldn't believe it, never thought killing on
that scale was possible. I thought humans were monsters.
Then I thought about their cities and how they need to feed
all those people, and I accepted it. But now I see them doing it
to their own kind, and for nothing. So I was right. They are
monsters."

Not being of a mind to dissuade him, I finished preening
him in silence, trying to imagine how my unstoppably optimistic brother Thomas Hardy might respond. But it was
impossible to imagine Thomas Hardy being here at all.

I was hardly the only new member of the 308th. As the summer tipped into fall, the regiment received replacements
from the 40th Infantry Division, known as the "Sunshine Division": strapping men—boys, really—from the ranges and
ranches of the western United States. Their tanned faces
were to supplement the conscripts from the Midwest who'd
arrived earlier to fill out the depleted ranks of the original
New Yorkers. The regiment needed to be at full strength, for
it was about to take part in a massive offensive that would
span the war's entire Western Front.

A lot of the new boys hadn't been supplied guns. The Ord-
nance Department had told the commanders not to worry: so
much of the regiment would be killed in the first few minutes
of the offensive that the survivors could take their pick of the
weapons of the dead and keep advancing.

I noticed that even when they weren't in the trenches, the
veterans of the 308th held themselves like hunchbacks, their
muscles remembering the low ceilings and the need to stay
down.

With one exception: a tall, thin man who walked upright
and with a self-possession that incandesced at the dim edge
of the Argonne Forest.

I saw him the evening we arrived but didn't realize who he was at first. His eyes hid behind his wire-framed spectacles in the gathering gloom. His build was gangly, his mien that of a friendly owl, his air scholarly and introspective even as he sat on a stump eating his rations and speaking softly to another soldier. His adjutant was a tiny, spry man with the appearance of an impish child. The vision of the two of them together—even seated, the former was taller than the latter—seemed designed to illustrate the surprising diversity of the human species.

"Before we go over the top again, Major," said the adjutant, "shouldn't you swap your captain's bars for your gold oak leaves? We don't have to make a big show of it. I can do the honors now."

"I suppose it's wise to wear them," he said, sticking his fork into his can of beans. His voice was higher than I'd expected, flat and reedy. "Does a major get better treatment than a captain in the hospital? But it's so dark you'd pin them on crooked. Let's wait."

"Whatever you say, sir," said the adjutant. "*Major* Whittlesey."

"Sleep well, Lieutenant McKeogh," he said. "Tomorrow could be the day." He squeezed the adjutant's shoulder, then strode away, tall as a sunflower.

I have always been fascinated by the human obsession with naming things. I have a vivid memory of John back at Wright Farm reading to us from one of their myths about the beginning of the world: *"Adam gave names to all cattle, and to the fowl of the air, and to every beast of the field."* In the wild, birds generally get by without them, but those of us who live among humans tend to find the names they give us useful and to use them among ourselves.

The army was particularly interesting in this regard, because each of the commanders had at least two names. Every time I joined a new regiment, figuring out which man went by which code name—names I'd hear as the messages I flew back Rampont were read back—felt like completing a puzzle. The Seventy-seventh Division, for instance, was called "Dreadnaught," and all their code names began with *D*. Its new commanding officer, Major General Robert Alexander, was "Dreadnaught One," and the commanders of the 308th were all variations on "Detroit," with Captain Kenneth Budd as "Detroit White" and Captain William Scott as "Detroit Blue," which left "Detroit Red" for Whittlesey. Humans usually name pigeons based on physical features or to evoke abstract concepts, so these code names confused me—Whittlesey was not red at all, but serene and pale, long and stately—until I caught the reference to the colors of the Americans' national flag.

The morning after our arrival, I met a man who lacked the tactical importance to be issued a code name but who would be the most important man in the regiment to me: the best pigeon man of whom Buck Shot had spoken, Private Bill Cavanaugh.

The 308th had three pigeoneers, but Bill was the nonpareil. The others were Omer Richards, who'd been with the regiment from the start, and Theodore Tollefson, known as Nils, who'd joined them that week, a youth from Minnesota who might as well have had a sign on his back reading FODDER, so ripe was he to be plucked by the guns.

Before I was sent to the front, I hadn't fully appreciated a key trait shared by my first caretakers, John and Corporal Gault: they had *chosen* to keep homing pigeons. In the trenches I and my fellow birds were in the custody of men who were feeding and protecting us because they'd been ordered to. Like us, they had been conscripted into service, to a greater or lesser extent against their will. Unlike us, they were performing tasks for which they had no innate aptitude and very little training.

Omer was trying to show Nils how pigeoneering worked on the battlefield, and I state without malice that it was a case of the dumb leading the dumber.

"What you want to do," Omer said, yanking Buck Shot's white wing in his hammy hand, "is pull 'em out and look for where to attach the message canister."

Nils looked on with a squint, as if perplexed by bird-handling that did not involve the wringing of necks and the plucking of feathers. "Kill me quickly at least, you oafs," Buck Shot said with a resigned groan.

"What have we got here?" said a firm but inquisitive voice, its accent that of the surviving city men who made up the core of the regiment.

"I'm trying to show Tollefson how to use these birds," said Omer, flabby-cheeked and grimacing as he pulled Buck Shot through the opening of the basket. "But I still don't trust 'em not to fly off and get lost."

"You can't lose a homing pigeon," said the voice. "If your homing pigeon doesn't come back, then what you've lost is a pigeon."

The speaker stepped around Omer and leaned in for a clearer look, and there was Bill Cavanaugh. His striking blue eyes had the intense forward focus of a predator's—the kind that produces instant alarm in us side-eyed pigeons—but they were set in such an open and sympathetic face that this initial effect was swiftly dispelled, then reversed. Bill's eyes were those of a self-taught naturalist. His movements were quiet and exact. Calm and bright.

With the air of a born teacher, Bill sought to improve the other pigeon men, not arrogantly but kindly, giving advice without giving offense. "May I make a suggestion?" he said, eyeing Omer's fumbling grasp on Buck Shot.

Omer was clutching my poor white friend too tightly. Buck Shot bulged his eyes, partly in jest, partly in earnest. "See?" said Buck Shot. "Bill's the only one who's worth a damn."

"If you can help it," Bill said, "it's best to hold the birds against your body or your forearm. Try to hook your little finger into the joint of their wing, then put your thumb and other fingers around the body."

He picked me up with ease in a warm, clean hand—no dirt under his nails, which given those conditions seemed as heroic an achievement as any battlefield victory—and brought me to his chest. "Hey there, pal," he said. "Hey there, Cher Ami. Corporal Gault tells me you're a brave one. Ten missions behind you and still ready to fly for us."

Nils smirked. "Now I guess you're gonna tell me it can understand you," he said, his rounded vowels laden with doubt. "They sent me on a snipe hunt or two back at camp. I know when I'm being hoodwinked."

"Oh, they understand us well enough," said Bill. "I read somewhere that in the Philippines they say that of all the birds in the world only the dove understands the human tongue."

I cooed and rubbed my head against his chest in affirmation, the fibers of the green wool coarse against my feathers.

"Whether Cher Ami understands the words or not," said Bill, stroking my back with his index finger, "she can hear the tone and the intent. See? We need to treat these little birds well, so they can do their job."

She. Bill had called me "she"—the only human to get that right. I wished I could thank him.

"If you grab them by the wings or the tail," Bill told Omer, "like you're grabbing Buck Shot now, then their muscles strain, which might keep them from flying well."

"Got it," said Omer, relaxing his hold on Buck Shot, who breathed an extravagant sigh. "I'm used to carrying chickens. When a chicken can't fly, that's not really a problem."

"I figured you've been around birds," said Bill. "I can tell by the way you feed them. Pigeons just take a little adjusting. Tollefson, let's see how you do." Bill took Buck Shot from Omer and put us both back in the carrier. "What's your pigeon know-how?"

"We raised 'em on the farm back in Minnesota," said Nils. Hovering uncertainly beyond the wicker, his face was as square as a block of wood. "But only for food. We didn't race 'em."

"That's too bad," said Bill, and then he seemed to drift into a reverie of wonderment typical of him. "How do they do it?" he asked, his question directed at me as much as the other soldiers. "Find their way home from places they've never been? Well, they figure out where they are. But how? Blindfold one of us, throw us in a truck, drop us somewhere in the forest with no map or compass—I couldn't find *my* way back. Could you? And these birds don't just fly home, they do it by the shortest route at the fastest speed. They don't quit till they get there."

Nils's squint had grown more contemplative. "I never looked at 'em that way."

"Have a go," said Bill, patting Nils on the back. "Take Cher Ami out of the basket. Smooth and gentle. She's a good bird, she'll play along."

Nils's hands were smaller, neater, and less shaky than Omer's, no doubt because he hadn't spent time yet on the front. Adept, he gripped me as Bill had shown him.

"There you go," said Bill. "Put her back in and try with Buck Shot. That's it, you've got him. Isn't he a pretty bird?"

"I suppose he's fine, on account of his plumage," said Nils. "He's like the kind they send up at fancy weddings. But no matter the color, they're dirty, ain't they? You see 'em in the cities, eating trash off the street."

"They keep themselves pretty clean," said Bill, diplomatic but passionate. "You see 'em in cities—where you *don't* see peacocks and parrots and penguins—because they're smart, and adaptable. They're there because people brought them there, and they learned to get by on their own."

"If they were plants," said Omer, "they'd be dandelions."

Bill laughed. "That's not far off," he said. "I happen to like dandelions, too. But keep in mind that while the birds we'll be carrying may look like those feral pigeons, they're modern racing homers, with the best qualities of eight different breeds. We've got hundreds of years of trial and error at our disposal. Now, let's take a crack at putting on the message canisters."

Bill scooped me out again for a demonstration, and Nils followed along, attaching a metal cylinder to Buck Shot's leg. "I won't do it now, of course," Bill said, "but if this were the real thing, I'd take Cher Ami and toss her. If you're sending both birds with a duplicate message—not a luxury we're likely to have on this offensive coming up—then wait sixty seconds between tosses. You want to give them every advantage of not getting shot and making it back to Rampont."

"I think I've got it," said Nils. "I guess I'll find out after we go over the top."

"Hey, Cavanaugh?" said Omer, consulting a battered scrap of paper. "That bird. The one that's just pigeon-colored."

"Cher Ami," said Bill.

"You keep calling it *she* and *her*. But the Signal Corps' waybill says it's a cock."

"Does it?" said Bill. "That's wrong."

"Huh," said Nils. "How the hell can you tell the difference?"

"Oh, that's easy," said Bill with a wink. "You just ask 'em. They'll let you know."

He took Buck Shot from Nils and returned us both to the basket. Omer stepped over and peered in with his topaz eyes, not unlike a goat's. "They'd be dandelions if dandelions lazed about in a basket all day," he said, tapping the roof of our carrier. "Eating peas and corn while we're being fed biscuits made of weevils and old straw."

Bill fixed him with a look, friendly but reproachful, as he finished securing our door. "Sometimes we look at animals and think they're doing nothing," he said. "But in fact we really have no idea what they're doing. Somebody who saw us sitting in our trenches would probably think that we're doing nothing, too." He stood, deftly tossed an empty message canister into the side envelope of the wool cap atop Omer's head, and walked away with a laugh.

Wait, don't go! I wanted to say. I hadn't felt so well understood since Baby Mine and I got separated. I don't know whether the men felt the same way, but for me, as bad as the danger and discomfort and privation could get, worst of all was the absurdity, the desperate impression that everything had careened out of control. Simply being seen and appreciated felt like a glimpse of blue sky through a squall line.

Bill was right: we pigeons were never idle but watched our humans always. We listened, too. To stave off boredom, I kept my collection of animal metaphors that I heard them use. A veteran soldier had called the Baccarat sector a sleepy old lion who only rarely awoke to stretch his claws—by contrast to the Vesle, a monster hellcat who scarcely ceased to spit and scratch. As they went about their work at night, the men often described themselves as ants, busy but insignificant. They dehumanized their enemy, too. Pigs, they called them. Dirty.

I shared these discoveries with Buck Shot, who didn't really care but humored me all the same.

The men said the gray uniforms of the Germans made them look like wolves. Both sides were so defensive in their tactics that the violence had no resemblance to the predator—prey dynamics of the animal world; it was more like prey—prey. Pray, pray you don't get hit by a shell: I heard many men under fire offering panicked prayers to a god whom, I gathered, they believed to reside in the sky. But I had spent a great deal of time in the sky and had never seen evidence of any gods there.

The men said machine-gun bullets chirped by like meadowlarks.

Sometimes they renamed animals as different animals. They called the canned corned beef in their rations "monkey meat" and referred to their body lice as "shirt rabbits." They'd pick the insects off one another, comparing themselves to apes grooming in some great gray zoo. I could tell that many of the men felt terribly lonely, helpless and estranged from their fellow soldiers, but they were never alone and never powerless thanks to all the life that depended on them, the lice and the rats and the mice. Each man was the miserable monarch of a kingdom that squirmed with vermin, one that consisted of the dirt and the bit of sky each one could see from the dirt, of their feet in their boots, of their boots in the mud—a kingdom all but indistinguishable from a grave.

On the morning of September 26, we quit the trenches for the forest. Well before dawn we had been awakened—as it seemed every sleeping thing in Europe must also have been—by the roar of an artillery barrage of unprecedented scope and severity directed at the German positions. We all knew then that the time had come to advance.

Major Whittlesey, his oak clusters now affixed, prepared us to go over. Outwardly he set about his command with utter conviction, but I could sense inward doubt about what the generals had demanded that he demand that his men do.

Within days it would be clear that his misgivings were warranted.

While Whittlesey was committed to following orders, as any successful officer must be, he was also quick to recognize the extent to which those orders were callous or unfair, and he'd try to bridge the gap between what was required and what was right through his own exceptional effort. The morning of the advance, he had had to close the company kitchens early in order to get the regiment into position, even though some men were still in line for breakfast. As we stood massed in the trench awaiting the signal to go over, he raced up and down the line handing out hunks of bread and cold meat; when he ran out, he stood directing the anxious mass to their places with his own dry slab of bacon as a baton.

Then, like some gaunt referee, he blew the whistle that sent us forward, leading the way with a pistol in one hand and a set of wire cutters in the other. The dawn was vaporous and dewy to the point of opacity, but he kept calling out through it, tall as a lighthouse, his confidence and good cheer shining like a beacon, drawing the men forward. He might have doubted his orders, but he believed in his men, and in turn they wanted to please him. That was another metaphor I'd collected: Whit, they said, was a lamb who fought like a lion.

The green darkness and tangled undergrowth through which we advanced convinced me that Whit was correct to be suspicious of his orders—not because they were ill-conceived but because the Allied commanders who'd ordered us to advance into the Argonne probably didn't believe that success was possible in the first place. The land was fissured with rises and ravines that were all but invisible beneath the thick woodland canopy. "'Copse' is only one letter off from 'corpse,'" said Buck Shot, his only comment as we proceeded through the trees: a fortress made of forest, snipers in the leaves.

The one bit of happy news was that the basket containing Buck Shot and me had ended up on Bill Cavanaugh's back. Whenever the guns would fire and everyone would pancake flat onto the ground, Cavanaugh would protect us, finding us cover, keeping us low. The men were dispersing into the mist like mist themselves, losing one another, losing their way—something that was not supposed to happen, which seemed to be the theme of the campaign.

The only thing that went right was that we succeeded in breaking through the German defensive line. And then even that turned out to be bad.

By the afternoon of the first day, we'd made it close to the stated objective, the *dépôts des machines*, a mostly abandoned but still-defended German railhead in the shadow of the inauspiciously named Moulin de l'Homme Mort, or Dead Man's Windmill. The troops seemed to be in bright spirits as

Whittlesey sent word down the lines that they'd done well and would dig in for the night, falling early due to the steep hills and sinister trees.

Characteristically, Buck Shot did not share in the good cheer, but in this case his dread proved unnervingly prescient. "We did *too* well," he said. "We're too far in front. We're going to get stuck here."

There was an abandoned bunker to shelter in, done up in legendary German splendor, complete with left-behind bottles of mineral water. Bill used some to fill the pan in our basket, and we were drinking it in, parched and shaking from the long day's advance, when Whittlesey angled his tall frame through the door, followed closely by McKeogh, his diminutive adjutant. In the weird atmosphere of the erstwhile enemy stronghold, the two looked even more than usual like a marionette act.

Bill rose and saluted. Whit noted the mineral water and our basket's full pan, and he failed to suppress a smile. "At ease, Cavanaugh," he said. "Lieutenant McKeogh has set up a runner chain to report our position and establish communications with HQ. But I'd like to send one of your trusty birds as our insurance policy. Though I'm concerned we haven't enough daylight left for them to navigate by. If they won't make it to Rampont tonight, then I'd just as soon wait till the morning."

"Oh, they'll make it, Major," Bill said. "The manual says to release them at least an hour before sundown. Once they get aloft they'll have twice the sun they'll need."

Cavanaugh opened his message kit and began to write according to Whit's dictation, the three men deploying ciphers and ellipses as the contents demanded. As he spoke, Whit slipped a long finger through a gap in the wicker to stroke my back. By then I had been with the army long enough to know how unusual it was to be touched by so lofty an officer. "Buck Shot!" I said. "Look! The major is mad for pigeons!"

"Not so fast," said Buck Shot. "*Cavanaugh* is mad for pigeons. And I think Whittlesey may be mad for Cavanaugh. Before you arrived, he'd talk and talk with Bill about us, as must anyone who talks to Bill for any length of time. He's a real poetic type, the poor man."

Whittlesey had taken barely a glance at Bill since he and McKeogh had walked in, and his voice remained crisp and official, but it was easy to see a softening in the set of his face, a warmth that I hadn't noticed before. It reminded me of my time with Baby Mine, of whom I tried not to think too often. What would be the point?

"You may be right," I said. "But I don't think the feeling is reciprocal in quite the way the major might like."

"Whit's in for a disappointment," Buck Shot said. "But then who among us is not?"

Whittlesey signed the message and slipped it into its canister, and Bill unlatched our door and reached in. "I'll send Buck Shot," he said. "He seems the more agitated by what we've been through today. If he can make it home to rest, it'll be good for him and good for us."

"I defer to your judgment, Private," said Whit, laying the metal tube in Bill's palm. Bill affixed it to Buck Shot's right leg opposite the identification band on his left, then smoothed his creamy feathers.

"So long, friend," said Buck Shot. I wished him good luck and promised to see him back at Rampont. Bill carried him out the doorway and tossed him two-handed into the sky.

We spent a miserable night in our funkholes, the rain and the cold clinging to us like an ooze. The next day we advanced negligibly, pinned down by German machine guns. No reinforcements arrived.

By the next morning, our situation unaltered, it became clear that our runner chain had been broken—which is to say that the runners had all been captured or killed—and furthermore that few of us pigeons remained. Buck Shot had been correct: we had advanced too far ahead of the rest of the 77th Division, and as a reward we'd been cut off from any hope of assistance.

If I may be forgiven for stepping back from my tale for a moment—for increasing my altitude, as it were, to provide a more expansive view of its landscape—I would like to add emphasis to a point that my casual visitors in the Smithsonian tend to miss. While most of them learn that the Lost Battalion was thusly named when it got cut off from the rest of the Allied forces, and while a few of them understand that this occurred because Whittlesey's men were uniquely successful in advancing as they'd been ordered to do, almost no one seems to grasp that this happened to the battalion not once but twice in the span of a week. The incident that I have just described was the first—the "Small Pocket," they would come to call it, in order to distinguish it from the larger one that lay ahead.

As Whittlesey's reports of success and requests for further instructions flew away on pigeon wings and received no replies, as his brave runners saluted smartly and charged into the forest and disappeared forever, the realization began to spread like an infection among the officers that we were trapped, that we had trapped ourselves, that our success was failure, that we'd been doomed not by our bad luck or poor performance but by a systematic deficiency within our own army, and that we were now living through a nightmare.

This was wrong. As we'd soon see, a true waking nightmare requires full knowledge that a disaster is about to happen—indeed, that it has happened before—and that this knowledge will do nothing to stop it from happening again.

Even as the extreme peril of our situation clarified, Whit never once let it show, on his face or in his words. Even, perhaps especially, under those circumstances his speech remained cool, with an anachronistic formality. Uniquely among the men, he never flinched or crouched when under fire; he wasn't foolhardy or reckless but simply seemed to accept his fate and to know that it would encourage his men to see him upright and unafraid. Best of all, he was funny—not rollicking but droll, an emperor of understatement. When a German machine-gun unit located us that afternoon and strafed us until their ammunition was spent, his equipoise remained uncracked. "*Most* unpleasant," he said to McKeogh, as though remarking on an inferior cup of tea.

The rain continued into the next day, with no word from headquarters. Without support we couldn't move forward, and without guidance we couldn't fall back, so we had to stay put and keep our cover, though there was no doubt that the Germans knew our position. Predictably, we came under attack again that morning, this time from artillery.

When the shells began to fall, Whittlesey, Cavanaugh, and Larney, the signalman, had been out in the open, puzzling over routes that might take runners back to American or French territory. With a combination of shouts, whistles, and gestures, Whittlesey directed the platoons into defensive positions as explosions rained splinters of stone and wood from the hillsides. Larney had the good sense to rush from the funkhole where we were sheltering to retrieve Whit before the Germans adjusted their trajectories; tugging on the major's belt, he looked like a mariner trying to strike a tall sail in a high wind. Whittlesey barely managed to fold his long limbs alongside Cavanaugh's and Larney's as a shell obliterated the spot where he'd been standing and buried his protruding boots in gravel and mud. "Why didn't God standardize me?" he wondered aloud once we could all hear ourselves again.

By that afternoon I was the last pigeon, all others having been dispatched with their terse but urgent messages. While I awaited my inevitable flight, I watched with interest as a gray mouse approached our funkhole, in search of the cracked corn that had slipped through the weave of my basket. Little four-fingered hands, little sniffy pink snout.

We did not speak, but I was grateful for the distraction. I

had to occupy my mind with something or I'd have gone mad there in my basket, passive, unable to move—which is how the men must have felt as well.

As the shadow of the ridge inched toward the bunker door, Bill broke my reverie. "Come on, Cher Ami," he said, slipping a message into a canister. "I've saved the best for last."

I flew with all my usual alacrity and then some, because this time Bill was the one who had tossed me. *Cher Ami!* said the voice, *Home to your loft by the airway! Home to Rampont!* as I flew above the horror, noise and smoke and screams made more eerie for their filtering up through the crowns of the trees. Still, I was glad to have my flight hidden from any marksmen and falconers who might be below, alert for the telltale clap of pigeon wings.

———————————

My eleventh mission. I made it back with no difficulty. How close Whit's trapped men were to Allied territory! On the ground the distance had seemed extreme and insurmountable, when in fact it was only insurmountable.

I slowed by flapping forward, stretched out my legs, and alighted on the landing board, then gave the bell a hard peck. Corporal Gault appeared instantly to collect my message, leaving me with fresh food and water and, as always, the smell of chocolate.

A flash of white beside me and a familiar morose voice. "Welcome home, Cher Ami."

"Buck Shot! You made it! When reinforcements didn't come, we were afraid that something terrible had happened to you."

Buck Shot fixed me with a look that said he was very happy to see me but that I was being very dense. "We all made it back," he said. "The pigeons did anyway. The runners were lost, I think."

"Well, if the generals had our position," I said, "why couldn't they send relief?"

"They could have," said Buck Shot. He gave me an affectionate peck and fell silent, leaving me to my thoughts.

By that point in the war, I had spent so much time with men—next to them in foxholes, carried on their backs—that I'd come to see us as part of the same flock, so much so that I'd sometimes forget the crucial differences between us. The greatest, perhaps, was that we pigeons had no choice but to perform the task we'd been assigned: when our baskets were opened and we were hurled into the air, we heard the voice and flew home, no matter the danger, even if we were wounded or sick. I do not mean to diminish my accomplishments; not all birds flew equally well, and I did what I had to do with effort and skill.

But men seemed to have a choice of whether to fight or not. They'd face consequences if they didn't, but it was hard to imagine that any could be worse than death, particularly the deaths I saw them suffer. Yet the majority followed all orders, no matter how stupid. Even when it became clear that they might be sacrificed at any time, whenever it was necessary or simply convenient.

I don't know whether my message helped Whit and his men in any way. One could never quite tell in the mess of the war when things happened for a reason or just happened because they happened.

But a few days later, Whittlesey, Cavanaugh, and the surviving men of the 308th Infantry Regiment were finally rescued. Not long after that, I was reattached to them, and we went into battle again.

CHAPTER 10

CHARLES WHITTLESEY

After our inculcation into the army tradition of hurry-up-and-wait, the rapidity of the orders and the intensity of the bloodshed in late September and early October were bewildering.

We'd lost so many officers in the Vesle sector in August that I received a promotion to major and was given command of the 1st Battalion, events that immediately renewed my sense of being an impostor. The fact that I was far from the only officer with limited combat experience commanding hundreds of men did nothing to diminish this feeling. So many of us were attorneys and bankers, leading bricklayers and stevedores against the battle-tested Imperial German Army. When I was a young lawyer, I had a recurring dream of suddenly finding myself before a judge, trying to argue a case for which I hadn't read the brief. The war felt like that but a thousandfold.

As always, McMurtry helped put me at ease—not with reassuring words, which I might have mistrusted, but simply by behaving as if my elevated rank and authority were entirely proper, barely worthy of remark. It was strange to think that I now outranked my friend, this man who'd charged up Kettle Hill with Roosevelt.

As we prepared to lead the regiment over the top and into that menacing landscape, I stood looking at the men—more my men now than ever before. Their lives, if they escaped with them, would be divided forever into Before the War, the War, and After, and between those divisions would stretch psychic no-man's-lands as desolate as any in France. The hoary generals remained well behind the line, preserved and protected in their sumptuous headquarters, with minimally inconvenient access to hot food and mistresses. They treated the war like an abstract game, as if they were avid school-boys learning craps, gambling for inconsequential stakes. Advances and retreats—safe at Bar-le-Duc, safe at Rampont—they indicated with candy-colored stickpins, stabbed into pretty maps. They'd clap one another on the back when the pins inched forward and make a show of concern if the pins reversed, but they didn't comprehend the mud-covered men who became their own memorial statues on the spots where they fell. The boys who died so the pins could move.

Of course, the enlisted men weren't always paragons of selfless decency themselves. My adjutant, Lieutenant Arthur McKeogh—known as Mac, though he did possess something like Arthurian chivalry—told me about a conversation he'd overheard between two privates in Lieutenant Revnes's platoon: a Brooklyn man who'd come over with us on the *Lapland* and one of the new westerners from the Sunshine Division. The latter was valorous, it seemed, but totally untrained. They came to us not knowing how to do anything.

McKeogh was a tiny man, five feet tall in his boots, who could be quite unobtrusive when it suited him, which it often did. "How does it work, though?" he heard the Sunshine private say, his folksy twang making the query somehow more desperate. "How do you put in the clip?"

"I'll show you," said the New Yorker, heedless of McKeogh's presence, "but it'll cost you five francs."

"All right," said the rangy man. "Which one's the five-franc piece?"

At this point McKeogh broke in. "Private," he addressed the New Yorker, "are you charging your fellow soldier to show him how use his weapon? This fellow who'll be giving you cover when you go over the top? You'll wager that against five francs?

I don't like to hear any man tell me what his life is worth—and I'll be damned if I'll let him set the price so low."

McKeogh oversaw the return of the five francs, improbable as it seemed that the westerner would survive long enough to spend it.

On that misty morning of September 26, the regimental postmaster moved through the line like a ghost, collecting our letters, including mine to my mother and my brother Elisha.

My trench watch told me that the hour drew near 0600; the bombardment would cease, and we would proceed soon. The brass whistle hung at my neck, heavy as a cross, but otherwise I felt too light. The orders of the night before had been to leave behind overcoats, ponchos, rain slickers, blankets, and shelter tents in favor of basic combat gear: rifle, bayonet, steel helmet, gas mask, short combat pack with two days' iron rations—four boxes of hard bread, two cans of corned beef—mess kit, entrenching tool, cartridge belt with a hundred rounds, a full one-quart canteen, and a first-aid pouch.

Headquarters—which had declared that the first phase of the offensive would be complete within seventy-two hours—had already begun to issue contradictory directives. As the last shells screamed through the soft gray dawn, I motioned McKeogh to my side. "Mac," I said, "have the company commanders make it understood: HQ's orders are that we're not to stop to give first aid. We continue forward regardless of casualties."

McKeogh looked surprised, then relaxed with a wry smile. My own age, but with the agility of a much younger man, he'd worked as a journalist in the city and had the cool cynicism engendered by his profession. "Yessir," he said, clapping a deliberate hand on the first-aid kit that our initial orders had insisted we all pack. Then he was off to spread the news, wraithlike in the mist.

The seconds ticked down, and I felt beset by the sort of agitated, blurry-edged fatigue that one experiences when one can least afford it. I was not alone in this. The regiment as a whole was weary and full of the flu, with more than half of us—including me—leaky-assed from dysentery. But the generals' plan made no allowances for disease.

I blew the whistle.

Beyond the trench line, we were greeted with an opaque curtain of fog. It further concealed already well-hidden enemy positions but also shrouded more mundane hazards, like snagging branches and slippery rocks alongside steep drops. Catastrophe struck immediately: one of our men—there wasn't enough of him left to tell whom—snared a bag of grenades on a clump of hazel, accidentally pulling a pin, and blew everyone in his clumsy vicinity to kingdom come. Nothing to do but brush off the shreds of flesh and keep moving.

The awful mist and the rough topography kept funneling us into bottlenecks, and a sniper or a machine-gun team awaited us at each. The New York veterans had learned how to spot machine guns masked under logs or rocks by watching for a thin bluish haze—the expended powder from a nest—or grass flattened by muzzles firing, but those tricks worked only under normal visibility.

As the mist burned off, I saw McKeogh huddled against a tree, and we both heard, between the chirps of the bullets, a drip-drip-drip on the leaves at his feet. It was not raining. Above him in the branches dribbled the remains of a German sniper. McKeogh jumped but stayed put until it seemed safe to move on.

By the end of that first day, we'd made it close to our stated objective, the dépôts des machines, and I prepared to write up my reports and to receive orders from the rear, were any to reach us. Given our positions, reporting to HQ meant sending pigeons, and sending pigeons meant an occasion to speak to Bill Cavanaugh.

Knowing he'd likely soon be needed, he'd dug in near the abandoned German bunker where McKeogh and I had spread out our maps. We found him seated next to his basket, speaking quietly to its occupants. On the side of the carrier, he had pasted two hand-printed labels bearing the birds' names: BUCK SHOT (WHITE) AND CHER AMI (BLUE).

"Nameplates, Cavanaugh?" I said. "I didn't realize this was a formal function."

Cavanaugh blushed. "If anything happens to me, sir, I want the other pigeon men to know what to call them."

I remembered the jittery white bird from the Vesle, but the trim and muscular blue one I hadn't seen before. Its round, intelligent head ticked toward me, and its gold eyes met mine in what felt like compassion. "New arrival?" I asked.

"New to us, sir, but not to the war. The Signal Corps says she's flown ten missions, all of them in near-record time."

"She?" I said. "Cher Ami? Somebody doesn't know French."

"More likely it's that somebody doesn't know pigeons, sir. She'll serve the battalion well, I think. Buck Shot's pretty keyed up, as usual. I'm trying to calm them. That was a hell of an advance."

"It looks as though they're calming you in turn," I said. Coos flowed from the carrier like the murmur of a stream. "Say, Cavanaugh, why don't you move them into the bunker for now? Lieutenant McKeogh and I will meet you there once we've finished our review."

By tacit agreement McKeogh moved ahead of me along the tracery of deer paths that linked our positions; following him, I felt like a giraffe in pursuit of a mongoose. Once we'd gotten the report from each of the lieutenants—our losses hadn't been as bad as I'd feared—we made our way to the bunker in the failing afternoon light.

I had Cavanaugh send a bird back to headquarters with our coordinates. The army's instructions were to always send two with duplicate messages in case one bird was killed or became lost, but I wasn't confident that we had two to spare, and I'd learned to trust pigeons more than the army.

Cavanaugh sent the white bird. I was glad that he didn't pick the blue one. I felt better having her with us.

McKeogh went to muster a scouting party, intending to make use of the twilight to spot German positions in the surrounding hills. That left me, Cavanaugh, and Cher Ami in the bunker. I had little to do at that point but wait, and the valley was eerily quiet, and I was tired and lonely and wanted the company of someone distant in the chain of command, someone with no apparent concerns aside from the welfare of his birds. I wanted the company of Bill Cavanaugh.

"How did you first come to fancy them anyway?" I asked. "The pigeons."

"You really want to know?" he said, smiling to reveal a slight gap between his two front teeth, a metonym for his general openness. "When I was real little, I got sick with pneumonia. A friend of the family sent two squabs in a pasteboard box. I lifted up the lid, and there they sat. Black and shiny, sending up little *peep-peep-peeps* when I let the light in. I'd been so sad and helpless, and then all of a sudden I was so powerful. Responsible, too—responsible for those little things. There's nothing needier than a baby bird, Major. In my neighborhood, squab's said to be good food for a sick kid, easy to digest, but I could never have let Ma make 'em into soup. They were the most wonderful things I'd ever seen, and they seemed to think the same about me. When I got well, I asked the old Irish guy who lived a floor above us, who kept racing homers, if he'd teach me how to train 'em. Old Dan, his name was. He's dead now. But he showed me how to build 'em a little wooden box on the roof next to his. Those two birds lived there a decade. I got more after that, but that pair would have been my treasures even if they never won a race. Annie's taking care of my flock while I'm away."

As always, I was somewhat at a loss as to how to respond to Cavanaugh. For the hundredth time since the deck of the *Lapland*, I wanted to write a letter to Marguerite testifying to this man's miraculousness. But such a letter was an impossible object, a message that could never exist lest it catch the voyeuristic eyes of the censors. I'd have to tell her about him when I got back to the city. When he and I both got back to the city. Maybe she could help make true my cockamamie dreams about the three of us having reason, somehow, to see each other socially.

"In New York before the war," I said, "I saw pigeons all the time, of course. I'd often walk to the East River or the Hudson from my office and see them squabbling with the seagulls. But I never paid them much mind. Here I think about them every day."

By then it was late enough to feed Cher Ami—for reasons related to their propensity to home, the army insisted that birds away from their loft be given food only once a day, a half hour prior to sundown—so Cavanaugh measured out a dry mix of peas and corn and placed it in the basket. His every gesture made me see how rare true gentleness was in a man, and how mesmeric. I blessed Cavanaugh for existing and cursed love, that joker, for dealing me an unplayable hand.

"It's kind of funny, I guess," he said as he worked. "Pigeons are doves, and doves are symbols of peace. And here we are using 'em to fight a war. Is that what you call an irony? That's a word I don't think I ever use quite right."

"Maybe better to call it an incongruity. Or a sacrilege, if that's not strong enough."

"Sacrilege is pretty strong," said Cavanaugh, refilling Cher Ami's trough from a bottle of German mineral water. "I guess it seems silly to feel bad about the pigeons who get killed in the war when all these men are dying around us every day, but I do. The men's souls at least have a chance to go to heaven, but the birds' . . . I don't know."

"The eschatology there is a bit beyond me, I'm afraid," I said, wondering what it might be like to have Cavanaugh's deep Catholic faith. He wore a scapular; I'd seen him undress.

"The first time one of my birds died," Cavanaugh said, "I asked our priest if I'd see her again when my turn came to go on to eternal life. He said no. He said that to think otherwise would be heresy. That animals have souls but not—how did

he say it?—not *rational* souls. They can't understand anything that's eternal, or universal, like divine truth. So when
they die, they're dead, and that's that."

"Since we arrived in Calais," I said, "and maybe even before, I've not seen a great deal to reassure me that the human
claim on a rational soul has any stronger basis than the animals' does. And what can we know of a pigeon's soul? Or any
animal's, really?"

Cavanaugh quailed a bit at this, as if in fear that our conversation was leading him out of his depth and away from his
faith, but he didn't retreat. "When something doesn't talk, I
guess we figure it doesn't think," he said.

And that reminded me of a little fragment from my studies
at Williams, something I jotted in a notebook and then largely
forgot, something I had never returned to because the paths
I'd followed—poetry, socialism, law, now war—never led me
back to it. It came to me like the memory of a charming street
in a strange city, one that I never walked down because it
would have taken me out of my way.

"It's not exactly doctrine," I said, "but I read a line once in
a sermon by the theologian Meister Eckhart. He wrote, 'God
becomes God when the animals say: God.'"

Cavanaugh turned his face up toward mine. His blue irises
were the two brightest things in the bunker, in the Argonne,
in all of France. "I don't pretend to know what that means,"
he said, "but I like it. I'm going to try to remember it."

His freckles, I noticed, were of two sizes: seven or eight
prominent flecks crossed the bridge of his nose amid a dust-
ing of tiny others in a pattern that seemed artful, deliberate,
gesturing toward significance. I shook off the impulse to
study them like some antique astrologer, knowing that any
meaning I found there would be entirely of my own making.

From the bunker door, a third voice unfurled into the silence, quiet enough to comply with the order for strict noise
discipline that I had issued yet still somehow resonant and
clear, as if it had been trained for the stage, which it had.

"Major Whittlesey," said Lieutenant Revnes, entering with a salute. "Did I hear you quoting a Heinie philosopher in the midst of this war? All the hicks and hayseeds we took on from the Fortieth won't know what to make of you."

I let his comment hang in the air, giving him time to appreciate how thoroughly it had failed to amuse me. "Eckhart's been dead for six hundred years," I said, "so we probably ought not to assume his endorsement of the kaiser. Much as I am unable to assume that you have a good reason for leaving your platoon unsupervised while it's holding a vulnerable forward position. Do you have something to report that a runner couldn't, Lieutenant?"

Revnes's unit was part of the 306th Machine Gun Battalion's D Company; he'd pleaded a special request to quit his safe job with the Argonne Players and take a combat command, landing there after his predecessor was shot through the neck. Marshall Peabody, to whom Revnes became second-in-command, had feared the worst but reported that Revnes had proved surprisingly brave and resourceful on the battlefield, if still self-important and duplicitous in his everyday conduct. Revnes was also known for looking after his men's interests, and he seemed to be well liked by them, if not quite respected.

Since I was the senior officer among all the units that had advanced with us, Revnes was circumstantially under my command. He seemed to intuit that in such perilous straits I wouldn't bother to reprimand him for petty insubordination and in his usual fashion had staked a claim at the edge of acceptable behavior. Now he was watching me with a smug and bright expression meant to suggest that he'd overheard my conversation with Cavanaugh. I had been cautious, and Cavanaugh was a complete naïf, and therefore I wasn't concerned, but I remained on my guard. I didn't figure Revnes for queer—his appetite for women was certainly pronounced—but he had the air of a man who'd spent enough time around the city's queer fringes to observe certain signs and gestures.

I could feel him assessing me, probing for a disclosure that he could use to his advantage. I wouldn't be giving him one.

"Well, that's just the thing, Major," Revnes said. "My gunners *are* holding their position. Given how many have the flu, or the shits, and can barely stand, much less run, I thought it best that I come myself. They know what to do, and they'll do it. But they'd feel a hell of a lot better with more supplies and more information. I figured I might learn things that a runner wouldn't."

"Lieutenant, this may not have been impressed upon you during your time on the stage, but you can say of any man anywhere in this war that he would feel better with more supplies and more information. If your troops are holding their position, keeping quiet and alert, and stretching their rations, then they know all they need to know. And they must be satisfied with that, or you wouldn't have left them under their own supervision. Which returns us to the question of what you're doing here."

Revnes unveiled a conspiratorial grin. "Oh, they're satisfied, Major," he said. "Most of them think we've stopped here to rest and regroup, and they're grateful for it. So long as they stay sharp, I'm not going to tell them otherwise."

"But you believe otherwise."

Revnes glanced at Cavanaugh, pantomiming doubt that we should be discussing this in front of an enlisted man. "Orders were to pack light," he said. "No rain gear, two days' iron rats. That's how you pack if the plan is to advance and keep advancing. We're not doing that. And we have no supply line. Which makes me wonder whether we're cut off."

I'm fairly certain I kept the surprise off my face. Revnes's analysis—which, we'd soon learn, was quite prescient—echoed a concern of my own, one I had barely discussed with the captains. "Lieutenant," I said, "I strongly recommend that you keep that pointless supposition to yourself. So far as you and your men are concerned, our present situation is as predicted: we are holding this position while we establish lines of communication and finalize plans for an assault on German fortifications. If you've nothing further, you are dismissed."

"I've nothing further, Major," he said. "I and my men will keep believing that, or acting as if we do." He saluted and turned on his heel. At the door he paused and looked over his shoulder at Cavanaugh. "Speaking of the mysteries of faith," he said, "lover boy, birdie boy, those pigeons aren't giving you kisses, you know. They're just pecking."

He was gone before I could reprimand him, had I been inclined to do so. I firmly believed that disrespectful behavior had a corrosive effect on order and morale and felt that I should say something to Cavanaugh, but he glanced up from his tending of Cher Ami with a reassuring smile. "Something my ma taught Annie and me," he said. "The punishment for being a guy like that is being a guy like that."

As I lay in the bunker that night, I remembered Camp Upton before the conscripts arrived, and the instruction that we officers received. They had told us that success in war was often determined by morale, coming down to the willingness of individuals and units to perform in combat: loyalty to the cause would secure the cause. I fell asleep forcing myself to think of what they had taught us and not what I was coming to know: that battle was not a struggle between opposing wills but a contest between material forces that cared not at all for the character of the humans involved.

———

The next day we moved forward as far as we could—which is to say not far—and dug in again, very near an enemy we could hear but rarely see.

The newspapers always called our temporary defenses "foxholes," but we seldom did so. To us they were funkholes. Holding one or two soldiers, they were supposed to be about five feet long and three feet deep, but the conditions under which we dug were hardly ideal, particularly in the root-webbed ground of the Argonne. At camp we had dug them in the soft Yaphank soil with our army-issue shovels. In France we often found ourselves without the proper tools, never having been issued them. We dug with the covers of our mess kits, discarded Boche helmets, our own bleeding fingertips— anything to lower ourselves from the paths of the bullets.

That afternoon the sun revealed itself for a moment. The rays filtering through the hills and trees seemed almost holy, fairly inviting the men to stand up and bask. A mistake.

"We look like a town of overgrown prairie dogs!" said one of the western men, rising from his hole to survey our layout. He turned toward me and was stretching with a slightly delirious grin when we heard the shriek of an incoming shell; a burst of blood and he was gone.

The artillery bombardment crashed around us, and we could do little but cower in our funkholes. I'd jumped into one with a medic, Private Irving Sirota, nicknamed "Baron" by the men, a Brooklyn pharmacist with slick black hair and a clipped voice. He'd spent a year in medical school before getting drafted: not enough training to put him in a field hospital instead of here with us. Sirota could hear the shrapnel tearing men to pieces; he also knew that he couldn't go to their aid until the barrage had quieted. I watched him crane his neck to survey the damage, figuring where he'd most be needed, whether he could risk a sprint now.

I could have answered that—a dead medic had no value to us—but I opted to distract rather than scold. "How are you holding up, Sirota?" I said, crouching next to him.

"I'm all right, Major," he said. "But after this a lotta guys ain't gonna be."

Cries of "First aid!" had begun to rise from every side, and I felt him flinch in frustration. "Sit tight, Private," I said. "Any man whose wounds won't wait for the shells to stop falling probably isn't going to pull through, no matter when you get to him. Wait till it stops."

"You're right, sir," he said. "I'll wait. But, sir, a minute here or a minute there can decide whether a fellow goes home with both legs or both eyes. So it matters, sir."

One has strange thoughts while immobilized in a funk-hole, and in that moment of stasis my mind began to assemble inopportune citations to refute Sirota's argument—John Stuart Mill, Immanuel Kant—only to cast them aside. "True," I said. "But everyone here knows what he's risking. Remember that a medic doesn't *cost* anyone anything or take anything away. The shells do all the taking. You're just giving these men back some of what they've lost. So go easy on yourself."

Sirota didn't respond, but his breath slowed and he settled into the dirt, his helmet low above his eyes.

When the shells finally slackened, he clambered out and set to attending the wounded with little more at his disposal than white gauze bandages; the recipients of his ministrations looked like pathetic partial mummies. I didn't see him again until after sundown, when he reported the casualties: dozens killed outright or too badly injured to move. I passed the night mostly sleepless, hearing their moans and pleas for relief, drifting off now and then only to be awakened by a renewed onslaught of shells.

The following day, September 28, brought a reversal of fortune, or seemed to. We advanced under our artillery's morning barrage only to meet little resistance, closing easily to within one kilometer of the dépôt des machines. Our scouts reported much German activity behind their lines but little incoming fire: they were falling back. Best of all, rations and water had arrived from the rear, along with stretchers and bearers to carry away the casualties. We were no longer alone: by midmorning McMurtry's Company E had joined us, and although we remained dispersed along the line, it was immediately reassuring to know that the old Rough Rider was with us. Suddenly it seemed as though the generals' improbable scheme might actually work.

But by the afternoon our luck had not held. We took artil-

lery and machine-gun fire, fought hard to dig the Germans
out of their nests, and then halted in a sudden, uncanny still-
ness. Although we could hear hard fighting some distance
beyond our flanks, the hill of Le Moulin de l'Homme Mort
just ahead had fallen silent: no sounds of other battalions,
friendly or hostile. We knew that the Germans were out there,
waiting. The whereabouts of the relief forces with which we'd
rendezvoused that morning remained a mystery. We'd learn
later that the 2nd Battalion had advanced too quickly and
been ambushed in a ravine: B Company had become entan-
gled with McMurtry's men, the line had gotten muddled, and
McMurtry had been forced to fall back. *The offensive will be
complete in under seventy-two hours*, headquarters had said. It
was complete, all right, with us isolated in deadly circumstances, victims of our own success.

It began to rain. McKeogh, his face red and raw and drawn,
reported that none of our runners had returned from any direction, a sure sign that our chain and been broken. "At least
our pigeons have most likely gotten through," he said. We'd
been sending birds to reinforce our runners and were down
to three, including Cher Ami, the blue one that was Cavanaugh's favorite.

"I wish we had more pigeons," Cavanaugh said.

McKeogh and I looked at each other. Cavanaugh's remark
was of a sort apt to draw a rebuke, or worse, from many a sergeant: the battlefield was not a place for wishes—the first
cousin of complaints—but rather for making do with whatever one had. Yet Cavanaugh was a good soldier, apparently
incapable of both despondency and stiff-upper-lip posturing.
And Mac and I weren't sergeants.

McKeogh's ears stuck out like wings beside his cherubic
cheeks; soaked and filthy, he was the very likeness of an urchin whom one might see outside Grand Central Station,
palm outstretched. "I wish they'd let us take our rain gear,"
he said with a sly grin.

I laughed, then coughed, the abrupt outrush of air having

convulsed my gas-racked lungs. "Well," I said when I could speak again, "I wish there were something more we could do than wait it out." I wiped my glasses with a handkerchief, which only made them blurrier.

But there wasn't, so wait we did. I envied the believers among us, who at least were able to occupy themselves by praying that the Germans wouldn't close in and finish us.

I awoke the next morning, somewhat surprised to be alive, and received an update from McKeogh: still no contact with any friendly forces. I had him summon our signalman, Private Larney, who appeared in an instant, as if he'd simply been folded into my musette bag. Larney looked as worn and high-strung as the rest of us from days of incoming fire but as tidy as a soldier could be under those circumstances, and poised for action.

Larney was from somewhere in upstate New York, which made him what the city men called an "apple-knocker;" I could tell—in the way one lonely person can recognize loneliness in another—that his small-town upbringing and his Catholic faith and his general reticence kept him somewhat apart from the other men in the battalion. I also knew that he was keeping a diary, a practice that army regulations strictly forbade lest the contents fall into enemy hands. He'd had one confiscated by the Signal Corps already, and this time he was being more cautious, hiding the pages in his mess-kit carrier. I supposed I had a duty to discipline him, but I chose not to. He understood the risks, and I took it on faith that as a trained signalman he also knew effective countermeasures: a personal cipher, perhaps, or enough misinformation sprinkled throughout to wreck its usefulness to the Boche. In any event I had a sense that the diary was the linchpin that kept Larney spinning straight. If it helped him do his job, then I wasn't going to take it.

"Larney," I said, "you're to keep this in strictest confidence and to discuss it with no one but Lieutenant McKeogh and me. The battalion is cut off, completely surrounded by hostile forces. In the event that we are overrun, you must be prepared to destroy any and all written material of a sensitive nature. Do not hesitate to do this on my order or when in your best judgment the time has come. Now, do you have the signal panels ready, in case they should send any planes over to search for us?" I honestly had no reason to believe that any planes were on the way.

"Yessir," he said. "I'm ready."

"Very good," I said. "Care to update us on your progress with the 'Mademoiselle from Armentières'?"

Larney started, surprised that I knew of his project, and then blushed.

For a man who himself displayed little inclination to joke, Larney had an almost Linnaean interest in humor, plumbing the depths of each issue of the *Stars and Stripes* for specimens, right down to the ads for Lowney Chocolates: *Not a "dud" in the box!* printed beside the image of a doughboy loading his rifle, *Lowney's Chocolates—Dig In!* above a drawing of a trench, *Get some before they Argonne! Ouch!* and so forth. But his quiet mania for documentation achieved full flower with "Mademoiselle from Armentières," a bawdy English song that had become omnipresent along the front, spreading among the Allied forces with the promiscuousness of the eponymous mademoiselle herself to spawn innumerable variations. It was odd to see Larney, who would under no circumstances breathe a word of the lyrics aloud, devote himself to compiling them with near-monkish solemnity. McKeogh had brought me up to speed on the enterprise, reporting with bemusement that although Larney dutifully recorded every version, including those that condemned the young lady—*"You didn't have to know her long / To know the reason men go wrong"* and *"She'll do it for wine, she'll do it for rum, / And sometimes for chocolate and chewing gum"* were representative examples—he seemed to prefer those that condemned the injustices imposed on enlisted men (*"The colonel got the Croix de Guerre, / The son-of-a-gun was never there"*) and the army's hypocritical embrace of religion (*"The YMCA they saved my soul / Yes they did—in a pig's arsehole"*).

Larney had recovered his composure. "Slow progress lately, Major," he said. "Not much time for singing during the advance. I hope you don't think my collection's too coarse."

"Not at all," I said. "I think it's a contribution to knowledge. When all's said and done, it'll probably tell the story of this war as well as any official report. I hope you'll keep it safe—"

I sharpened my gaze a bit.

"—while making certain that any other writing in your possession that might be of value to the enemy is destroyed. All right? Dismissed."

Banter with the enlisted men did not come naturally to me, as it did to McKeogh or McMurtry, but as in my Williams days I could excel at it by effort, showing that I took an interest. My interest was sincere, though unless I worked at it, my efforts fell more on the side of awkward than adroit. I felt more comfortable with Larney than with most; he was nearly as peculiar as I, and far less skilled at concealing it. Plus, I found that I increasingly shared his baffled fascination with the bizarre and macabre humor of soldiers, which dogged the army's rigid official cant like a mad twin.

After long tense stretches interrupted by halfhearted enemy shell bursts and machine-gun fire, by midafternoon our passivity was becoming unbearable. The men had consumed the limited resupply of rations and were weakening from exposure. The early autumn had remained unseasonably damp and cold, as if the very earth had taken understandable offense to our activities and was defending itself however it could.

Then, somehow, something changed—the light through the clouds, or the distant sounds, or the mood of the unseen Germans as they watched through the trees. I was sure I was imagining it until I glanced at McKeogh, who was looking at me wide-eyed. He'd felt it, too.

"What do you think, Mac?"

"They're moving," he said. "Not to attack. They may not even know we're here. I say now's the time to break out, Major."

I studied the forest and the rocky outcroppings behind it, their peaks yellowing in the oblique sunlight. "If they trip over us, we'll have quite a mess," I said. "Send word down the line that the men aren't to engage the enemy unless it's absolutely necessary for self-preservation."

"Yes, sir," he said, but made no move to depart. He knew I'd have another order, just as I knew how he'd choose to execute it.

"As soon as that's done," I said, "muster a scouting party. They'll need to slip through the Boche at our rear and make contact with regimental command, give our location, and restore our lines. We won't have a second chance, so use the best men for the job. I defer to your judgment."

I knew he'd use a three-man team and that he'd pick himself to lead it. The mission fell under the category of suicide—not what I wanted for Mac. But he was the most likely to make it through. Back in high school, I occasionally saw a basketball team that was conspicuously dominated by a single scoring player whose fellows trotted uselessly behind him. McKeogh's short stature strained the comparison, but there were many days during the Argonne Offensive when my battalion felt that way: we held our position while McKeogh and a few handpicked men disappeared into the woods to destroy machine-gun nests, kill officers, and collect German documents. He was a gifted soldier, fearless and buoyant; more than that, he was funny, dearly loved by all the men, and a hell of an administrative assistant. That last may sound inconsequential, but so much of the war was fought on paper, and Mac was excellent at recordkeeping as well as at the odious but necessary censoring of letters. By then I'd witnessed many occasions when a fine and promising man was killed or maimed owing to some stupidity of the army's, but usually this happened without warning. In this case I could see it coming; I was ordering it into being.

McKeogh returned as dusk drew near—the time to make a break if there would be one. "Who've you picked to go with you?" I asked.

"Two stand-up guys," he said, waving the two men over: Private John J. Munson, who'd by then largely recovered from the gas attack that had skinned him alive, and Private Jack Hershkowitz, a scrappy man whom I remembered faintly from Upton.

The successful owner of a dried-fruit factory prior to being conscripted, now a successful soldier, Hershkowitz was a Romanian-born Jew who was fluent in German; he was also deathly sick with influenza. "If I stay here, I'm a goner," he said, swaying and weak. "Might as well die on my feet."

Munson, too, was unafraid. "Trying to get out is better than staying," he said. "If a bullet's got my name on it, then it's got my name on it."

"But we'll strive," said McKeogh, "to keep our noses clear of all bullets."

Before they set out, I called on Cavanaugh to send our last pigeon, Cher Ami, while there was still enough light. "She'll get the word through if anyone can," said Cavanaugh.

I swear I saw the bird nod at me before he tossed her.

We watched her circle up and away. Unless a hawk or a bullet caught her, she'd be back at her mobile loft within the half hour. It was like magic. So far as we were concerned, she might as well have been bound for the moon. I was struck by a sudden visceral understanding of why the ancients regarded doves as messengers to and from the divine.

Her flight gave me a quick thrill of hope, but when she vanished over the ridge, the feeling did as well. We were really down to last things now: last pigeon, last scouts, and soon, perhaps, last bullets and last breaths.

But despair didn't strike until I turned toward Cavanaugh, who was sitting beside his wicker basket, both now emptied.

The tiny door gaped—no point in closing it—and Cavanaugh looked lost, senescent, a hundred years old.

Now he was an ordinary soldier like the rest of us.

————————

The last day of September dawned windy and wet and still quiet, too quiet. Then the woods roared to life—not with the fatal attack we'd been expecting, nor with the artillery barrage that preceded every attempted Allied advance, but with a liquid rush of American troops from nowhere and everywhere, blowing up German positions, establishing their own machine-gun nests, whisking our dead and wounded to the rear and water and rations to our front line. They met so little resistance that I wondered for a moment whether McKeogh and I had spooked ourselves, imagining an enemy that had never been there.

In the confoundingly arbitrary way the war had of unfolding just like that, five days after we'd set out on the advance, we'd been rescued. My men emerged from their funkholes like worms flushed by a hard rain, teeth chattering, barely able to grip their rifles. Had I encountered the battered and unkempt troops who relieved us in civilian life, I'd have guessed them to be vagrants; by contrast to my own men, they looked like Olympians, hale and bronzed.

McKeogh, Munson, and Hershkowitz had made it through—as had Cher Ami, hours ahead of them—and we had the four of them to thank for the white bread, Karo syrup, and bacon that the supply wagons were now passing around. McKeogh's little party had spent a wild night in the woods, slipping through the middle of a German encampment and killing a half dozen of the enemy to deliver the news of our whereabouts to the regimental command post by daybreak. McKeogh's war was over: he'd been shot in the hand, and the surgeons judged his usefulness in combat to be at an end. Hershkowitz's was as well: he had walked out of the woods at the point of collapse, running a fever of 105, and been remanded to the infirmary. Only Munson, gas-flayed and lung-burned though he might have been, was sturdy enough to rejoin us. All three men would later earn decorations for their valor that night. Cher Ami would rejoin us, too, though she received no medal. Her honors, like my own, would come later.

Word was sent down the line: Colonel Cromwell Stacey, the new commander of the 308th, wanted to see me posthaste. By the time I'd organized our resupply, the sun was very much down, the area still very much suspected of containing German units, and I made my way to HQ through the blackest night, passing from reserve post to reserve post in silence, holding the hand of each successive guide. After so many days of lonely terror, I liked this hand-holding; it was fine indeed to feel rough human skin, the sense of being led instead of leading.

The regimental adjutant handed me a hot cocoa and a ham sandwich and sent me straight to Colonel Stacey, an ax-faced man who invited me to warm up by the potbellied stove in his cozy office. Steam rose from my drenched uniform as if I were subliming. Amid those simple comforts that the past five days had made strange—warm mug, soft bread, smell of burning wood—my body felt as if it were not my own, and I considered that I might have died without noticing.

Stacey remained standing; indeed, it was difficult for me to imagine him seated. He looked intensely uncomfortable to be indoors at all. Under the bare lightbulbs strung across the ceiling, his skin was uniformly brown and lustrous, the color of varnished walnut.

I knew him by reputation. A veteran of the Marine Corps and the coast guard as well as the army, with which he'd seen combat in Puerto Rico and the Philippines well prior to the current war, he'd been in France only since March and had already earned the Croix de Guerre while helping to thwart the German advance on Paris. He'd made no secret of his contempt for some of his superiors' decisions, and rumor had it that his candor had gotten him transferred here to the 77th, a command he did not want. He'd spent a couple of furious weeks idle at Divisional HQ and then had abruptly taken over the 308th when his predecessor, Colonel Austin Prescott, had botched the commencement of the Argonne Offensive so badly that General Alexander ordered him taken into custody. Stacey was by all assessments a capable and courageous commander. I could feel him struggling against automatic contempt for me, a bespectacled major from Wall Street, just as I tried to moderate my own suspicion that he was a bloodthirsty psychopath.

"Damn good work at l'Homme Mort, Whittlesey," he said. "Your men kept their heads in a sticky spot, which is a real credit to you and to your little lieutenant as well."

"McKeogh, sir."

"That's the man. He turned out to be quite a killer. But then small men often do. Sorry to see him go, but this fight will be over by the time that nick on his hand has healed. He'll be of more use back home, as an instructor. It's a very different war we've got here, Major. Very different from the wars I've known."

After the combat surgeon invalided him, McKeogh had been spirited off toward Calais and would soon be convalescing aboard a transport ship. I wouldn't see him in person again until nearly a year later, when we'd meet for dinner at Rector's in Manhattan.

"With the war ending soon," I said, "I suppose the men whom McKeogh trains will never have a chance to apply his lessons."

Stacey looked at me with a flash of suspicion, as though I were mocking him, which to some degree I suppose I was. "Oh, they'll apply them," he said. "You can be sure of that. I hope you don't hold with those fellows in the newspapers who say this war will cure us of our will to fight. When Germany surrenders, Europe will be a goddamned mess from Paris to the Urals. For every soldier in those trenches who swears he'll never fire a rifle again, there'll be another who's found that he has a taste for it. Mark my words, Major, we'll be over here again."

I didn't have the energy to argue, wasn't sure I disagreed anyway. "About McKeogh," I said, "I'm recommending him for commendation. Munson and Hershkowitz, too. Up to and including the Distinguished Service Cross. We wouldn't have been rescued without them."

"I'll support that," Stacey said. "Good for morale. But let's have no more of this talk of 'being rescued.' That's not what happened. You took a position and you held it. Your lines were cut, temporarily, as will happen in battle. Other units extended the advance to your position. And with the Boche on the run, we'll soon push even farther ahead."

"So the advance went exactly as planned? That's the official line?"

"That's the truth, Major. Fret about precision all you like when you're practicing law. Out here we're only concerned with end results. And the plain fact is that we are exactly where General Pershing expected us to be."

"I'm sorry, Colonel, but it seems to me that that was my battalion's trouble. We *were* exactly where General Pershing wanted us to be. Our mistake was to get there on schedule, forty-eight hours ahead of everybody else."

Stacey laughed. "You're not wrong, Whittlesey. And now you've shown the rest of these laggards how it ought to be done. Starting tomorrow I think you'll find that the quality of your support has increased quite a bit."

The ham went dry in my mouth, and I swallowed with effort. "Tomorrow, sir?" I said. "Sir, my ranks are depleted and exhausted. They ought to relay to the rear. They can't go over the top again tomorrow."

Stacey stepped closer and put a hand on my shoulder, his expression that of a parent preparing to share some difficult news about Santa Claus. "Of course they're depleted and exhausted," he said. "They ought to be. They're fighting a war. This is the last push, Whittlesey. From the Meuse to the Argonne, this offensive cannot spare a man. Your battalion fought like hell to take and hold l'Homme Mort, Major. Relaying them to the rear now would be an insult, not a mercy."

I returned my half-eaten sandwich to its plate and stood. I knew that Stacey had a reputation for resisting orders he thought stupid; I was well known for hewing to duty, but also for speaking up when my superiors overstepped, and I hoped he would esteem that.

"Respectfully," I said, "the men are badly shaken. They have experienced a psychic blow out of proportion to their actual casualties, substantial though those have been. They did as they were told, and as a result they were trapped in the midst of enemy territory with every reasonable expectation of doom. They feel betrayed, as if they cannot rely on their army to support their efforts, and therefore they will now be reluctant to make those efforts. They ought to be reassigned to a support role, and not to the vanguard."

As I spoke, Stacey's leathery pioneer face clouded with anger, but this dissipated into something more like pity.

"Major Whittlesey," he said, "you are an outstanding battlefield commander. That opinion is unanimous throughout the 77th Infantry, from General Alexander down. I'm told that you lead from the front, pistol in hand, and that you stand tall under fire. I lead my boys the same way. It gives them courage, which is the one supply we don't have to haul in from the rear. You know that, Major. That's why I'm damn sure—sure as we're standing here—that you never let your men know they'd been surrounded. They've been cold and wet and hungry for five days, but they never felt lost, or betrayed, or hopeless, because you never let them. *You* felt that way, and you still do, I'm sure. The 'psychic blow'—is that what you called it?—was yours, not theirs. You and your adjutant carried that weight, as you should have. You didn't shift it onto your men. Because that's command. No matter how dire the straits, you keep your men up. Now, sit down and eat your food, will you?"

"I'm finished, sir. Thank you."

He gave me a good-humored, reproachful glare, then reached behind my back, picked up the remains of the sandwich, and took a bite. "By tomorrow morning," he said, muttering through the meat and bread, "your men will have had a full night's sleep, and they'll be warm and well fed, ready to stretch their sore legs and take another kick at the kaiser. And you'll be ready to lead them. You're to proceed north along the Ravin d'Argonne from your present position, then east up the Ravin de Charlevaux to take Charlevaux Mill. It's time to push on, Whittlesey. Finish this and go home."

The bare bulbs cast their light on Colonel Stacey's face as he chewed, impassive and leonine as a sphinx. "It'll happen again," I said, as evenly as I could.

"Put it out of your mind, Major," he said, drifting over to his desk to study his maps. It was clear that he needed nothing else from me.

"This is not well planned," I said. "Advancing in the ravines makes sense if you're studying a map of France. Look any closer and it's suicide. Those ravines are edged with mortars and machine-gun nests. Every path is snarled with barbed wire. The Germans have fallen back tactically, with the very aim of luring us there, and now we're obliging them. We'll have no support on our flanks. It will be l'Homme Mort all over again. We'll be cut off."

"You're getting panicky, son. You'll have support from the 307th on your right and the French on your left. We'll snip the Boche like pruning shears."

"Shears have two blades, Colonel: the 307th and the French. Why put us in the middle?"

"Major," Stacey said with a sharp rap on his desk. "We'll have no further discussion on this subject. Let's both stop pretending to be fools. It's a damn tough job, which is why it's been given to you. Have I been clear?"

His anger wasn't all meant for me. He knew that the order was stupid—that the only strategic advantage to be gained from sending us into the ravines was a demonstration to the enemy that we could afford to squander our troops and were willing to do so. The army had already shown Stacey how much it valued his opinions, and it valued mine even less. His irritation was that of a father whose impotent hypocrisy has been flushed into the open by the insistent questioning of a child.

"All right," I said, placing my hand on the doorknob, hard and cold. "I'll attack. But whether you'll hear from me again, I don't know."

———

Stacey would, of course, hear from me again. So would a whole galaxy of others who'd never had a reason to think of me before.

The colonel was quite right: that first encirclement at l'Homme Mort—we'd start calling it the Small Pocket after we'd been trapped in a larger one—had been terrifying for me. But because we'd been lucky, because it hadn't ended in a massacre, the incident wasn't worthy of note to the generals or the press.

The second encirclement would be a disaster, and it would win me commendation and international fame. It would leave my brain full—as it is now, here on the *Toloa*'s deck—of visions of pleading faces and ruined bodies, of phantom agonies that scour the parts of my consciousness where I once held hope for the future, like the pains that plague a maimed man where a limb's been cut away.

On that last night of September, though, I was just a field officer sent back to his battalion alone, no hands to be held. I found my men with great difficulty in the darkness. I visited myself upon them like an unwelcome shade whom they wished they could unsee.

Or so it felt when I made myself say, "Orders are to advance at daybreak."

The men actually took it like champions, just as Colonel Stacey had assumed they would. No barracks to be had, we nodded off where we sat to the common refrain—uttered softly, like a lullaby—up and down the trench: *It's a great life if you don't weaken.*

CHAPTER 11

CHER AMI

〰〰〰

Take the thing that bothers you and place it in parentheses.

I've told myself that a thousand times since we got stuck in the Pocket. Bracket the death that spatters against you.

But not a day has slipped by these past hundred years that I haven't recollected my final flight. And now, on the eve of their centenary, here in the darkened museum—Sergeant Stubby asleep beside me, climate-controlled air sighing around us—those events replay behind these glass eyes that I can never close.

"Leaders, get your men up!" yelled Whit on the morning of October 1, his blue eyes metallic in the pewter dawn behind his wire-rimmed spectacles.

Low clouds, an autumn chill—the sky had poured the night before. Many of the men scrambled to reattach bayonets that they'd removed in the night; weary, waiting for the order to go over the top, they'd kept nodding off and almost falling on their own blades.

As we lurched forth again—Buck Shot and I on Bill Cavanaugh's back, he like all the men already exhausted, covered with cootie bites, feet festering with sores—we understood the orders as the sergeants hollered them: *Advance until the last man drops!*

We pressed through an apple orchard under heavy sniper fire: fruit exploding, and skulls as well. Somewhere ahead a soldier trilled a jaunty tune as the German bullets hissed through the branches.

"Good grief," Bill muttered over his shoulder toward our basket, "some ghoul is whistling the *William Tell* Overture."

He promised to explain the joke later but never did.

Our advance stuttered and stopped, stuttered and stopped. The trees were too small for hiding, and the bullets seemed to come from everywhere at once regardless. The smell of apples—fresh apples burst by bullets, brown apples stomped into the dirt, no orchard keepers left to harvest them—cut through the battlefield reek, reminding me of the cider mill back on Wright Farm.

The men picked up the wounded and carried them along. In some cases there was nothing left to carry. As we paused on the steep slope of a north-south ridge from the forest into the valley, the officers trying to determine how best to proceed, one soldier struck a match to light his buddy's cigarette. A shell hit the kid holding the smoke bull's-eye in the chest, blowing his organs all over the ground, knocking the boy with the match unconscious.

With the conditions too dangerous for us to either keep moving or remain exposed, Whit halted us and had the men dig in along the Binarville Road, a Roman highway made of stone blocks—fifteen hundred years old, Bill told us. An artifact of the dawn of human order in Europe, an order now collapsing. The dense forest that crowded the slope behind it was thick with underbrush, giving the Germans cover to approach by slipping from tree to tree.

A little railroad snaked through the ravine. Log sheds, splintered ties, and a few dead Germans were scattered along a narrow path of open ground. The enemy appointed their outposts in greater luxury than we did ours: this encampment seemed a regular village, complete with an empty mess hall, bathhouses, latrines, and a sort of church for makeshift services. Whit set himself up in a three-room log cabin and put the commander of the supporting battalion, a steady-handed captain named George McMurtry, in a concrete dugout two hundred yards away. If a shell dropped on one, the other might survive.

"Do you sweethearts smell that?" said Bill, finishing a

funkhole large enough for himself and the basket of us. "Something stinks worse than a Gansevoort sewer."

"It *is* worse than a sewer," said Larney, pointing to a boxcar on the narrow-gauge tracks.

A decomposing German lay inside, head out one end, feet out the other, his face a purple mass squirming with maggots. In swift unspoken agreement, the men gave the car a shove, Bill making the sign of the cross, as if asking forgiveness for his crassness. The offending odor rolled along about a hundred feet, then tipped off the warped track.

It was comforting during that long night to hear Bill and Larney chat as if they were old friends catching up over dinner, even though their meal was limited to two sticks of chewing gum.

Their topic was wireless telegraphy, as radio was called then. Larney was complaining that the militaries were not wise enough to adapt new technologies as readily as old. "Even naval telegraphy can't transmit voices," he said in his low, measured tone, his accent so different than Bill's. "Only Morse code. No offense to your birds, but I wish they could go both ways."

"I know," said Bill. "They probably do, too." He stuck a finger through the slats to pat my head, and I cooed agreeably, although in truth the idea of homing in two directions was perplexing, and rather disturbing if I thought about it too much.

"Well, they're a blasted sight better than signal lamps and panels," said Larney, folding and refolding his empty gum wrapper. "And the telephone cable. You unwind it and it gets instantly broken. I want a portable two-way radio. It's coming, I know it. But it's not going to help us in this war."

"Lately," said Bill, chewing his gum slowly to make it last, "whenever I think about it, I can't imagine *anything* getting through. To the commanders in their châteaux, I mean. Tooling around in motorcars, surrounded by their yes-men. Oh, sure, the messages get delivered—Company X advanced, hooray, Company Y got wiped out, tough luck—but we can't ever tell them the most important thing, which is that this entire war is goddamned insanity."

"I read that Joffre always insisted on a two-hour lunch," said Larney, his voice rising slightly. "Haig still takes his daily horseback ride. Hindenburg gets ten hours of uninterrupted sleep a night. How can you get men like those to understand cold rations and lice?"

"Here we are at the line," said Bill, putting the canvas sack over our basket, preparing us to turn in for the night, "and yet not more than a mile or two away, everything is French beauty. Beech forests. Vineyards. Leaves starting to turn. That's what's really fucked."

Larney didn't blanch at Bill's profanity but declined, as always, to use any himself. "It reminds me a touch of home," he said, quieter again. "The trees. Anemones and cowslips underfoot. No sounds of battle, just the whispering of the leaves."

Their damp uniforms crumpled, yielding up a little smell of sweat as they curled against each other and did their best to pass the night in sleep. I let my own breathing deepen and synchronize with Buck Shot's and tried to do the same.

Starting the next day, time became featureless, a fever fugue of suffering punctuated by German attacks. Those arterial pulses of horror only underscored our swampy passivity: the routine of the ordeal. By then the battalion had stopped receiving resupplied rations, which meant no mealtimes to give structure to the hours, and so they dragged. It seemed increasingly likely that the men would begin to consider our corn and peas as a source of food—and us as well. But I trusted Bill to keep us safe.

That morning Colonel Stacey sent a runner saying that a one-hour barrage would be followed by the resumption of the infantry attack. "'You will press on to your objectives at all costs,'" our major read aloud to McMurtry in his reedy voice. "It's déjà vu, George. Going over again with no blankets, no raincoats, no reserve rations."

"No coffee either," McMurtry said. "No rum. No experience, in the case of most of these fellows. My boys who had the best skill at this sort of fighting are all in infirmaries now, or in cemeteries." He clenched his beefy hands into and out of fists. "You can see what's happening plain as day, but damned if you can stop it. The krauts are going to maneuver to pinch us off."

Whit sent the runner back with confirmation that he had understood his orders, along with a request for rations and ammunition that would never come.

The customary barrage flew over our heads: tons upon tons of shells loaded with shrapnel and high explosives, bringing detonations and pandemonium to the territory we'd be advancing through, concussing the men's skulls. "I hope this doesn't hurt your bird brains as much as it does mine," said Bill, adjusting his helmet and hoisting our basket, where I nestled next to Buck Shot. I was touched by his concern, unable to reassure him that our pigeon heads were better insulated than men's, less apt to be rattled.

Slightly behind us, though we couldn't see them, we heard sergeants up and down the line saying, *Get ready, gang!* and then the whistles blew and everyone stumbled forward, men falling everywhere, the air blue with bullets and hung with cries of *First aid!*

The battalion advanced, sending its wounded to the rear. Every prospective path forward was snarled by underbrush or barbed wire or both, often in tangles deeper than the men were tall. The forms of these sprawling barriers seemed to reflect the madness of the war, antic and perverse and sometimes wickedly clever: one soldier tore his shins on a jagged strand strung beneath the surface at a river crossing. The men cut the wires when they could, but it was slow work and

had to be done while they were exposed to fire from the surrounding hills.

Traversing the valley, we came upon a young German soldier, wispy and blond, too young to grow a beard. Surrounded
by Americans, he raised his hands and yelled, *"Kameraden!
Kameraden!"* in a cracking voice. Rather than kill him, as I'd
seen other commanders do for the sake of convenience or re-
venge, Whittlesey took him along, keeping him nearby. One
of the men, a German-speaking replacement from Minnesota, asked the prisoner how he liked the war. "Not very
well," he replied in listless English, scuffing through the decaying leaves. "But there are more of us quite close. We will
destroy you."

As the battalion advanced steadily along the river, the
men's trepidation seemed only to increase. "We're getting
close to the spot where the Argonne and Charlevaux ravines
meet," Bill whispered to us as we hunkered behind a dead
oak, waiting for the signal to move. "There's a hill there. You
can probably see it if you look. From that hill the Germans
can hit anything in the valley. And we have to get around it.
So when we advance, keep your little heads down. A lot of us
aren't going to make it through the next few hours."

But toward the end of that second day came unexpected
good news: one of Whit's scouting parties had found a hidden path to the hilltop and cleared the German defenses
there with little resistance. When Whittlesey and McMurtry
ascended to take a look, they expected to find a machine-gun
nest; what they found instead was a wide double trench that
stretched farther than they could see. This was the vaunted
line of fortifications that they'd been dreading for weeks, apparently abandoned.

The men's spirits were high, but so were their casualties,
and with night falling, Whittlesey and McMurtry ordered
their companies to dig in. We proceeded down the hill's steep
opposite slope toward Charlevaux Brook, where the men established a perimeter near a small grove of pines—a box

about three hundred fifty yards long and seventy yards deep—as the sun began to set behind the fat gray clouds and the bald white hill of La Palette. The trees on the hillside had begun to take on their autumn colors. As Bill dug and Buck Shot and I ate our evening meal, I noticed a mossy wooden footbridge that spanned the brook a short distance away; then the dusk swallowed it.

Our spot was well chosen. The brook provided a source of water, and the stony bulk of the hill that we'd descended shielded us from the arc of the German artillery. Though death and injury had thinned our ranks, the losses were offset slightly by the addition of troops who'd wandered in after being separated from their parent outfits: a company from the 307th Infantry and two from the 306th Machine Gun Battalion. Whittlesey finished the day with about seven hundred able-bodied troops, perhaps another hundred too ill or badly wounded to function, and a handful of German prisoners.

Just as he'd been taught at Camp Upton, Whit set up machine guns and rifles to cover the flanks, then sent a water detail to fill and lug back canteens. He sent a runner—a man—and a messenger—a pigeon, one I'd never seen before and would never see again—to relay our coordinates to Colonel Stacey. He ordered the men who still had them to eat their iron rations and to share with those who didn't. He did everything right.

As night wrapped around us like a gray German uniform and the men made their usual jokes about digging their own graves, McMurtry squatted at the edge of the major's funkhole, a short distance from where Bill had dug us in. "Well, Whit," he said, "we seem to have broken the Giselher Stellung as if it were paper!"

"'A steel band'—isn't that what their propaganda calls it?"

"Not so steely without anyone to man it."

"Evidently not. You suppose they've all turned tail back to Luxembourg?"

McMurtry smiled. "Seems unlikely, doesn't it?"

"Something's amiss." Whit took off his glasses to rub his eyes, then replaced them, studying his map before the light vanished.

"A tactical withdrawal," McMurtry said, looking over Whit's shoulder. "But to where? And to what end?"

"It looks like we're half a kilometer from Charlevaux Mill and the Binarville Road. If we're lucky, then they've fallen back that far and will be waiting for us in the morning."

"But we've probably used up our luck for the day."

"Probably," Whit said, folding the map. "Which means they're all around us. And that we're out by ourselves. Just as we were at l'Homme Mort."

Had I been the pigeon chosen to fly back to Rampont that afternoon, I could have looked down to see that the battalion had created what's known as a salient: a line of attack that projects into enemy territory. Yet again the troops under Whit's command had been the only ones on the entire Western Front to advance as planned. Despite the clear orders given by every Allied commander—anyone who retreated would at best be court-martialed, at worst be summarily shot—the French who were to protect our left flank had collapsed at the commencement of the day's advance, and the American troops to our right fell back by midafternoon. None were so devoted as Major Whittlesey's battalion was to him, none of their commanders so bound to duty as he. Whit engendered such pride and confidence that his men routinely achieved impossible results and did so without ever quite realizing the difficulty. In this they found their ruin.

The last message we received from headquarters—a runner sent by way of Colonel Stacey—relayed a curt and uncomprehending response from General Evan Johnson, the brigade commander, about our self-destructive advance: *Congratulations.*

McMurtry had a good laugh at that, and he and Whit exchanged sarcastic handshakes and backslaps. Then McMurtry retired to his own funkhole, puffing an imaginary cigar as he stepped into the night.

Memory heaps hindsight, but I swear I really did have a sense of foreboding looking across the valley toward that opposite hillside.

"I am going to die here," said Buck Shot, his demeanor evoking a handkerchief soiled and washed too many times. "This is a place of death."

"Buck up, Buck Shot," I said, looking up at the witch's cloak of broad-leafed trees. Between the looming hills and the encroaching clouds conspiring to mute the moon and stars, the ravine was profoundly dark. "Every place we've been has been a place of death. There's no reason to think this spot's special."

His once-shiny eyes gazed dully across the Pocket, now pockmarked with funkholes and small berms of earth. "I can see it coming for me," he said. "I can feel it. I won't get out of this place alive."

I didn't try to dissuade him further. There was a decent chance that he might be right. No birds sang; even our fellow pigeons in their dispersed baskets fell silent, waiting. The forest was exceedingly peaceful, still in a way that nature never is.

A couple of hours after darkness had fallen, one of the sentries woke Major Whittlesey up with a half-panicked report that he'd heard voices only a few yards from him, voices speaking German. The sentry had been stationed at our rear, up the slope of the hill we'd passed over late that afternoon.

Whit took in this account groggily, told the sentry that he was probably imagining things and that he should return to his position and keep on his toes. The major's instructions were clearly meant to give courage, not to show doubt. The sentry saluted and padded silently back up the hill.

Star shells sparkled us in white light that night: we were being watched.

———————

The next morning an airplane circled, buzzing like a mosquito before flying off.

"German?" said Bill, removing our canvas cover in anticipation of Whittlesey's call for a messenger.

"German," said Larney. "We're in for it."

We were. Within half an hour, an enemy barrage raged like a lethal thunderstorm. Because Whittlesey had dug us in on the reverse slope, most of the large shells missed us, flying loud and close above our position, exploding in the dirt road beyond. But somewhere nearby, the Germans had a small trench mortar—a *Minenwerfer*—that hurled high-angle shells unimpeded into our close-packed funkholes. "Flying pigs," the men called those shells: fat and gorging on human targets.

A wounded boy babbled again and again for hours, "What is this war? What's this war for? What is this damned war?" his voice growing weaker over the warren of men until he died.

The speech of the mortars: "loud" doesn't do it justice. The sledgehammering booms came across distances so vast that we half expected them to knock a hidden star or two from the daylit sky.

Whit called for a pigeon, and a brown-and-white bird named Antoinette carried the message: *We are being shelled by German artillery. Can we not have artillery support? Fire is coming from the northwest.* I'd find out later that Antoinette made it but the army made no effort to oblige until the following day.

Human language inevitably organizes as it communicates, and thus the hell of the Pocket sounds tidy when I describe it. It wasn't. Events that my account sets down straight-edged were jagged as they happened. I can list the major episodes: A private's teary report that our runner chain had been broken and all the men along it killed. Whit's order to Captain

Holderman of Company K to reestablish communications with the 77th Division, Holderman's failure and frustrated return. Whit's optimistic charge to Lieutenant Schenk of Company C to take out the German trench mortar, his staggered expression when Schenck came back to report all his outfit dead and the mortar still in action. But these were only incidents, and taken together they fail to capture the quagmire of feeling that was our actual experience of that day.

The men were so brave. Whit was as struck as I was by what he would later describe as the heroic fortitude of the bleeding soldiers whose stifled moans floated over the dark hillside. These words bridged the chasm between the horror of the events and the prideful grief of the families of the fallen, words that he and only he would regard as insufficient, compromised, unworthy.

The wounded men strove to grit the little devils of anguish between their teeth, for cries provoked sprays from the German machine guns. I heard McMurtry stop to check on one who'd been shot through the guts, who looked up and said, "It pains like hell, Captain, but I'll keep as quiet as I can."

I can say without hesitation that those dragging days were worse for the men than for us birds. Men can't bear time the way pigeons can. We pigeons were used to being kept on a light diet, since the army knew that hunger made us more likely to home.

Also, we could groom ourselves without accoutrement, though Buck Shot had stopped doing so, too depressed. Among the men, only Whit kept his face clean-shaven; how he did it in the absence of privacy and clean water, I'll never know. I also knew that our major kept up a strong front during the day, his cheer unflagging, but wept uncontrollably while asleep in his funkhole. By that time I had learned much about the courage of men, and this sound frightened me more than the explosion of any weapon. If Whit's men heard it, I felt sure, their faint hope of survival would gutter.

Noticing everything, as homers do, Buck Shot and I looked at sunset toward the Charlevaux Valley: marshy at the bottom, deep green and brown up the opposite slope, and beyond that La Palette's bare hill, protruding blue in the west, with a gray streak of road across it. The scene might have been charming if not for the war and the weather.

"Rain, rain, rain," Buck Shot chanted. "Slanting rain, sideways rain, misty rain."

He was shaking and skinny. No matter that Bill slipped us extra corn, Buck Shot couldn't eat. I didn't know what to tell him.

"At least we're not horses," I said, and thought of the animals I'd seen in other battles, their screams even louder than the men's. Their dilated nostrils and stringy manes. Their viscera trailing like the soldiers', long and crimson. Little in their plight seemed to offer encouragement, even its contrast with our own. "The horses need blankets," I said. "All we need is our canvas sack." It was the best I could do.

"I know, I know, I mustn't mope, Cher Ami," he said. "You really are a friend, a dear friend, my dearest friend, and I'm sorry I can't take this the way you can."

"No," I said. "You're right. It's a mess. It's less strange to get upset by it than not."

If Buck Shot was still listening, he didn't reply but only kept watching the dusk through the basket's gaps as the crescent moon rose to blur the deepening blue.

When the morning came, I could hear the buzzing clouds of blackflies above the bloating remains of men and beasts. One of the crates of pigeons, the one Tollefson had carried, had been smashed by an unexploded flying pig, all the birds crushed.

I could smell the miasma of men relieving themselves wherever they could, despite Whit's strict orders to use the latrines he'd had them dig. Excrement mixing with the rot and the gas. I could see the soldiers' skin taking on a claylike pallor.

I could sympathize with the men who fell asleep with their faces against the actions of their rifles. Fluffed in my little basket, at least I had relative warmth and shelter. The rainy vapor of France chills you to the hollows of your bones, then works its way into your marrow, and you're colder than you've ever been, a cold of wretched permanence, like you'll never be warm again.

I did not fancy myself invulnerable, though. The roar of the fighting that morning became a kind of synesthesia, a gray and obscuring cloud of sheer noise. I could feel the quivering of the ground and the spatter of flying dirt, and if one of the shells hit our basket, then we'd die, too.

During a brief break in the German assault, one of the western replacements spoke, seemingly to no one. "It seems like we ain't nowhere at all," he said, "but slugging along through some kind of black dream what don't have no end."

The major looked up from his trench map, and for a moment we all thought he might reprimand the westerner for complaining. But Whit just nodded, in that way he had of showing someone that he'd truly been heard. "Keep slugging, soldier," said Whit.

"Yessir, Major," said the westerner, blinking as if snapped out of a trance. "Wouldn't dare to quit."

Some of the men, it must be said, really were very daring. Private Philip Cepaglia, for instance, a tiny, tan Italian who bore the nickname Zip. Fiery-tempered and impulsive, he found the wounded's moans for water unbearable. Wiry and athletic, he could move like a shadow—silently, swiftly— and twice that morning he strung a dozen canteens together and made his way through sniper fire to Charlevaux Brook. On the second trip, some of the canteens got hit, their precious contents fountaining out, but Zip himself came through untouched.

Whit refused a drink, told him to take the water to the injured. "You'll get a medal for that trick, Cepaglia," he said.

"No, Major," said Zip, shaking his statuesque head—large eyes, beaked nose—beneath his helmet. "It's good to have something to do that's not sit here and wait to get whacked."

But Whit, as always, later did as he said he would, and Zip got a Distinguished Service Cross for feats of valor in water-fetching.

After what would have been lunchtime—had there been any lunch—Whit had McMurtry circulate the message to all his commanders: *Our mission is to hold this position at all costs. No falling back. Have this understood by every man in your command.* Amazingly, the men followed the order with vigor. Sirota, the medical officer, who had long since run out of bandages, figured out a method to handle the casualties strewn across the hill after the latest onslaught. The men's uniforms had wraparound pieces that started at their feet and spiraled over their trousers—surely provided by the quartermaster because they looked smart, and kept debris from going up the pant legs, and because whenever washing was possible, the pieces could be washed. Sirota took them off the dead—and eventually the living—because the wool wraparounds soaked up gushes of blood and could be wound tightly about torsos and the stumps of legs and arms.

"That's the kind of resourcefulness that's going to get us out of this, Sirota," said Whit. "Hold our boys together a little longer. Remember, two million Americans are pushing up to relieve us."

"I just hope I've gotten the wool clean enough—that I'm not wrapping them in infections," Sirota said, and hopped grimly to the next funkhole.

In the lulls Whit detailed men to bury the dead, partly out of respect but also because leaving the bodies where they lay threatened to murder morale. "These men," he said, "deserve a last earthly tribute."

Not to mention that aboveground they began to stink.

But the Germans took to targeting the burial parties with machine guns—"Very unchivalrous," remarked Whit to the

young German prisoner, who shrugged—so even this obser-
vance soon became impossible.

———————

Though any catalog of events must misrepresent how baggy
that extended passivity in the Pocket felt, one incident in
particular was so grotesque as to give shape to the rest.

On the afternoon of Friday, October 4, our own artillery,
the Americans who Whit had promised were pushing up to
relieve us, began firing. The hail of shells started at the top
of the hill that sheltered us—Hill 198, I'd later learn they
called it back at Rampont—before crunching down to the
Charlevaux Brook. The men loosed expletive-heavy cheers,
including some in Italian from Zip, as the bombs chomped
their way through a few German snipers.

When the fire crossed the brook, the water erupted in gey-
sers of liquid and mud, as if an invisible giant were trying
to skip stones. But these were missiles filled with shrapnel
and high explosives, and they didn't stop at the water but crept
up the other side of the valley and into our own hill.

The cheers turned to cries of *"No!"* and *"Stop, stop, stop!"* but
the shells kept coming, digging into our funkholes, unburying
our dead, flinging shards of steel as they burst. The spot that
Whittlesey had picked to dig in might have been well protected from German shells, but it was quite exposed to American ones.

Nils Tollefson was struck by shrapnel while conferring
with Bill, his square-as-a-block-of-wood face splintered bang
apart. Buck Shot hunched as far as he could to the back of
our basket, but there was nowhere we couldn't see Nils lying
in the mud, his head half gone, never again to return to Minnesota and his family's farm.

Splashed with gore, Bill crouched for an instant in mute
horror and then with a single desperate cry began to move,
snatching up our basket to take us to the major. We were the
last two homers remaining in the Pocket.

"It's friendly fire, Cher Ami," said Bill, maintaining his own grip on the situation by explaining it to us. "Buck Shot, our own artillery is firing on us."

"Wrong coordinates," said Omer Richards, the third pigeon man, flat-eyed, staring at what was left of Nils.

The soldiers always said that you can't avoid the shell with your name on it. The shells fell and fell and fell and fell, ruining brawny bodies and scrawny ones alike.

Then the shell with Bill's name fell.

A yellow cloud burst overhead, and he toppled. Buck Shot and I reflexively belled our wings and raised our feet as our basket twisted, dropped, and crashed to the ground, coming to rest on its side; we bumped hard against the wicker and each other, but weren't badly hurt. I knew right away that something awful had happened. Once I'd found my footing, I cocked my head sideways to peek through the gaps in the weft.

A half-inch shrapnel ball had hit Bill in the stomach. The impact knocked him backward; had he not managed to pivot in his fall, he'd have landed atop Buck Shot and me. As it was, his shoulder struck the mud alongside us, and he rolled free, ending faceup at the trench's midpoint as more projectiles shrieked overhead. Slippery pink guts bulged through the hole in him.

Panicked, I began to keen—a high, harsh sound I hadn't made since I was a fledgling, begging food from my mother's throat. "No! This can't be!" I said. "Someone help him! First aid!"

But Buck Shot, in shock, ignored me. And the men could not understand.

Omer ran to grab our basket, then stood over Bill, looking sick and helpless.

"Get away," said Bill, his hands, which had held me with such gentleness, now slick and sweating and clutching his abdomen. "Get the birds to the major. They're the last ones. Send the message before they kill us all. Go!"

Omer staggered with us to the major's funkhole. Though

calm as a lake of incalculable depths, Whit was bleeding considerably from a wound on the bridge of his nose.

"Good man, Richards," he said, wiping blood from his lips and chin and dictating his message to Larney, his even voice faintly fissured with emotion. *We are along the road parallel to 276.4. Our own artillery is dropping a barrage directly on us. For heaven's sake, stop it.*

Larney rolled it up and handed it over. "A bird, Richards, and quickly," Whit said, holding the scroll with his usual fastidiousness so as not to obscure the message with blood.

Omer reached in to scoop me out—which Bill would never have done, wanting to keep the best for last—but he faltered.

Buck Shot, from the corner, rose wild-eyed to his feet. I saw what he was about to do, but pinned tight by Omer's filthy fingers, I couldn't make a sound.

"Madness!" Buck Shot screamed. "I have to get out of here!" With a lunge and a frantic clap of wings, he vaulted Omer's arm, flying up and away, the container on his orange leg empty.

Now out of the basket myself, clutched too tightly against Omer's ribs, I joined the men in watching the white daub of Buck Shot go, though I alone could see how his getaway would end. Wings cramped from his scrambling takeoff, he was fighting the air, flapping hard but moving slowly. His panic had driven him too high and too far over the German positions; now he turned toward home, which made him nearly stationary relative to their rifles.

Usually a pigeon's release produced a hail of bullets from the enemy's side, but this time we heard only one shot, from a sniper who'd been eyeing our trench.

It was enough.

A great cloud of small feathers showed that Buck Shot had taken a direct hit, and with an abrupt drop of altitude he was gone. In his interrupted flight, he'd looked like a shuttlecock struck badly in a game of badminton—an image I remember vividly but that strikes me now as strange, as if only through comparison to a man-made bird could I accept my friend's death in this man-made war.

Sorrow I felt, but not surprise. Buck Shot had prophesied his own demise, and like many such prophecies made in war, his had fulfilled itself.

I was the last. Whit glared wordlessly at Omer, who continued to crush me against his side. Our major affixed the message himself and said, "Cher Ami, you're our final hope."

I cocked my head to look into his light blue eyes and blinked in understanding.

Richards gave me an awkward toss.

It's odd, the things you notice in a crisis. As I flew up, I saw a blood blister, small and black, on Whit's finger from where his pistol had pinched him; it looked like a poppy seed. This was the last I'd see of him for a long, long while.

I flew a short distance, keeping low, and then perched in a walnut tree to smooth the feathers that Omer had disheveled. The men began to yell, throwing sticks and rocks between shell bursts to get me to leave, but I only shifted from one branch to another.

I'd flown eleven missions prior to that day. I'd survived them by being patient and by having excellent judgment of speeds and distances. I was cautious and quick-thinking, mature and coolheaded, and I'm not bragging—just explaining the facts. The American fliers, Eddie Rickenbacker especially, were said to possess these same traits, and I like to imagine that they would have understood what I was doing on the walnut tree. My infantrymen, however, assumed that I was dawdling because I was an idiot, or afraid. That's not why I stopped. I was thinking.

Poor Omer began to climb the tree, an undertaking that seemed likely to get him killed—with some justice, perhaps, since it was mostly his manhandling I had to recover from. But ready at last, I took to the sky.

At once the sky betrayed me. A massive explosive shell

struck the funkhole directly beneath me, blowing the five men there to pieces and wrecking the cushion of air beneath my wings; I dropped like a stone through the plume of hot gas.

For a moment I lost all sense of myself. When feeling returned, I was huddled on the edge of the fresh crater, well speckled with mud and ash, my vision blurred, my hearing gone. For what seemed a very long time, I sat unmoving as my perceptions returned to me: the shouting men, the falling projectiles, Bill lying pale on the earth.

I shook mightily, casting the grime from my feathers. Then I rose, bringing my wing tips together with a terrific burst of claps. The air above me was deformed, chaotic, utterly disordered by the detonating shells. I found still air, and I dug my wings into it. I found billows of heat, and I rode them up.

I circled to get my bearings—feeling out the cleaner air seeping through the blood and the gun smoke, alert for the dark smell of fungus and fallen leaves from the deep forest to the south, the tang of years-old manure in the fields farther on—and I soared above the maelstrom.

In moments of extraordinary difficulty, one rises above oneself; one becomes an aura, overcast and vaporous. Above the ooze and above the bursts, above the horizontal hailstorm of bullets from the hills.

The German snipers had had plenty of time to take aim. Each bit of lead that caught me sent me tumbling, then rebuilding the cushion of air that kept me aloft. My movements became gooey; I tried not to think about why. Kept flying. Wing bones, long feathers still intact.

They shot out my eye. Head wrenched to the side, I blacked out, arced back toward the mud like one of those hateful shells. Then snapped awake, half the world gone. Kept flying.

I heard a despairing shout from bucktoothed Omer, bumbler to the end. "They've got him! He's done for!"

They had gotten me. But I was not done for.

In my intact brain echoed the voice: *Cher Ami! Home to*

your loft by the airway! Home to Rampont! A vista opened in front of me, almost as if I'd willed it. I thought of everything I could to not think about dying.

Flying over fields, thinking of the peasants not there to harvest, the harvest itself not there, the earth out of which it would grow blown to smithereens. Thinking of the heads of the men, like stalks of wheat themselves, chopped by the reaper.

The mist rising and falling dove gray over the fields. No, not over the fields but over my surviving eye. The hollows of my beak, gore-clogged, caught no odors beyond those of my own wounds. I thought I really might be dying. I did not want to hang in the air, then meet eternity. I wanted to make it. I hurtled forward, following the voice. Over the familiar sites to Rampont.

Grim farmhouses, bare and hard, frugal and efficient to the point of starvation. Everything once pure now besmirched, everything sordid. The hens in the henhouses distressed, brooding. Roosters and rabbits. Very few cows. The sheep and bigger animals all eaten. I was not going to die; no one was going to eat me.

Wrecked churchyards. Graves upturned, old bones mixing with the new, and me starting to feel like a corpse myself. I thought of Bill, and of Buck Shot, and of Larney and Whittlesey, and President Wilson and Wright Farm, John and the soldier son he wanted me to save, and my parents and my sweet vain sister Miss America, and my lost Baby Mine. I was not going to die; no one was going to bury me.

Though my pain was so overwhelming that I hardly recognized it as pain, I made it. Me, NURP 615, back to my loft, alighting on the board—a graceless landing, since I could only put weight on my left claw, while my right wiggled uselessly.

I pinged the little bell with my beak to announce my arrival, just as I'd been trained. In my state of complete collapse, I showed no signs of panic. Behavior of the highest order. Major Whittlesey would have been proud.

Corporal Gault was on loft duty, thank whoever should be

thanked for such things. "Cher Ami!" he said. "What have they done to you?"

He spoke to me, low and comforting. He said he'd been worried ever since he'd learned that I was attached to the Lost Battalion—that's what they were calling us already, the Lost Battalion—and that he'd feared he'd never see me again or, by probable extension, ever hear from Whittlesey. He did his best not to hurt me, a blood-smeared fluff of feathers. The message holder hung by a few shreds of flesh to what was left of my right leg, and he took some of the tendon when he lifted the canister off. "I'm sorry, I'm sorry, I'm so sorry," he kept saying. I could see him holding back tears. I must have looked quite bad.

"My God, no," he said when he'd unrolled and read the thin paper note. He could hardly hold the telephone as he relayed it to Division Headquarters. "Major, listen to this one," he said, and read the message aloud, in code, only to have whoever was on the other end tell him to repeat it in plain English, no matter who might be listening.

Within a minute the clamor of the guns had died down. The division had phoned the artillery and ordered a stop.

I had no way of knowing whether any of the men had survived.

"I wish we could figure out which triple-distilled idiot authorized that friendly barrage," Corporal Gault said, turning back to me, his eyes aggrieved and determined. "Come on, Cher Ami. You're going to be all right."

I had seen enough men die to notice that this was a thing that soldiers always told those who were surely dying. It never seemed convincing, but it seemed to make them all feel better, and that was worth something.

Long afterward, glowing with patriotic pride, Gault and a number of his commanders would tell me that I had flown forty kilometers in twenty-five minutes that day.

In war it is difficult to know anything beyond your immediate surroundings. As Gault worked to clean me up, even those became unknowable to me. My mission done, my brain emptied at last of all but Gault's soothing voice, I let myself slip into a restful blackness, with no expectation that I'd ever emerge.

It would be quite some time before I learned what happened after that.

CHAPTER 12

CHARLES WHITTLESEY

—◇◇◇◇—

Take the thing that bothers you and place it in parentheses.

I've told myself that a thousand times since we got stuck in the Pocket. Bracket the death that spatters against you. Set that clotted mess aside and do not look at it anymore.

But hardly an hour has slipped by these past three years without my recollecting those five days under fire without food or water, when we, the 308th, bled out, only to rise again like revenants as the Lost Battalion. Unkillable, at least in the public's mind.

Even here on the windswept deck of the southbound *Toloa*, even looking into the glass-green ocean, I see those incidents. This afternoon I can bear it, because soon I'll have sneaked free. War renders all parentheses porous, slipping out and asserting itself not merely as a clause but rather as the entire contract. I signed one with no termination provision and no limitation of liability that obliges me to live publicly with the memory of the Pocket.

Tonight I am breaking it.

While Cher Ami sat in the walnut tree preening her blue-gray feathers before flying away with my message, I swear I could see her *thinking*. Her golden eyes stared straight into my mind, and then she took wing.

As I watched her go, the leafless branches of the trees looked like skeletons' fingers, their foliage shredded away by our artillery. The gnarled hands pointed the way out but clasped us in. Desperation rose like bile in my throat, and I wished I could vomit it out. But I steeled myself.

We saw Cher Ami get hit, but we saw her keep flying, and

as she passed from view, I was seized by a near-frenzy of relief, one that I dared not demonstrate for fear of encouraging
the men toward carelessness. Richards was wrong, as usual:
Cher Ami did not appear done for. If she didn't make it, we'd
all surely die.

Why was Richards here? I felt a spasm of dread. "Where's
Cavanaugh?" I yelled above the din as our second-rate pigeon man dashed back to cover.

"Wounded, Major," said Richards. "Looks pretty bad. He's
in your funkhole. It was the nearest one to where he fell."

An unseen hand reached beneath my ribs and crushed all
it found there. I could not speak, and for a moment I stepped
outside myself, surprised in an oddly clinical way at the intensity of my anguish.

"Major?" said Richards. "With your permission, sir, I'd like
to eat the leftover bird feed? We ain't got any homers left, and
I'm near to starving."

I nodded, and Richards began tearing into the packets of
yellow cracked corn and dried maple peas, first weighing
them in his palms to judge how best to ration their contents—
using what formula I could not imagine—then flinging
pinches of each into his mouth, crunching them with his
back teeth as his buck incisors chewed the air. The sight
made me irrationally angry at him for being incompetent
and ugly and unscathed, unlike Bill Cavanaugh.

A little after four o'clock, about an hour and thirty-five
minutes after it had started, the monotonous torrent of agony
from our own army's guns finally ceased. McMurtry and I
looked at each other. "Praise be to God and to that blessed pigeon," he said, wincing as he lifted his burly frame from his
squat.

"Cher Ami," I said, looking across the Pocket where a few
men's heads emerged like moles from their holes. "Let's get a
count of who's still alive and see if her work was in vain."

Sirota, our medic, had run out of wraparounds. He moved

about the hillside transferring crusted bandages from the dead to the soon-to-be-dead.

I made my own rounds, trying to say—without sounding cockeyed—that the friendly barrage had conferred one benefit: now the generals really knew where we were, or perhaps more accurately knew that we were still there, holding our ground. Unable to bring relief from pain, I tried to bolster morale, moving from man to man repeating, *Remember, there are two million Americans pushing up to relieve us.* The words had long since slipped free of their specific meaning and become pure ritual, both for me and for my listeners.

Two million Americans to the rescue or not, our own numbers were grim. A pair of lieutenants from the 306th Machine Gun Battalion—Marshall Peabody, my friend since our Camp Upton days, and Maurice Revnes, of whom I had worked hard to keep my strong dislike in check—had been together in their command post up the slope when a shell exploded on the edge of their hole, blowing off part of Revnes's left foot and tearing Peabody's left leg to pieces. Overwhelmed, Sirota and our other two remaining medics had been unable to respond to their cries for first aid. Peabody had managed to put a tourniquet on his own mangled limb, and one of our corporals had come to help Revnes, but that help had consisted of two handkerchiefs covering the wound, held in place with used bandages from a first-aid kit. Peabody and Revnes had been two of my last three machine gun officers.

I assigned control of our automatic weapons to a Sergeant Hauck, whom I knew not at all, as he'd joined us the week before. Peabody, his face a mask of suppressed pain, refused to be moved to shelter and attempted to resume command; I had to order him to accept that the duty had passed to Hauck. "Yes, Major," he said, sweat beading on his square jaw where his dark beard grew. "I'm sorry I got hit. If you can have someone help me keep it loaded, I can still use a rifle to fight off the Boche."

"We'll see to that," I said. "And you needn't apologize. Just hold on, and remember, there are two million Americans pushing up to relieve us."

"Two million goddamned Americans my ass," said Revnes under his breath.

Having larger problems to deal with, I pretended not to hear and continued on to the command post to confer with McMurtry. We were down to so few officers that I was unsure of how we'd go on. During the barrage McMurtry had received a contusion in the knee that left him hobbling, and Captain Holderman had been cut badly by shell fragments. He insisted on remaining in command, and having no replacement, I let him.

On my way back from taking stock of the disaster, I found a private named Hollingshead, called Holly, squatting to relieve himself at the base of a tree. I was furious. With so much now out of my control, having my few remaining applicable directives ignored filled me with unaccustomed rage.

"You're violating a direct order, Private," I said, interrupting him in mid-shit. "Use the latrines we dug. Have some respect for yourself and for basic sanitation."

Hollingshead, mortified, soiled himself in a scramble to simultaneously pull up his trousers and salute, succeeding at neither. "I'm sorry, sir," he said.

"A man who defecates against a tree is a man who declares that he is no longer part of the army, that he is in fact no longer part of civilization. What do you think we're fighting for, Private? Do you think you're going to die here, Hollingshead?"

His lower lip quavered, his face crumpled in tears. "S-sir?" he stammered.

"You will *not* die here, Private. You will continue to shit and to fight in this army as ordered, like the well-trained infantryman you are. You will do so with pride and with dignity. When you return to your unit, make it known to your fellows that any such future act will be punished. Now, go and clean yourself up, Private."

"Yes, sir!" said Holly, his face flushed pink, fastening his pants as he rushed away.

Alone for a moment, I leaned my forehead against the oak's splintered bark, took long breaths, and absorbed the sickening odor of what Hollingshead had left as it danced with other battlefield stenches.

I returned to my funkhole as dusk was falling. Larney and Richards saluted as I approached, and their grim and wary faces told me before I could ask that Cavanaugh was beyond help. My first sight of him—gutshot, curled in anguish—confirmed it. Straight-limbed and charming Bill, so full of joy, now already smaller, the way that the dead shrink up.

The two privates slunk off without a word spoken, and I sank to the earth at Cavanaugh's side. "She did it, Bill," I said. I had never called him by his first name before. "Cher Ami, your favorite. She got them to stop."

"Cher Ami was the best one," he said, his voice faint but emphatic. "I said that, didn't I, Major? I knew she'd come through."

"You were right," I said, smoothing the damp yellow hair off his forehead. "Try to rest."

It was early yet, but there was no food and nothing to do, nothing but yell at men about their poor sanitation and watch the best of them die, killed by their own slipshod army. By then we had all learned that the hours between dawn and dusk took an eon to pass. In the absence of proper sleep—I hadn't had any of that since we'd left Camp Upton, didn't yet realize I'd never have it again—the texture of dreams began to steal into our waking lives whenever the light died in the skies.

With the responsibilities of command in suspension, I'd look at the faces of my men and be tormented by my superfluous schooling. *Famine is in thy cheeks*, I'd think: a fragment from Shakespeare. Romeo to the apothecary. Act 5, scene 1.

"It's funny, Major," said Bill, his sapphire eyes glassy. "I woke up starving this morning. Now I'm just cold. I used to think about Rector's and all the food I'd eat there when I got home. Crabs and yams and cantaloupe, steak and straw-berries."

"We'll go to Rector's," I said, a thing I had wanted to tell him for months. "When we get back to Manhattan. And you'll be my guest, not my waiter. We'll split the entire menu."

"I tried to think of it like a sacrament," he said. "Being stuck here with no food. Like fasting. But what are we sorry for? This isn't Lent, it's a war."

He stopped talking and clutched my hand, squeezing until it hurt. I had wanted this touch—rather more than I'd admit-ted to myself—and some shamed and superstitious part of me wondered whether my want had caused this, like a wish twisted by a wicked djinn.

All around us the men tried to sleep, piled like puppies in their funkholes.

"I been wondering," said Bill, delirious. "You've got more learning than I do, Major. Do sunrises and sunsets really look different? Or do we only imagine they do?"

"Cavanaugh," I said, and stopped, unable to steady my voice.

"That was my last one, Major. I should've taken a better look, I guess. I'm sorry I can't hang on. It's an honor. Make sure, in your letter, you tell Ma and Annie how I loved them. Tell them please to take care of my birds. It's been an honor, Major. You've been good."

"No, Cavanaugh. You're going to make it. You're going to survive to tell them yourself. Two million—"

I couldn't get the rest out, wasn't sure he could hear me anyway.

"You're going to see your birds again," I said. "After we stuff ourselves at Rector's, you'll take me to Hell's Kitchen. I'll meet your mother and Annie. *Both* Annies. We'll talk about the close call you had in the Argonne and how the sur-geons stitched you up. You'll tell them what a great com-mander I was."

He smiled his gap-toothed smile, his teeth enormous in his sunken face. "All right, Major," he said. "I'm going to close my eyes for a minute, then."

I listened to his shallow gasps. Sunrises or sunsets—trapped as we were, it didn't seem to matter. War occurs in the dimensions of time and space, just like everything else. "In military operations," said Wellington, "time is everything." In our case time was all we had, waiting in our tiny space for reinforcements to arrive or for the Germans to finish us. Two burning fuses of unknown length.

The next enemy assault came that night at around 9:00 P.M. Flares lit up the slope, sinking toward us on their small parachutes while the Germans hid from their own lights in the nearby brush. I ordered everyone who could still shoot to remain calm and not fire until the enemy came into view. They did so perfectly, to the Germans' vexation.

"*Kamerad,* vill you?" called a voice during a lull in the fighting, the first of many requests for surrender that we'd receive.

"Come in and get us, you Dutch bastard!" yelled Holderman. I ordered the men to open fire on the spot where the voice had come from, and the attackers withdrew.

Fragmented sleep, fragmented dreams. Bill huddled against me to borrow my warmth in the chill of the night. I kept waking up to see if he was still breathing, his familiar smell of hay and tobacco now cut with desperate sweat, metallic blood.

———————

The following morning, October 5, dawned with us lying cheek to cheek. Mine warm, his cold.

Bill Cavanaugh was dead.

I held on to what remained of him a while longer. His corpse did not repulse me; in the limited way that circumstances had permitted, his was a body I loved. It filled me instead with inexpressible melancholy, melancholy that I have never put aside. I did not pray, so instead I quoted Shakespeare—"Alas, poor world, what treasure hast thou lost!"—a fragment from *Venus and Adonis*. It was not something Bill would have known, and that seemed fitting, given his enthusiasm for discovering new things.

I moved Bill's body off my lap and stepped from the funk-hole into another battlefield dawn. He was hardly the only one who had died in the night. In spite of my innate intelligence, in spite of my education, how little I understood our circumstances except that they were bad, very bad. The colossal scale of the war made it impossible to know more. It had been created by men, but by men in the aggregate and not by the kings and kaisers and presidents whom we soldiers comforted ourselves by imagining in control of it. Even the generals could be only as the blind men judging the elephant, taking it for its parts, never comprehending the whole.

The earth lay before me like a bare idea, a wasteland that we could not traverse. We had to stay put. The brook babbled as it always did at the foot of the ravine. The sound seemed like mockery now, but the mockery was in my head. Water was still only water.

Men woke up nearly mad from thirst, their mouths leathery, but I posted a guard to keep them from trying to scramble to the brook, lest snipers pick them off like squirrels.

The living rose from their holes and turned out the pockets of the dead in search of cartridges. We were on our way to starving to death, the men's eyes popping out, their cheeks caving in. I joined them, moving from spot to spot, citing the approach of my two million. My repetitive behavior, heedless of circumstances, had come to resemble that of a ghost.

As I was reviewing the reports of the surviving commanders with Larney, McMurtry staggered up, sturdy and unflappable amid the filth and butchery. His bruised leg had stiffened during the night, and he approached the project of walking on it as if it were a challenging new hobby that he'd taken up, like golf or billiards. His bulldog jaw, far leaner than it had been in Baccarat, retained its customary tenacity. The men and I adored him for that.

"Morning, Major," he said. He must have noticed something in my face that gave him pause. "Cavanaugh?"

I shook my head.

He puffed a short equine sigh, then nodded. "Damned good pigeon man," he said.

"The best I've known."

"His bird saved us, I suppose. Which, to my way of thinking, means that *he* saved us. Or had quite a hand in it anyhow."

"And so my report shall read," I said.

He allowed an interval of respectful silence before he spoke again.

"Well," he said, "you'll be pleased to know that I managed enough sleep last night to have those clichéd dreams of mashed-potato mountains and gravy lakes, butter-pat meadows and trees with trunks made of porterhouse steaks."

"Now that I think of it," I said, trying to elevate myself to his bluff, unruffled manner, "our grenades do resemble little metal pineapples if you look in the right light."

Larney followed this exchange, probably trying to determine whether it merited inclusion in his compendium of war humor. As usual, his own contribution was sincere but devoid of wit, well meant but at cross-purposes to our own remarks. "Some of the men are eating twigs and acorns and roots," he said. "They're rolling up dry leaves and smoking them. It's nothing like a Camel, they say."

Jokes and pranks did occasionally break the tedium of our confinement; unfortunately, they were all played by the Germans and thus rather cruel. Late that morning Captain Holderman saw one of the Company K privates hop from his funkhole, don his pack, and dash toward the rear. Holderman grabbed him by the belt and asked what he thought he was doing; the private replied that he'd gotten word along the line that the 77th had been driven back and that I had decided to withdraw our command.

"Remind the men," I ordered when this story was relayed to me, "that among the enemy are many English speakers who will attempt devious ruses. The men are to confirm the truth of any directive that arrives from nowhere and always to use common sense. They should be particularly skeptical of orders to withdraw, as this battalion shall be doing no such thing."

The German ploys continued, with diminishing artfulness. Around midday a heavily accented voice cried out *"Gaz masks!"* Infantry Drill Regulations included no such command. One of the men responded with a shot into the underbrush, and the trickster died with a howl.

By the late afternoon, the Germans had abandoned fake commands in favor of sham orders given to their own imaginary troops, intended to persuade us that we were surrounded by a vastly larger force. *"Bring up ten machine guns on the left!"* they'd yell, and the German speakers among us would holler back *"Wint Beterben!"* which I gather translates loosely as "a bunch of fart-bags."

Throughout, my men's spirits seemed not to flag, which made me feel both better and worse—better because they had committed themselves to fight to the last man, worse because it was I who had brought them there, who was inspiring their sacrifice.

Toward the end of the day, our American artillery started up again, causing us to fear a repeat performance of friendly fire, but this time it hit the enemy. It seemed only to goad them into redoubling their attack on us, this time with grenades. We staved them off but took still more casualties. One man, a replacement whose name I never knew, had his legs blown off and lay there while the rest of us fought, crying *"Mama!"* until he died.

At dusk I slumped in my funkhole, my palm bruised and throbbing from my pistol's recoil, and joined McMurtry in watching Larney lick grains of coffee from a discarded can. This in turn reminded McMurtry that he still had a small piece of fatty bacon—it couldn't have weighed an ounce—that he'd used to grease cuts on his hands from the ubiquitous barbed wire. He pulled it from his overcoat, picked off the lint, and sliced it in two, giving me the second bite.

That night we heard machine guns firing to the south. This was unusual only in two respects: first, that they weren't firing on us, and second, that they weren't German. The German Maxim gun is fed by a belt and rarely misfires; in action it sounds like a monstrous stock ticker. The guns we heard chugged unsteadily, rarely managing a half dozen shots in a burst, and were firing past Hill 198: it was our own 77th Division, attacking the Germans with the despised Chauchats. Though none of us spoke a word, a glance from funkhole to funkhole in the moonless dark revealed countless pairs of American eyes widening in excitement as the realization spread.

But our prospective rescuers were still far away and likely had little sense of our exact location. McMurtry slid along the dirt to whisper in my ear. "A flare's no good," he said. "They won't see it for the damned hill."

I listened as the distant Chauchat was answered by nearer German guns. "A bit like the bagpipes of Lucknow, isn't it?" I said.

McMurtry gave me a look that confirmed we'd had the same idea, then motioned Larney over.

From all my years in classrooms, the lessons that have stayed with me most vividly have been digressions, asides, anecdotes told mostly to relieve the lecturers' own boredom, and officer training at Plattsburgh was no exception. There I'd heard about the bagpipes supposedly played by Highlanders in the relief force that broke the siege at Lucknow during the Indian Mutiny and how they had alerted the trapped British of their pending rescue. McMurtry and I reasoned that if we could hear the Chauchats of the 77th, then perhaps they could hear ours. I had the nearest lieutenant—William Cullen, who went by Red—fire bursts from his own Chauchat during a period of quiet: four bursts of five rounds each to empty the clip. It was a risky use of ammunition and an obvious signal that provoked another round of shots from the enemy. Worse, the sound of the American guns ceased shortly thereafter, and my hopes of relief anytime soon were dashed—though I kept my discouragement off my face.

The temperature plummeted to nearly freezing, and I forced myself to crawl from funkhole to funkhole in the trickling drizzle before the men made their nightly attempts at sleep, repeating my refrain about the two million Americans, embellishing it with the tale of Lucknow. Those surrounded British troops had held out for forty days, I told them, and we'd been in our spot only four, so we could stick it out a while yet.

As I moved on through the darkness, I'm sure I left the men baffled by my military scholarship, wondering where the fuck Lucknow was. If they thought of our circumstances in any sort of historical terms, then they probably compared our enemy to a rather different group of Indians and imagined me as analogous to Colonel George Armstrong Custer.

That night I was awakened by McMurtry's hand on my shoulder, and I rose with a start to address whatever the trouble was. My vision was blurred, my throat rough, and I realized that I had been sobbing; he had only sought to quiet me before the men heard.

October 6, the fifth day, was foggy. I felt as if I had slept wrapped in damp towels that had frozen overnight. The weariness in my eyes must have been clear to Holderman and McMurtry, who did their best to cheer me.

"We're beaten up but far from licked," said McMurtry, clapping me on the back. "When he hears 'Stand to,' every man still jumps from his funkhole to take his place on the firing line."

"Isolation, starvation, heavy casualties—if those haven't broken the boys yet, then they're not going to," said Holderman. "It's like any other misery: it seems intolerable, and then you get used to it. Hell, by the time those two million soldiers finally break through, our guys won't *want* to leave. They'll be building themselves fishing lodges."

I laughed obligingly at this. The two captains didn't know—and I didn't want to worry them by telling them—how many men had come to me directly in their hunger and despair to request permission to try to break through the German lines at our rear and make it back to Division Headquarters. This would have been suicide, but the men clearly knew that, and I didn't insult them by pointing that out. Instead I assured them that such adventures were better left to the scouts and that I needed them here. They always nodded in understanding and returned to their posts, but I knew that soon they'd stop asking and just leave.

Marshall Peabody had died during the night. He'd held on far longer than any of us had expected and had remained lucid through his agony, taking occasional shots at the enemy until his hands grew too weak, then exhorting those around him to fight like hell. His destroyed leg was swollen and filthy, and it was obvious that infection would kill him if blood loss didn't. As it happened, blood loss did; his tourniquet slipped, and he was gone.

His death struck the few surviving men in his machine-gun company hard. Even wounded he had functioned as a moral center of gravity for the 306th, and when that gravity dissipated, they began to drift.

Around midday Private Sidney Foss—a youth with thin lips and beady eyes who absolutely should not have been appearing at my command post at midday—appeared at my command post. He saluted perfunctorily and presented me with a note written on a field message pad. *Major W,* it said:

If our people do not get here by noon, it is useless for us
to keep up against these great odds. It's a horrible thing to

think of, but I can see nothing else for us to do but give up—
The men are starving—the wounded, like myself, have not
only had no nourishment but a great loss of blood. If the
same thought may be in your mind, perhaps the enemy may
permit the wounded to return to their own lines. I only say
this because I, for one, cannot hold out longer, when
cornered as we are it strikes me that it is not a
dishonorable thing to give up.

Revnes

I read it a second time, very closely, then handed it to Mc-
Murtry without a word. He read it and returned it to me, and
I folded it into my pocket.

At the commencement of the Argonne Offensive, General
Alexander had issued an order declaring that any man who
called for his unit to retreat or fall back was a traitor who
should be shot by his commander or by any patriot who happened to be in the vicinity. When I read it, I was stunned—
under the Articles of War, it was flagrantly, almost luxuriantly
illegal—and I opted to ignore it, the way one might ignore
flatulence at a white-tie dinner. The order came back to me
vividly as I read Revnes's message, because at that time I was
nurturing a strong impulse to walk over to his funkhole and
put a bullet in his chest.

"Looks as though Lieutenant Revnes is a little scared," I
said, as quietly as I could, then turned to Foss and asked,
"Where will I find the lieutenant, Private?"

McMurtry looked concerned. "Do you want me to—"

"Stay here and rest your knee, Captain. This errand isn't
worth the discomfort."

Foss led me through the Pocket to where Revnes sheltered
among other injured men. I had expected to find him reclin-
ing open-shirted, brooding like Byron, but instead he was
pale and clenched, obviously suffering. Staring down at his
crippled foot, I felt pity vie with rage.

Revnes was seated next to Herman Anderson, a sergeant from my own Company A. Both men watched me sullenly, while the soldiers on either side of them shrank back to whatever extent their injuries would allow.

"Now, listen, men," I said. "Everything looks good for reinforcements to get through, and it will be a little matter of time before we rejoin the division. Please don't be scared."

I didn't have Revnes's talent as an orator, but I think I did a fair job of addressing my entire audience while giving the impression that I was speaking to the three conspirators. I then reversed this approach and allowed the men to glimpse the degree to which I was restraining my anger. "You are probably all aware," I said, "that Lieutenant Peabody died overnight. You will also remember the encouragement that he offered to all of us, even after being badly wounded. Not many of us are as brave as Lieutenant Peabody. But I think we can all appreciate his bravery and can resolve not to dishonor him by abandoning the example that he set. I hope every man here will continue his defense of our position with vigor and with pride, because—let me be quite clear— there is going to be no surrender. Sergeant Anderson, do you still have ammunition for your sidearm?"

"Yes, sir."

"Good," I said with frightening cheer, and looked him full in the face. "If you see any signs of surrender from anybody— a white flag, upraised hands, anything like that—you shoot him."

Anderson looked as if he'd been slapped. "Yes, sir!" he said.

Revnes grimaced but nodded in acknowledgment.

I issued my customary assurances about the impending arrival of two million reinforcements and the resilience of the British at Lucknow and left the men to their thoughts. By then the applicability of the Lucknow episode had been lost even to me, but I went on repeating it. Though I'd never say it aloud, I'd begun to think instead of Leonidas dying with his Spartans at Thermopylae, Eleazar Ben Yair and his men killing one another rather than surrender at Masada, and Paladin Roland fighting to the death in Charlemagne's rear guard at Roncesvalles. I could not resurrect my dead men, I could not restore their destroyed limbs and eyes and faces, but I could still safeguard the notion that their sacrifices had been made in service to some worthy end, even if it meant the loss of all that remained. We would fight until we were all dead. No other option was conceivable.

As I was headed back to the command post, another German attack: machine guns strafed us with suspicious indifference, clearly providing cover for something—and there it was, a group of perhaps a dozen of the enemy who'd worked their way onto an overhanging cliff to fling grenades at us. I was lucky, spotted them quickly, got my whistle into my mouth at once. It was rare for our men to actually see gray German uniforms, and they opened fire with enormous pent-up anger and considerable accuracy. The Germans' luck was as poor as ours was good: a couple had pulled the pins on their grenades as they were hit, and their fellows were unable to kick them off the ledge before they exploded. Gore rained on us, painting our faces as we cheered.

What a thing to find joy in.

I met McMurtry outside our funkhole, receiving a sergeant's report regarding our casualties from the attack, which were thankfully few. As he turned to point out his best guess as to how the Germans had ascended the cliff, I was alarmed to see a dark line of blood down the back of his service coat.

"What have you got there, George?"

"How's that?" He pivoted toward me again.

"No, turn that way again, let me have a look."

Perplexed, he obliged. At the top of the dark line, between his right shoulder and his spine, an object protruded by a couple of inches. Without thinking I gave it a yank, and out it came: part of the wooden handle of a potato-masher grenade.

McMurtry let forth a howl that must have been audible in

Berlin. "Murder!" he screamed, turning on me with a rictus of shock. "If you do that again, I'll wring your neck!"

We stood looking at each other and at the bloody fragment in my hand, and both began laughing uncontrollably until everyone around us joined in. "I won't do it again," I reassured him once I could speak. "There's only one. Go get it dressed. Didn't you know you were wounded?"

"Someone might have mentioned it to me," he said and limped off.

After their humiliation on the cliff, we expected retribution but were surprised that the enemy's next assault was of a more psychological cast. Late in the day, Private Hollingshead— dirty, non-latrine-using Holly—materialized at the edge of the Pocket. He was blindfolded, using a cane, limping toward us while his free hand waved a white flag tied to the end of a stick. A cloth bundle hung from his neck; when he reached us, we opened it to find two packs of cigarettes, a loaf of black German bread, and a typewritten note.

None of us had seen Hollingshead since that morning. He and seven other men from Company H had disappeared; to the limited extent that we thought about them at all, we assumed they had deserted. Unsurprisingly, they'd been captured by the Germans, who had decided to send only Hollingshead—the only one still ambulatory after the violence of their capture—back to us with a message.

In the funkhole where McMurtry and I squatted with Holderman and Larney, Hollingshead poured out his story. "You know the airplanes?" he began, trying to keep eye contact with me and failing. "The ones been dropping packages nearby?"

Our army had been trying to get supplies to us by air, but day upon day they'd missed the mark and the drops had landed behind enemy lines. *Chocolate!* the Germans would cry out as they opened the boxes. *Chewing tobacco! Canned beef! Jam! Thank you, Americans! Please tell your pilots how we love their presents!*

"We know the airplanes," I said. "Hurry it up."

"Well, a few of us went after them food parcels. Because an officer from Company H ordered us to." This was a blatant lie; there were no officers left in Company H. "The Fritzies ambushed us. Four killed, four wounded. They asked us questions, but don't worry, Major. We told 'em we outnumber 'em ten to one."

"I hope you lied to them better than you're lying to me. Come to the point."

"They sent me back on the condition I deliver this message," he said.

In my bloodstained fingers, the linen paper's pristine whiteness made it seem like an object from a more advanced civilization.

The German commander had mistakenly addressed his message to the 2nd Battalion, but we took his meaning:

Sir:

The Bearer of the present, Lowell R Hollingshead has been taken prisoner by us on October 7. He refused to the German Intelligence Officer every answer to his questions and is quite an honourable fellow, doing honour to his father-land in the strictest sense of the word.

He has been charged against his will, believing in doing wrong to his country, in carrying forward this present letter to the Officer in charge of the 2nd Batl. J.R. 308 of the 77th Div. with the purpose to recommend this Commander to surrender with his forces as it would be quite useless to resist any more in view of the present conditions.

The suffering of your wounded man can be heared over here in the German lines and we are appealing to your human sentiments.

A withe Flag shown by one of your men will tell us that you agree with these conditions.

Please treat the Lowell R Hollingshead as an honourable man. He is quite the soldier we envy you.

The German Commanding Officer

I handed it to McMurtry, who read it and handed it to Holderman, who read it and handed it back to me. We looked at each other and smiled. "Private Larney," McMurtry said, "this may be of interest to you."

For there was humor—sardonic and typically Teutonic—in this letter, particularly in the words "human sentiments." We had plenty of human sentiments toward the enemy who had killed or wounded more than half of our besieged command over the past five days. But they were not sentiments likely to inspire acquiescence.

McMurtry began to chuckle as he handed Larney the message, then to guffaw. "Hell and blazes, boys," he said, "we've got 'em licked! Otherwise they wouldn't have sent this!"

Holderman grinned. "Combat failed, so now they're begging!" he said. "We've got 'em right where we want 'em, Major."

Larney had taken on the bright-eyed look he got whenever he was working hard to memorize details for the diary he wasn't supposed to be keeping. "You want me to write up a response, Major?" he said.

The men had seen Hollingshead's undignified return, and now a crowd had gathered to see what was afoot. I had to use the moment correctly.

"They don't deserve one. We're Americans. We *can't* surrender. Larney, I want you to take in the signal panels immediately. We can't have them mistaken for white flags. Commanders, have the men keep anything white—bandages, handkerchiefs, anything—hidden away."

Once I was sure that I had made my point, I told the gathered men to go back to their posts, and word spread quickly. *The sons of bitches!* the men said, and *Kiss our American asses!* and far worse. *We'll never surrender!*

The Germans had miscalculated. Five straight days of torture had not broken us. This latest overture did not crush our resolve but rather set it aflame. The target of our suffering and anger now seemed hittable.

There remained the matter of Hollingshead. "You had no business to leave your position under any circumstances without orders from a superior," I told him. "And we'll listen to no more lies about that. Go back to where you belong."

Hollingshead seemed half asleep, less humiliated by this debacle than he had been by the tree-shitting incident. Perhaps he'd used up all his shame. "Yes, sir," he said. "Oh, sir, about this stuff." He held up the bread and cigarettes. "Should I split . . . ? And how . . . ?"

"No one else in this encampment," Holderman said, forming his words with extreme precision, "will touch that fucking bread."

Hollingshead skulked back to his hole, ate his bread, and smoked one of the gold-tipped cigarettes that his captors had given him. He immediately became sick and began to complain. "Shut up," I heard another man say. "Here you are, kicking because you're puking. Hell, I ain't got nothing in me to puke."

Larney returned from pulling in the panels. The men's spirits were elevated; mine were not. "The Germans won't like this much," I said. "At this point they *must* attack. And it'll be a big one. So be prepared."

"After all this pain," said Larney, "you become like an animal." More thoughtful, as ever, than most gave him credit for, he shook his head at the men's profanity but also in fellow feeling. "Does one wild animal surrender to another?"

The assault came before sundown. My men—little more than hungry scarecrows—repulsed it as if nothing gave them greater joy. Never mind that they were severely wounded or too weak to stand. Every man remaining steadied his aim and fired into the enemy. Those who could not hold weapons loaded the weapons of their fellows.

When the Germans, confident of their victory, sent two soldiers with flamethrowers to finish us off, we shot them, the liquid fire sizzling through the underbrush, the soldiers carrying the weapons going up as torches. With the aid of the added illumination, we dispatched the rest in a tornado of rifle fire.

Ammunition was running low. I heard Holderman cry again and again to charge bayonets, and the men did as he said, hungry for the chance to plunge a blade through German gray, to avenge their dead friends. Those with no bayonets used rifle butts or their boots and fists. Between airplanes and mustard gas and machine guns, every battle I had fought in to that point had felt terrifyingly modern, as if history had tipped off its axis. The killing that evening felt a thousand years old.

The Germans must have thought they'd raised the dead. Frenzied and bleeding, bearded and tattered, the remnants of our battalion fought until the last German fled. Intoxicated by their own ferocity, the men collapsed into their holes and hugged their comrades and cheered their victory. The exultation was immeasurable, and transformative. I thought of folktales in which men become beasts in the light of the moon. Faces I had seen every day for months came toward me in the dark, and I did not recognize them, nor they me.

If called to, we could not do it again. We had fewer than two hundred fifty men left with any strength, and it was no longer certain that they could be effective in battle. Five of our six machine guns were wrecked; even if they hadn't been, they could serve only as clubs, since we had no ammunition.

I let the men rest that night untroubled, or at least untroubled by me. A few were making out their wills—on field message pads and scraps of magazines, on Bible pages and strips of clothing. With no writing utensils around, they wrote their testaments in blood, available in abundance.

On the morning of October 7, I asked for a volunteer to

make his way back to Division Headquarters—a doomed job, I thought, if ever there were one, but I had no better options and no shortage of volunteers.

I sent Abraham Krotoshinsky, a Jewish private from the Upton days, quick and brave, whom I trusted completely. "If you get through," I told him, "tell them we have not surrendered but that help must be sent at once."

"Yes, sir," he said, so much shorter, looking up at me. "Can I leave most of my equipment behind?"

"You're the one doing this job," I said. "Do it any way you please."

He saluted, clearly thrilled to be getting out of the Pocket, to be doing something other than defending himself. Like many of the men, he seemed to have concluded that death would be an improvement.

I felt certain that that was the last I would see of Abe Krotoshinsky.

––––––––––––

Sometimes the moment we are about to cease believing in something is the moment that that thing proves itself to be true.

Unbeknownst to me, even as I was sending Krotoshinsky on his way, my promised two million Americans were pushing up the Argonne Ravine to relieve us.

By noon several companies had maneuvered through a gap in the German wire, and a lieutenant by the name of F. A. Tillman was leading Company B of the 307th Infantry Regiment northwest, supported by Companies A and M.

I'd been worried that the relief forces, if they got close, wouldn't be able to find us, but Tillman assured me afterward that our nauseating stench let him know he must be close.

Upon arriving at the perimeter of the Pocket, he promptly fell into one of our sentries' holes, landing on one of our men, who instinctively tried to kill him with a bayonet. "What the hell's the matter with you?" Tillman managed to choke. "I'm looking for Major Whittlesey."

"Go fuck yourself," the sentry replied.

"I'd rather not. Listen, you damn fool, you're relieved. I'm with the 307th. We'll have food up to you right away."

I was talking to McMurtry when the sentry ran up with the news. "Major, a lieutenant is here," the private said. "He spoke the words we've been dreaming of for days."

I didn't believe it and crawled to the perimeter to investigate, anticipating the springing of a German trap at every inch.

But it was an actual fact. We were relieved.

As if he were performing a vaudeville gag, Tillman produced a steak sandwich from his musette bag, and I stood eating it slowly until McMurtry, keen that something was up, found us.

"For God's sake, give me a bite of that!" he said, taking the sandwich from my hand.

As we passed it back and forth, Tillman updated us on his advance to connect with on our right flank. "We're pretty happy to rescue you," he said, hale and blond, practically fat in comparison to our emaciation.

"Rescue, hell," I said, unable to stop myself. "If you had come up when we did, you wouldn't have put us in this fix."

He didn't reply to that, probably attributing my outburst to my being half crazy from the ordeal. He placed his men as a protective screen on the heights of the road, and McMurtry and I supervised the distribution of about sixty cans of corned beef hash to our officers, who measured out each mouthful to ensure that everyone got some.

The wounded got fed first. I watched as realization dawned on the haggard men, most too stunned and too dehydrated to cry. Stepping from the funkholes that they had expected would be their graves, they shook hands with one another, spread the word, fell to their knees in prayer.

"It's like being reborn," said Larney, trembling.

"I feel like a cat," said Holderman, slightly hysterical, "having all nine lives at once."

I handed the heel of the steak sandwich to McMurtry, who seemed to eat it in one bite, like a snake with a trick jaw. I felt an extraordinary lightness, like drunkenness but pure, as if I could float over this place of death, like a blimp above the Channel. I was happy. Truly happy.

It would be one of the last times.

CHAPTER 13

CHER AMI

~~~~~~~~~

In my first dream after the Pocket, I dreamt of a cemetery without name or end, and its tall columbarium, those memorial structures modeled on dovecotes, with small drawers set into the mausoleum walls: little crypts for the ashes of the dead.

But in the dream each box contained the taxidermied body of a pigeon whom I had known and loved: President Wilson, Buck Shot, Fast Time, Lady Jane, Big Tom, Miss America, Thomas Hardy. Last but not least, my long-lost darling, Baby Mine.

Some of the drawers contained the remains of men: Bill, and Whit, and Omer, and Nils, and Corporal Gault. Not their ashes but their bodies, stiff and shrunken like dolls, now no bigger than doves themselves.

I'm not sure how I was opening those drawers.

I woke up looking into the face of an army doctor with sandy hair and pimples on his nose. I woke up and thought, *Am I a human now?*

Because they were doing human things to me, things I had heard of them doing to save wounded men. I could not believe I was not dead. Coming back into my body, seeing out of my single golden eye, trying to struggle upright, I realized that they had removed whatever had remained of my right leg. It tingled and pained, but there was no limb there, only air.

I felt the veterinarian—he was a vet, I knew that, I was still a pigeon—stitching up my feathered breast as best he could.

"He's awake," the sandy-haired man said. "Chloroform, please. We can't have him thrashing."

A hand put a tiny cloth over my beak, stinking and faintly sweet, and I felt my consciousness vacate—a mercy, because the needle and thread passing through my flesh was too much, even for a racing homer accustomed to physical suffering.

I dreamt again—of lavender clouds tinted with yellow, yellow clouds tinted with gray, silver clouds tinted with pink, clouds unscrolling in a sky of powdery blue, clouds I'd never fly among, not if I became human.

When I next awoke, they had finished sewing and I was alone, nestled softly among paper and straw in a private cage. Not in the mobile loft with the other birds but in an office, atop a table near a potbellied stove. I felt not well by any means, but better.

Before I remembered all that had happened—Bill gutshot, the walnut tree, the exploding shell, the bullets, the voice calling me back to Rampont—everything seemed distant but okay, like I was seeing it through a thick dawn fog, rosy and blurred. Then came clarity: what I'd been through and my present and permanent incompleteness. One eye, one leg.

Corporal Gault—who was seated at a desk across the small office, the kitchen of a converted village house—heard me stirring and came over to stroke my head, unable to hold me because I was wrapped in a bandage. His kind eyes stared down at my maimed and ungainly body, and he forced a smile beneath his chestnut mustache.

"The bandage is to keep you from pecking at your stitches," he said. "My poor Cher Ami." His face seemed enormous, corpulent, but I realized that I had just grown accustomed to the starving men I'd left in the Pocket, their skin taut against their skulls.

Gault kept up with his duties—supplying the mobile lofts with food and water, retrieving messages whenever bells chimed—but seemed to spend all his free time talking to me. "You're a hero, do you know that?" he said. "You're famous. The most famous pigeon that ever flew. You're in all the papers, from the *Stars and Stripes* on up to *The New York Times*. Look down if you don't believe me."

Sure enough, the crumpled newsprint insulating the bottom of my cage contained headline after headline about my death-defying flight, partially obscured by excrement and a few drops of my blood.

"Don't worry about the mess," said Gault. "I'm keeping my own clippings. So's every pigeon man in Signal Corps, probably. These are just for you."

Though perplexed that Gault had lined the cage with the papers rather than hanging them where they'd be easier to see, I appreciated the gesture—and he'd assumed that I couldn't read them. From the datelines I deduced that I'd been slipping in and out of consciousness for several days.

"Now take a peep at this," said Gault. He removed something from his pocket and held it up to show me: a tiny wooden leg. "A guy in the Quartermaster Corps who's handy with a knife made it for you. To thank you for everything. He says he's not sure if he got it right on the first go, but he'll keep at it until it works. As soon as the doc says you're ready, you can try it on. With some practice I think you'll be able to walk again—and land, too." Gault shook his head, his voice soft and wondering. "They're treating you like you're a regular soldier. Better than they treat some humans, I guess. You're a lucky bird! But you deserve it. The Lost Battalion sure was lucky to have you."

Gault was speaking to himself more than to me, puzzling over questions that would come to occupy me for much of the next hundred years. At the time, though, I wasn't thinking in those terms. I didn't want to be human. I only wanted to know what had become of some of my favorite humans, what had happened to the men after I'd flown home.

I cocked my head in curiosity, and Gault seemed to become conscious of the deficiencies in the newspaper accounts. After a pensive silence, he told me what had happened.

Following the halt of the friendly barrage, it had taken

1st Army a few days to fight their way to Whit and the Lost Battalion. They'd dispatched the Fiftieth Aero Squadron to try to establish the men's position and reopen communications by parachuting in a crate of pigeons, but one of the aviators got shot in the neck and the birds were never dropped. Thus, when reinforcements finally reached the Pocket, they weren't sure what they would find.

What they found was a scene of horror that had been unimaginable even to seasoned soldiers. The smell had reached them first. Men who knew about such things from their civilian lives likened it to a slaughterhouse, one that had never been cleaned. The distribution of food to survivors was greatly aided by the fact that none among the relieving force could imagine eating in the presence of that stench; they happily gave up their rations.

Medics who'd seen every type of violence done to human bodies on the Western Front had still never before encountered so many wounds that had been festering for so long. They took regular breaks in their ministrations to vomit. Worst of all was the unsettling sense that the usual triage categories had been blurred beyond recognition: the Lost Battalion couldn't be easily sorted into the walking wounded, the invalid, and the dead. A soldier who'd taken a shrapnel ball through the chest might fully recover, while another fellow shot in the hand might be dead of blood poisoning within the hour. Life and death commingled, traded places, relaxed their borders. Even the few men who had come through the incident largely unhurt looked like shades, greeting the new arrivals with yellowed grins and vacant eyes.

Of the 600 or so who went into the Pocket, only 194 emerged on foot, with another 144 carried out on stretchers. The rest were dead or vanished into the woods. Trapped in that confined space, the battalion had buried the corpses in a shallow grave near where the wounded lay until they lacked the manpower for even that. When the relievers arrived, they buried the putrefying dead wherever they had fallen.

"Only one pigeon man came through," Gault said, his eyes shining. "Omer Richards. The rest didn't survive."

Bill Cavanaugh, my sweetest human friend, was dead. This was news I had already intuited, but hearing it was like being shot again. I huddled in my nest and closed my eye.

"That's right, Cher Ami," said Gault, placing a cloth over my cage, his voice growing muffled. "Rest up and get your strength back."

That night I dreamt of John on Wright Farm. During my racing days, he always promised that I would make a name for myself, and it seemed that I had, to a far greater extent than he ever could have imagined. In the dream John was smiling, silent. He certainly knew about my famous flight, but I had no way to reach him except in dreams, no way to hear what he'd say about my achievement, no way to learn what became of his son.

Corporal Gault told me that my name would live forever in American history.

Forever, I can say now from inside my display here in the sleeping Smithsonian, turns out to be a lot less long than it sounds. Almost nobody remembers me now.

Truly nobody remembers the Mocker, a gargantuan cream-colored bird, fluffy as an overstuffed pillow, whom I met during my convalescence at Rampont. Gault brought him in and set him on the table next to me at the beginning of November, when the shortening days cast the converted kitchen in violet shadows.

"This gentle giant flew fifty-two missions before being wounded," said Gault by way of introduction, turning the great bird's cage to face me. "We can't put you together, lest you mess each other's dressings, but maybe you'd like the company."

A good idea in theory but less than satisfying in practice. Though the Mocker's wounds were less severe than mine from a bodily standpoint, they were mentally much worse. He'd lost his left eye and part of his cranium to a rifle bullet; the vet had given him a lopsided turban of gauze to protect his exposed brain where the bullet had carried the bone away. The bandage swooped down over his missing eye, and the other didn't focus on anything.

I tried to strike up a conversation. "Fifty-two missions!" I said, looking into his face, drab and void. "You're a much bigger hero than I ever was. And I don't just mean your size."

"I was born in 1917," he said, puffing his chest. "My name is the Mocker."

I blinked at him, puzzled by his response, and tried again. "It seems that we're both lacking an eye," I said. "I find that I'm adjusting, but I won't really know until I've flown again. I'm terribly anxious about it, to be quite honest. How long has it been since your injury?"

"I was born in 1917," he said. "My name is the Mocker."

Over and over. To every question.

He recovered more rapidly than I did. After two weeks they put him on a transport ship among thousands of wounded men and sent him to the Army Signal Corps pigeon lofts in New Jersey, a place that I wouldn't see for months.

Along the way the army awarded him a Distinguished Service Cross, and the French gave him the Croix de Guerre, both of which he damn well deserved, but I was happy to see him go. Through no fault of his own, he gave me the creeps. His missing brain chunk must have contained the better part of his personality, because the husk of the bird I met was utterly unreachable.

Many years later, when a lay historian with a particular interest in homing pigeons came to see me at the Smithsonian, I overheard her say that the Mocker died on June 15, 1937. *That can't be right*, I thought, but she went on to confirm it: he'd been the last of us pigeon heroes of what was then still known as the Great War, though with armies massing in

Europe again it wouldn't be for much longer. He lived for al-most twenty years in that eerie eternal state.

Shortly after the announcement of the unbelievable Armi-stice, Corporal Gault rushed in, radiant with good news. "Not only is the war over," he said, "but they're sending us away, Cher Ami, away from this backwater! We're going south, to a hospital on the Riviera!"

"I was born in 1917," said the Mocker. "My name is the Mocker."

"We're not taking you, I'm afraid, my huge heroic friend," said Gault, for all the difference it made. "But, Cher Ami, you're renowned enough to merit a personal escort, namely me. I'm to stay there tending to you and overseeing the other recovering birds! You're my feathery ticket out, dear friend. You've earned us warmth and sunshine."

I had heard of the army hospitals in the South of France, first from President Wilson at the lofts in Langres, cocky President Wilson who somehow knew everything, and then from the men of the various battalions to which I'd been at-tached, who spoke of them often. They featured among the myriad stories that Whit had used to comfort his injured men, saying, *You're going to make it. You'll be down on the Riv-iera while we're still soaking through these woods.*

I was keen to be going, mostly because it meant that I was finally well enough to travel and that soon I could start train-ing again—for my own well-being, not for resumption of the horrible business of battlefield messaging. But mostly I was happy for Corporal Gault, who was fairly afloat at the pros-pect of relocation to that airy southern clime that the men spoke of like a land in a fairy tale.

The Riviera was a landscape that encouraged enchantment.

Once upon a time, a busted-up blue pigeon who most men mistook for a cock, who had been grievously injured but by

some magic survived, went with her human protector to a
rainbow land of azure sea and turquoise sky and shimmery
cliffs and the scratchy-fresh smells of wild lavender and
thyme. Fishing boats and palm trees, jasmine and mimosas.

In the vast army lofts near one of the hospitals where Corporal Gault oversaw us—recuperating birds from across the
Western Front—the hot, high drafts of scent intoxicated us.
Our tolerance for beauty was so low, given the grim gray
ditch we'd come from, that almost any hint of loveliness
would have sufficed to make us drunk.

And amid that profusion of perfume and color, I was still
able to detect the smell of white roses at the edge of happiness.

In the luster of the Mediterranean light, Baby Mine basked.

At first I could not believe my eye, thinking perhaps that
my lack of depth perception was causing me to imagine
things. But as I inched closer, hobbling unevenly between
my real leg and my wooden one, I could see her pink-tinted
feathers and intelligent beak. I wanted to fly to her, hesitat-
ing only because of my wounds. My beechwood prosthesis
gave me the staggering gait of a tortoise, translating my former grace into pitiful comedy. But this was no time for van-
ity. I called out her name.

She turned and flew to my side, and the air we breathed
became oxygenated with joy.

"Cher Ami!" she said. "Dear Friend. Your name is like the
start of a letter that a soldier might write. Whenever I carried
a message for the army, I imagined that I could send one to
you, too, and I thought of what it might say. It helped me get
through, I'm sure of it. But what happened to you? Are you in
much pain?"

"I am," I said, honest with her, as I always was and would
always be. "It's low in the background, a smoldering fire but
always there. I'm all right, though. I'm surprised you recognized me."

"Of course I did," she said, our wings touching.

"You look unchanged," I said. "But none of us is unchanged. You're recuperating?"

"Somehow I wasn't wounded," she said in her ashy voice. "I'm here because of my dumb lungs. From all that damp in the trenches—all that northern French rain—they got infected again. But Gault thinks the Côte d'Azur will cure me if anything can."

"Gault knows what he's doing," I said. Suddenly self-conscious, I dipped my beak to smooth the feathers over the scar on my breast. "I'm sorry that I look this way."

"It makes me sad," she said, tilting her head to gaze evenly into both my remaining eye and my feathered-over socket. "You're too smart for me to lie to you, and I'm too smart to think you'd to want me to. But I'll say this honestly: to be grotesque is to possess an almost magical ugliness. Now you possess it."

I kissed her neck with my beak. "I'm still myself," I said. "Even more now than before. I love that you understand that."

She kissed me back with a certain solemnity. "I've learned that everything that thinks and feels," she said, "grows by subtraction. Detachment brings perspective. Wisdom comes from letting go. It's true for humans, too, but most of them seem to struggle with it."

"Their world is very complicated," I said.

"They've made it that way. Just look at what they've done."

At first I thought she was talking about the war—which was all but erased by our current surroundings, present only in the injuries it had inflicted, transformed into a symptom, or a specimen, not unlike the transformation I'd undergo later, upon arrival at the Smithsonian—but she wasn't. She was talking about the lofts, the hospital, the hotels, the streets, the harbor, the palms that lined the quays—the entire human project to remake the world, of which the war was a shadowy, ineradicable part. We watched it in silence for a while, marveling at the sweetness and sadness that underlay all we saw.

"I wish I could let go of this feeling," I said. "The sense of being at war. They say the war's over, but it doesn't feel over. It feels like it was always there and always will be. Do you know what I mean?"

She nodded her glossy head. "It's hard to put aside the anticipation and dread. The thought that the next minute might be your last. You learn that when you're under fire—the agitation keeps you alive—but when all the shooting stops, you can't unlearn it. It lives in you, just like the voice that tells you to fly home. But it's over now, Cher Ami. It can't hurt any of us anymore."

As she finished, we both jumped at a voice that came from behind us—startling, even though it was familiar.

"President Wilson," said President Wilson, "reporting for duty at the Langres loft reunion."

Though wounded, he was still black as an oil slick and authoritative as ever. Aside from the eye, the two of us had been shot in exactly the same spots, only his damage had all been sustained on the opposite side of his body: my dark mirror of injury. He regarded us boldly, with no self-consciousness, as he told us his tale.

"I was assigned to the Tank Corps at first," he said. "Sometimes they dropped me from airplanes to men on the front lines. Things got most exciting when they transferred me to the 1st Division. I saved the lives of many soldiers. But I owe my present appearance to my final mission. November fifth."

"Oh, no," said Baby Mine. "Only six days before the Armistice."

"Fate, she is cruel," said President Wilson. "Some infantry units on the Verdun front became cut off. They sent me with their coordinates so the army could locate them. I found my way to my loft at Cuisy through fog and heavy fire. The Germans gave me these souvenirs—"

He stretched to his full height to give us better views of his absent foot and the bare patch on his breast, his black feathers glinting in the honeyed sun.

"—but I got my message through."

We filled him in on our own experiences. Always attentive to his keepers' discussions, he had heard about the Lost Battalion, but like all who got their news from official outlets, he had no sense of the true dimensions of the horror that occurred in the Pocket. For once he seemed to be at a loss for a response.

So the three of us fell silent, looking at one another and out toward the sea, watching a few white cloud puffs hurry toward Corsica. Learning to accept again that life could be pretty.

———————

The following two months unspooled like an idyll. The loft men all believed I was male, so they did not think to interfere with the fact that Baby Mine and I had mated up. If anything, they thought our union sweet: war pigeons in love.

I learned to fly again, thanks to the patient training of Corporal Gault. When not swimming through the aquamarine sky, I whiled away the hours catching up with President Wilson and Baby Mine. We talked about the pleasant features of our present, and we could speak freely about the unpleasant features of our past, which was a solace. Gault never had us fly significant distances, and Rampont receded in my mind, supplanted by our clement new home.

One day in December, still warmer and sunnier than anywhere we'd come from, an unfamiliar human voice wafted in through the wire squares of the flypen where Baby Mine and I exercised. "I heard you were here, Cher Ami," it said.

I flew to the perch nearest the man: a soldier in a wheelchair, being pushed by a nurse with marcelled red hair that peeked from her white cap. Both of the man's legs were missing below the knees.

He looked surprised that I had responded to him, that I seemed to be—and in fact was—listening to what he had to say. The flash of delight in his eyes was pushed aside by grief and doubt, and the nurse placed a reassuring hand on his shoulder.

He looked at her, sheepish. "This is probably silly," he said. "It's harder than I thought."

"I don't think it's silly at all," she said. "Look, he's listening."

The soldier turned to me and cleared his throat.

"Cher Ami," he said, "my name's Lionel Blendheim. From Stockton, California. I'm a private in C Company, 1st Battalion, 308th Infantry. I was with you in the Pocket."

He stopped, then reached a hand across his chest to his own shoulder, placing it atop the nurse's.

"I read in the *Stars and Stripes* that you'd be here," he said. "Since I'm here, too, I figured I ought to come pay my respects. I guess we both had a rough time of it, didn't we? But you look like you're doing pretty well now. And so am I, with a lot of help."

He was really talking to the nurse, not to me, but that was fine. They were obviously in love, and as a fellow in-love being I was happy for them.

"I wanted to say thank you," he said, his eyes full, his voice barely steady. "You really saved us that day. And all of us who came through, we all know it. Me and the guys, we took care of each other in there as best we could. And I guess we did okay. But there's something about getting saved by . . . well, by a bird, no offense, that really gives you a funny perspective on things. I'm not a churchgoing fellow. I don't think in those terms. But it sure makes me wonder if there's things in this world I ought to have paid better attention to."

He was talking to me now. I cocked my head, focused my golden eye.

"They almost missed me when they were evacuating us," he said. "Those olive-drab army rags sure blend in with mud and dead leaves, which was swell when the Germans were shooting at us but not when the medics were getting the wounded out. I couldn't hardly make a sound—it'd been so long since we'd had any water—but I kicked up as much of a fuss as I could, and the major, Galloping Charlie himself, he saw me and sent the stretcher-bearers. Now I'm here. Like he promised me I'd be."

He hunched forward with a grimace, then stretched out a hand to put a finger through the wire. I hobbled closer and gave it a light peck on its tip. The soldier and the nurse both laughed, then cried.

"I wish you could tell us your story, little bird," Blendheim said. "I'll bet the newspaper version isn't quite right. I know what they've done to *my* story. They're trying to tell me it was the Germans who took my legs, but I know it was friendly fire. All the worst hits we got were from our own guns. I don't blame those artillery boys—I'm trying not to anyway—but the lying about it sure sticks in my craw."

He settled back in his chair again. "Anyway," he said, "thank you. Me and the other fellows, we won't ever forget you. And as I'm working to get better—to get strong again—I'm going to think of you. Flying again, with your little wooden leg. If it helps, I hope you'll think of me, too."

"You're welcome," I said, though he could never comprehend it. "And thank you."

The nurse kissed his forehead as she turned him around. "Lionel," she said, "I'd swear he understood every word."

Her low heels clicked as she wheeled him away.

In 1918, my last Christmas, Baby Mine and I were cast in the local pageant. The Riviera villages, like many throughout France, followed the tradition of the crèche begun by St. Francis of Assisi, that lover of animals, the first to organize a spectacle re-creating the birth of Christ in Bethlehem.

I can never think of St. Francis—his love and respect for all creatures—without thinking of Bill Cavanaugh.

Some of the village children had befriended us pigeons over the previous weeks. Corporal Gault had taught them how to change our water and feed us, even how to train us to home: to release and time us. When the parish priest began accumulating animals to march alongside the children who were to play roles in the Christmas drama—Mary and Joseph, the angels and the wise men—they beseeched him to include pigeons. A benevolent man beloved by the townspeople, he conceded that while none of the Gospels made specific mention of homers being present at the birth of the Lord and Savior, it would be in the Franciscan spirit to include birds alongside the traditional cows and donkeys.

The French children carried Baby Mine and me in our basket through the candlelit street to the church. While I was as mystified as ever by human religion and its tendency to answer simple questions with long, strange stories, that night I felt almost blessed.

It could not last. On an uncharacteristically overcast day late in February, Corporal Gault came into the loft with an announcement.

The army had previously declared its plans to send the American Pigeon Service soldiers home to the States later that spring. Now they'd decided that they needed a few heroes to make the return earlier. "Ceremonial purposes," Gault explained to President Wilson and me. "Pershing wants to give you a medal, Cher Ami. Plus, the army's got some scheme about a goodwill tour. It's still taking shape, and it'll be a while before the orders make their way down to me. But I'll be shipping back across the Atlantic next week, and the two of you are coming with me. Well, I guess it's fairer to say that I'll be going with you."

"America!" said President Wilson. "The first time for you and me, eh? Off to the New World! The glorious land we have served with distinction. We shall be paraded through the streets beneath their skyscrapers. Schools shall be named after us. Prepare yourself for fame, my friend."

For all his knowledge, President Wilson could be oblivious to the feelings of others, and had Gault's announcement not stunned me so completely, I might have bristled at his enthusiasm.

I didn't want to go to America. I supposed I'd been assuming that when the war ended, I'd be sent back to Wright Farm, just as most of the surviving conscripted men would return to wherever it was that they came from. Over the past months, whenever something remarkable happened, I'd imagined how I'd describe it to my family and to John's other homers when I saw them again. Whenever I flew back to my mobile loft in difficult circumstances or in record time, I'd imagine the news reaching John and how he'd praise me for my achievements when we were reunited. I never subjected these fantasies to an instant of practical thought.

Had I done so, I would have realized that we pigeons were not conscripts like the men. We were matériel; we were property. The army hadn't borrowed us but owned us. During the war it needed us as messengers, and now that the war was over, it needed us as celebrities.

I would never see Wright Farm again. That realization was a blow, but not the main source of my anguish. What I most wanted in the world was simply to stay in the Riviera with Baby Mine—or, if that wasn't possible, to go wherever Baby Mine would go when her rehabilitation was complete.

Pigeon handlers, even kindly ones like Corporal Gault, regularly separate birds as it suits them, assuming that they'll go on to bond with others. They're usually correct: while pigeons are famously monogamous, most will pair with another mate if parted from a partner. But not I. Such matters were not so simple for me. And I knew I'd never find another like Baby Mine.

President Wilson had realized all this before I had. In truth, he had little more desire for fame than I. But he understood that going to America would cost me more than it would him, and in his graceless way he feigned enthusiasm for the trip to try to keep my spirits up. The fact that such sensitivity did not come easily to him made me appreciate it even more, and I told him so.

"I am glad that we can be frank with each other, Cher Ami," he said. "Though we have carried our last messages and dodged our last bullets, though we have earned the right to rest and happiness, our duties are not yet discharged, which means our war is not yet over. I fear the two of us shall never run out of applications for the phrase *'c'est la guerre.'*"

Baby Mine grieved when I gave her the news.

"It's not fair," she said, burying her face in my shoulder. "Look at what happens to the men who served. Look at Lionel Blendheim, who lost his legs and found a wife. The army isn't forcing *them* to part."

I didn't know what to say—but Baby Mine understood that nothing could be said, or done. Though our bird hearts were breaking, it is in a pigeon's nature to carry on stoically. The morning they put Corporal Gault and President Wilson and miserable me on a train bound for Brest, Baby Mine and I kept our parting dignified. "I will always love you, Cher Ami," she said.

"And I will always love you, Baby Mine," I replied.

As Gault scooped President Wilson and me into our travel basket, my remaining eye watched her steadily to record every detail of her pink feathers, my bullet-rattled sinuses strained to capture the last inkling of her white-rose scent. I seized on these sensations as if they were clues that might one day guide my flight home, though my only return to Baby Mine would come in dreams.

Honors ennoble those on whom they're bestowed, but they also ease the guilt of those whose commands made them necessary in the first place. A medal is a mirror, reflecting a glory that we force ourselves to believe in.

Such were my thoughts upon receiving the silver medal from General Pershing.

The army had no official award for valorous animals, but Pershing's hand had been forced by the French, who'd given me the Croix de Guerre. Like every power that had taken part in the global war, they were terrified of the energies that its horrors had unleashed in their populations: the Russian and German empires had already collapsed in revolution, and every nation seemed susceptible to a similar crackup. The French, however, were quick to notice that public revulsion at the waste of thousands of human lives could somehow be swept away by the story of one heroic animal. In a strange reversal of the tricks men used to depict their enemies as beasts to make them easier to kill, honoring the deeds of birds and dogs and horses made the idea of battlefield sacrifice simpler, more straightforward, easier to enjoy.

So Pershing needed a medal and had an idled silversmith work one up. At the ceremony, as the general held me in his hands, I understood that I was no less a prop than the bogus award, that we were all putting on a show to bolster the morale of the men in France awaiting their return and their even more impatient families back home. Along with the medal, Pershing presented both President Wilson and me with army pensions, a gesture clearly meant to reassure the troops that the U.S. government would keep its commitments. If the army could afford to give pensions to pigeons, then the men had nothing to worry about.

Pershing saluted us at the gangway of our transport ship, the *Ohioan*. "See that these birds make their journey in an officer's cabin," he ordered Gault. Such arrangements had long been settled, but the general had to make theater out of it.

Still, as we crossed the ocean westward, I had to admit that the cabin was one of the finest places I'd ever been. A petted passenger aboard that colossal vessel crowded with American troops, my experience was far more luxurious than our Channel crossing had been, with our basket lashed to an open deck. Our journey to America took over a week, and Gault whistled and smiled the whole way; he was from New Jersey and eager to be home.

I never discussed it with President Wilson, but I had begun to suspect that I was no longer a pigeon. In practical terms I had become something else, akin to a plush horse whose ostensible retirement would consist of being trotted out and ridden hard to the end of the line, with the accompaniment of waving flags and stirring speeches.

I think that that was when I started to become what I am now, here in the halls of the Smithsonian. A piece of suspect evidence. A symbol of something I never really was.

The ship was so vast that I had trouble understanding it as a thing rather than a place. The watery expanse we crossed was so featureless that my homer's mind failed to grasp it. Instead I thought of doves and the sea, of doves and boats, of pigeons and Noah, of pigeons and olive branches. A little piece of a tree, a little piece of peace. I felt lonely and unwell, not only in my heart but also in my body, which had never ceased hurting. Even in the midst of our cosseted journey, I felt that death could not be far from me and that I'd be at peace sooner than anyone might think.

As it happened, I was right about death, if not about peace.

CHAPTER 14

CHARLES WHITTLESEY

⸻

In my first dream after the Pocket, I dreamed of a cemetery without name or end and its tall columbarium, those memorial structures modeled on dovecotes, with small drawers set into the mausoleum walls: little crypts for the ashes of the dead.

Each box was printed not with a dead man's name but with the same graven gold label:

SAFE FOR DEMOCRACY
SAFE FOR DEMOCRACY
SAFE FOR DEMOCRACY

When I pulled the looped brass handles, the boxes wouldn't slide open, wouldn't budge. My little sister, Annie, came in, the same age she was when she died, though I was grown, thirty-four. She said, *Charlie, don't cry*, and opened one drawer, and Bill Cavanaugh emerged to stand behind her. He put his hand on her shoulder and said, *You don't need me to, but I forgive you.* Annie touched his hand with her own and said, *History will forgive you, then forget you.*

I woke to McMurtry shaking me, saying, "Rise and shine, Major. You were muttering in your sleep. Come on, it's breakfast time. Bet you never thought you'd hear me say that again."

Stiff and cramped, I rose from the ground, and the lingering uneasiness of the dream soon gave way to relief at our rescue and unaccustomed hunger for the hot chocolate and greasy potatoes that awaited us.

In the hours immediately following the arrival of the
307th, the realization that I was no longer about to be killed
routinely jumped from hiding to startle me like a roguish
child. The most mundane sensations—the smell of food, the
crunch of dry leaves, a puff of wind—would leave me near
laughter or tears simply because I was alive to experience
them. On being rescued, our main priorities had been distributing water and food and arranging the evacuation of
our wounded, but I had also assigned soldiers to gather and
secure our remaining weapons and ammunition. That night
they confirmed with ghoulish amazement what I had already
suspected: we were down to two working machine guns, no
grenades, a handful of rifles and pistols, and so little ammunition that our few functioning weapons would have consumed
it in a few minutes of hard fighting. "Couldn't have cut this
any closer, Major," they said.

The previous night had provided the first sound sleep that
most of the men had gotten in seven days, since we'd begun
our advance on October 2. Many of us, including McMurtry
and me, chose not to avail ourselves of the opportunity, instead waking periodically to keep the wounded company, repeating the whispered incantation, *Hang on, buddy. A few more
hours. Hang on, hang on.* We did so from a sense of duty—and
of responsibility, which is not the same thing—but also because, at least in my case, deep sleep didn't seem trustworthy,
or earned, or even particularly desirable. It seemed decadent,
like breaking a fast with cake instead of bread.

The morning light revealed that many of the men had died
anyway, before the stretchers and bearers reached them. I
had thought that knowing relief was on the way would sus-
tain them, but the body quits when it must, regardless of the
mind's exhortations. I'd soon learn that the reverse also ap-
plies: the body will go on living against the mind's wishes
and will.

Even then, heartless as it may sound, I had an inkling that
for the most mangled and irreparable it was better to die than

to live on in agony. What has surprised me in the years since is my own inability to predict these outcomes. Some of our most grievously disfigured men went on to lead full and happy lives. Whereas I, who came through with only wrecked lungs and a few scratches, am now here on the deck of the *Toloa*.

But on that Tuesday morning, as I gulped my first coffee in a week, the sickness that had infected me was still dormant and life seemed incalculably rich, incalculably fragile. The morning air was frosty, and whenever anyone exhaled, his breath escaped in a white cloud, like ectoplasm at a séance or spirits leaving a body. I had to remind myself, *No, these men survived*.

The valley came alive with the engines of trucks and the calls of ambulance drivers. McMurtry, Holderman, and I worked with the officers of the rescuing companies to prepare the men for departure. The YMCA distributed chocolate.

Holderman, his cheekbones so sharp against his sallow skin that they threatened to slice through, kept refusing food, passing it to the hungry men. "Captain," I said, standing next to him in the clearing where they'd parked a water truck, "don't make me order you to take sustenance. You're no help to me or the army if you faint."

"I'll get something for myself shortly, Major," he said with a grin that was meant to be reassuring and was anything but. "For now it's a sight for sore eyes to watch the men."

I couldn't disagree. I hadn't seen my men eat since the first day in the Pocket, when I'd watched Larney and two other privates sit at the edge of a funkhole and debate with the gravitas of congressmen whether they should eat one cracker apiece then or half a cracker each and share a cigarette. Judicious, they settled on the latter. Then Larney unrolled a copy of *Adventure* magazine from inside his signal panel—he had carried the flimsy publication through the entire advance—and read his fellows a story about pirates on the coast of New Guinea.

A familiar Brooklyn voice jarred me from the recollection. "Major! I made it!"

It was Abe Krotoshinsky, leading an officer from the 307th to our clearing. "I made it back to Division HQ like I said I would. I told 'em that you hadn't given up, Major, and that they'd better come get you, and fast!"

News of Krotoshinsky's return passed through the clearing like a wave. Crazed with joy, the nearby men dragged themselves to their feet to hail and touch him, as if they were witnessing a miracle, and perhaps they were. A private named Fein—who'd been all but inseparable from Krotoshinsky since Camp Upton—clasped his arm and said maybe a dozen times, "Gee, I never thought I'd see you again!"

I had to turn away to keep from crying.

From writers: that's how most of us citizen-soldiers had learned about war before we fought in one, whether that writing appeared in sensationalist magazines and cheap novels or in the *Iliad* and the *Aeneid* and the blood-soaked pages of the Old Testament.

It seems childish now to confess, but my own notions of battle all came from literature. When we arrived in the Argonne, I viewed the landscape through the lens of the pastoral poems I knew, ticking off correspondences and variances. No shepherds or sheep but plenty of birdsong: larks in the morning, nightingales at night. Ravaged rustic houses. Rural landscapes sundered cataclysmically, to no apparent purpose.

But the bold and hearty youths at least turned out to be much as the poets had described them—and I, chaste and masculine, had enjoyed the proximity to great male beauty. *Et in Arcadia ego*, though: Bill Cavanaugh, the best and most beautiful of them all, was gone, and his ugly death simultaneously confirmed the truth and proved the obscene inadequacy of those pretty verses. In life he had elevated all who served with him, and as he bled out shivering in my funkhole, the poison of war that killed him seeped into every good thing he had touched.

It was fitting, then, that the story of the Lost Battalion was told not by bards plucking lyres but by a pack of harried journalists who scurried like chipmunks through our glade that morning, eventually finding me seated on a stump next to what must have looked like an unprepossessing group of grimy, bearded infantrymen.

I had read these scribblers' accounts of doughboys going over the top with "throaty cheers" and shouts of "Remember the *Lusitania*!"—descriptions that squared badly with my own memories of men marching forward while eating and smoking, yelling a far less romantic vocabulary. Tableaux like the one our rescuers found never made the papers or the newsreels. The dead looked so small, and there were so many. The living were weary and stinking, shambling when they could walk at all.

The reporters seemed eager to get quotes from me, presumably since I'd been the commanding officer. I shooed them away; I didn't want to talk. "Don't write about me," I said. "Write about these men. New Yorkers and westerners. All fine."

Most took the hint, resolving to content their editors with what I assumed—correctly—would be preposterous accounts of my valor and humility and racing off in the hope of filing their stories first.

But one, a skinny fellow in a strange uniform, refused my brush-off. His hair was parted to the side and slicked across his wide forehead, and his ears stuck out like the handles of a jug. His lips were curled in a studied wry expression that suggested long experience with soldiers and with writing on deadline, an expression that I'd soon see belied his curiosity. His hair glinted in the sun with the shine of the well-fed.

"Better get yourself some iron rats, Major, before you keel over," he said, theatrically tucking away his notebook to show that we were now just two guys talking. "You want to take care of these mugs, sure. And just maybe you figure having something to do is the only thing still keeping you on the rails after the hell you went through. I'm seeing this a few times now, Major. My advice, for whatever it may be worth? If you're gonna crack up, do it soon. You'll get back on your feet faster."

I glared at him for his presumptuousness, then realized that he was trying to provoke me. For some reason I resented this ploy less than I appreciated his willingness to engage, to talk to me like a man instead of a monument. "You've seen this, have you?" I said with a vague wave at the reeking, cratered clearing. "A few times now?"

He smiled. "Well, not *this* exactly, Major," he said. "Nobody has quite been seeing *this* since maybe the Battle of Agincourt."

"Is that how you plan to write it up? 'We few, we happy few, we band of brothers'?"

"That, more or less, is the angle I'm working, all right." He extended a hand, which I took. I had forgotten that human skin could be so clean. "Runyon is the name," he said. "With the *New York American.*"

"Runyon," I said. I pictured myself in Mrs. Sullivan's parlor on a summer morning some years earlier, reading every word of a piece that I'd meant only to glance at. "Damon Runyon? I've read your writing on baseball. I'm not very interested in baseball, but I've read it."

"At your service," he said, touching his cap. "I have stepped away from the stickball beat these days, as you can tell."

"Bad luck for you, I'm afraid. You'll have to find another fellow for your Prince Hal. I've said all I need to say today."

"Sure about that, Major?" he said, patting the pocket where the notebook had gone. "The story gets written regardless. You prefer not to give me a quote, which is okay. This army is full of guys who love to see their name in the paper and who *heard* you say something one time, or *think* they heard you say it, or anyway can *imagine* you saying it, and what I need can be had from them. Now, I do not care to write bunkum, Major, so I wanted to chin with you for a minute to get the fix on what sort of egg you are. Neither do I make threats—not against war heroes anyway—so I will not have you thinking that that is what this is. I just want to tell you what is about to happen before it in fact happens."

Given the state I was in, it took me a moment to follow what he was saying. "I don't understand," I said. "Just write it up and leave me out of it. If you need a hero, there must be twenty or thirty men in this valley who'll fill the bill. George McMurtry. Neb Holderman. Krotoshinsky. Cepaglia. What do you need me for?"

Runyon looked as confused as I was. Then he laughed, not unkindly. "Sorry, Major," he said. "That particular horse has already come to exit that particular barn. While you were busy trying to keep your guys alive, ink-slingers like me were making you famous from Paris clear to Honolulu."

I felt nauseous. For the past few days, I had mostly forgotten that a world still persisted outside the war, and now that world was rushing at me before I'd had a chance to think about rejoining it. "Runyon," I said, trying to strike a sincere balance between kidding and serious, "as you may know, I'm an attorney in my civilian life. When you're drafting your story, you may wish to consider the ease with which I can litigate." I forced a toothy smile, which I imagine was perturbing. "That *was* a threat. Now, with the understanding that everything we say is off the record, can you tell me how the hell it came to be that everybody knows who I am?"

"Sure thing, Major," he said. "That only seems fair. Mind if I have a seat?"

Without waiting for an answer, he sank to the dirt beside my stump, folded his legs, lit two cigarettes, and handed one to me. I hesitated, then took it, sucking hungrily at the tobacco and collapsing in a coughing fit. He waited for me to finish before he spoke again.

"Probably one out of every three reporters covering the

Argonne," he said, "is a guy like me, in the employ of some New York paper."

"Which basically makes you press agents for the 77th Division," I said, "given how many of our men hail from New York."

"The army pays a sight better than what Mr. Hearst will give me," Runyon said, grinning to reveal a set of surprisingly white teeth. "Otherwise you are on the trolley. I know the 308th has many a westerner, too, but San Diego to Omaha is a hell of a paper route, so New York is where our bread gets buttered. You really are as smart a guy as they say."

"Flattery's appreciated," I said. "Though it will get you no comment."

"A fellow can't be blamed for trying," he said. "But yes, whatever the five boroughs' very own National Army Division does is damn well interesting to folks back home. Plays pretty good in Mr. Hearst's other papers at that. When your tenement boys turn out to be the best backwoodsmen this side of Daniel Boone, for instance . . . well, that sells a subscription or two."

"Because nobody expected it."

"Nobody," he said. "No offense meant. You fellows are full of surprises, and that always makes great copy. But Kidder Mead is the gent you really have to thank for your newfound notoriety. Know him? *New York World* before he enlists, now a press officer for First Corps. Hell of a newspaperman. You'll like him, Major: another fellow does his job a bit too well for his own good. The guy writes two releases a day, and they all read like dime novels. Anyway, early this week a UP reporter following the 77th gets wind of the pinch you and your guys are in and cables it to the bureau. His editor comes back with, 'Send more on Lost Battalion!' And the name sticks. The generals do not seem to like it very much—a lot about this episode will be hell to explain if anybody pushes them on it, which nobody will—but this fellow Mead, he picks headlines like handicappers pick horses, and he is never wrong. So he plays up the Lost Battalion angle. And that, my friend, is how you and your men come to be a batch of bona fide heroes."

As Runyon lit another cigarette off the one he was finishing, I watched the other reporters rove among the survivors. "What if we'd been wiped out?" I asked. "We very well might have been. How would Mead and the rest of you tell the story then?"

He shrugged, then removed the spent smoke from his lips, crushing it out on his boot heel. "Well, in such a case, it is no longer Agincourt," he said. "Instead we have the Alamo of the Argonne. The bigwigs can use that, too. Just like they used the *Lusitania*. The important thing is that you guys do not surrender. That is everything in a war like this. A war that is frankly, if you will pardon the expression, a fucking mess."

"Can't print that in a family paper."

"Add that," he said, "to the quite lengthy list of absolutely true things you can't print in a family paper. Listen, Major, on the level, things are about to become very strange for you and your men. Up till this week, you are just pieces on the checkerboard: dispensable, sure, but at least you know what your mission is. Now you are the big story. Something that nobody ever talks about is this: the folks back home are fretting not just about what to do if Johnny never comes marching home again but also about what to do if he does. They know that a very bad business is in progress over here, and they are scared about what exactly it does to their fine sons. The army is in sore need of guys like you, to show that it is all okay, that the sweet fellows who come over are the same sweet fellows who come back. And the showing of that is a mission with no end. If I know the newspaper business, you and your men are going to be watched for the rest of your lives. Every time one of you passes through any turnstile whatsoever—birth, marriage, death, new job, political appointment—your picture will be in the papers next to two or three columns, probably not too accurate, about the Lost Battalion. Are you following me?"

I nodded. "It'll be the same sort of hullabaloo that England makes over the survivors of the Light Brigade."

"You really are a brainy one," said Runyon. "Williams and Harvard? But your snoot isn't up in the air. Watch your step, Major, or you could end up a congressman. You got a doll at home, waiting by the fire?"

I gave him the rueful laugh that was my set response to this question, the one I'd been rehearsing since high school. "Nope," I said. "No doll, no dame, no tomato, no broad. However the current parlance puts it."

"Damn shame," said Runyon. "For both of us, that is. These stories always play better with a love angle. But this is off the record anyway, right? Speaking of which, if you will excuse me, Major, I need to go find someone I can quote."

"Naturally," I said, shaking his hand as he stood, relieved that he was leaving. "Thanks for giving me the lay of the land."

"Thank *you*, Major," he said. "For your time and for what you did here. When the army starts slinging the applesauce— and it will—try to remember that you held these fellows together and got them through. Good luck to you."

And he shuffled away, cool but eager. It was obvious that everyone was going to talk to him, and I hoped for the best result.

Not long after Runyon and I parted ways, I looked up to see Major General Alexander himself stomping toward me across the clearing, holding a starched handkerchief to his nose to shield it from the stench. His small eyes squinting, his eyebrows knit in a permanent frown, he congratulated me in his gravelly voice. I saw no cause for congratulations, but I thanked him.

"I'm pleased to promote you to the rank of lieutenant colonel, effective immediately," he said. He held out his hand to his adjutant, who filled its palm with my new insignia, silver oak clusters to replace gold. He took a half step forward as if to pin them to the shoulder loops of my ruined uniform, then realized that my height, which exceeded his by more than a foot, would require him to stand on my tree stump to do so. He grabbed my wrist instead, thrust them into my hand, and clapped me on the elbow as if trying to rouse me from unconsciousness.

Given that over half the men under my command were dead, promotion was the last thing I felt I deserved. I wondered for a moment whether the army would have made me a full colonel had *none* of my men survived.

I thanked Alexander again.

Reticence makes the talkative awkward; they trip trying to fill the silence. Even when they're major generals. "What a godforsaken pit you had your men dig into, Whittlesey," said Alexander, his arms akimbo, looking from the hill to the brook and back.

"It was actually rather pleasant when we arrived, sir," I said.

"Had you made it a bit farther, past that road," he said, pointing north, "then our 1st Army airplanes wouldn't have had such a hard time finding you in this thicket."

Rage narrowed my peripheral vision, like black tunnels closing in, a rage I hadn't known I felt. My pistol-bruised fist tightened around the new silver leaves, and I struggled against the impulse to hurl them into the mud—or to stuff them down the general's throat. My mouth fell open in a snarl as my mind assembled a response likely to land me in the stockade.

But Zip Cepaglia spoke before I did. "First Army artillery sure found us real good, General," he said. "Found us no problem."

Alexander wheeled like a hunting dog in the direction of Cepaglia's voice. Cepaglia stepped forward, chin up, to save him the trouble of guessing. The general stalked toward him but shifted his attitude as he became conscious of the many reporters within earshot.

"My boy," he said, laying a paternal hand, thick and paw-like, on Cepaglia's wiry shoulder. "That was not our artillery that fell on your position. It was the French. The French! Let's have no confusion about that."

He turned and raised his voice, speaking partly to the men, partly to the newspapers, mostly to himself. "You men have had a hell of a week," he said. "A hell of a week indeed. And we won't forget it! No we won't. You've made your nation proud."

The men were not favorably impressed by this performance, beyond being moved to try it themselves. "You hear that, Sarge?" J. J. Munson all but shouted, ostensibly to Red Cullen, who was standing right next to him. "It was the French that shelled us! Don't that just beat all?"

"Well, I'll be," said Cullen at the same volume. "I wonder how in the hell they got set up southeast of us when they were supposed to be southwest, on our left flank?"

"I guess war's plumb full of goddamn mysteries, ain't it, Sarge?" said Munson.

The general marched away, pretending not to hear, just as the men were pretending not to be speaking to him. I looked over at my three soldiers and tried to give them a cautioning smile, but with each flash of the sun off Alexander's spotless boots my mind returned to the helpless fury I'd felt while we were being shelled: the inferno of noise, the enemy watching in glee. Through all their cruelty, I never harbored an anger toward the kaiser's troops to match what I felt toward my own commanders at that moment.

It was a good lie, whoever had come up with it. Blaming the Germans wasn't an option—too many incriminating duds still littered our funkholes—but since the French 75-millimeter gun was also the main field weapon of the American artillery, guilt could be plausibly shifted in that direction. No one who'd actually been in the Pocket would believe the explanation, but that didn't matter. We were symbols now, no longer in control of our own stories.

After we got back to the States, many former members of the Lost Battalion would drift into my law office and beg me to lead a campaign to set the record straight. *Forget it*, I'd tell them, *The war's over. Leave it in the past. Make a life for yourself.* Advice I was no better able to follow than they were. They'd leave unsatisfied.

I hope these men were pleased when, a couple of years later, the army finally confessed that its own shells had indeed done the most grievous harm to the soldiers in the Pocket. By that time I myself was indifferent, well beyond satisfaction.

After watching General Alexander tramp through the clearing, receive and return salutes, and address a pack of reporters, Runyon among them, I became aware of a voice beside me.

"Major," said Cepaglia, low but insistent, as though he might have been saying it a while. "I done a thing that's maybe bad, and I want to talk about it. Okay?"

I shook myself alert. "Private," I said, "if General Alexander tries to argue that your behavior today was insubordinate, you can rest assured—"

Cepaglia was waving a hand in the general's direction as if shooing flies. "No, no, no," he said. "Fuck that guy. Fuckin' asshole. I don't come over to you to insult no generals. I gotta come clean about what I done."

This was the longest string of consecutive English words I had ever heard from Cepaglia, and I marveled at how much he'd learned since he'd first staggered off the train to Upton in his red shirt. "Of course, Private," I said. "What is it?"

Cepaglia looked suddenly overwhelmed to have my complete attention. His lower lip quivered: the only sign of weakness I ever saw in him. "It's about this coat," he said.

In a vague way, I'd been aware that Cepaglia had been wearing an oversize army trench coat, too large for his lean frame, but finding an explanation for this had been vanishingly low on my list of concerns.

"Red—Sergeant Cullen—he come in with it," Cepaglia said. "Against orders, I know. Not s'posed to bring no coats. But real good to have. Then Peabody, Lieutenant Peabody, his leg got smashed up. And he was such a big prince about it! You remember? It hurt him so much. But he never showed it. All the time he laughed, he said jokes. He kept us up. He kept the men up. We all said, 'That guy's gonna get a big medal.' Well, time goes on, and then we know: Peabody ain't gonna see that medal. Ain't gonna make it. So we give him the coat, the one Cullen had. The one coat in the whole outfit. It was our medal for him, for being brave. When he died, we don't know what to do. With the coat, see? Munson says it's bad luck to take a dead man's coat. But I says, 'I can't have no worse luck than I got right now,' and Munson says, 'Dibs on the coat, then.' And we take turns wearing it."

Cepaglia said all this while staring into the Pocket, his eyes steady and bright. It was already becoming hard to remember where our funkholes had been, the exact locations of certain momentous events. I'd lost track of Bill Cavanaugh's body; he was in a shallow grave with the other men who had died at around the same time, perhaps now partly uncovered or more deeply buried as falling shells and rain had moved the mud that had covered him.

"Cepaglia," I said, "I'm an officer, and I can say that you didn't break any rules. I'm an attorney, too, and I can say that you didn't break any laws. I'm not a priest, and therefore I'm in no position to absolve you, but it seems to me that you didn't do anything wrong. I knew Marshall Peabody pretty well, and my guess is that he'd be sore if you fellows *hadn't* taken your coat back. And I don't have Munson's expertise on luck, but yours seems damn fine."

Cepaglia sniffed, nodded sharply, and gave me a bashful

smile. "Okay, Major," he said. "Shit, Lieutenant Colonel, I mean! Thank you. I feel okay. I think you understand. We train and train, you know? We got pretty good, right? Pretty damn good soldiers. But then there's luck. And there's what we do for luck."

"We all have our superstitions," I said, thinking of Bill and his scapular. "Mine were my glasses. I told myself that if they didn't break, then I'd survive. I've never told anyone that."

His dark eyes grew solemn beneath his bunched eyebrows, charcoal black, still not much darker than his battle-smudged skin. "This army is a lot of fuckin' bullshit, sir," he said. "But I'm glad they make you a colonel. That's good. The guys, they all like you, and they're gonna be real proud."

With that, Cepaglia saluted crisply and zipped away, true to his nickname.

As it happened, his good luck would continue after the war. Munson's wouldn't, but I don't believe that his fate depended on the coat.

Major General Alexander ordered us rotated to divisional reserve, just as I had requested we be after the Small Pocket episode. Given our condition, I don't suppose there's much else he could have done with us.

This took us off the front lines, but it still left much work to be done, particularly by me. The 308th had to be drastically reorganized: new officers promoted to take the places of the many who'd been killed, replacements arriving from Calais incorporated into existing units. McMurtry had wanted to assist, but his bruised knee was getting worse, and he could do only so much. Regretfully, and at my insistence, he limped off to the infirmary.

Busy though I was, being in reserve gave me time to think in a way that had been all but impossible in the Pocket. I discovered, however, that thinking had become difficult. For seven days I'd been constantly possessed by an urgency to keep my men and myself alive under the threat of imminent attack. Now the threat was gone, but the urgency remained— and without any specific cause to warn against, it adhered to everything, like static electricity. Mundane administrative chores that I normally enjoyed and excelled at became nearly insufferable; they seemed pointless, even indecent in light of the slaughter under way a few miles to the north. I had trouble concentrating on these now-joyless tasks, and in my frustration I became quick to anger. I had never been an angry man before. It didn't suit me; I wasn't good at it.

Though it was no longer in any way productive, I thought constantly of the Pocket. In an effort to stop recalling the carnage and misery that I'd witnessed—that I had led my men into—I tried to think in more abstract terms. I wondered, for instance, at our popular epithet, as Runyon had explained it. Why had the "Lost Battalion" caught the public's imagination? Why "Lost" rather than "Beleaguered" or "Surrounded" or "Encircled"? "Lost" was, I supposed, the most romantic option, evoking ruined cities and sunken galleons. The idea disgusted me, and I was angry again.

But the plain fact remained that if the moniker hadn't caught on, we might never have been saved at all. I knew from my days training at Plattsburgh that one weak battalion didn't count for much from a tactical standpoint; four years into a war that appeared eternal, the British, the French, and the Germans had all sacrificed vaster quantities of men, and Colonel Stacey had made it clear that the army was prepared to do the same to us if it suited the generals' purposes. But the boisterously democratic American public was not yet inured to such imperial ruthlessness, and with news of the Lost Battalion flashing through headlines from coast to coast, certain gentlemen in Congress and the War Department had become skittish. Reports of our situation reached General Pershing from the top, not the bottom, and populated his thoughts with the disastrous consequences to home-front morale if we surrendered or if the army simply left us to die. Thus he ordered us rescued, no matter the cost. In a very practical sense, we owed our lives to Runyon and his ilk.

Though I made no attempt to seek it out, it took only a few days for someone to hand me an edition of the *New York American* that included Runyon's story. It exhibited the predictable degree of restraint: *Out of the fog of fighting that hangs over the Forest of the Argonne came limping today Whittlesey's battered battalion which made the epic defense in the dark glades and beyond. Out of this scullery of war*—scullery?—*the American infantryman is emerging as the greatest fighter the world has ever seen.*

As I read, I half expected a Sousa march to begin playing from thin air, like an enchantment in *The Tempest*.

A bit farther down, I found Runyon's account of the German request for surrender that hapless Hollingshead had delivered, and I was surprised to learn that I had responded by telling the Germans to "Go to hell."

At the time this was a source of amusement and mild irritation; I had no means of anticipating the number of occasions in the coming years when I'd be referred to in print or introduced at events as Charles "Go to Hell" Whittlesey.

In fact I had made no response whatsoever to the Germans' request, as I told reporters whenever they bothered to ask. McMurtry consistently corroborated my accurate account, often joking that as a thrifty New Englander I had chosen to conserve our remaining paper.

But Runyon hadn't lied exactly when he said that he didn't write bunkum. He had a source for the quote, and he wasn't alone, as it appeared in the less artful stories of other reporters, too. It had come, unsurprisingly, from no less lofty an authority than Major General Alexander. *What did Whittlesey say to the Germans?* the reporters had shouted at him in our bloody clearing, already knowing my answer and that it was insufficient for their purposes. *Well, I imagine he told them to go to hell,* said Alexander, and a dozen pencils sliced into a dozen notebooks. If any among them had scruples enough to omit the phrase, I imagine his account was simply drowned in the flood of consensus, dragged down by the dull weight of fact.

Today, aboard the *Toloa* as it steams slowly south, I can flourish my contempt for this cavalier approach to storytelling. The truth is that I was guilty of it myself.

When I emerged from the Pocket, I returned to regimental HQ, slept for the better part of two days straight, and awoke to find a fat stack of correspondence waiting for me, bound neatly in twine. A few letters—the first of many to come— were from complete strangers who'd read the early stories and written to thank me for my service. Most were from my family and my friends in New York, all of whom had reasonably surmised based on newspaper accounts that they might never see me again. Evidently they had decided that if I made it through alive, I should find assurances of their love and admiration immediately at hand.

I tried to read them and found that I could not. Each statement of praise made me feel more unworthy, more fraudulent, more guilty over the many soldiers whom I had not saved, the many dead men who had trusted me. In time I stopped trying, made careful records of the addresses to which I'd send vague but sincere thanks, and threw them all away.

My first response was to Bayard Pruyn. The fact that he'd been my law partner as well as my closest male friend somehow made it easier, providing a comfortable professional idiom wherein to cloak my disquiet.

Had I made any effort to communicate the true nature of what I'd experienced, it's doubtful that the censors would have let it though. But I made no such effort. I opted instead to allay concern—to convince him that I and all the others were holding up handsomely—and in so doing I nearly convinced myself.

I appreciate your last letter, I concluded, moving the pen slowly to control my tremulous hand. *If I said it any other way,*

I'd be trying to put into words what I cannot write. Because out here in the woods, Pruyn, where the hidden things of life begin to show, one learns new things. Friendships that can reach across five thousand miles and jog your elbow become pretty real and fine. And believe me, I felt your cheery voice when that letter reached me, at the end of a day that had been—oh, well, "some digging." It's a great life. Finest thing in the world, and we'll never have the same small outlook on men when it's over. Some of these fellows are just finer than anyone can say.

And yet, and yet.

I signed it, examining my signature closely in the hope that its familiarity would convince me that I remained who I had been. Then I folded it and slipped it into an envelope, leaving it unsealed for the army to read.

A collection of largely indistinguishable days passed, and then Major General Alexander summoned me for an audience.

I reported to his new headquarters, an elaborate complex that the Germans had built and then been forced to abandon in their retreat. He'd set up his command post there a day before he'd disregarded the misgivings of both Colonel Stacey and Brigadier General Johnson and ordered our advance up the Ravin d'Argonne. While we'd been in the Pocket being pulverized by our own artillery, he'd been exploring his new amenities: kitchens and mess halls, bathhouses with hot and cold taps, moving-picture theaters and bowling alleys. Even setting aside our misery in the Pocket, Alexander's present comforts compared favorably to the day-to-day lives that most of my soldiers led back home: plenty of the city men lived in cold-water flats, and plenty of the westerners had no running water. Little wonder, then, that he'd looked so jolly as he marched into our clearing. Even when directly confronted by it, he found our suffering beyond his grasp. He simply had no sympathetic imagination, which probably made it possible, or at least more pleasant, for him to perform the daily task of sending men to die.

In his office that evening, a fire roaring in the stove, I saw his high-handedness once more on display. "The 308th will be back in fighting form in practically no time, I hear," he said from behind his capacious desk. "Well done, Whittlesey. General Johnson didn't think there'd be much of a foundation left to rebuild on, but we've proved him wrong as usual, haven't we?"

Alexander's rhetorical question was so dishonest in its assumptions as to be unworthy of a reply. "We're ready for our orders, sir," I said. "When do we move out?"

"The regiment moves out," he said, consulting his watch, "in thirty-seven hours. You, however, move out tomorrow morning. I trust that gives you enough time to pack your things."

I made no attempt to hide my alarm, or my irritation. "Pardon me, sir?" I said. "You're separating me from my regiment?"

"You're damned right I am," he said. "Come on, man, you can't be surprised. You think we're going to send you to the front lines again? Did you lose your damned mind in that ravine?" He laughed as if what he said had been extremely clever. "You're a hero now. But you're a funny sort of hero, in that all you really did was survive when no one expected you to. Now, take that fellow Rickenbacker, the pilot. If he's shot down—as I expect he will be sooner or later—then all his victories still stand, don't they? But if we rescue 'Go to Hell' Whittlesey against all odds only to get him killed by sending him to the front again . . . well, that spoils everything! Particularly after all the losses we took trying to recover your command. That would amount to pure goddamned foolishness. You're valuable to the army—quite valuable—but not as a dead man. No, you'll stay behind the lines. More than likely you'll go back to the States."

I'd been prepared for stupidity and callousness, but the prospect of being parted from McMurtry and all the rest hadn't occurred to me. "What'll I do?" I asked.

"You'll train more men," said Alexander, as if this were as plain as his salt-and-pepper mustache. "A massive offensive

is planned for the spring, and we're going to need every soldier America the Beautiful can provide. The men you trained
at Upton turned into quite a bunch of bushwhackers, and we
can use more like them. Sergeant," he barked to his adjutant,
"the lieutenant colonel's travel orders, please."

Papers rustled, a typewriter chimed. "What about the others?" I asked.

"How's that?" Alexander said. "What others?"

"The two hundred men who walked out with me, General.
The Lost Battalion, as the papers have it. What happens to
them? Do they go back to the States as well?"

"Now you're being deliberately daft. We can't spare two
hundred souls purely for propaganda purposes. Besides, two
hundred names haven't been in the headlines of every newspaper in America. One has: yours. We'll try to keep the 308th
in supporting positions until the fresh conscripts have
learned the ropes and the memories of your adventure have
faded a bit. But we still have a war to win."

The adjutant slipped the typed forms beneath the major
general's hand, and with a stroke of Alexander's pen I was
out of the fight.

My train left at 11:00 A.M. the following day. I scarcely had
time to bid good-bye to my men. I worried what would become of them, as well as what they'd think of my departure.
They all seemed to admire me and to understand why I was
leaving, concepts that continued to evade my own grasp.

Before heading to the station, I turned in paperwork recommending an unusually large number of my men for decorations. I also filed a report on Revnes's conduct. I hesitated at
first to do so; I didn't necessarily want him to be court-martialed,
which his petition in favor of our surrender might well have
warranted. But recognition for the actions of the brave dimin-
ished in value when contrasting actions were not also faithfully
recorded, so I wrote up the account—avoiding prejudicial language, being sure to mention Revnes's commendable service
earlier in the advance as well as the extenuating circumstances

of his serious injury—and attached the note from him that Private Foss had delivered.

Then I boarded the train. As I seated myself in the club car, the luxury was so far removed from the HOMMES 40, CHEVAUX 8 boxcars we'd taken from Calais that I had to laugh, but the laugh was mirthless. I stared out the window in silence as we roared west to Brest.

From that sheltered port city on the Breton coast, I followed the deeds of the 77th Division as it fought on without me and captured Saint-Juvin, as well as Grandpré. While I didn't miss combat, I missed the satisfaction of discharging my duties. I felt guilty, at loose ends: I was safe and comfortable, war and all its dangers receding.

So, too, did I feel lonely, lonelier than ever, in a life that had been filled with considerable loneliness. I dispensed quickly with the few tasks that the army assigned me and spent my days roving the streets, crossing and recrossing the Penfeld River in the long shadows of the city's squat tower and ancient castle, their massive walls testifying to the assumption of a permanent state of war. I worked, and I walked, and I waited for the bureaucrats to sort out my fate.

One Saturday evening I went to a show in the American camp: skits put on by a troupe of army performers much like the one to which Lieutenant Revnes had been attached before he'd sought a transfer into a combat unit. The show was okay, amateurish but lively. I lurked in the back, as was my habit—partly because my height obstructed the views of other men but also because I didn't desire to be recognized.

My drifting attention was recaptured by a skit near the end: two soldiers in olive drab, portraying two soldiers in olive drab—not exactly an opportunity for thespian wonderworks but relevant to the audience's concerns and easy on the costume budget to boot.

"Gosh," said one of the players, brandishing a bare forearm, "I lost my wristwatch!"

"That's nothing!" said the other. "A major over in the 77th lost a whole battalion!"

Huge laughs. After an instant of shock, I laughed, too, and then became aware of my own laughter, which as a result began to seem, and then in fact became, forced. I'd known in an abstract way that people had been talking about me—more than that, that I was now a common subject, a topic upon which complete strangers might converse—but to watch it happen was unsettling, like haunting my own funeral. The sarcasm stung, but at least it seemed honest and thus less of a torment than adulation might have been. *Go on!* I wanted to shout. *Be skeptical of my heroism! I don't believe it either!*

My cheeks grew hot, and my mind flashed on a similar sensation: the inferno that bloomed in the Pocket when the two wounded *Flammenwerfer* operators incinerated themselves during that final German assault—their strangled shrieks, the smell of burning hair and melting flesh, the pulse of the blaze on our cheering faces through the cold and dirty air.

I slipped into the night. Passed the hospital tents with their smell of carbolic soap. Walked until the blush subsided from my skin, down by the waterfront. From the doorways of houses, prostitutes—all female—called to me, and I murmured, *"Non, merci."*

Amid the masonry wharves of the harbor, stone beneath my seat, I marveled at how soft I had stayed. Battle was said to harden a man—during my youth I'd heard this stated in the same offhand tones used to discuss First Communions and debutante balls—but in my case there had been no hardening, only a constant effort to hold together despite proliferating cracks.

Every noise made me jump, and the harbor was noisy, even at night, little creaks and slaps among the boats, along the waterline. We soldiers learned vigilance until our technique was flawless and thoughtless; we learned it or we died. But then what? Once we'd ingrained it so deeply as to make it automatic—stay alert, sleep light, trust nothing—we couldn't unlearn it when the danger had passed. Through discipline we had put our vigilance beyond our own control, out of the realm of skill, into the realm of instinct.

The days wore on, and each seemed to bring me more commendations, more reassurances of my unimpeachable leadership. In his official report on the Pocket, Colonel Stacey concluded, *There is not the slightest criticism of Whittlesey's splendid conduct.* In a newspaper story that my mother clipped and mailed, Neb Holderman called me—or was quoted as calling me—*stout-hearted, and as game as they make them. He seemed to be cool and calm in the Pocket as though we were back at a rest area, and my hat goes off to him for being a good soldier and a true American.* Every one of these sincere and well-meant statements helped convince me that I was losing my mind.

I sailed for New York on Halloween—a relief, because it meant that I was finally doing something, even if I wasn't sure exactly what.

I leaned against the upper deck railing of the transport ship—reading Frost's *Mountain Interval* and remembering as I did so my first encounter with Bill Cavanaugh. I was imagining the conversation we two might have had had he been there with me, alive and bound for home—when the news came that the war was over.

An armistice had been signed, putting to an end those fifty-two months of hubris and idiocy. In light of this announcement, the blue-gray expanse of the Atlantic continued to look exactly the same.

Eventually American lighthouses came into view—Chatham, Nantucket, Montauk—and then Long Island and the yawning mouth of the Hudson in the dawn light. When the transport ship chugged into the Upper Bay, I saw the Statue of Liberty, her huge turquoise form at dramatic variance from the tiny gold likenesses of her that adorned the shoulders and helmets of the 77th. Here was something else that Alexander had taken from me and portrayed as a gift: the chance to share this with my men, to see their faces as she came into view. Our New Yorkers had worked as clerks, tradesmen, civil servants, chauffeurs for Standard Oil in Brooklyn, engineers at Otis Elevator in Yonkers, electricians in the Brooklyn Navy Yard, Western Union messengers, insurance adjusters, detectives with the NYPD, saloon owners, bookkeepers, post-office clerks. The upstaters had been farmers but also machinists, customs inspectors, and college students. The westerners had been rivermen, stock raisers, horse breakers, miners, timber cutters, and railroad brakemen. Some had been lawyers like me, and as I planned on going back to be. I thought of those men as we crept upriver, and also of all those who'd been with me on the *Lapland* but would never return from France.

At the North River Piers, they didn't discharge me immediately, but they did send me home. With the Armistice signed, there would be no spring offensive and thus no training for one. Major General Alexander would soon have to vacate his lavish German-built quarters. Unlike my comrades, who would languish in France for weeks, then months, as 1st Army, unprepared as ever, grappled with demobilization, I was free.

Or so I thought.

Mrs. Sullivan—overcome with joy to see me, insistent on furnishing me with a seemingly limitless breakfast—didn't have my room ready yet, so I took the train to western Massachusetts to visit my family. I'd carried a photo of my mother in the upper-left pocket of my uniform all through the war, and the face that greeted me at the door was unchanged, which didn't seem possible. I reminded myself that I had been gone only seven months.

As soon as she finished hugging me, my mother handed me an invitation to appear at a "War Night" celebration of the Williams College Club in Manhattan the following week.

"You'll go, won't you, Charlie?" she said. She seemed to understand my combat service as dangerous and demanding but otherwise not essentially different from times I'd spent away at school. It occurred to me that my letters home had never given her any reason to think otherwise.

While at that moment the prospect of addressing fellow alumni in the familiar confines of the Williams Club seemed as alien as sprouting wings to frolic in the clouds or gills to root through the unlit abysses of the sea, I could not think of any polite way to decline. The exercise of trying to invent a plausible conflicting engagement made me aware of how devoid of order my life had just become, and the resulting panic convinced me that renewed sociability was the wiser course to pursue. I wrote my reply with my mother looking on, and she mailed it before I could change my mind.

The announcement of my appearance packed the club with over three hundred Williams men. Even shifting the event into the main hall from the small clubroom left spectators spilling into the vestibule and clustering on the stairways. My fellow speaker, Alonzo "Zo" Elliot—the evening's original main attraction, who'd composed "There's a Long, Long Trail," a song every British and American soldier knew by heart, and who had then gone on to Stateside service in the Signal Corps— was gracious about being upstaged, and indeed seemed honored to share the bill. With a chorus of six doughboy veterans, he sang his own beloved composition, as well as "The Star-Spangled Banner" and the Williams College fight song.

In that unruly atmosphere, more evocative of a football game against Amherst than a reception in polite society, the club president gave me an introduction built entirely around my famous fictional reply to the German request for surrender. "It was a command, a malediction, and a prophecy combined!" he cried.

The crowd cheered for what the bulletin of the alumni society later assured me was a full five minutes; to me it felt like weeks, akin to paralysis in a nightmare.

This was not the event I had prepared for. Had I known that I ought to prepare for it, I still wouldn't have done so—peppy patriotism was not my style—but at least I wouldn't have been caught by surprise. In my speech I spoke not a word about the ordeal in the Pocket. I could feel the audience grow restless as I praised the kindness of the French civilians. I fear that my face must have looked quite melancholy as I sat down again.

As I did, Zo Elliot, a natural cheerleader with the best of intentions, attempted to rescue me by yelling, "But did you tell those krauts to go to hell?"

I'm ashamed to admit that I nodded. By then I was prepared to do anything to get the night over with. A whoop went up, and several men hollered, "But did they go?"

And three hundred voices answered, "They sure did!"

I resolved to be more careful about my engagements in the future.

After respectfully declining a few invitations to serve as a jingoistic prop, I agreed to appear at the opening of the Union Peace Jubilee at the Sixty-ninth Regimental Armory, an audience and occasion that I hoped would be better suited to my demeanor. Six thousand Episcopalians attended to hear remarks from me and Treasury Secretary William G. McAdoo, President Wilson's son-in-law. Few in the crowd recognized me—with my slender build, my stooped shoulders, my scholarly mien—as "the foremost American military hero of the Great War" until McAdoo introduced me, calling me "a modern Cincinnatus who had laid aside his sword to go back to the pursuits of peace." But they gave me a three-minute standing ovation. Fidgeting, waiting for the cheers to subside, I could tell that the speech I'd prepared wouldn't be any better received than the one I'd given at the Williams Club. But that, I reasoned, just meant they needed all the more to hear it.

"The American soldiers are not going to come back hating the Germans," I told them. "No man who has been out in the frontline trenches facing the enemy is going to return with malice in his heart. The paramount trait of the American soldier is kindness. If he met the kaiser on the road, he would be as willing to share his cigarette with him as with anyone else."

In the pauses where I had left space for applause, I detected only coughs and the shifting of posteriors in seats. Peace Jubilee or no, no one had come to hear a call for compassion. When I sat down without delivering the rousing war story all had been anticipating, the Episcopalians sat baffled until McAdoo's headmasterly clapping goaded thousands of pairs of hands to join in.

And yet at the reception afterward, I was inundated by further requests to speak. Why would they want me, having seen me for what I was: an officer who'd failed as a tactician and was failing as a rhetorician, a man who'd lost his battalion and now couldn't find his voice?

What these smiling, handshaking people wanted, I decided, was simply someone with a famous name—or, more precisely, they wanted to be the sort of people who could *get* someone with a famous name—to show up at their events. They didn't care how well I spoke; it didn't matter if I spoke at all. I could sit quietly, on display, like a hunter's trophy or an exhibit in a museum. I was proof of something.

Still, didn't I have some responsibility to testify—even if only mutely—on behalf of my men? How might I assist them? What would they have me do?

On Thursday, December 5, at Fort Dix in New Jersey, the army gave me my honorable discharge: I was a civilian again.

But my life and my name no longer belonged to me and never would.

I resolved to agree to appear at Liberty Loan drives and Red Cross fund-raisers, but only if I could remain silent on the topic of the war. I vowed to take every opportunity to deflect attention from myself in the direction of those who were more deserving or in greater need.

On Boston Common on Christmas Eve, snowflakes floating

down like feathers—*Cher Ami*, I wondered, *where are you now?*—Major General Clarence Ransom Edwards, Commander of the Department of the Northeast, pinned the Medal of Honor to my chest. When the journalists hit me with their usual barrage of Lost Battalion questions, all I said was, "I don't know what I would have done without Captain George C. McMurtry."

McMurtry was also among the first to receive the medal, but his was awarded with little fanfare. Holderman wouldn't get his until 1921, following years of humiliating pleas from me.

After the ceremony, alone in a city that was not my own, it occurred to me that I could quite easily find a place to change out of my uniform, then stroll through the crowds, pick someone up, and end my many months of celibacy. But I was being watched too closely. I was watching myself.

Instead I took a train to my parents' home in Pittsfield.

The snowflakes shivered outside my window. I found it unbearable to think about the fact that so many people were thinking about me, but I couldn't stop thinking about it. I couldn't stop thinking.

CHAPTER 15

CHER AMI

~~~~~~~~~

Patriotic parades are for politicians and civilians, not for soldiers, not for pigeons.

My early-spring arrival in the United States had been disheartening in ways I'd expected—Baby Mine and I had been parted for good—and also disorienting in ways I hadn't. At first America had seemed particularly but not essentially different from Europe: new trees, new birds, new insects, new flowers, all behaving as such things behaved. But the difference in the human sphere was more profound. Certain smells that I had always relied on to lead me toward civilization—the weathering of quarried stone, ancient metal tools buried in the earth, soil that had been tilled and retilled since before history began—were all but absent here. The cities felt provisional, contingent, and frankly fake, as if everything I saw had been assembled to fool me. Or someone. Or everyone.

In those joyous days after the Armistice, the Americans seemed to move in impromptu rhythms, agitated and poorly fitted to my own dark mood. My thoughts, if I let them, took up a drumbeat of death and loss, loss and grief. Humans, particularly groups of humans, prefer their cadences and their abstractions to be upbeat. Heroism. Democracy. Peace peace peace.

And so the powers-that-be decided that shortly after its return home—and despite its weariness after languishing in France, despite its soldiers' freshly cultivated distaste for marching on pavement—the 77th Infantry Division would parade through the streets of New York City. On the appointed day, over a million people gathered along a five-mile route in beautiful spring weather, amid dogwood flowers and the scent of lindens.

With a whistle blast signaling a rattle of snare drums, Major General Alexander started the cavalcade up Fifth Avenue, leading astride a shining black horse, looking as proud as a conquering caesar. Twenty-five thousand soldiers poured from the side streets behind their commander into a column massive and precise, coordinating by invisible signals, like a shoal of minnows or a murmuration of starlings. I imagine that the soldiers and onlookers alike were almost unanimously thrilled by this display and felt themselves to be part of something noble and unstoppable.

Those among us who did not experience this thrill felt very lonely indeed.

We pigeon veterans occupied a position of honor near the front. Corporal Gault carried us—President Wilson and me—in an elevated ceremonial basket with a gapping weave that ensured we could be admired. Behind us stretched a living river of gleaming steel and olive drab, the men marching with a swing and a snap through the brisk, clear morning in canyons walled with claps, tears, and cheers.

Before us marched the surviving ambulatory remnants of the 308th Infantry Regiment, at least those who hailed from New York or who'd stayed in the area after being officially deactivated; most of the westerners had gone back west. But it was the hometown fellows—the Liberty Boys, New York's Own—whom the crowd really wanted to see, the men who'd grown up in the nearby tenements, who'd been expected in their lives to amount to little or nothing of significant value, who'd trained and traveled and fought and finally kicked the kaiser hard in the hindquarters, showing the French and the Brits a thing or two in the process. If the lowest of New York's low could do that, then what might their best be capable of?

Walking in front, as if promising an answer to that very question, was Lieutenant Colonel Charles Whittlesey, fully a head taller than most other marchers. I saw him before he saw me: the flash of his round glasses, then his features in profile as he glanced at the crowd, features somehow made more mature by lines of tragedy. He appeared as alert and intelligent as always, shy and mild, the unlikeliest of warriors. He also seemed uninjured, which made me glad but also aware of the stitched-up wreck I had become. I watched his long stride until I was almost hypnotized.

The men did an eyes-left at a reviewing stand on the steps of a grand public library dripping with red-white-and-blue decorations, then continued north to the edge of Central Park, where bands played cheerful tunes from temporary platforms. In the lulls between their brassy blasts, I heard the two-note spring calls of male chickadees going about their business in the trees; they sounded slightly taunting.

A delicate breeze riffled the petals off the cherry blossoms, and the men looked snowed on. I thought of Buck Shot, his feathers fluttering to the mud.

The parade's initial tidiness had begun to relax, the soldiers becoming individual men again. Ruddy and suntanned faces aglow, they were happy to be home and glad to show it. I noticed them noticing the younger adult male spectators in civilian clothes, wondering—perhaps with resentment, perhaps curiosity—why they had not fought.

As we passed a reservoir at the park's north end, a tottering man—probably a vagrant, certainly a drunk—stumbled from the crowd to point at the Statue of Liberty patches sewn on the shoulders of the men's uniforms, gold against a field of blue. "Is that Lady Liberty?" the man shouted. "Or a French mademoiselle with a candle, huntin' for your Lost Battalion?"

"If I weren't hauling you two," Gault said through a clench-toothed smile, "I'd haul off and sock him."

The parade concluded in Harlem, where the abundance of brown faces in the crowd prompted grumblings and muttered slurs from some of the men. It is perhaps unnecessary to say that we pigeons, a species characterized by dramatic

individual variation in color and form, find the human preoccupation with small differences in skin color very con-
founding. Throughout the war I noted with disappointment
how frequently soldiers would use sex and race to shore up
their own fragile concord, as if any acrimony might be
smoothed over through agreement that women and darker-
complexioned persons are weak, stupid, and unreliable.

"On such a happy occasion as this," said President Wilson,
fluffing his feathers, "might one be forgiven for wishing that
human bigotry be suspended for the day? Or for a few hours,
at least?"

I agreed. Some among the 308th became quite vocal in
their racism after the Small Pocket incident, during which a
Negro regiment, the 368th, had been unable to advance to
cover their flank, thereby becoming a convenient repository
of blame after Whittlesey and his men were surrounded. As
a few fair-minded soldiers pointed out, given that the 368th
had been furnished little training and even less proper
equipment than its white counterparts and had been ineptly
led by its white commanders against an unusually tough
German position, it had performed quite creditably under
the circumstances. This, however, had not been an argument
that most of the regiment was prepared to entertain, and it
was swiftly buried in the self-serving nonsense of officers'
reports. I thought about telling President Wilson this story
as the parade came to an end—it was rare that I knew about
something he didn't—but didn't see the point.

The alleged failure of the 368th at Binarville, coupled with
the manifest unwillingness of most white American soldiers
to serve with Negro units, persuaded the army to assign
those units to the more legitimately egalitarian French,
where they generally excelled. One in particular, the exten-
sively decorated 369th—the first American unit to reach the
Rhine—hailed from the very neighborhoods where our
parade concluded. A few weeks earlier, they had paraded
this same route up Fifth Avenue into Harlem to be met by

cheering crowds and signs reading MAKE AMERICA SAFE FOR DEMOCRACY. President Wilson and I wouldn't hear a word spoken about them until many years later, during our mutual tenure at the Smithsonian.

From atop his steed, Major General Alexander made a show of reviewing his troops a final time: twenty-five thousand hands saluting him spiffily.

In the mild unruliness that ensued, the men falling out of formation, I saw Whittlesey full on, his body in shadow, his face in light, looking even taller in his peaked cap. The right kind of eye contact can feel tactile, like being physically touched, and so it was when the pale blue eyes behind Whit's spectacles met my remaining golden one. An unmistakable thought passed between us: *That one, I fear, is not long for this world.*

"Corporal," Whit said, tapping Gault's shoulder, "I know that bird! Cher Ami, I mean."

"Everyone does, Colonel Whittlesey," Gault said, laughing, then holding our basket toward Whit for a better look. "Just like everyone knows you. It's an honor to meet you."

"Thank you," said Whit. He didn't quite seem to be listening, just staring fixedly at me, although I knew he had stopped seeing me. I knew what—whom—he was thinking of. I was thinking of Bill, too.

"I—" Gault said, then cleared his throat. "I was on duty when Cher Ami came in with your message, sir. I telephoned it to Major Milliken, my CO, and he rang the 152nd to stop them. Cher Ami flew fast, sir—very fast, when you consider the shape he was in—and we relayed the message right away. I know they say it was the French, sir, but I know it was us. I think it's terrible, the way the army has—"

"She," said Whit.

"Sir?"

"The shape *she* was in," said Whit. His reedy voice, slightly raised, sounded both distracted and unhinged. "Corporal, on behalf of all of us who were in the Charlevaux Ravine, I'd like to thank you for your fast and accurate handling of my message. As bad as the incident was, it might have been a good deal worse. I'm satisfied that you and your commanders did a fine job, and I hope you'll give them my thanks."

"Thank you, sir. That will come as a great rel—"

"Now, about Cher Ami," said Whit. "May I have that pigeon, please? I understand that she would need to be formally designated as surplus material. I'm familiar enough with the process, and I'm happy to assist with the administrative end of it."

Gault froze, his mouth agape.

I flapped my wings to get the men's attention and poked my head between the basket's wide warps, cooing to signal that I was in favor of this idea.

"What on earth are you doing?" asked President Wilson. "Have you gone mad? That officer won't know a blasted thing about keeping birds."

"He'd learn," I said.

President Wilson was correct, of course: there was no way that Whit could take care of me remotely as well as Gault and his colleagues at the Camp Vail lofts, especially given the special care that my injuries required. That didn't matter to me. I was in pain all the time, not sure how much longer my body would hold up even in the custody of the army's best veterinarians. And I felt as though Whit and I belonged together.

Understandably, Gault decided to take the request as a joke. "Oh, that's a good one, Colonel," he said. "But these little fellows can be a lot of trouble and a real mess besides. Wouldn't you rather have a dog?"

"No," said Whit, and then he stopped to cough rackingly before going on. "I have some sense of what would be required. I knew her handler, a man called Bill Cavanaugh. Very knowledgeable. Enthusiastic. Perhaps I could assist you as a volunteer first, until I know the ropes. I work as an attorney, but I can come to New Jersey on weekends. I'm sure I could learn to take excellent care of her."

"I understand, sir," said Gault, although he clearly did not. "I'll check with command and let you know."

Whit flinched, coming back to himself, like someone who'd been drifting off to sleep, speaking without realizing it. "Sorry," he said. "What's your name, Corporal?"

"Gault, sir. George Gault."

"My apologies, Gault. I'm afraid I got a bit carried away by my comic scenario. I'm a New Englander, and our senses of humor are very dry. And I must admit that I'm a bit overcome by the sight of my old pigeon comrade."

"That's quite all right, Colonel," said Gault. "The two of you went through hell together."

Whit put a finger through a gap to stroke my wing, and I could feel a small but constant tremor, one that his fellow men couldn't see but that went to the core of him. He bent his towering frame to lean closer, and I saw myself reflected in his spectacles. "You're looking well," he said, "all things considered."

"The Vet Corps really performed a miracle on him—on Cher Ami," said Gault, avoiding the question of my sex without conceding the point. "And that wooden leg really works. I wouldn't have guessed. Cher Ami is flying quite well. Getting used to the missing eye, too."

But Whit wasn't talking to Gault; he was talking to me. "Thank you, dear friend," he said. "I'm glad of the chance to see you one last time, for old times' sake."

I often wish that humans could understand me, but rarely so painfully as in that moment. Though I spent only a few days with him in the Argonne—scarcely more than a week—Whit had impressed me as one of the finest men I'd encountered: brave and capable, perceptive and kind. His participation in the war helped me understand the genuine values that humans used to justify it, and seeing the waste it made of him— even after it left his body all but unscathed—convinced me of its essential malevolence, its ability to shape individual and collective human will to its destructive purposes, rather than the other way around. I wanted to tell him that.

I wanted to tell him that when we made our separate Channel crossings into France, we'd both been younger than seemed imaginable; a few months after the Armistice, we were both old beyond our years. Our status as heroes had made us strangers to ourselves, transfiguring us into icons of victory, undefeated and indestructible, not subject to the limits of living beings. But so too had fame's spotlight pinned a shadow to each of us that no one else could see, an uninvited guest who sat at our meals, woke us from rest, and impelled us to return again and again to the battlefields we thought we had escaped.

I wanted to tell him that I understood.

"Good-bye, Corporal," Whit said, forcing a funny little smile. "Thanks for putting up with my jest. Good-bye, Cher Ami. A finer bird never flew the skies."

His voice broke with what might or might not have been another cough, and he hastened away without waiting for Gault's reply. I watched him go, moving steadily through men he had commanded and men he hadn't, waving and returning salutes, until he made an abrupt turn and almost collided with another soldier, one nearly as tall as he. The two men spoke, then walked off in step.

Gault, perplexed by the entire exchange, lifted our basket and carried us in the opposite direction, past the row houses toward Lenox Avenue, where motor trucks waited to return us to our lofts in New Jersey.

And that was the last I saw of Charles Whittlesey.

Five miles in from the Atlantic, with rail sidings out of Hoboken and access to the port of Little Silver, Camp Vail was an ideal site for the Army Signal Corps School, and to the humans in charge we pigeon veterans were ideal teaching tools.

Those among us who were not too seriously injured could help soldiers learn the care, handling, and training of homers. Those who were fertile could breed, building up the pigeon army within the human one. And those who were simply heroic messes—who could neither fly well nor breed successfully—could be deployed to educate the public about the importance of keeping a supply of carrier pigeons at the ready for when the next war came.

The next war. An acrid glop of vomit rose in my crop whenever I thought about it. We were often assured that the Great War—"great," they called it—had been the war to end all wars, but this was spoken far too often to be true. It was widely known that the treaties formalizing the end to the fighting were not being written with an eye toward preventing future hostilities, and the U.S. Army had resolved not to be caught short of pigeons again.

President Wilson and I shared our home loft with fellow battle-tested veterans: Lord Adelaide, a blue-checkered cock, and Blanchette and Petite Rosette, twin red-checkered hens who'd made it through still healthy enough to be bred. Aside from these, dozens more came and went.

Baby Mine was not among them.

To a casual observer, it might seem that we wounded heroes had the lightest duties, but a mascot's work is the killing kind. The damage I'd sustained on my last flight to Rampont lingered. Every morning I woke up weary.

From an anatomical standpoint, we homing pigeons are architectural perfection—our physiognomy ideal for what we're supposed to do—but my architecture was wrecked. Whenever I flew, my torn muscles and dented ribs nearly pulled me apart from the inside; whenever I *didn't* fly, my body tensed and sickened from its innate desire to be airborne. I became like one of the shell-shredded cathedrals we'd sometimes see in France: my soaring arches and unsullied lines were still visible, but they'd never regain their wholeness.

Rest might have helped, but I got little. Monday through

Friday the Signal Corps took me by train or motorcar to elementary and high schools, town-hall meetings and ice-cream socials. Though the physical exertion was minimal—I sat in a basket—the experience of repeatedly traveling a certain distance from Camp Vail and calculating the route and speed and elevation of a return flight that I would never be allowed to make became mentally taxing.

But I had a duty to perform. Civilians demand heroes to process vast loss.

These events were monotonous, except when they were harrowing. One sunny morning Corporal Gault carried me not to a waiting car but to the auditorium of the Signal Corps School, where the folding seats had unfolded beneath the torpid forms of disfigured men. Incapacitated veterans. As Gault walked up the aisle to place my cage onstage, I cataloged their wounds, comparing them to my own by instinct and in sympathy.

A man whose jaw had been torn off by a bullet. Another whose teeth had been shattered by shrapnel. Another whom mustard gas had blinded. Wheelchairs lined the walls, containing men with rolled trouser legs, empty fabric pinned to itself. Sleeves hung limp and vacant, fingers and hands and forearms and arms blown off by explosions or lost to gangrene and amputation.

The army had brought them here to educate and cheer them, to convince them that their future could, and ought to, be bright.

I hunched in my basket as a press officer took the podium.

"Rehabilitation offers the promise of living an independent life as a contributing member of society," he said. "We have brought you here to assist you. There is a way forward. Our victory in Europe has proved what the world has long suspected: this will be the American century, an era of unprecedented opportunity and prosperity. Others like you are already integrating themselves back into the engine of our national economy. You shall watch some of them here, in this short moving picture."

He raised his hand to signal the projectionist. The lights dimmed, and we watched a brief film that might as well have been called *So, You Got Maimed in the War!* Images of injured doughboys flashed between intertitles of soothing assurances that their lives could proceed normally.

The press officer read the words in a lockjawed Yale accent for the benefit of the sightless. "'I will never become a charge upon public society,'" he said, ostensibly on behalf of the man on the screen, who was missing a leg—his right, like mine. "'When the government fits me with a new limb, I'll be good as new. As soon as I can learn to use my new leg handily, I'll go back to the machine shop once more.'"

Though the human audience couldn't recognize the sound as such, I couldn't help but burst with ghastly laughter at a scene near the end: a group of amputees, beaming cheerfully, hobbling about a grassy field in a staged game of baseball. One-legged soldiers hopped around the bases while their wheelchair-bound comrades cheered from the sidelines, as if the ability to go through the motions of the national pastime were conclusive proof that everything would be all right for these men.

"'In veterans' hospitals,'" read the press officer, "'men learn to use prosthetic limbs, undergo reconstructive surgery, and receive care for respiratory ailments. The blind receive special assistance in the learning of braille.'"

When the lights went up, the press officer asked whether the men had any questions.

One blind veteran spoke toward the sound of the officer's voice. "All the special assistance in the world," he said, "won't change the fact that I'm a charity case and always will be. I sit in the hospital all week, forgot, till every Sunday, when the volunteers come out to read to me. Feeling guilty after church, probably. Feeding the blind ape peanuts."

"If your question is what the army can do to help," the press officer said, "then we'll see to it that you get some information on braille. You won't have to rely on others to read anymore. Next question? You, Private, in the front row."

The man stood up. The lower half of his face had the texture and sheen of melted candle wax; the army surgeons had done their best, but it had not been very good. "In my city," he said, "they've passed an ordinance, a law, that says people with severe facial injuries have to wear masks or hoods in public, so as not to scare women and children. They'll fine you if you don't comply. What am I supposed to do?"

"Our army doctors are creating specially designed masks that hook around a patient's ear to add an anatomically correct chin, nose, or cheek to a face," said the press officer. "We'll have more information on that and a variety of other salutary developments today after lunch. But first—"

"Not about the mask," the private said. "About the law. How do I get them to change the fucking law?"

The press officer's assistant hastened over to quiet him. "*But first*," the press officer said, "we have a special guest, by the name of Cher Ami. Corporal?"

Gault looked mortified, apologetic for still being ablebodied. He lifted my basket and carried me to the podium, where he delivered a speech that I had heard dozens of times, synopsizing my heroics, detailing my honors, then running through the list of wounds from which I had gloriously recovered. Although the speech was always the same, the catalog of injuries had a sicker resonance than usual and seemed almost scolding. *If this pigeon can get better, why can't you? There you go, enjoy your moral.*

At that point Gault usually held me in his arms as schoolchildren filed by to pat or squeeze me, but these men were in no shape to file, so he made his way up the aisle instead. Any man who wanted to could examine my wounds; the blind could lay their fingers upon me. As I was passed around like a relic or a fetish, gentle hands touching my feathers, I considered how many of these men would spend their lives alone. Even given the war's substantial winnowing of the population—over a hundred thousand Americans killed, over sixteen million dead worldwide—it would be hard for disfigured men to meet women or to marry. I sympathized. These men and I had been poorly used.

But between us was one crucial difference so far as the public consensus was concerned. To marriageable women, and indeed to everyone else, I was cute, even with my wounds. *Especially* with my wounds. In the beginning I was honored to appear before these men in the hope of lifting their spirits, but it quickly became apparent that that was not the point of putting me on display. By showing me to the injured men, the army told them, *This fluffy, cooing thing with its wooden leg is what the public will know of the ravages of war. Your task is to remain unseen.* By showing me to the public, the army told them, *War is a game, and its costs are light enough to be borne by even this little bird.* The burgeoning American empire demanded sacrifices; my job was to help make them acceptable, even entertaining.

In that limited and perverted sense, I continued to function as a messenger pigeon.

———————

After my communion with the maimed, I felt more exhausted than ever, which mattered not one bit to whoever made my busy schedule. The following day we were traveling as usual, to a public high school in Perth Amboy.

These propagandizing excursions were always variations on a theme. In a hot gymnasium with squeaking waxed floors or in a hushed auditorium plushed in red velvet, Gault told the story of the Lost Battalion, which I did my best to ignore in the hope of keeping memories at bay. The story he told was largely about me, but it was not my story.

Then the time came for me to be embraced by the students. I loved them so much, these American children, even the obstreperous ones of middle-school age, even the high-schoolers acting tough. *Don't let them convince you that this was good, or worthwhile,* I'd try to tell them, but they couldn't understand and probably thought that I was just an exceptionally friendly bird.

In Perth Amboy, Gault tailored his banter to our location, as he always tried to do. Since the school was on Eagle Avenue, he began by saying, "The eagle is the emblem of our proud United States, but it's the pigeon to whom we owe our present state of liberty."

Before I got coddled and patted, a tall and scholarly young man with a mien that reminded me of Whit's stood to ask, without any hostility, "Can an animal truly be devoted or brave? Or does it just act as it's been bred to act?"

Smiling, Gault stepped forward to provide some studied, dismissive answer, but then the gym filled with unintelligible voices, soft but sharp: the student's peers, taunting him for having the temerity to question this fun new national myth.

"Now, hold on," said Gault. "That's a good question. A real good question." He stepped back, resting a hand on top of my cage. "If we ask that question about animals," he said, "then we ought to ask it about men, too. If you think that Colonel Whittlesey was brave—and I do—or that his men were brave—and I do—then I believe you can think the same of Cher Ami. There's a lot of fancy words we could use to talk about bravery, but I think it comes down to what your teachers would probably call determination and what most of us in the army call pluck. When I was learning about war pigeons, my sergeant told me, 'No bird will home unless it has plenty of pluck,' and I endorse his opinion. See, I don't think it's the magical ability to navigate—to know where they are and how to get home—that makes these birds special. I think every pigeon has that, even the ones you see on the street. No, what makes our birds special is the plain fact that they'll do it—no matter the distance, no matter the danger. The men of the Lost Battalion knew they could give up and raise the white flag at any time, but they didn't. They got through because

they had the pluck to stick it out. And Cher Ami isn't any different. He took his licks and he did his job, a display of pluck
that'd be phenomenal in a human being. Now, maybe that
kind of pluck comes from good breeding, or good training, or
heaven above, or somewhere else. It's interesting to think
about, but in the end I don't know how much it matters. When
you and your buddies are in a pinch and you need pluck to
pull you through . . . well, wherever it came from, it's inside
you. It's your character. This bird's got it, and I think if we
pay attention to their example and stay on the up-and-up,
then we'll have it, too."

The auditorium applauded. Gault looked pleased, and surprised at himself. Careworn as I was, I felt touched by his
answer.

In my heart, however, I could feel myself failing, the old
wounds paining. On the journey back to Camp Vail, past the
pine trees and over the river, I kept imagining myself less as
having pluck than as *being* plucked, feather by feather.

It is the nature of a homer to adjust quickly to new surroundings, but I was still surprised to discover how soon I began to
feel American, despite my English origins and my fancy—
Americans always regarded anything Gallic as fancy—
French name. The expeditious mixing of those from diverse
backgrounds was something that I admired and still admire
about my new country, and as other pigeon veterans arrived
who'd served in every theater of the conflict, I found that I
could readily connect with them.

We each had our own way of dealing with our memories,
however. As summer approached, I found myself looking
backward more than forward, and although I maintained my
sociability, those who knew me could tell that something was
amiss.

"You're not eating, Cher Ami," said President Wilson one
evening when we were momentarily alone. "And these seeds

that Gault has brought us are really quite good. Not as sustaining as peas and corn, but a pleasant change. Flavorful. I am imagining myself as a wood pigeon, or a turtledove. Try some."

"Oh, don't worry about me," I said. "I ate earlier."

"Earlier? This morning? In France? When earlier?"

I laughed, a hollow sound that any veteran bird would recognize and respect. "Old friend," I said, "you and I and all these pigeons have been through hardships, and by them we have been changed. But in my case I fear that these changes have been for the worse."

I knew I could count on President Wilson to refrain from pious claptrap. "Human beings," he said, millet crunching in his beak, "seem powerfully invested in the notion that suffering improves or ennobles the sufferer. This is, of course, childish nonsense. Dishonest and irresponsible."

"I was never so airy as my sister Miss America," I said. "Nor so optimistic as my brother Thomas Hardy. But until the war I always felt delighted to be alive."

"The thing to do," said President Wilson, staring east toward the sea, "is to try to be decent to everyone. It sounds simple, but becomes quite tiring, no?"

"It is not so easy to be good and kind when one is in constant pain," I said.

"I, too, have found this to be the case," he said.

We lapsed into silence, grateful not to be suffering alone.

My sulks grew longer, my temper shorter. And though their bullets were the proximate cause of my pain, I should clarify that I bore no ill will toward the defeated enemy: toward the Germans or, for that matter, toward their birds.

Late in May, as Camp Vail prepared for Decoration Day, Corporal Gault brought in an Imperial Army pigeon who'd been captured before the Armistice. "In you go, Kaiser," he said, placing him in the loft. "Time to make some American friends."

The other birds hung back, though not because the newcomer was German; they didn't adopt our keepers' rampant nationalism any more than I did. Rather, they were circumspect lest his sadness prove catching.

Kaiser was depressed. I was, too, though I hid it better. For most of my life, the chance to make a positive change, however tiny, had struck me as a gift; by the time I made it to Camp Vail, it seemed almost pointless, as did everything else, but I hoped that behaving as if I still cared might rekindle some warmth in my cooling self—and, failing that, at least make Kaiser feel welcome.

While contemporary humans insist on deriding us as filthy, we pigeons are fairly meticulous—which is how I knew how badly Kaiser suffered, huddled on his perch, insensate to his own waste. Only a despondent bird would shit on his own feet as Kaiser had done, above the crushed corncob litter. Even in his abject state, he was impressive: slate gray, with a few feathers the pale blue of a mountain pond.

"Greetings, Kaiser," I said, the first to approach. "Please make yourself at home here. I like your name, though it's rather on-the-nose for a German bird, isn't it?"

"Your American soldiers gave it to me," he said. "Very creative."

"Fair enough. What's your real name?"

"I'd rather not say. If Kaiser is who they want me to be, then what does it matter?"

"Well, it matters to me," I said. "But you don't have to talk about it if you don't want to. How did you end up here?"

He wouldn't look at me. "Germany lost the war, obviously," he said. "I am the spoils."

"What about before the war?"

His eyes remained fixed on his soiled feet. "I was born in Cologne," he said. "Son of a long line of racing homers. The Imperial German Army trained me for special missions. The Americans killed my handler and captured my basket during the Battle of the Meuse. Your demobilization was incredibly disorganized. It took them until now to send me here."

"I can see why the Signal Corps would want you," I said,

trying to be encouraging without being ingratiating. "You're a very clever and beautiful bird."

At last he looked up, squinting with pained suspicion. "And who are you, if I may ask?" he said. "The elected dignitary of welcoming the pitiable?"

"I'm Cher Ami," I said. "I didn't choose my name either, but I like it, and you can call me that."

His eyes widened a bit, revealing vivid red irises. "Of the Lost Battalion?" he said. "I suppose I ought to have known by your injuries, which are quite famous, as is your final mission. A hero bird. Not shamefully captured. Why are you wasting your time talking to a prisoner?"

I flapped in good humor and then leaned in gently to crush a few mites that I had spotted on his neck. "It doesn't matter how any of us got here," I said. "You're with friends now, if you want to be. You're able-bodied and a brilliant flier, I'll bet, by the shape of your wings. You're going to be okay."

From his reaction—an instant of relaxation that became a complete collapse—I gathered that it had been a long time since anyone had told him that. His neck shrank into the cushion of his breast, and he took deep, ragged breaths, each ending in a high quiet note that recalled the sound of a desperate chick. The other birds watched and then began to fly to us, one by one, puffing their feathers and lending their bodies' warmth. And Kaiser was home.

His strength and confidence grew even as my own faded, and he more than repaid our welcome by becoming a source of cheer for all of us. Before long he ended up the mate of Petite Rosette, and they were prolific parents. A happy pigeon couple can raise as many as eighteen babies in a single year, and their descendants went on to great success in competitive races. Some carried messages against the Axis Powers in the next world war.

Kaiser died in 1949, at thirty-two years of age. In the wild a pigeon lives only about three or four years, but in the relative safety of captivity the average life span is twenty.

Not for me, though.

Owing to my battle wounds and the stress of my many appearances for the army, I died when I was little more than two years old, on June 13, 1919, there in the Signal Corps lofts at Camp Vail, New Jersey. One week after Congress passed the Nineteenth Amendment, which would eventually recognize the right of women to vote. Pigeons do not vote, but as a female being I felt a degree of investment in the fortunes of other females.

The heartbeat of a healthy pigeon is faster than a human's, but regular and steady. That early-summer morning, with the wind blowing salty from the Atlantic and the first roses springing open, I felt my pulse slow.

At the same time, I felt a flutter along my scarred breast where the bullet passed and the vet stitched me. I do not think it overliteral to say that it was the spark of life that all beings possess seeking to leave my body.

Humans release pigeons—the white ones they call doves— as symbols of hope and loyalty at their weddings and civic ceremonies, and at funerals as representations of the soul's final journey. But for the most part, the humans who attend such events don't know what they're witnessing. Those birds circle dramatically above the scene and vanish, but they don't simply disappear: they orient themselves in those spirals, and then they fly home.

I felt my spark of life starting to circle.

Kaiser and President Wilson alighted by my side, pushing up next to me in the straw where I lay in the loft's corner.

"Dear friend," said President Wilson, "we've come to comfort but not to interfere. Go if you must. Your rest has been earned."

I could no longer speak, but I was aware and recollecting. Big Tom and Lady Jane. John from Wright Farm. The tobacco-and-hay scent of Bill Cavanaugh's hands. The anxious face of Charles Whittlesey. The first time I kissed my long-lost Baby Mine, our eyes closed in the fullness of the moment. The hint of white roses at the edge of happiness.

I felt Kaiser's beak, quite close to my earhole, whispering.

"My real name is Pumpernickel," he said. "I'm grateful that you asked, and I'll never forget you."

In my final living moment, I couldn't tell if I was laughing or crying.

Among pigeons the sound of a pair of wings clapping is a call to action. The noisy departure of a single bird is a kind of nonverbal *Let's go!* to the flock. I heard this sound from somewhere, and my spark of life rose on wings of its own to follow.

In that instant—which had to have been longer—I felt my spark circling, circling, circling, and I expected soon to experience nothing.

And then I heard the voice. *Cher Ami! Home by the airway! Home to your body!*

Flashes flew at me, winking in and out of focus. Withered lips, a face like a wooden carving—the features, I'd soon see, of the taxidermist hired by the Signal Corps to preserve me.

After a confusing interval of uncertain duration, I became fully conscious again to discover that I had become part of a grand exhibit on the Pigeon Service of the American Expeditionary Forces in France. All my pain had gone, but otherwise my sensations were a general extension of the loss of my leg: my mind would try to move my body, but nothing would happen.

This paralysis sounds nightmarish, but just as I had lost my locomotion, so, too, had I lost all the bodily drives and impulses that would have made such fixity intolerable. What's more, my awareness had become quite sharp and no longer tethered to my old perceiving organs; I found that I could simply expand my consciousness to explore my surroundings, permeating them like steam coming off a warm pond. I've learned that I can wander quite far and that the voice—the old voice—always calls me back.

At first I believed myself to be completely alone. I tried to broadcast myself toward birds whom I knew to still be living: President Wilson, Kaiser, Baby Mine. No replies. Then toward birds I knew to be dead: Buck Shot, Thomas Hardy. Silence again. I felt, I realized, a bit as Whit had felt in the Pocket, unsure whether my messages were being received. I wondered whether those I loved were still thinking of me.

Now they're all dead, and I no longer wonder.

Other taxidermied animals, I discovered, could hear and would answer me. As in life my greatest successes were with other domesticated creatures, especially those who'd had a strong emotional engagement with distances and locations: horses, dogs, my fellow homers.

Ten years passed like a gust of wind, President Wilson appeared next to me in the display case—perched rather impressively by his taxidermist atop two crossed branches—and we picked up where we had left off. When Sergeant Stubby, that brave pup, arrived to join us, we all became fast friends. President Wilson and I are separated now, but I feel certain that some clever curator will one day reunite us, if only for a while. Time stretches infinitely. Death has taught me patience.

So here I remain, at once a pigeon and a statue. Quite strange when I think about it, but after a hundred years I don't think about it often. Humans and the multifarious complications of their lives have always fascinated me, and nearly four million of them from all over the world walk through my museum each year. I read them like I once read the weather, attentive to signs: what has changed, what has remained the same, what the future may hold. I keep watching the show.

CHAPTER 16

CHARLES WHITTLESEY

Patriotic parades are for politicians and civilians, not for soldiers, not for pigeons.

The parade in which the 77th Division marched on May 6, 1919, was a crowd-pleasing concoction, though it did not please me.

For five straight miles, the crowd stood dozens deep on both sides of Fifth Avenue, drowning out the thumps of our boots with their cheers. The army had replaced the ammunition in a few of our caissons with mounds of spring flowers—a powerfully symbolic gesture, even if insincere—but the crisp air of the morning aggravated my lungs.

At the end of the route, as the parade was breaking up, I embarrassed myself by asking a corporal from the Signal Corps if I could have Cher Ami.

I thanked her keeper and hurried away, shaking off the encounter like a punch, nearly running into a tall soldier, a corporal whom I didn't know.

Large dark eyes. "Colonel Whittlesey!" he said, his sharp jaw dropping. He looked abashed out of proportion to our near collision. "It's an honor. Please forgive my clumsiness."

The right kind of eye contact can feel tactile, like being physically touched.

"Not at all," I said. "The error was entirely mine. Corporal . . . ?"

"Corporal House," he said. He had the precise, resonant voice of a college man. "Stephen House. I served with the 305th Field Artillery Regiment."

Distracted as I was, I didn't immediately catch the significance of what he'd said.

The 305th was the unit that had rained the friendly barrage down on the Pocket.

I paused. I wasn't angry—not at the 305th at any rate—since I didn't blame them for carrying out their orders. Much of the war's waste and misery arose from the actions of men who sincerely thought they were coming to the rescue.

Even that morning, when greeted by Major General Alexander, I had found no reserves of disgust for him, only pity. That spring morning, as the distant willows on the Harlem Meer swayed in the breeze, I could no longer summon enmity toward any individual man. The war itself had been the real antagonist.

Anyway, in that instant I was studying Stephen House.

Recognizing men who are attracted to other men bears a certain resemblance to reading poetry. It rewards an attentiveness to multiple layers of meaning—the confidence to discern what is being communicated and to react accordingly. Corporal House was undeniably poetic: athletic, masculine, but with a mild and bright sensitivity. My type, I guess. I discovered myself to be not only lonely but full to my edges with lust, unexpressed.

"Pleased to meet you, Corporal House," I said.

Several incompatible shades of discomfiture, I noticed, had hit him at once. He'd been ambushed by my celebrity, unsettled by the uncommon experience of standing beside someone taller than himself, alarmed by my open look that suggested I'd figured him as queer, and even more alarmed by the inkling that I might be, too.

And of course an ugly intruding subject twisted between us like a loop of barbed wire.

"Colonel, I'd just like to say—" he started. "I'm not sure you know this, but—"

I didn't particularly want to discuss the subject he was trying to raise. "You have nothing to apologize to me for," I said, rather more abrupt than reassuring.

He looked as if I'd dropped a key through the bars of his cell. "Sir?" he said.

"Really, House, let's get that straight right off the bat. Neither you nor any other member of the 305th has anything to apologize for or to feel guilty about."

House was dumbstruck. "Thank you, sir," he managed. "It's really been eating me. I can't begin to tell you how many nights I've lain awake—"

He kept his voice steady and his head high, which I appreciated, but his eyes had begun to fill, and I leaned in to put a hand on his shoulder—to buck him up and because I wanted to touch him. "You did your best with the orders you were given," I said. "We all did. We did things that caused harm that we didn't intend or we failed to do things that might have helped. It doesn't matter. It was war. You're forgiven. Put it out of your mind."

"I can't thank you enough, Colonel. I—"

"Whittlesey," I said. "Or call me Charles. I've had my fill of being called Colonel. I'm not in the army anymore. You're walking south, I assume?"

I gestured, he nodded, and we fell in step. "They gave me my discharge last month," he said, his sloe-eyed glance meeting mine. "So apart from ceremonial engagements like this one, the army's leaving me alone. I can finally go back to work. Luckily, my firm held my job."

"That *is* lucky," I said. "What kind of work do you do?"

"I'm an engineer. Bridges, tunnels."

"Should be quite a demand for that, the way the city's growing."

"That's the hope. Pretty mundane stuff by your standards, probably. You're a Harvard man, I hear?"

"Harvard for law, Williams for my bachelor's," I said. "That's not as impressive as it sounds either. I don't make impassioned speeches to rapt juries. I just try to keep bankers out of trouble." I took a deep breath. "Listen, I'll be dining at the Williams Club this evening. Would you care to join me?"

"Absolutely, yes," he said, looking at me directly. "It'd be an honor. What time?"

"Seven," I said. "It's at 291 Madison Avenue. I have duties to attend to now, but I look forward to seeing you then."

Damp under my arms, heart beating fast, I watched him walk off. His ready acceptance had assured me that my hunch was correct.

———

Stephen House showed up in civilian clothes punctually at the heavy oak doors of the Williams Club, as did I. Freshly shaven and easy of manner, he seemed to be one of those constitutionally happy people.

We were shown to my usual table in a dark, cherrywood corner. Meeting publicly in one of my regular haunts might seem bold, but I counted on plain sight being the best place to hide.

The staff knew me to bring guests, and unlike in other restaurants—where it was commonplace for strangers to clap me on the back and shake my hand and thank me for my hallowed stand in the name of America, thereby obliging me to neglect both my companions and my food—the waiters and my fellow clubmen treated my presence as routine.

Stephen House lived up to his surname. Speaking with him engendered a homey feeling, a casual rapport that I could move into comfortably. Over steak and potatoes and English peas, he and I talked about harmless things: my work in contract law, his in engineering, the warming spring weather, our fondness for the city.

I was too nervous to eat much but had an extra brandy. I hadn't been with anyone for more than sixteen months, since my leave from Camp Upton that New Year's Eve.

Stephen asked me back to his place.

———

His chambers were cozy, with a private bathroom but without a private kitchen; there was a restaurant on the ground floor. Convenient—for him to live in and for me to get to and get away from. It reminded me of Marguerite's and wasn't far from her place, actually.

As we settled into his sitting room, he poured me a scotch, and the weight of the cut-glass tumbler anchored me. Stephen House seemed a steady and discreet type of man; he'd hew to the code of honor to never reveal another man's secret life. As a civil engineer, he, too, had a career and a reputation to protect.

"It's a treasure to have found the company of a fellow veteran," he said, sipping his drink. "I was at a wedding last week, and I tried to explain to one the guests that all the stories he'd read about us doughboys had been crammed full of bunk. I hadn't exactly expected gratitude, but he clearly resented having the stuffing knocked out of his favorite myths."

"Before we shipped for Europe," I said, "my parents threw me a farewell dinner and presented me with a canteen made of silver. A silver canteen! Can you imagine how that would have gone over with the rank and file? Now that I'm back, they don't want to hear a word about how unrefined it all was."

Stephen laughed at that, with the appropriate measure of bitterness. "I've tried to be honest with myself about it," he said. "It's no fun to think you might have been played for a sucker. But the more I learn, the clearer it seems that the war was motivated less by any desire to safeguard democracy than by plain greed. While Wilson was supposedly keeping us out of the war, the banks were loaning billions to England and France. They sent us over there to secure those loans. But you work on Wall Street. I'm sure you know more about this than I."

"You're not wrong about greed," I said, the scotch warming my throat. "But I led my men there anyway, as ordered. Beyond creating a lot of widows and orphans and invalids, it made no difference. That's why you never stop hearing about the Lost Battalion, you know. Why we lead parades. Not because we helped changed the course of the war but because we didn't, and the army knows it needs to justify the waste."

"I'm not sure that's exactly true," said Stephen. "You under-estimate the symbolic value of what you did. You and your men inspired the rest of us."

"Inspired the hawks. The politicians. Inspired other men to think that it's noble to die abjectly. Respectfully, Stephen, you may think that just because you're meant to think it." My anger welled aimlessly. "None of this matters now," I said, finishing my scotch in a gulp. "I want to forget the war." I leaned forward to set my tumbler aside, involuntarily rising.

"Don't leave," Stephen said, next to me in an instant, tak-ing the empty glass, placing his warm hand on the back of my neck. "I didn't bring you here to talk about the war."

He smelled green, like vetiver, and a bit sweaty. It was heady. We stumbled toward the bedroom, two tall drunk men, tugging off clothes.

We fucked on his iron-frame bed, squeaking but sturdy against my thrusts, and by the time I pulled out to come on the small of his muscular back, I'd managed to forget every-thing for a fleet few seconds. It was excellent.

When I returned to myself, twisted against him atop his sheets, Stephen lit a cigarette and looked at me expectantly.

"So," I said, rusty at pillow talk but sensing it was called for, "you don't sound like you're from New York. Where's home for you originally?"

"Detroit," he said, exhaling away from me, as fetching in profile as straight on. "That's where I went to college, too. Wayne State. I grew up near the Detroit River, which is the only thing about the city that I miss. I couldn't wait to move here and start my real life."

"What's your favorite memory of Detroit?" I was genuinely curious.

"The Belle Isle Bridge," he said without hesitation, brown eyes on the middle distance, as if he could see it. "I once watched a man—a rich entrepreneur, one of the heirs to the Scripps publishing empire—fly an airplane under it as a stunt.

It was a Curtiss Model F, a kind of flying boat. Quite something to see."

I smiled, but I could already feel the past reaching for me: buzzing overhead, and Larney saying, *We're in for it.* My last swallow of scotch had caught up with me and wasn't helping.

"That sounds like a fine memory," I said. "I can't think of airplanes without thinking of the war." I couldn't stop myself. "For a moment today, I felt certain that the being who understands me most in this world is a pigeon."

"Cher Ami?" Stephen said. "He's a military aviator of sorts himself, isn't he?"

"She," I said. "I think about Cher Ami. I think about all of them."

"Charlie," he said, freighting the two syllables of my name with such compassion that I felt crushed. "I understand why you'd feel that way. But you're not being fair to yourself. You weren't responsible for the deaths of any of your men. Blame the Germans. Blame the army. You *saved* half your command."

I'd said far too much. I'd taken him for a young and erudite bon vivant, but now I saw a serious urgency underpinning his fun.

"I could have refused the order," I said. "I know the law. I could have gone to the stockade and taken my dishonorable discharge. Today I might be representing hoodlums and swindlers instead of bankers, but that would be okay. No one would know who I am."

"And somebody else would have led your men into the Pocket," Stephen said. "And instead of blaming yourself for what happened while you were in charge, you'd be blaming yourself for not being there to help."

He wasn't wrong, but that didn't make me feel any better. I looked away, shifted in the bed so we were no longer touching.

We fell silent for a while. I could hear raindrops against the window, and I wondered when the weather had blown in; the day had been so clear.

I pulled away gently, swung my legs to the floor, reaching for a sock.

He sat up against his pillow to watch me dress.

"When we were in France," I said, "we heard that church bells from all over Austria had been collected and taken to the Vienna arsenal to be melted down and converted into munitions."

"I think we all heard that story."

"But what happened to the bells *after* the war?" I said, buttoning my shirt. "I cannot imagine that the Austrians have restored them to the peaceful forms they had before. The churches will get new bells. Or they won't. And the old bells will remain tools, or shells, or cannons. Irrevocably altered from their original shapes. I am a repurposed church bell."

"The papers may be full of lies," he said, "but you're just as good a man as they say you are. And I'd like very much to see you again."

I permitted myself a few seconds to look at him. He really was quite handsome. And kind. Exactly the sort of man whom in my youth I might have idly imagined myself meeting. But I had not met Stephen House in my youth.

"You haven't any idea what kind of man I really am. I shouldn't have come here. It's too risky. And it's not fair to you. I'm a hero. Everyone is always watching."

"I would never say a thing. If that's what you're worried about."

"You seem like a good man, Stephen," I said, pulling my jacket from the back of a chair. "I thank you for a very lovely evening and for your continued discretion. But please don't come to the Williams Club again, and don't try to see me anywhere else. I wish you much continued happiness. Good night."

Naked still, he couldn't very well follow me out into the misty street. The rain had moved on.

Walking past the golden warmth of cafés and bars, I imagined myself among those inside, laughing without a trace of bitterness. Instead I went back to another solitary night, coughing in my drab room. I drank another whiskey. Undressing, I noticed I'd buttoned my shirt incorrectly in my hurry to leave.

On those summer mornings, sunshine poured into my chamber like lemonade into a glass. The beginning of every day was the best, before it all came back.

To bathe and shampoo, to shave and dress for another day seemed a bit too much at first. But I did it. Weekend or weekday, I accomplished whatever was expected of me and then some.

Autumn came. On the anniversary of the Armistice, I agreed to issue a statement: *When an individual shows courage under stress, we feel a thrill at his achievement, but when a group of men flash out in the splendor of manliness we feel a lasting glow that is both pride and renewed faith in our fellow man.*

I strove to be chaste, failing only rarely, and succeeded overall in giving the impression of being vaguely prudish. Two or three times a week, I attended funerals of men who had finally died of their wounds. And month after month I was showered with honors. That metaphor—"showered"—as if I were expected to receive that rain like a parched desert, when in fact it burned like acid. I turned down requests for appearances that numbered in the thousands. Politely, but never without regret.

I tried to practice enough law to earn a living.

In August of 1920, John J. Munson stumbled into my law office on Rector Street. In itself this was hardly unusual. I was visited weekly by veterans from every division of the American Expeditionary Forces, not just the 77th.

As he pushed past the secretary, demanding that I see him without an appointment, I hardly recognized him. During the war he'd been blandly attractive, with abundant dark hair whose maintenance seemed one of his fondest hobbies; though mustard gas had left terrible scars on his arms and back, it had spared his face. The man whom I ushered into my private office was thin and sinewy; when I took his hat, his scalp showed beneath greasy strands. His shirt gave off a ripe unwashed smell, and when he spoke, his once-mellifluous voice quaked like an old man's.

"I need your help, Colonel," he said. "I need you to pull some strings."

"Whit," I said. "Please, call me Whit. How can I help?"

"I'm still not over it," he said. "Let a door slam, and me, I jump like I'm stung."

Munson looked every inch like the drunk that he'd become.

"Did I ever tell you about the shell?" he said. "A shell hit right beside me, right in my funkhole. French 75, high-explosive, sticking out of the ground, closer than I am to you right now. I sat there and waited for it to explode. Trying to be ready. How do you get ready for something like that? It was a dud. But now it's like I'm still waiting, listening. Waiting for the explosion."

"Well . . ." I said, but it didn't seem to matter whether I was there or not.

"I jump at sounds, normal city sounds. The rumble of the elevated. Train whistles. The pneumatic drills putting up skyscrapers and fixing the sidewalks. A pneumatic drill sounds like a machine gun."

I could smell gin on his breath. Prohibition had to be hard on him. Like many respectable citizens, I had a prescription at my pharmacist's for as much whiskey as I required for medicinal purposes, but poor Munson was no longer in any way respectable, and a mere prescription wouldn't be enough for him even if he were.

"The first thing I'd recommend," I said, trying again, "is getting yourself a shave and a new suit." I opened my bureau drawer to access the petty-cash box; I'd reimburse the firm later, after I got Munson on his way. "Here," I said. "We can

call this a loan. Pay me back when you're on your feet again."
I knew it would almost certainly be spent on more liquor, but
figured I owed him a chance to turn himself around.

"No, no, no," he said, waving the bills away. "I just need
someone to listen to me while I figure it out. I've tried to push
it from my brain. But it comes crashing back, like a cupboard
full of tin pots clattering to the floor. Wherever I am. They've
still got us surrounded. We're still lost. That shell—the fuse—
it's a long fuse. It's still burning."

He lurched from his chair.

"Remember how we came up on that hill? We thought we
were dead men. Remember? You kept us up, but we knew.
That was supposed to be the toughest defense on the German line, and the krauts had cut and run! It was all ours, not
a shot fired! Do you remember that feeling? All I wanted in
the war was to stand on top of a hill—stretched tall, fearless—
but now look at me."

Despite all my training in argument and rhetoric, I was
flummoxed; it was pointless to persuade a shell-shocked man.

"I'm sorry," he said, running a hand over his sweating
forehead. "God-awful sorry you're seeing me like this. My
life is all apologies and disappointments now. I can't get it to
make sense anymore, civilian life. Remember when we didn't
call it that? We just called it life? I don't know how to talk to
people anymore, but I talk to my dead friends all the time. I
think about the things they loved and will never have again.
Freddie hated the food at training, but he loved the shredded
wheat with raspberries and cream on sale at the canteen."

He made a great deal of sense, paraphrasing thoughts I'd
had myself, fairly precisely describing my own experience.
Were I a man of passion and expression like Munson, not of
discipline and reserve as I'd been raised—then I might be
living his life.

"Now, look here," I said, with a firmness meant to reassure
myself more than him, "let's lay this out calmly, one problem
at a time. Since you find that—"

"Calmly?" he said. "I *am* calm! Calm as can be. I didn't think you'd be like all the rest, thinking I'm crazy. I thought you'd understand, since you were there. Maybe it's a different experience for an officer than for us enlisted men. I thought the same shells fell on all of us, but maybe not. Maybe every man has his own shell."

A rap came on the privacy glass of my door, and Bayard let himself in; he must have been standing there the whole time. "Everything all right?" he asked, raising an eyebrow.

"Of course not!" said Munson, snatching up his hat and pushing past him. "The colonel here gawps at a man so he feels like a fool. Nothing's all right, and it never will be again. Good day, sirs!"

Then he pivoted and walked away with a drunk's exaggerated care, like a debutante demonstrating her posture.

"You all right, chum?" Bayard asked.

I looked down at my hands, surprised to find them shaking. "I'm sorry about that," I said. "He was a good man. Lost Battalion. Not one of the pretenders. I couldn't help him."

"He seemed past help. Why don't you take the afternoon off?"

Work had come to be the thread that fastened me to my own sanity, so I declined Bayard's offer and got back to the contract I'd been reviewing, reading the same clauses many times without comprehension.

Shortly thereafter I informed Bayard of my intention to dissolve our partnership and transfer to the firm of White & Case. He evinced an appropriate degree of sadness. I'd be only two blocks away, I pointed out, and we could still meet for lunch. We both knew that I hadn't been pulling my weight since I'd shipped home from France. He needed someone whose attention wasn't being drawn and quartered, and I needed to be an associate somewhere, not a partner, in order to balance my obligations. My new firm seemed convinced that my name brought them prestige, and they promised a light workload on very favorable terms. When Bayard and I announced my departure, we said it was because White & Case had more work in my chosen specialty of banking law.

Something less than a year passed, another year of appearances and accolades and funerals and the occasional bit of contract review. I tried to take solace in my circumscribed life.

The Lost Battalion had finally been scheduled for release in conjunction with the upcoming Fourth of July holiday, and I and the other soldiers who'd played ourselves in it were invited to a July 2 screening at the Ritz-Carlton Ballroom, along with an assortment of generals and studio executives.

At dinner the preceding Friday, I invited Marguerite to be my date. She hesitated.

"Charlie, you know how I enjoy your company," she said. "But lately—and I hope you'll hear this in the spirit that I'm offering it—you have become short-tempered. Snappish. Hard to be around, to be quite honest."

This hurt me severely, because she was correct. I thought I was doing a fair job at impersonating my old self, but I'd been wrong. I imagined myself as a grand old building: marble façade intact, interior dilapidated and overrun with rats.

"I'm profoundly sorry, Marguerite."

"There can be no question of my love for you, Charlie. But I haven't the heart to let myself be ill-used." An acute awareness of months—years—of unhappiness I had caused her rushed over me, and I was ashamed. "I'd be honored to go to the screening with you, yes. If you can try to be kind."

I promised I would, and I was. I held her cool, dry hand to steady myself in the dark during the scenes that were difficult to watch, which turned out to be all of them.

A newspaper write-up the next day said, *"The picture seemed to please the many notables who were present, with the thrills and smiles and tears of a retold story. Of course there was no villain and all were heroes from 26th of September when the Yanks climbed over the top and penetrated the German lines."*

The reviewer seemed to have a promising future as a diplomat.

I sent to Marguerite's office a vase of dark pink roses—the symbol of gratitude—along with a note of thanks and vowed never to watch the picture again.

CHAPTER 17

CHER AMI

I remember in the Pocket hearing one soldier ask, "Hey, buddy, what time is it?" and another soldier answer, "What the fuck do you care? You're not going anywhere."

Both that desire to know and the dismissal of that desire are relatable now. I won't be going anywhere for a long, long while.

After I woke up in my glass display, I struggled to understand my condition—the weird circumscribed immortality I'd accidentally been granted—but also, and relatedly, I tried to understand where I was: what a museum was and what my function was inside one.

Apart from the few joyous days I spent with Baby Mine, my existence has been and continues to be defined by the uses to which humans have put me. This seems unjust, and perhaps it is, but I console myself by considering that the existence of nearly every creature is defined by what other creatures make of it.

For just as humans use us animals as companions, servants, laborers, factories, and food, so, too—as my brother Thomas Hardy once observed, on the train to London—do they use us in order to know what to make of themselves, by way of comparison and contrast. This practice has a long intellectual history that I now have the time and the ability to explore. Aristotle, I have learned, described animals as illustrative of certain human traits, particularly irrational impulses. Descartes, extrapolating from Aquinas, regarded us as mere machines, since we supposedly lack immortal souls. Darwin studied pigeons closely and inclined to agree with Aristotle.

Humans seem to have a pronounced tendency, even a need, to draw distinctions between opposites and to zealously maintain them, even when evidence suggests that those boundaries are quite blurry indeed: man and animal, life and death, moral choice and innate instinct.

What I missed most, at least at first, was the sense that every day might turn out to be momentous, that for good or ill my life might be abruptly transformed. I soon understood that barring the occasional change in the museum's hours or the periodic cleaning or rearrangement of my case, things are going to remain pretty much the same.

As compensation I have my expanded capacity for seeing and knowing. In the early days of my after-death life, I chose to look in on some of the men whom I had encountered during my time in France and see how they were faring. I figured that keeping an eye on those men might provide me with clues regarding what that war had meant to them and therefore what I had come to mean.

My observations were interesting, if not quite enlightening. Some of the men came through their wartime experiences in fine spirits, grateful to have survived and eager to resume the lives they had lived.

George McMurtry was one of the lucky ones, as he'd be the first to insist. He resumed his prewar career as an attorney, then went on to earn a fortune in the stock market, maintaining homes on Park Avenue and in Bar Harbor, as well as memberships in all the best clubs.

Those who'd known McMurtry before the Great War were surprised to detect upon his return to civilian life a new gentleness in his manner, one that became more pronounced with the passage of years, along with an occasional hint of wistful melancholy. When asked on such occasions if he was feeling all right, he would always say that he was remembering a friend.

After his conviction and bad-conduct discharge were reversed, Maurice Revnes returned to the States, got married, and had a moderately successful career as a producer of films and plays. His wife was afraid to sleep in the same bed with him, for he'd wake in the night thrashing and sometimes screaming about his missing leg—upsetting in itself and somehow all the more so given that he had kept his leg and lost only the majority of his left foot. Revnes died in Florida at the age of ninety-five; newspaper obituaries identified him as a World War I veteran but included no mention of the Lost Battalion.

Many of the men—particularly, for whatever reason, the westerners—never married, unwilling or unable to burden a woman with their broken bodies and erratic minds. Many spent their remaining years in tumbledown shacks outside dead-end towns on the desolate prairies from which they'd come, guarding their solitude, keeping clear of the currents of history. One or two of these men lived long enough to be awakened by a flash of light, a fireball rising over the distant desert, and a sudden rush of wind declaring that history had found them anyway.

Of all the men I'd known, the one I found myself following with the greatest interest was Charles Whittlesey.

I watched him on the streets of New York City as he walked to work and hoped not to be recognized. Even as he avoided people, he seemed drawn to the city's feral pigeons, feeding them on his noon break from his law office, naming those who congregated on the ledge outside his rooming house. They seemed to make his existence bearable when the days were sloppy and the clouds were gray and he hated the meat loaf he'd had for lunch and felt that no more happiness would be forthcoming.

I watched him take longer and longer nighttime walks, and I understood that he was cruising—or rather, that he was passing his former cruising spots without ever picking or being picked up, without even any intent. When he encountered and identified men he once would have approached, he riveted his eyes to the pavement, walked on. Whit in stasis.

This went on for a while. He seemed to be deliberately trying to lead the same sort of ghostly death-in-life that circumstances had forced upon me.

―――――――――

And then it was the fall of 1921 and Whit was on a train,
heading my way. To my disappointment he was bound not for
the Smithsonian but for Arlington National Cemetery, where
he had still more war-hero obligations to meet.

He had come to serve as a pallbearer for a soldier who'd
been killed during the war in France and whose remains
could not be identified.

It was a crystal-blue day better suited to a picnic than a somber service. The event reunited Whit with George McMurtry
and Nelson Holderman, between whom he sat joylessly while
President Warren G. Harding led the ceremony. General Pershing and Marshal Foch were there, too, both spewing gran-
diloquence, decorating their speeches with platitudes—*in
honored glory*, et cetera—evidently untroubled by asserting the
authority to speak in the presence of men who had fought in
the trenches.

But Whittlesey, like McMurtry and Holderman, wasn't listening to the oratory. Whit and I were both thinking of one
soldier in particular, one who most probably lay in the
Meuse-Argonne under a cross inscribed HERE RESTS IN HON-
ORED GLORY AN AMERICAN SOLDIER KNOWN BUT TO GOD. Yet there
remained—and Whit chose to dwell in—the sliver of possi-
bility that the soldier whom he and his fellow pallbearers
carried to his grave that November day had once been Bill
Cavanaugh.

"I should not have come," I heard Whit murmur to McMurtry. "It has been too unnerving."

McMurtry smiled and reached over, playful and reassuring, to jostle Whit's knee. This he regretted immediately: it
felt like a scarecrow's limb or the frame of a barn overdue for
collapse.

President Harding pinned a medal on the flag-covered coffin, and they laid whoever the Unknown Soldier was to rest.

As he walked away from the tomb, Whit was thinking of how fine it would be to be unknown.

I watched him on the train ride back north, seated next to McMurtry, saying, "They're always after me about the war. I used to think I was a lawyer. Now I don't know what I am."

I watched him visit his family in Pittsfield the following weekend, speaking nothing of the burial—as if an event with the Great War's victorious commanders and the president of the United States merited no remark—until after dinner, when his impatient father asked him about the ceremonies. "They made a deep impression," Whit said, and fell silent again.

I watched him attend a Red Cross fund-raiser, where he was praised for his efforts—relentless, compulsive—to assist with the enrollment of a half a million members between Armistice Day and Thanksgiving. At the dinner he turned abruptly to the major seated next to him—another combat veteran—and asked, "How do you get through the day? Raking over the ashes like this revives all the horrible memories. I can't remember when I've had a good night's sleep."

The next day I watched him attend a fancy reception at the New York Hippodrome for Supreme Allied Commander Marshal Ferdinand Foch, where he shared the stage with armless and legless veterans, paying tribute to one of the war's chief architects with the mute testimony of its costs. Whit wondered, not for the first time, whether all the work he'd done since the war had mostly served to reinforce the notion that it had been just and good and therefore had made the next war easier, inevitable.

I watched him return home alone that night to the usual racking cough that woke the other residents of his rooming house, all of whom cursed him under their breaths but none of whom broached the issue with him or with the landlady, in deference to his heroism.

As always, Whit knew that he was waking them.

Yet something had changed.

When he finished his nightly liquor and turned out the light, I saw that his face had relaxed, untroubled to an extent I'd never seen before.

I watched him return to work at White & Case, laughing genuinely at his colleagues' jokes, not worrying about his cough, which, ironically, caused him to cough much less often.

I watched him stay late that afternoon to bring all twelve of the cases he'd been working on up to date. He left notes, not in plain sight but easy to find: *"Look in upper-left-hand drawer of my desk for memoranda of law matters I have been attending to."*

I watched him visit the Pruyns the following afternoon, Thanksgiving Thursday, appearing, as they would later say, in unusually cheerful spirits. It was also the one-year birthday of Patricia, the Pruyns' daughter, Whittlesey's godchild. Whit's dearest friend, Marguerite, was present, and she, too, would later report that Charlie had been in a very high mood. He'd brought baby pins for the little one, had laughed and played peekaboo.

I watched him start his last full day in New York City by using the office telephone to contact an army press officer who owed him a favor in order to find out how to contact the German lieutenant who'd sent the surrender request via Hollingshead while they were in the Pocket.

Whit being a famous war hero, they tracked the man down. His name was Heinrich Prinz, and he had gone to work for the American occupation after the Armistice. They arranged for Whit to speak to him by telephone. Prinz had lived briefly in Seattle, of all places, and his English was superb.

They forgave each other everything.

I watched Whit type up letters. He was a skilled and meticulous typist, even in an office well outfitted with secretaries.

Later, in response to frenzied queries from every reporter

in Manhattan, the recipients of these notes would remain united in their commitment to keeping the contents confidential, issuing a joint statement to *The New York Times*: *"The letters contain only personal farewells and in no instance attempt to explain the reason for his departure."*

I watched him tell his colleagues of plans to visit his parents in Pittsfield again, because both his father and his brother Elisha were ailing. Later that evening he'd tell Marguerite the same thing.

After he was gone, Marguerite would remark, "I think that was about the only lie Charlie ever told in his whole life."

They'd been particularly eager to interview Marguerite, because she was widely assumed to be Whit's fiancée—and because a story of despair caused by thwarted love is easy to write and readily intelligible to their readership—but she would assure them that that absolutely had not been the case. The reporters would observe to one another, but would not write, that Marguerite seemed oddly wonderstruck, and even slightly amused, as if appreciating what Whittlesey had done as a clever magic trick and an elaborate practical joke.

Given my current state, I was able to see all this for myself, but as it happened, that final item also came to me: an elderly curator arrived early, pulled up a chair beside my case, and read me the article in its entirety.

"I thought you should know," he said. I learned later that one of his sons had been killed in France.

I am a stuffed pigeon, so despite my intimate association with Charles Whittlesey in life, in death, and in history, no reporters ever asked me for comment—not that they would have been able to understand me anyway. Still, it would have been nice.

I'm not sure what I would have said then, and I'm not sure now. During their time together at Camp Upton and in the early days of the war, Whittlesey and McMurtry would chide each other good-naturedly on the subject of religion, McMurtry being a relaxed and tolerant Presbyterian and

Whittlesey being a relaxed and tolerant atheist. During their few idle moments in the Pocket, they renewed these discussions with greater urgency. "What do you say over the dead?" McMurtry asked. "Since you have no faith of your own, I mean? Our chaplain can't keep up with this killing, so I step in when I can, but without the churching I've got, Whit, I think I'd be lost at sea. What do you do?"

Whittlesey seemed perplexed by the question. "I say whatever they would have me say," he replied.

"That's all well and good for the fellow who's dead, I suppose," McMurtry said, "but what about you? Let's be honest: we say these things to hold ourselves together as much as to safeguard anybody's immortal soul. What do you say to yourself?"

Now Whit understood, and he nodded and blushed a bit. "It's not something I'd expect everyone to adopt," he said, "but I sometimes think of a line from Catullus, the Roman poet. *'Atque in perpetuum, frater, ave atque vale.'* That's 'So forever, brother, hail and farewell,' more or less. It's held up for two thousand years, so I suppose it'll carry me through this."

I've returned to it often. It doesn't promise the comfort of heaven, and it doesn't evoke the glory of war. It doesn't assert that the death was necessary, or valuable, or just. It just declares admiration for the dead and grief at the loss.

Best of all, it addresses the dead as "brother," thus erasing nearly all the distinctions that might have separated Whit from the fallen in life: rank, class, background. Even species, I like to imagine.

I don't know where Whit went—where he is now, if he can be said to be anywhere. I stretch myself out into the cold darkness toward him, but I get no reply.

While I'm hesitant to apply my own experience to Whit's, I draw on my memories of homing: of the intense, convulsive need to return to my loft and the translation of every sensible thing into routes and impediments. Once I was launched into the air, the world in all its plenitude seemed no more than a thing to be traversed and endured on my way home.

I think that may be how Whit felt about the world before he found his route out. Bill Cavanaugh, whom we both loved, used to say, *Pigeons fly faster to a happy home.* Wherever Whit is now, I hope he's happy.

Hail and farewell, brother. I salute you, and good-bye.

CHAPTER 18

CHARLES WHITTLESEY

———— ·≈≈≈· ————

I remember in the Pocket hearing one soldier ask, "Hey, buddy, what time is it?" and another soldier answer, "What the fuck do you care? You're not going anywhere."

Both that desire to know and the dismissal of that desire are relatable now. These past three years, I've tried to keep my life precise and circumscribed, even as I have remained as attentive as a metronome to the passage of time, the days ticking by in excruciating sameness.

But today the moments rush past like a cataract, and I am going somewhere. The *Toloa*—newest and largest of the United Fruit Company's Great White Fleet—churns beneath my feet, carrying itself south. I am making my trip in luxury. "Only one class, sir, and that's first class," the agent said when I bought my ticket.

The weather was wet and chilly in New York the morning we left, but this afternoon the sea is calm and the weather clement. After the *Toloa* makes its stop in Havana, it'll proceed on a two-week cruise. The deck, though hardly crowded, is meandered over by people set on enjoying their vacation—*"five thousand miles of sunshine among the quaint countries of the Caribbean,"* the poster in the American Express office had promised, along with *"many delightful shore excursions."* They stroll and gaze, alone and in pairs.

One of them approaches, clearly having recognized me as Charles "Go to Hell" Whittlesey. Broad of shoulder and dark of complexion, he wears an impeccable slate suit with a red pocket square. As he gets closer, I see that he has eyes of cobalt blue, like a perfume bottle, glinting in his deep-brown face. I recall my first glimpse of Bill Cavanaugh's eyes aboard the *Lapland*, and for the first time since the Pocket the memory is sweet, not agonizing.

"I'd heard a rumor that we have a war hero on board," the man says, extending a hand, warm and dry. "But I didn't expect to have the good fortune to run into him this very afternoon."

Up until a few days ago, being recognized would have made me irritated and anxious, but now it doesn't trouble me; I'm already feeling freer.

The man's name is Maloret. "I'm from Puerto Rico originally," he says, "but my father was American. I'm a veteran, too. I fought in the Spanish-American War. On the U.S. side, if that's not clear."

Those eyes flash again, scattering light like a semiprecious gem. Maloret is older than I am but seems younger than I've ever felt. He's not really my type, but he has an endearing guilelessness and a misshapen charm, a languor of gesture.

"What brings you aboard the *Toloa*?" I ask.

"I have business in Havana," he says. "Exceedingly boring business, I promise you. What are you doing for dinner?"

"Dining at the captain's table."

"I am as well. I was just going to invite you. Farquar is an old chum of mine," he says, using the captain's first name to show the depth of their friendship, or simply that he's the sort of person who prefers first names. I still don't know his. "I'll look forward to seeing you there and to making more of your acquaintance."

Mr. Maloret, of Puerto Rico, who has business in Havana. He walks away, leaving behind the peppery scent of his cologne. He seems as though he might be interested in an assignation. This journey has suddenly taken on the cartoonish dimensions of a classic temptation narrative.

I never miss the Army-Navy game, I'd said to the captain's

man when he invited me to dinner—it was a rivalry that continued to interest me despite all the misery the army had inflicted—so could the captain arrange for me to listen to the broadcast on the wireless? It was uncharacteristic of me to make requests like this, selfish and unnecessary, but as a war hero I knew they'd never say no. I listen to the game alone in a small lounge, not another soul around. It is bliss. Navy wins, seven to nothing, but that's okay. That success can manifest itself in the right kind defeat is one of the underlying premises of my voyage. I rise, prepare my room, and wash up for dinner.

When I emerge from my cabin, gaiety suffuses the early-evening air. We're now beyond the reach of Prohibition: U.S. law extends only three miles out to sea, the length of a cannon shot. We're well past that now.

I make my way to the captain's table and enjoy every bite of food, from the iced celery and assorted olives to the stuffed lamb cutlets to the vanilla blancmange. We talk easily, the captain and I, the captain and Maloret, the handful of other honorary guests whose names I luxuriate in forgetting the instant I hear them.

As the dessert plates are cleared away, the captain excuses himself and returns to the bridge, cigar in hand, leaving me with Maloret, who suggests that we head to the lounge. I see no reason to disagree. It's early yet.

We sit in the smoking room of the steamer and talk a little about the war. We have a drink and then another. We speak of his time as a soldier in Puerto Rico and of the time he spent in Paris as a supplier of the American Expeditionary Forces, the extent of his role in this most recent conflict.

I feel remarkably self-possessed.

"I don't much care," I say, swirling the ice in my glass, "for how some journalists have already started to call it the First World War. As if they're already eager for the next one."

"I must say I am impressed," he says, "given the extreme

difficulty of what you endured in the Argonne, that you have remained so easy in your bearing and able to speak of the war with such calmness."

I want to tell him that he should not assume the presence or absence of another being's pain simply because it is not being manifested in a manner that he recognizes. I remember Bill Cavanaugh saying, after Lieutenant Revnes made one of his frequent references to the pigeons as "dumb animals," that while he couldn't say how exactly how his birds felt, he was sure that they preferred comfort and safety over pain, like any of us, and that it wasn't hard to respect that.

What I say instead is, "Thank you."

After an hour or so, the conversation lags, and I don't seek to revive it. My watch says eleven fifteen. "It struck me suddenly how weary I am," I say, rising. "I apologize, but I must retire to my room."

"I hope to enjoy the pleasure of your company again," says Maloret, blue eyes holding mine for an extra beat. "If not aboard the ship, then perhaps I can show you a good time in Havana."

"Perhaps," I say.

On the starboard side of the upper promenade deck, a few shreds of fog blow along the ship's rail, much as it did those mornings in the Argonne Forest. The night is partly cloudy, and there are a few people about, either gazing out to sea or into each other's eyes. Filtering starlight and international romance.

I look up at the stars, and in my relative good cheer I feel like the teenager I once was, poetic and romantic and excited about the world.

The railing feels cold in my hands. My service pistol is in my pocket just in case, but I'm not going to need it. Its weight—a bit over forty ounces on the scale—will help to pull me down.

The wind picks up. We are too far out to sea for there to be any gulls. With my face in the air, I feel like I'm flying.

I try to picture the face of every man in the 308th. Hail and farewell, brother. I salute you, and good-bye.

Then I jump.

I fear that as I fall—a dark blur against the ship's white hull—my mind will spill over with every horror that I witnessed during my brief life, but this does not occur.

Instead I think of feathers, and then nothing at all.

CHAPTER 19

CHER AMI

〰〰〰

No flowers are laid upon my grave, but I'm not complaining. I have no grave. I am my grave.

No flowers are laid upon Charles Whittlesey's grave either, and neither is he complaining, for he got what he wanted.

"He was a victim engulfed in a sea of woe," said one of the partners from White & Case by way of eulogy. The extent to which this metaphor was unintended or simply in poor taste is not clear, but it was true enough at any rate.

Humans have no monopoly on grief. Dolphins carry their dead on their backs for days. Giraffes refuse to eat. Elephants cry.

Whit carried the dead on his back for years. For life. I'll carry him on my flightless wings always.

Back on Wright Farm, John once told us that hummingbirds are the only birds who can fly backward. Here in the museum, backward is, in a sense, the only way I fly.

Through the years of my stay here, the quantity of material that surrounds Sergeant Stubby and me has accordioned, growing longer and shorter according to what the culture deems most important. The Great War exhibit stretched long and expansive through the twenties and thirties. In the forties the curators compressed us into less and less space. The defeat of Hitler and company can be presented as a quest far more noble and necessary than the First World War, the obscure origins and anticlimactic end of which are befuddling even to superlative armchair historians.

The tenor of the exhibit on our war material has changed over the years. For a while the wall bore a quote from a letter that General Patton sent to General Pershing: *"War is the only place where a man really lives."*

I would look at it and think, *Please let that not be true.*

In the seventies I heard a reporter interviewing Great War veterans for a television documentary. One of them was Zip Cepaglia, wrinkled but dignified, still with the trace of his Italian accent. "What are your feelings about the Battle of the Meuse-Argonne?" the reporter asked.

"Well, I think it was a fucked-up mess," Zip said. "And that's a very generally held opinion among the guys like me, the guys who been there."

That didn't make it into the museum.

The army stopped using pigeons as message carriers in 1957. Fifteen living heroic birds were donated to zoos, and about a thousand of the others were sold to an eager public that was then still enthusiastic about breeding and racing us.

When people believe in animals, what do they believe?

Whit goes unmentioned in my display.

James Larney—the signal-panel carrier who kept a diary during his days on that hillside above the brook in the Pocket, who collected the soldiers' jokes and songs in the belief that they would reveal something about the war and those who fought in it, something hidden to themselves—had a hard time dealing with Whit's death. He had by then become a political bigwig in upstate New York: very civic-minded, active in the American Legion, a real stand-up citizen.

But when he heard the news, he took a break from all that and he bought a ticket on the *Toloa* to Havana. The same ship, the same route, even the same cabin that Whittlesey had taken, all to try to comprehend what had happened to his beloved commander. A pilgrimage of sorts.

He stood at the railing all night, staring up at the moon and down at the waves.

But when the sun rose over the ocean, he still couldn't understand.

Maybe you can?

Historical Note

World War I has always saddened and fascinated me with its colossal scale and the destruction it wrought, and the way it opened the door to the subsequent horrors of the twentieth century. But my inspiration for this book came from an unexpected place.

I teach a class at DePaul University called "Drift and Dream: Writer as Urban Walker." Back in 2013, one of the students in that workshop, Brian Micic, turned in a poem that contained an almost throwaway line about pigeons: "This was no Cher Ami story. (Look it up!)" I appreciated the good-natured ribbing—I am forever reminding my students to look things up—so look it up I did.

What I found astonished me—despite my years of reading books and watching films about the Great War, I had never heard of this bird, nor had I heard anything at all about the Lost Battalion, the nickname of the group of American soldiers she helped to save from a friendly fire incident in France's Meuse-Argonne Forest in October of 1918. I also knew nothing whatsoever of that group of men's commander, Charles Whittlesey, a person who gave his all not only in that ordeal but also in his civilian life upon returning to the States.

The size of their bravery in life and the depth of their forgottenness in death made me realize that I needed to tell their stories. I went to see Cher Ami in the Smithsonian Institution in Washington, DC, and was stunned by how small and smart she looked, even stuffed, and I kept her picture as the wallpaper on my computer as I wrote.

Cher Ami really was one of the many highly decorated homing pigeons to be deployed by the United States Armed Forces during World War I, thanks to these birds' reliability and accuracy in relaying information from the front lines to the rear. She really did receive grievous wounds while carrying the message that saved Charles Whittlesey's Lost Battalion. And she really did manage to live on for a few months after that, stitched up by army medics and using a tiny wooden leg. Taxidermied after her death in honor of her high level of service, her body really does remain on exhibit at the Smithsonian in their "Price of Freedom" exhibit.

Charles Whittlesey, the courageous and compassionate commanding officer of the Lost Battalion, really did receive the Medal of Honor for his leadership during that harrowing incident. Sadly, upon his return to the States, he really was unable to adjust to the demands of serving as a high-profile war hero and took his own life by leaping into the Atlantic from an ocean liner in 1921. His body was never recovered.

To be clear, this is a work of fiction and not a biography of either Cher Ami or Charles Whittlesey. Though largely based on newspaper reports and other published accounts, the specific circumstances of the novel are invented and the attitudes and opinions expressed by both pigeon and soldier are entirely imagined.

That said, I encourage everyone interested to learn more about this once famous and now largely unsung episode in American history, perhaps by visiting the Smithsonian in DC and the National World War I Museum and Memorial in Kansas City, Missouri, and by reading the following books, which were indispensable in the writing of this one:

Cher Ami: The Story of a Carrier Pigeon by Marion Benedict
    Cothren (Boston: Little, Brown, and Company, 1934)
*Finding the Lost Battalion: Beyond the Rumors, Myths and Legends
    of America's Famous WW1 Epic* by Robert Laplander
    (Waterford, WI: Lulu Press, 2006)

Five Days in October: The Lost Battalion of World War I by Robert
  H. Ferrell (Columbia, MO: University of Missouri Press, 2005)
History and Rhymes of the Lost Battalion by Lee Charles
  McCollum (Chicago: Buckley Publishing Company, 1919)
History of the 308th Infantry: 1917–1919 by Louis Wardlaw Miles
  (New York: G.B. Putnam's Sons, 1927)
The Lost Battalion: A Private's Story by John W. Nell (San
  Antonio, TX: Historical Publishing Network, 2001)

Last but not least, unrelated to World War I, but very much
related to Cher Ami, I recommend *The Pigeon* by Wendell
Mitchell Levi, published by the R. L. Bryan Company in 1941,
for being a marvelous compendium of pigeons and all the remarkable things that they—like humans—can sometimes be
capable of.

ACKNOWLEDGMENTS

Thanks beyond measure go to:

Lisa Bankoff, Abby Beckel, Logan Breitbart, James Charlesworth, Christen Enos, Elisa Gabbert, Virginia Konchan, Caro Macon, Eric Plattner, Mitchell Rathberger, Beth Rooney, Martin Seay, Rachel Slotnick, Kimberly Southwick, Margaux Weisman, and Becky Wills; my family, especially my mom and dad for instilling in me a lifelong fascination with history; all the poets who do Poems While You Wait; the staffs of the National World War I Museum and Memorial and the Smithsonian Institution; my students and colleagues at DePaul University; and anyone who has ever talked with me admiringly about birds in general and pigeons in particular.

Much gratitude, too, goes to Coo d'Etat and Walter Pigeon, the pigeon couple who built their nest under the eaves of our condo as I was writing this novel, and who taught me up close about the love and loyalty of pigeon parenting as they raised their kids, Feather Locklear and Molly Wingwald. Wherever you all are now, I salute you.

Also, to my former student Brian Micic, who introduced me to the story of Cher Ami in the first place. One line in his poem written during the fall of 2013 has changed my life forever for the better, and for that I will always be grateful.

Reading Group Questions and Topics for Discussion

1. The book opens with two epigraphs: one from Aristotle and one from General Joseph Joffre. Why do you think the author chose these to precede the story? What themes do they set you up to expect?

2. Kathleen Rooney chooses to tell the story in the alternating voices of Cher Ami, a pigeon, and Charles Whittlesey, a human. How would the story be different if she had only offered one perspective? What do the two interwoven perspectives do for the impact of the overall narrative?

3. Do you consider yourself an animal lover? Does that love extend to pigeons? Did this book change the way you look at pigeons or other animals? If so, how?

4. Cher Ami speaks, from inside the Smithsonian, of "World War II, which happened even though the horrors of the Great War were said to have obviated all future war" (page 7). Did you know much about World War I, aka the Great War, prior to reading this book? If so, how did this book make you see it anew? If not, what shocked you in this book's depiction of that conflict?

5. Compare the attitudes that the animals have regarding their role in the war to those attitudes held by the humans. How are they similar and how are they different?

6. When he's an undergraduate at Williams College, Whit writes in his yearbook that the purpose of a college education is "learning to judge correctly, to think clearly, to see and to know the truth, and to attain the faculty of pure delight in the beautiful" (page 50). How do his youthful idealism and his excellent education prepare him—or not—for the horrors of trench warfare?

7. Both Cher Ami and Whit fall in love during their time on the front in France. How do their relationships to their beloveds—Baby Mine and Bill Cavanaugh, respectively—compare and contrast?

8. The media, including Damon Runyon and others, plays a complex role in this story in that it makes the men—and animals—of the Pocket so famous as to require them to be saved (when, under other circumstances, they would have been sacrificed), but it also paints a simplified and damaging picture of their heroism and what they endured. How should people on the home front think about the experience of soldiers at war, given that the information that they receive will always be suspect?

9. After she is shipped to the United States, Cher Ami is used by the army as a public relations tool in order to make people feel better about the war. How does that make you feel?

10. Whit returns home from the war with negative feelings about the decisions made by his commanders, yet he is extremely generous with his time and his fame whenever the army or other organizations request his assistance. Why do you think that is?

11. Whit chooses not to tell anyone of his plans to board the ship to Havana, not even his most trusted friend, Marguerite. Why do you think he opted not to tell even her, and what might have happened if he had?

12. When James Larney, the signal-panel carrier who kept a diary in the Pocket, hears about Whit's disappearance, he buys a ticket for the *Toloa* to try to understand what happened to his beloved commanding officer—but he does not feel as though he is able to comprehend it. Did you come away from the book with an understanding of what happened to Whit?